FALLING FOR THE BACHELOR

AMY ALVES

AMY ALVES BOOKS

ISBN: 978-1-7780263-3-1 (ebook)

ISBN: 978-1-7780263-4-8 (paperback)

https://amyalvesbooks.com

Cover Design: Kiwi Cover Design

Editor: Little Tweaks

Proofreader: Little Tweaks

❀ Created with Vellum

VAUGHN FAMILY & FRIENDS TREE

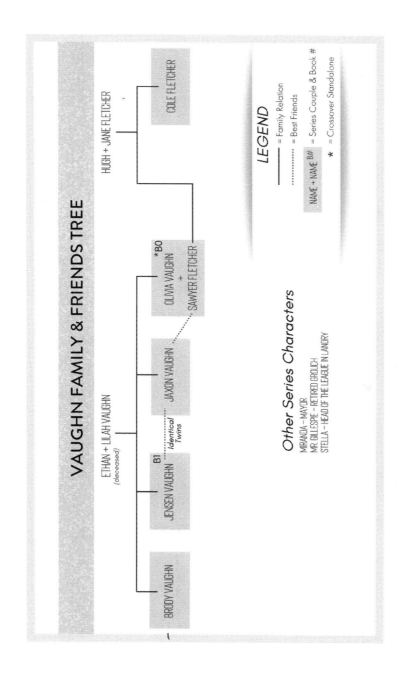

HUGH + JANE FLETCHER

COLE FLETCHER

ETHAN + LILAH VAUGHN
(deceased)

*B0
OLIVIA VAUGHN
+
SAWYER FLETCHER

JAXON VAUGHN

B1
Identical
Twins

JENSEN VAUGHN

BRODY VAUGHN

LEGEND

——— = Family Relation

·········· = Best Friends

NAME + NAME B# = Series Couple & Book #

* = Crossover Standalone

Other Series Characters

MIRANDA – MAYOR
MR GILLESPIE – RETIRED GROUCH
STELLA – HEAD OF THE LEAGUE IN LANDRY

CHAPTER
ONE
SAWYER

TWO MONTHS AGO . . .

T he town's busiest busybody sits in my waiting room, ready
to pimp me out.

I take some comfort knowing that in a few short months, I'll
have nearly thirty miles between us where I can focus on my new
business back in my hometown.

*Vaughn has its own group of meddlesome townsfolk too—stop kidding
yourself.*

But I'll celebrate this small win, even if it means trading one
interfering small-town group for another. At least in Vaughn, I've
never had anyone try to manufacture a specific future for me. Or
sabotage my dates—demolishing any positive remnants of my
dating track record. Or try to take over my pet adoption event and
turn it into a singles meetup for animal lovers.

"Dr. Fletcher, so glad I caught you."

"Stella, something wrong with Puss Puss?" Am I glad she
adopted a cat from our event last year? Yes. Do I think Stella
should be allowed to independently name a pet? Absolutely not.

"Pussy Puss is just fine."

She also gave the cat a nickname that's technically longer than her real name—and more horrifying.

I wait, hoping she's not in the mood to be coy.

"I checked with Belinda to make sure you didn't have any other appointments. We need to have a little chat. It's long overdue."

Shit. I've been ducking out of this conversation for nearly a year.

"No need, Stella. Water under the bridge, completely forgiven. I've got a pickup game I'm heading to tonight." Technically, I have a squash game in Vaughn with Jaxon and Anders, but I don't give out those details. Who knows what she would do with them.

"It won't take but a minute. Plus, what could be more important than your future happiness?"

"I'm already perfectly happy, Stella," I assure her.

She snorts, which has my eyebrows raising. Do I come off as unhappy? *Am I* unhappy?

"You keep telling yourself that, but I've known you for nearly a decade, and you've never been surlier. Either it's been too long since you cleared out the man pipes, or you're unhappy with something—or thing*s*—in your life. As a married woman, I can only help you with the latter. Starting with your love life."

"No," I tell her firmly. Her smile drops and her head tilts. "Thank you though," I add, softening the blow.

"The League wronged you. In a bit of a matchmaking mix-up, you inadvertently became, uh, collateral damage. And it racks me with guilt that those couple of blips set you on a path to monkdom. Which is at least partially on me, as the head of The League."

"Monasticism," I mumble.

"Pardon?"

"The life of a monk is called monasticism."

Her hand slips into her bag, and she pulls out a tiny notepad, frowning while scribbling a few notes. As the head of Landry's information and community network—The Landry Life League—Stella's use of her little notepad is foreboding.

"What did you write down?" I ask.

"Don't worry about it." She waves me off.

Oh shit.

"Sawyer. I'm going to be honest with you." She slips the notepad back into her bag as my heart races, the need to flee rising. "We have already announced you as the next bachelor in our *Love in Landry* event."

"Love in Landry?" I ask, hoping it's not what I think it is.

"The council's legal team informed us we can't call it *The Bachelor: Landry Edition* anymore. Something about copyright. So we've had to rename it."

Fucking great. This again. Maybe I could say I can't participate because—

"The League wants to try to right our wrongs. We want to see you happy in love, not only in your career."

Little does she know I've made changes there too.

She digs out her notepad again. "Is there anyone you'd fancy as a potential contestant?"

"At no time did I agree to this. In fact, during the first—and I'd hoped final—Landry Bachelor event, you approached me and I turned it down. I believe my answer was, 'Thank you for considering me. My answer is no—forever, no.'"

"Pssh! Who knew you were so dramatic?" *I'm* dramatic? A lengthy sigh leaves her. "I didn't want to bring this up, but it's become necessary." I frown at her and take a step back. "The unfortunate ending of your last relationship was an accident, Sawyer. And I'd hate to think of that *mishap* turning you away from finding love."

If I had it in me to gasp, I would. She's got me by the balls, *if* she is aware of everything that happened.

"How did you hear about that?" I casually ask.

Goddammit, was there a tremor in my voice?

"Her family is grateful you didn't press charges. It would have been humiliating. For both of you, I imagine."

"Her family assured me the details would remain private."

She purses her lips, eyes darting away.

Well, fuck me.

"It can definitely still remain private. But considering you haven't dated since then, people are starting to ask questions. Best way to shut them up is a distraction. Say . . . a town event? Don't you think?"

"No," I answer, crossing my arms. *Hell no.*

"Wheels are already in motion, my dear. Unless, of course, you already have someone you're seeing?"

I could lie but then there would be follow-up questions. "No."

"Are you sure? There's no one from your past—a missed opportunity? Someone recently single maybe?"

Okay, now I'm confused. I thought she was here to convince me to be their bachelor for the Love in Landry event.

The more things she says, the more my instincts are telling me to slowly back away and escape out the back exit.

"No . . ."

She studies my face a few moments longer than is comfortable. "All right. If you're sure." She sets her shoulders, her wide smile returning. "That problem will be solved in a matter of months, then." She taps my forearm with her pen. "You'll see. This is going to be the best thing to ever happen to you, Dr. Fletcher. Sometimes these little surprises in life are exactly what we need, don't you think?" She sighs dreamily. "And what could be a better surprise than love?"

"I've had plenty of surprises in the love department. I'd rather choose how I go down that path on my own."

Or avoid it altogether.

"So you've mentioned. But the beauty of this dating show is that you'll get to choose who to fall in love with. Win-win."

"Not sure love works that way, Stella." I adjust my collar, a little short of breath.

Her eyes sparkle with a knowing gleam. One which guarantees an additional dose of chaos into my perpetually tumultuous dating life.

CHAPTER
TWO
OLIVIA

PRESENT

My best friend's husband just wiped a booger from her nose for her. Then they smiled dreamily at each other before kissing.

Most days their love fills me up.

On the day I want to celebrate finalizing my divorce and moving back to Vaughn—not so much.

Would my ex-husband have groomed me in such a disgusting display of a love that knows no bounds? Absolutely not. Also, I probably wouldn't have wanted him to. Drew tends to hold things over someone, even something small, albeit gross, like wiping a nose.

Which is *one* of many reasons he is now my *ex*-husband.

"You two are absurdly cute. Though, the booger-wiping triggered my gag reflex a smidge. Let's keep the level of PDA to a minimum, all right, love birds?"

"Liam, we talked about not being overly lovey-dovey. Our girl recently ended her marriage, and here we are shoving ours in her face. Sorry, Livvie."

Ellie and my brothers are the only ones who can get away with calling me Livvie. It was sweet as a child, and I'm used to it from them since it's what they've always called me, but some days I wonder if I should have leaned into "Olive."

Nope. Nevermind. I hate it. It's what Drew sometimes called me when he was trying to be sweet.

"Yeah, sorry. It just kind of happens. Not my fault your best friend is so fucking beautiful. Now, look away, I'm going to give her another kiss—with tongue—and then I'm going to take off and let you ladies catch up."

"You don't have to do that, Liam." He quirks his head to hint he'd rather pluck his own toenails out than stay for our girls' night, likely turning into a man-bashing evening. I laugh and shoo him away with my hands, "Go on. You are relieved of your husband-slash-friend duties to go do more exciting things."

"Oh! Can you unclog my hair from the tub, sweetie? It takes fourteen minutes for the tub to drain. I timed it last night."

I snort. "Sure you don't want to stay and hear all about how my marriage fell apart, and that if one more person looks at me with pity, or shares their unsolicited life advice, I'll scream?"

His lip curls, and he says, "Yeah, I'm super good with goopy, smelly drain hair," before turning to Ellie, and laying an indecent kiss on her eager mouth. "Call me when you want me to pick you up," he whispers against her lips while giving her hair a quick, possessive tug.

Watching these two makes me a little hot. And ashamed.

Mostly that last one. I haven't had someone's lips on mine—their breath teasing my mouth, sparking the fiery burn of want and need—in a long, *long* time. And I miss it. And not only the physical intimacy either.

It's all the things I never had that I yearn for most. The cuddling, inside jokes, thoughtful surprises, knowing exactly what the other person is thinking.

Drew and I never had that. It wasn't the kind of relationship he wanted—or appreciated.

My ex-husband is a big, dumb jock who behaves like he's still twenty-two, not thirty.

We were hot and heavy in college, but it was mostly physical. That part definitely worked. Well, at first anyway—when I had no expectations, and getting off as much as possible was both of our primary objectives.

Honestly, I never considered Drew "husband material." Years ago I would have been consumed with guilt for letting that thought creep back up, but now the sweet tinge of vindication seeps in, and I'm appeased because I was right.

Even if I stupidly married him anyway.

Ellie sweeps her long white-blond hair over one tanned shoulder and settles back into the booth. She's always been petite, delicate, and the most lovable human being I've ever encountered. Which makes it hard to hate how perfect she is.

People often comment on how we are near opposites. We are both small chested, but from there, we diverge. My hair is a deep auburn, my eyes a vibrant hazel, my skin blindingly pale. I'm also what I like to call "bottom heavy"—all ass and thighs—with a slender upper body and a nipped-in waist that only serves to accentuate the curves of my lower half. Finding dresses that fit in all the right places is a bitch.

Our server, Max, comes over, and I immediately prepare myself. I can barely blink before I'm plastered against the ex-MMA fighter's chest. "Hey! I didn't realize you were still in town. How much longer are you here for?"

I never should have stayed away this long, but I'm prideful and stubborn.

"I'm going to stay for a bit longer I think. I miss it here."

I've been here for a week, but I'm keeping a low profile—to avoid all the questions I'm not ready to answer. Mostly because I don't know what to say. All I want is to move on.

Plus, I stupidly promised my ex-husband we'd keep the details of our divorce private, especially from his family. While we'd both rather not have the demise of our marriage plastered all over The Vine—our online source for town events and community information—the mystery has sparked a lot of conjecture and discussion. And while I'm thankful he decided to stay in San Francisco, I'm the one who's left fielding all the questions.

"Well, let me grab you both drinks. On the house."

"Thanks, Max. You need to run that by Harper first?" I laugh as he scowls at me.

"She's in the back making the schedule for next month. And she put *me* in charge." Max likes to dole out the free drinks, and as the manager of Rocky's Tavern, Harper enjoys tearing him a new one whenever he does. And we love it.

I try to keep my face impassive and order my drink instead. "All right, then, I'll take a wheat ale. El, you want a negroni? Mojito? What are you feeling tonight?"

"Oh. Um. Actually, just a sweet tea. Or maybe a lemonade? Wait, do you have ice cream to make floats? Because I could really—"

"Ellie! No. Absolutely not." I lean forward and whisper, "We're man-bashing tonight, so liquor is required."

She chews nervously at her lip. "Right! Of course. Definitely." Squaring her shoulders, she looks at Max and says, "Please bring me one of those drinks she mentioned." But then she winks at him and shakes her head ever so slightly.

I throw my hands up. "Ellie, why are you—Ohmygodyou'repregnant!" It all comes out in a rush. She even had tea yesterday when we met for brunch—herbal tea. And the way Liam was with her earlier was beyond his usual doting.

Her eyes widen, and a hand is quickly slapped over my mouth. "Shhh! Max, you heard nothing." She glares at him and holds out a hand. "Oh! But please bring me a root beer float. After mentioning it, I now need one."

Max's gaze bounces between us before he slowly backs away, miming zipping his lips.

I stare at her, mouth gaping.

"We haven't told anyone yet. I wanted you to be the first to find out. It hadn't seemed like the right time yet. Which is totally fine because it's still so early in the pregnancy. But, since you're planning on staying, I was hoping you'd be our midwife?"

My eyes sting as I suck in a breath. "Of *course*. Even if I'm not living here for whatever reason, I'll be here whenever you want or need."

She was possibly keeping this to herself for the last several weeks, feeling like she couldn't share their wonderful news while I was being miserable. I'm a horrible friend.

"El, I always want you to tell me everything. Even when I'm being pathetic."

"You're not pathetic. You're angry and disappointed. And you have every right to be."

"I refuse to let my shitty life choices overshadow your exciting baby news. That's it. Plans have changed. No more man-bashing night."

"No, Olivia. That's not what tonight is about."

"Drew fucked up a large portion of my twenties. I'm not going to let him mess this up too."

She huffs before a shy smile spreads across her cheeks. "You sure?"

"Absolutely. Now tell me everything. Have you seen a doctor at all or were you waiting for me? How many weeks are you?"

My life has gone to hell, but I take comfort in the fact that my best friend is living her dream with a man who adores her. And baby news definitely trumps whining about my jerk-off ex-husband who I am very glad I *didn't* have a baby with.

CHAPTER
THREE
SAWYER

Today is a good day. Not for Taps, or Mr. Dwyer, or the owner and employees of Taps, our local bar and grill.

But for me? There's a little bounce in my step and a wry smile on my face.

Mr. Dwyer and his wife recently purchased an RV and were about to take it out into the Cascade Mountains. They stopped to pick up supplies on Main Street, parking on a side street to be courteous about parking space.

Martin Dwyer has never driven an RV in his life.

And he backed it up straight into the side of Taps, smashing through windows, damaging structurally integral support beams, destroying the flooring, tables, chairs, and all kinds of interior elements.

The initial ramming of the building incurred a fair amount of damage—but I was told it was mostly contained to windows and exterior. The rest of the damage occurred when Mr. Dwyer attempted to "free" the RV from the wreckage. According to the town, Mrs. Dwyer was sobbing so loudly, her husband panicked and ended up reversing instead of pulling forward. Sean, our local heavy duty mechanic, had his tow truck come and haul out the half-buried RV.

It shouldn't make me happy.

I might be an asshole for being so damn happy.

The renovations at Taps will likely take weeks, maybe even months. Which means they'll have to shut down. Staff will be out of work for a while, residents won't have their favorite place to go to drink, dance, eat, and hang out, and there will be loud construction on our quaint, quiet street.

So yeah, I'm an asshole.

But I'm also keenly aware that Taps is the main venue location for *Love in Landry*.

And by the time the project is complete, I'll officially no longer be a resident of Landry. Not to say I won't miss it. I have friends here, my parents still live in the area. But it's time for a change. I've been stagnant . . . stuck—in the clinic I took over for my dad, in a town I never truly chose to live in, with residents who have interpreted my quiet discontent as a lonely, loveless life.

What they've blatantly ignored for the last six months is my insistence on keeping it that way—for a while at least. I have no desire to invite more chaos into my life. *Or* any more meddlesome matchmaking.

But I did need a change, and focusing on my career has been the right choice for me. Which is why last year I began researching shifting toward solely small animal and shelter medicine.

My dad typically focused on large animal care, and I ran the small animal clinic. But ever since a past intern of mine introduced me to the idea of shelter medicine, I've been wanting to make some changes.

I've partnered with Sonoma County's Humane Society to offer veterinary services to animals in need within our area. Last month I found a building for my new clinic in Vaughn to be able to accommodate those needs. Renovations start this week, and although the grand opening is approaching, I have more than enough time to help the new doctor I recently hired some time to adjust to his new position at the Landry clinic.

The bell above the clinic door rings, and I glance up from the front desk where I'm browsing the rest of the appointments for today while Belinda is on her break.

Perfectly coiffed golden hair shines in the afternoon light, her large handbag bumping into everything and everyone the newcomer walks near to get to me.

"Mama." I greet her with a warm grin.

She leans over the front desk, waiting. I stand up and plunk a kiss on the top of her head. Jane Fletcher is barely five foot, three inches, and a ray of freaking sunshine. I'm not sure how I turned out even remotely independent because this woman absolutely babied me. Some might say she still does.

And I couldn't care less. She's the best woman I know, and if she ever changed, I'd be crushed.

"Hi, sweetheart. I'm in town helping out, but thought I'd stop in and bring you some of my homemade granola." She holds out the container.

I snatch it out of her hands and crack the lid, sniffing it. "Thank god, I'm starving. Thanks, Mom. I missed lunch, so I doubt this will last long." I had stopped by The Sandwich Shop to grab something to eat when I got caught up with news of the commotion at Taps and forgot about lunch.

She twists her head to the side, assessing me. "You missed lunch, yet you look downright cheerful today. Your grin—full dimples. That's too happy to be about my granola. Though, it is amazing, if I do say so myself." She raises her brows at me in question, but before I can say a word, her whole face lights up. "Oh, I know what it is. I think my boy already heard the news."

"What news?" Technically, pretending I don't know and asking a simple question is not lying.

She chortles in an adorably unladylike way. "There was an incident at Taps involving an RV that will require extensive repairs. Apparently, construction crews can't get started for another couple of weeks, and the actual work will take at least a month. Something about ordering in new windows is causing the delay."

I try to hide my smug smirk but fail miserably. "I might have heard something about it. Terrible. Thankfully, no one was injured."

"Mm-hmm. Well, you'll be interested to know that they have not fully shut down." The breath stalls in my lungs. "The kitchen will remain open for takeout and catering services."

"Great news." And it is, truly. Eases my mind slightly about being an accident celebrator earlier. However . . . "And the dining and rec area?" They combine these areas for events, and it's the planned location for my upcoming romantic doom.

"Sadly, the rest of Taps will be closed until the end of next month."

Fuck. Yes.

The glee must be all over my face because my mother grins at me.

"You must be wondering about what will become of the *Love in Landry* event—the one you committed to months ago. If the event were canceled, tickets would need to be refunded and event coverage would be too, resulting in less funds for Dogwood Animal Rescue. That was the charity you requested as a condition of participating in the event, remember?" Mom's tone is even, sweet, but moderately reprising.

Shit. In my relief, I may have forgotten one major downside to this event being called off.

"I'll check in with Stella and see what can be done. I've got a few ideas as to who in town can fill in." Mom nods at me and then hands me a sheet of paper.

"Tentative plans have already been made."

"For a new bachelor? Great. I mean, by the time they get Taps up and running again, I won't even be living here anymore. I'll try to make my way back to town to catch the first night though." I let out a relieved breath. "This actually works out well. My schedule will be too crazy in a couple of months once the Vaughn Vets & Pets Clinic is open."

I'm treated to my mother's part sob, part whine. It's the noise she makes when she's displeased and pouting about something. She does it every time I bring up moving.

"Mom. I'll only be twenty minutes farther. You and Dad don't even technically live *in* Landry. You're on the outskirts. Plus, you're in Vaughn almost as much as you're here." She visits her best friend at least once a week. And I'm there just as much, if not more so, because some of my closest friends still live there too.

"Not the point."

"I'm not trying to poke a sensitive spot, but I think this might be fortuitous timing."

"Yes, well, Stella thinks this will work out quite well too." She stares pointedly at the sheet of paper still clutched in my hand.

Glancing down, I scan the note. It's a photocopy of a handwritten list of dates, times, and locations. I quickly skim back up at the heading, *LoveVine*.

"LoveVine?"

She nods. "The show is becoming a combined charitable event effort between The League and The Vine—LoveVine's 'producers'. Vaughn's Town Council had an emergency meeting once they heard about Taps and voted in favor of cohosting, allowing The Vine to coordinate production and the online coverage of the show. The group date nights for the show will be held at Rocky's

Tavern in Vaughn. However, a few of the *solo dates* will be held in Landry."

My forehead is tight, my chest itchy. "When did they reschedule the event to?"

"They didn't reschedule. You're still our Hometown Hottie, sweetheart. Now there are two towns joining forces to find you a *lover*."

I flinch in unexpected repulsion. "Please don't say 'lover' like that."

"I heard Delores's granddaughter recently graduated from college and has applied to be one of your '*lovers*.'" My receptionist chimes in, apparently back from her break. "She might be young, but apparently those enormous knockers are all natural."

"That's—" I have no response. "Thank you, Belinda. My mom and I are heading to my office. Give me five minutes before you send Mrs. Sarturo and Zeus into Room Three."

I reach across the counter to quickly and gently guide my mom toward the back of the clinic.

"Mom, we've talked about this. In order for me to believe you are non-sexual—which is exactly how I prefer to think of you and dad—you need to not say things like 'lover.' Especially around my staff, who will probably think this is an acceptable topic of discussion."

"Tough titties, my boy. Sex is great, especially in the morning." She winks at me and I shudder in horror. "So make sure you call ahead before stopping by—especially since your dad is stepping back to half-time." She places her hand on my arm. "Enough about me, let's talk about you. Specifically your love life—or lack thereof—and the reasons for it."

"Pass."

"Fine. My turn. Your romantic life is nonexistent, and knowing you, this means your sex life is also nonexistent. While I'm proud of the gentleman you've become and appreciate that you prefer committed, monogamous relationships, you're only in your early-thirties. It's time to shrug off the few relationship mishaps and open up your heart. And legs—of the right lady, of course."

"Mom. Wow. I love you, but we have leaped over all mother-son boundaries here." I slash an imaginary line between us.

"Well, sounds like the damage has been done, then. We might as well take in the new mother-son discussional terrain."

But behind her determined smile lurks concern.

I take a breath. "I'm fine. I simply need a change. Let me get properly set up in Vaughn, then I'll have time to devote to dating again. I'll even let you set me up on a blind date. *One* blind date. I know how much you've always wanted to do that."

She clasps her hands under her chin. "I really have." Eyes the exact same midnight-blue hue as mine lock on me. She sighs and drops her hands. "Here's the problem, sweetheart. This charity event is happening, and if you bail like I know you want to, I'll understand. I'll be disappointed, and the proceeds to the Humane Society of Sonoma County will be impacted, but if you feel you need to pull out, I'll support you. I only ask for you to give it some more thought first. If you could lean into the idea of finding someone—even just to spend some time with, nothing serious. Someone who might interest you. The way these dates are designed and how the candidates are fielded, there's a strong chance you'll meet more than one woman who piques your curiosity."

"Yeah, and with my luck, I'll pick the craziest of the bunch. Or some environmental catastrophe will strike while on our date. Or one of us will require emergency medical intervention."

"That's very unlikely to happen to you again, honey. Plus, we have off-duty EMS personnel who have agreed to attend each of the events. It's all been very thoroughly planned."

"EMS? It better not be Jaxon." As one of my closest friends, he would definitely jump at the chance to watch me humiliate myself.

"I'm not in charge of staffing," she evades. "I'm mostly helping in the candidate approval process."

"So you're . . ."

"Helping to choose your future wife? Yes."

We've gone from *lover* to *wife*. Jesus.

"This isn't *The Bachelor* show, Mom. I will *definitely* not be proposing at the end."

"I meant girlfriend. Sorry. But how amazing would it be if—" She cuts herself off after glancing my way. "If you got to meet fully vetted women, went on a few dates, and just felt out who you have chemistry with. No planning, hassle, or pressure."

"*No pressure?*" I ask, scoffing. "The whole town—people I know and see often—are going to be witnessing me dating, what? Four . . . five women?"

"Twelve."

"Sorry?"

"Twelve women. There will be twelve candidates to start."

"Great." That likely more than doubles the chances of disaster striking.

Because what my mom and Stella don't seem to understand is that I am inexplicably unlucky in love. And they are taking all of my awful love mojo and making a spectacle out of it. Bringing in more women, more potential for bad luck to crop up and decimate any romantic situation I might find myself in and then putting it on full display.

"Yes, it *will* be great. Just keep an open mind, okay?"

"So this is for sure still happening?"

"Ticket holders will be notified tonight. And because Rocky's is a bigger establishment, we were actually able to open up ticket sales for Vaughn residents as well."

I rub my forehead and wait for my mom's usual positive spin.

"That means an extra twenty thousand dollars for the animal rescue. Isn't it exciting?"

It is. And I'm going to hold onto that thought.

Because for two glorious hours, I believed I was off the hook.

It figures my first direct involvement in this "find Sawyer a girlfriend" town endeavor would wind up being a freak accident that causes the event to nearly double in size, allowing many, many more people to witness my dating downfall.

CHAPTER
FOUR
OLIVIA

I don't even look up from my plate until I'm halfway through my funnel cake. The owner talked me into drizzling caramel sauce on it, and I was unsure—being a traditional funnel cake lover—but the loud moan I let loose into the cluster of picnic tables at Food Truck Friday alerts Larry that it was a damn good recommendation.

"Larry. You are a funnel cake genius," I shout, my mouth still partially full of cake.

"Told you!" he hollers from somewhere inside the Funnel Me truck.

I hum contentedly and take another bite, caramel dripping down my chin.

"You look like a two-year-old who just ate their first, well . . . funnel cake. Hold on, let me grab a wet wipe, and I'll clean you up," a deep, mocking voice interrupts my blissful sugar-devouring privacy.

My eyes flick up to find my brother with a hand cupped around his mouth. "Larry!" he shouts. "You got any of those wet wipes for the littles? This one was a bit too eager."

A joyous laugh comes from the truck.

"Fuck off, Jaxon," I whisper-yell, making sure no kids are hanging around. Thankfully, most are on the playground. The food trucks bring a mixed crowd on Fridays. There's kids who play at the beach, water lovers who enjoy the lake, and residents from Vaughn and surrounding areas who come from various places along the expansive shoreline, stopping at Horton Beach for a treat.

And because it's a licensed event, people also show up for the drinks.

"What are you doing here? Mom canceled on me, and I was looking forward to eating all of this in sweet silence." She requested I bring her back a funnel cake though, and I have yet to decide if the one I have in the to-go container will make it to the house or not.

I've been staying at my mom's house the last couple of weeks, and the guys are there *a lot*. Partly because she feeds them whenever they stop by. The other part is that they are checking in on us. Ethan Vaughn was a staple in this community, a local legend, and the best dad. He's been gone for ten years, but we still feel his loss every day. My brothers have been making up for his absence as best they can, especially Brody, who has been taking on some kind of misplaced blame about what happened, which is also why he returned home immediately after his military contract ended. So they show up, doing things Dad used to, keeping Mom company, being protective over me. It makes us all feel a little closer to what things were like when he was still with us.

"Unless I'm on shift, I'm here most Fridays. Anders often comes with . . ." My brother's voice trails off, little more than background noise as something in my peripheral vision captures my attention.

My head tilts as I take in the broad back of a tall man with incredible calves and a bubble butt I'd one hundred percent bite if given the opportunity. I drag my eyes up to identify who the biteable ass belongs to and find a head full of sun-kissed chestnut hair. It's not trimmed down as short as some men keep it, especially at the tail end of the summer. It curls slightly at his nape, just long enough to run my fingers through.

Huh, he almost looks like . . .

Mr. Biteable turns around and reveals the face of my brother's best friend, Sawyer Fletcher. For years he was the boy next door —literally and figuratively—with floppy hair, and a bright, disarming smile.

Back when I was barely a teen, he didn't pay me much attention. Our four-year age difference felt huge then, especially since I was turning fourteen when he was already an adult heading off to college.

He was always sweet to me, and the age barrier disappeared once we were both in college. The dynamic shifted—we became closer, friendlier, conversations came easier. But at the time, I was in an intentional bad boy phase, followed by an athletes phase, which regrettably ended with Drew.

Nice guys with incredible smiles and bubble butts weren't on my radar back then.

I shove more funnel cake in my mouth, mumbling, "Idiot," to myself. Powdered sugar flies from my mouth, sprinkling the checkered table cover. I swipe at it, hoping no one saw.

"I'm the idiot? I'm not the one who's going to have a sugar crash and pass out drooling on mom's couch."

"I wasn't talking about *you*. Plus, I got the baked mac and cheese to counteract the sweets." I gesture toward the cheesy goodness and scoop some into my mouth. "See?"

"Then who were you . . ." He glances around, and Jaxon waves Sawyer over after spotting him. Sawyer points to Beer Me—yes, it's co-owned by Larry—where he's waiting in line to get his drink.

Licensing Food Truck Fridays for liquor was probably one of the Town Council's better ideas.

"So, little sis, you're finally out and about, huh? I only see you for family dinner lately. When are you planning to announce you're back for good? Keep in mind that I'm shit at keeping secrets, so you've got another few days, tops."

I roll my eyes at him. "I've inquired with some of the midwife practices in the area and plan to ask around if the birthing center at the hospital has any positions available. So you can talk freely about my move back home. Except we're not talking about Drew, okay?"

"No promises," he grumbles, adding some colorful expletives about my ex-husband. I should be glad my brothers aren't aware of the explicit details of our split. "Well, that's good timing since Miranda typically comes out for a bit and would have had questions. She has a group thing in the trails she does on Fridays."

Miranda is the eccentric mayor of our small town. Along with a few other Town Council members, she is rumored to be one of the mysterious contributors of The Vine.

"A group thing?"

"It's called Forest Feelings Friday."

I frown, trying to figure out what that could possibly mean.

"They shout their feelings into the trees," he explains. "It ends up being a bit of a bitch fest. I mean, the premise is sound but the execution is questionable."

I laugh, determined to stay to witness all the Vaughn quirks I've missed.

When Sawyer approaches the table, he gives me a genuine smile. There are no signs of overt curiosity or sympathy. He either doesn't know why I'm back home or doesn't care. Either way, I'm grateful.

His eyes dip to my assortment of food truck delights. When his nose scrunches at the sight of the deep-fried pickle, I almost laugh. While Sawyer Fletcher has always been handsome, smart, and reserved, I've always found his food particularity especially adorable.

"Hey, Liv." He holds out his hand like we might do some kind of man-shake or bro-pound or something. Solid no. Plus, my fingers are covered in caramel sauce.

"Uh, hey." I hold up my messy hands, suddenly wishing Larry had given Jaxon those wipes.

He does this weird pat thing to my arm instead. The pat turns into some kind of caress, our eyes connect as goose bumps break out over the exposed, overheated skin of my upper arm. He snatches his hand back and looks away.

"Welcome back." He clears his throat and takes a swig of his drink. "How long are you here for? My mom said something about a Vaughn family dinner sometime later this month?"

The fact that my family's last name and the name of the town are the same is no coincidence. My ancestors founded this town back in 1869, and we've stuck around ever since.

"Actually, I've officially moved back to Vaughn. You're one of the first to know."

"Before Miranda? She's going to be pissed, but I bet your mom is pretty happy to have you home. And hey, turns out I'm moving back too."

"I heard. And you're the one opening up a new clinic?"

"Yeah, over on Ross Street. I've partnered with the Humane Society to provide some shelter care as well."

"Daisy and I will have to check it out." I almost wish I'd brought her out with me tonight. She makes for a cute, furry buffer but is also an unapologetic treat thief. "Sounds like a lot of exciting changes for you. How are Jane and Hugh handling your move?" I've known his parents since I was young, and I can imagine they'd have thoughts about their son leaving the clinic Hugh owned for nearly twenty years. Sawyer's dark eyebrows dip low into a frown I rarely see on him. "They took it badly, huh?"

"No, they've been truly supportive. Dad is helping out at the clinic until we get our new vet settled in. And Mom was upset I'd be farther away, but she's here all the time anyway." He rolls his eyes. Jane and my mom spend at least a few days a week together. "I'm excited about the move, and the clinic is looking great. Leaving Landry, however, isn't going quite as smoothly. I got on The League's radar last year, and they aren't done with me yet," he explains, a soft smile aimed in my direction in an attempt to defuse his obvious frustration.

"Yeah, Livvie. Didn't you hear about our newest, most eligible, *single* resident becoming the Hometown Hottie?"

I scrunch up my nose. "What's a Hometown Hottie? I've been avoiding almost everyone in town like the plague to avoid questions, so I haven't heard much."

My brother's eyes light up. "Vaughn and Landry are cohosting a matchmaking event inspired by *The Bachelor* reality TV show. They're calling it LoveVine due to The Vine's involvement with planning and production."

"Huh. That sounds a bit familiar, actually. Did The Vine put it on their website? Or maybe I got an email? Something about a bachelor or contestants?" I take my phone out and start searching. "I'm looking it—"

Sawyer's big hand reaches over and smacks the phone down.

All right, then . . .

"Let me catch you up," my brother offers. "Fletcher here volunteered to be this year's Hometown Hottie, meaning he has two towns finding him some lady love—since he obviously can't do it on his own."

Sawyer swipes Jaxon's keys and throws them into the long grass surrounding the gravel picnic area. "You know I didn't volunteer, asshole."

"Aw, come on. You knew I was going to give you shit about this," my brother says, chuckling as he stands to retrieve his keys.

One of Sawyer's wide shoulders gives a lazy shrug. "Where's Anders?" he asks, looking over at Jaxon. "Doesn't he usually join you on Fridays? He'd be a much more reliable brainstormer."

"Wait." I stop licking the sugar off my fingers long enough to ask, "You didn't volunteer? But they made you the Hometown Hottie anyway?"

When I peer up, Sawyer's gaze is on my fingers, then my mouth. He quickly turns away, saying nothing. He's a little rosy at the tops of his cheekbones, somehow brightening the endless depth of his dark blue eyes. What has color rising on his cheeks, I'm not sure, but I'm going to guess it has something to do with the matchmaking event he signed up for. Or maybe my sugary mess is driving him nuts. Either way, flushed is a good look on him.

Sawyer puts his hand down after a quick forehead assault. "Yeah, well this was mostly Stella's doing. She organized an event in Landry last year where the town found suitable female candidates for one of our most eligible bachelors. The event had to be moved to Vaughn, but *LoveVine* will still have a live audience for all group dates and ceremonies, and a film crew for solo dates."

Oof. "That sounds tragically amazing." I pick my phone up again to hunt down some information. "Maybe there's a link to event tickets on—"

Sawyer yanks the phone out of my hands, sliding it into his back pocket.

"Sorry, Livvie, they're sold out for the welcome night and the first one-on-one date anyway," my brother tells me. "But there will be tickets for virtual viewing that will give you access to all recorded nights."

I raise my eyebrows at him, a wide grin pulling at my mouth. My chin hits my propped up fist. "I never knew you were into reality TV or committed relationships, Jax."

My brother looks away, his cheek twitching slightly.

"Ainslee wants to go," Jaxon defends.

I know for a fact that his best friend does *not* enjoy reality TV.

"Pfft, yeah right." My attention returns to Sawyer. "Sorry, continue. The paying audience gets to perv on your girlfriend-picking ceremonies. Then what?"

"At the end of the show, I choose a girlfriend. Mostly against my will," Sawyer mumbles.

"Why didn't you say no?" Jaxon asks. "To be clear, though, I think you should let this play out. And not only because I've already got tickets to a few of the nights and work a couple others as on-site medical staff."

"Dude, I'm not sure if you think this is how a supportive friend behaves, but let me enlighten you . . . it's not," Sawyer tells him.

"So, did you tell them no?" I ask, trying to get us back on track.

"Yeah, I turned them down for months. And then . . . well, it doesn't matter. I'm in it now, and the proceeds are going to a charity I chose, so I'd feel like a complete asshole if I backed out. Especially since there's only a couple of weeks until the opening event."

Jaxon's phone dings, and he digs it out of his back pocket, giving it a quick glance. "Oh shit. I have a date I forgot about. Tell Anders whenever he gets here that I'll be at Rocky's later. You coming too, or are you heading back to Landry soon?"

"I'm sticking around for a bit. I'll head over with Anders."

Jaxon smacks Sawyer's arm and rises from the table. "I'm going to drop some knowledge on you before I depart to enjoy some enthusiastic female companionship."

"Gross." I lightly gag.

He ignores me. "Finding someone to share time with is as easy as you make it, man. Decide what you're looking for, and if you can get anywhere near that with one of these women—women who, I'd like to remind you, are vying for your attention. Or if that doesn't work, temporarily change what you're hoping for." He slaps the impressive bulge of Sawyer's hunched shoulder and then darts off.

As we both watch the idiot get in his truck, I say, "I think what my obnoxious brother is trying to say is that you could make the most of this if you wanted to."

"I get it. And maybe at one point in my life, I would have welcomed it. But between the move and my aversion to dating, I'm wondering if a surprise long-distance girlfriend would be a believable out."

Looking like he wants to crawl out of his own skin, I decide against asking any probing questions about that, and instead I ask, "I'd back you up. Make up a name and a whole backstory about your sordid, overseas love affair . . ." The warm glow of satisfaction spreads through me when his dimples make an appearance.

"I can't even imagine what either town would do if I announced I have a girlfriend, regardless if she lives here or another continent."

"They'd probably insist she apply as a candidate to officially win your love." I flutter my lashes at him.

He shakes his head, and I bite down on a smile.

"Yeah. Which means there's no getting out of this. Not without disappointing a lot of people. Especially my mom. She's excited about me participating in this, dating again." His jaw ticks and I lean forward. There's a story there. "I don't know how to tell her this event will likely crash and burn, leaving us all single, frustrated, and publicly humiliated."

"Oof. Way to go negative." The eyes that flick up to mine are full of dread. "If they *actually* think you're going to find true love by dating a smattering of single, willing women they've chosen for you, they're delusional. They can't know who you're going to fall for or feel a spark with. Anyone can look good on paper, but I'm a firm believer in needing to make sure everything checks out between the sheets too. If they're not making you groan for more and leaving you with your legs twitching, the sports they played in high school, their favorite food, or the countries they've traveled to probably won't seem quite as interesting anymore."

Those cheeks darken under his golden tan again. Why is it so attractive? Flustering him might be my new favorite thing to do.

"Look, people shouldn't jump into relationships they're not ready for. But maybe you go into this with an open mind, meet some women, go on a few dates, leave the door open a crack for whatever happens. And unlike my brother, I'm not just saying that because I want to personally witness your extreme discomfort."

"That sounds reasonable in theory, but I really don't fucking want to. I'd love to be open to the possibility of meeting someone one day. But that day won't be during this town matchmaking event. It just—I can't. They think they're helping me, righting wrongs for the dates they've sabotaged, but they don't know the half of it. And now they're tormenting me with more dates, high expectations, and plenty of witnesses. It's a nightmare."

I nod and twist my lips into a sympathetic frown. Then it occurs to me . . . a fake long distance girlfriend might not work. But maybe a fake contestant?

"Well then, you need a ringer," I tell him.

One of his eyebrows lifts. "A ringer?"

CHAPTER
FIVE
OLIVIA

I hide my amusement at the desperation in his eyes.

"Yes. A ringer . . . a fake contestant. Someone who will be on your side, willing to help you get through this event by being the person you choose for your solo dates. She can be the contestant you end up with but there won't be any expectations, obligations or real feelings being put at risk. She can be your safe out. Essentially, she'll be your Jules."

"Jules?" he asks, confused.

"Your fake long-distance girlfriend I was in charge of naming —keep up!" I nudge him under the table, and as if by reflex, he traps my leg between his. I swallow awkwardly, nearly choking. He releases it, and I find my words again. "That way if all goes to hell—"

"It will," he grumbles.

"—you'll have your ringer to end up with."

"How would that work exactly? And why would she agree to it?"

Shit. Good question. Why would someone he barely knows, if at all, help him convince the town he has fallen in love?

"Is there a prize at the end?"

"I may have agreed to a couple's weekend trip to Lake Tahoe," he grumbles.

"Like camping? Skiing? Hiking? Spa? What kind of trip?"

He shrugs. "Whatever, I'm easy. I'd be up for all of that."

He'd definitely be able to convince one of the contestants to go along with this for a nice Tahoe vacation. Well, he'd be able to convince someone like me anyway. I guess it depends on what kind of women they find for him. Hopefully they know him well enough to choose some outdoorsy, nature-loving ladies.

"I mean, I'd sign up for a guaranteed, all-expenses-paid weekend of nature, adventure, and pampering in Lake Tahoe. Divorce is expensive, so a vacation is not in the budget this year."

"Yeah, I heard about that." His sympathetic eyes hold mine. "Mom mentioned you'd separated and were keeping it quiet."

"Keeping things like this quiet in Vaughn only works for so long. We'd actually been separated for almost a year before the divorce was finalized a few months ago. Once the house sold, I moved back here, and I'm sure by now most everyone knows."

He nods, thinking for a moment. "Well, for what it's worth, I'm sorry. You doing okay?"

"I am, actually." I pull my shoulders back. "This was a good thing. But I'm not sure how the town will react, which was why I was laying low. Lots of people here love Drew. Might make things a little awkward."

"That's shitty." He takes another sip of his beer and scans the beach area. "I don't know a single person who would side with your ex over you, no matter what happened. But people here are going to have their opinions and make sure to share them with you."

The roped muscles in his forearm flex as he sets down his drink. I haven't seen him in at least a year, and either he's more rugged or my eyeballs have become thirsty pervs.

I follow the lines of his arm up to his sculpted shoulder. He's not burly or wiry. He falls somewhere in the middle. Toned, fit, a much lower percentage of body fat than I'll probably ever see up close again any time soon. The golden skin that deepens in the summer from hiking and enjoying the beach is incredibly warm and inviting.

He must attract a ton of female attention. What's happened for a man like this to still be single?

"Do you have a list of who they've chosen so far so you can determine who would be best to approach? I can help you narrow it down if you want. Getting information in this town should be pretty easy, so that's one of the upsides."

"I don't find out who the contestants are until the first night of the show."

Dammit. "Okay, so you have two options. One"—I hold up a finger—"you roll the dice, approach one of the contestants after the first night, and hope she will go along with this plan. This is risky because by then, if it doesn't work out, you're on your own, doing the show without a safety net. Or it could even blow up in your face if she lets it slip what you're trying to do." His nose scrunches while he rubs the skin above his eyebrow again.

"What's the second option?"

"Option two is planting the ringer."

His head tilts as he considers what I've said. Leaning forward across the table, he peeks around, checking for eavesdroppers. In Vaughn nowhere is safe.

"Tell me more about option two," he whispers.

The desperate, serious expression as he leans in, his face mere inches from mine, has giggles erupting from somewhere deep inside me.

"You'd find someone to apply to be a contestant."

"Okay. What if the organizers don't pick her?"

"They will. You have to be strategic. Drop her name a few times, ask about her in front of the *right* people. But don't make it too obvious."

"This sounds like it will require top-tier deception tactics, and I'm not a great liar. Plus, my mom will know something's up."

His mom is amazing, and I love her to bits. But yes, she sniffs out trouble from a mile away. Growing up, the boys rarely got away with anything in front of her. Though, that could be because Sawyer is a total mama's boy and caves the moment she looks sideways at him. It's sweet, but it makes this plan more challenging.

"Think of it as setting the stage to put on a great show for the residents and raise money for charity. You have to believe in what you're doing, and that you're doing it for the right reasons. The people on reality shows are acting, at least to some extent."

His jaw clenches as he thinks it over. Picking at the label of his beer, he asks, "They sent out a bunch of applications last week. Do you think we could get our hands on an application so we know what's being asked? Then we can ensure the fake contestant aces the application and I won't have to lie or bring her up awkwardly in front of anyone."

"I think I might've actually been sent one." That was probably the email I got which mentioned something about participants. "But if not, I bet the moment Miranda finds out I've moved back, she'll ask me directly. Town Council has been trying to corner me to ask questions and 'help' me through this 'tough time'. Pretty sure they think I haven't moved on from Drew and am living a sad, dejected, spinster life."

"Come on, you're not a spinster. You're not even thirty and definitely won't have any issues moving on. Unless . . . I mean, I don't know a lot about your relationship with Drew, but if you're still hung up on—"

I cut him off with a laugh. "Nope. Not even a little. But it's not like I'm going to tell anyone I've had my rounds of rebound sex and don't need to be thrust upon the most eligible bachelors in town. Can you imagine the follow-up questions they'd have for me?" He grins at my exaggerated grimace. "Plus, we want those application questions." Then it occurs to me that Sawyer's mom and the leaders of each of our town's planning committees might find it odd if Sawyer is suddenly on board with this idea. "Do the organizers know you aren't interested in dating and don't want to be their Hometown Hottie?"

"Yeah, they're clear on that. Well, Stella is. And my mom. But they also believe my reluctance to date stems from their interference in a few of my past dating experiences and this is their chance to balance the scales. God only knows what they'll escalate to when this all goes to hell too."

"Blind arranged marriage?" I guess.

"Probably."

"But maybe you get through this and they'll leave you be after?" I say, trying to be positive but my tone comes out high-pitched and uncertain.

"Already made that part of the deal. Still feeling the harsh sting of buyer's remorse though."

"And you won't tell me why you caved? Stella has something on you, doesn't she?"

Those expressive brows dip into a frown before he grumbles, "Not exactly."

A laugh bursts from my mouth—the kind of laugh I haven't experienced in a long time. "That's a yes."

"It's a 'kind of.'" He sighs, but there's a smile playing at his lips. Raking a hand through his hair, he says, "Shit, maybe Jaxon's right and I do need to change my expectations and the types of women I like. Maybe then I'd already have someone in my life."

I scoff. "No. You should absolutely *not* listen to my brother. He is the ultimate player, which is something you've never been and should be proud of. Jaxon may treat them well—if he didn't, I'd lay into him—but not one of those ladies ever sticks, and he's never sad to see them go. I mean, look at who he spends most of his time with. Ainslee is basically his perfect woman, but he's oblivious." I rest my elbow on the table and prop my chin up on my fist. "So maybe don't take his advice to heart. Or even mine. We are not shining examples of emotionally fulfilled, love-savvy adults."

He grins. "I think I could probably do worse—and have."

My eyes widen, silently begging him to explain. Whatever has put him off dating can't be as bad as he thinks, right? One day I'll get him to spill.

"Whoever we find would have to agree to remain single for the next, what? Two months?" I ask.

He nods. "And she'd have to convincingly pretend to be into me and be available twice per week for the duration of the event."

I nod, making mental notes for later since my phone—where I usually jot down notes—is currently cuddling with his ass.

"It doesn't include the stuff we'd have to do outside the event days to make it seem real. Staged encounters, cheesy flirtations, and maybe even some physical intimacy."

"Sex? That might send the wrong message to the organizers that you're interested in dicking around, not finding a relationship. And you don't want to make it seem like you're intimate with more than one or maybe two participants. Lastly, I think fucking your fake contestant would be a *really* bad idea. She might think it's more than it is."

"Whoa. I'm not fucking anyone," he shouts, a little too loudly. "Shit." He searches for onlookers, lowers his voice, and leans forward again. "What I mean is, I'm not hooking up with any of them, in any way. But we'll have to make it look like we're into each other, and that might involve some closeness, hand holding, a kiss or two."

"Okay, so you need someone comfortable with you, who can think on their feet and isn't bothered by a little physical contact."

"Right." His brows pull way down as he thinks about the situation. "What happens after though? Won't people expect the relationship to continue after I make my choice at the end?"

"Maybe the excitement of the Bachelor event kept things exciting in the moment, but in reality, it no longer felt right? Or maybe you find out you're not compatible sexually. Or one of you likes pineapple on your pizza and it makes the other one gag."

"Pineapple on pizza is a deal-breaker, huh? Shit, I'd just want her to not hate dogs, talk in a baby voice, hit on my friends, or confuse real and mythical creatures."

A choked laugh leaves me. "I'm flat-out riveted, Fletch." I lean forward on the tabletop, our arms nearly touching. "That list begs a lot of questions, while setting the bar for female companionship shockingly low."

"Yet the list still exists, and for good reason."

"Well, you have Stella and Miranda vetting candidates, finding you the perfect match. That doesn't ease your mind?" I say, voice high and full of sass.

He gives me a playful glare in return. "Hell no. I need a ringer. Preferably someone from Vaughn. Miranda and the rest of the Town Council might be a bit unconventional and eager oversharers, but they don't have quite the meddling force of Stella and her group. The ringer will need the thirty mile buffer." I've only met Stella a handful of times, but if there's a whole town full of Stellas over in Landry, he's right. "Shit. That means I'll need to find someone this week."

"If you're in a bind, I could do it. I mean, if it wouldn't be too weird." His mouth opens to speak but then snaps closed again. His fingers resume picking at the beer bottle label. "Nevermind. Of course that would be weird. I just got invested in seeing this through, helping rescue our town stud from all the women wanting to get their hands on you." I know where my hands would start . . .

Goddammit, Olivia! Focus.

I laugh awkwardly to ease the tension, but it ends with a snort.

Mentally I slam my head against the wooden table.

"First, 'town stud'?" His lip curls in distaste. "Sounds like I'm being set up as a breeding stallion."

I raise my eyebrows, tilting my head. He's not wrong. He clearly has great genes . . .

A rough, frustrated groan escapes him. "I'll admit your idea makes a twisted kind of sense. We know each other, and then there's the fact that our pineapple preferences are compatible." He grins at me, the hint of a dimple showing. Those freaking dimples are distracting. "But we'd probably have to kiss at some point. And hold hands. We'd have to get close, flirt, touch. I'd brush your hair off your face, like this . . ." His fingers find a wayward piece of my deep, red-hued mahogany hair. Prickles of sensation rush along my temple and cheekbone where his fingertips gently make contact. "Let my hands wander, almost innocently, like this . . ." He follows that piece of hair around my ear, down the side of my neck, skimming my shoulder down to my arm as he releases the wavy strand. The pad of his thumb sweeps down to my wrist before interlocking our hands.

I didn't realize I'd been avidly watching his every move, staring at his hand as it lightly caressed me into a stupor.

My heart is thudding in frantic beats. I drag my eyes up to his, and instead of the hint of a blush on his cheeks, there is something else entirely. Heat. Intent. Intrigue.

And I wonder if maybe he wasn't blushing before—maybe he was trying to lock down this scorching intensity.

"Yeah." He clears his throat, pulling away. "Too weird."

My brain finally switches back on in time for me to agree. "Yep. Weird."

Dammit. Be cool for once. This man witnessed some of your most embarrassing pubescent stages in life. As a grown-ass adult, you're supposed to be a remarkably well put-together goddess.

"Well, I should sneak off before Miranda catches sight of me and forces me to join in on Feral Feelings Friday or whatever it's called." I stand, hastily grabbing my takeout containers.

"Smart," he says, his voice clipped but kind as he too stands. He slides my phone out of his back pocket and holds it out to me.

With a smile, I take it, appreciating for a moment that his residual butt warmth is probably the closest I'll ever get to touching his perfect ass.

"Hope Anders gets here soon and helps you figure out a better solution. Maybe you can convince them to find some bachelors for a Hometown *Honey* instead? I'd volunteer," I quip.

He sidles up beside me, taking the stack of containers from my hands, piling them on top of his.

"I'll make sure to tell Miranda next time I see her. Maybe she'll plan one for this winter."

I glare up at him. "Don't you dare. I'm not that desperate. Not yet anyway."

His shoulder nudges mine, and we start walking toward the parking lot. He lags a little behind, looking deep in thought.

"When it comes to relationships, you've always been the private, quiet type. Is that why relationships have been harder for you lately?"

In a low, rumbly voice which does unseemly things to my insides, he says, "I'm quiet in my public life—not in my relationships, and definitely not in the bedroom. That's part of what has to check out 'between the sheets,' as you put it."

Holy. Shit.

What does he say? Does he grunt? Moan? Growl filthy things? Whisper sweet, sexy praise?

Sweet goddess of all things naughty, I'm a sucker for a dirty-talking groaner.

My feet stop working, and the gravel under my sandals almost takes me down. A firm grip on my elbow keeps me upright as I begin to tilt.

"Whoa," I say as a gush of air leaves my lungs. And I'm not sure if I'm responding to his alluding to his bedroom dirty talk or how hard I almost went down.

"Sorry. That was a stupid comment. I've been spending too much time with Jaxon."

"Mm-hmm. I can only tolerate guy talk in small spurts." My cheeks flame at the word "spurts." *Did you really just say spurts? Fuck, Olivia! Get it together!* "Anyway, it's totally fine, no worries."

It's not fine. *I'm* not fine.

"Yeah, I'm sure nothing surprises you after spending time with your brothers."

"Nope. I'm immune." Not to dirty talk though.

Anders's infectiously boisterous laugh carries through the valley.

"Anders made it. Maybe he'll have an idea of who you can ask to help you out and be your fake contestant. Or maybe he'll treat you to one of his insane hookup stories, and that'll convince you to lean into the 'finding a real girl-friend' idea—even if it's through this town bachelor setup thing."

"Ha. Unlikely." He walks me the rest of the way to my small hatchback. "Thanks for listening tonight. And for the brain-storming."

"Of course." I open my car door and get in.

"And welcome back. You were missed."

"Thanks, Fletch," I say with a smile.

Hands in the pockets of his well-worn jeans, he walks back-ward a few steps, in the way hot-as-fuck guys pull off.

"Hey, Liv?" he calls, tipping his chin up.

I lean out of my open car window. "Yeah?"

"Fuck Drew. I never liked him anyway."

My smile stretches wider, drawing more heat to my cheeks. I bite down on my lower lip, attempting some restraint.

"You don't even know what he did."

"I don't need to. Night, Liv."

"Night, Fletch."

On the drive back to my mom's house, I wonder what the *hell*

I was thinking offering to be a fake contestant among a sea of women vying for a position as his girlfriend.

The last thing I need is to tempt the love gods, or whatever potential powers that be, and risk their wrath for pretending to fall in love.

Which means I shouldn't participate in a pretend relationship with someone wanting to actively avoid relationships.

That's the kind of fucked-up relationship karma I can't afford right now.

Maybe I could view it as helping a friend, supporting him through an event he's obviously dreading. Maybe I could even get us both excited about dating and giving a relationship a chance again.

It's a step forward.

An awkward, somewhat misleading step forward.

CHAPTER
SIX
SAWYER

A loud squeal comes from outside the clinic, and I can't tell if it's a person or an animal.

A burly figure enters the clinic, and I recognize the dog before I recognize his owner. Sammy strides in, tail wagging, sniffing at all the shoes. Sean Wentholt follows close behind, a leash in his hand.

Sean adopted Sammy at the last pet adoption event. Technically, he adopted the pup for his roommate—who is now his fiancée. Somehow the mechanic gets the perfect girl to fall for him because of a dog, but me—a veterinarian with two dogs—nope, no falling in love over here. I haven't even been able to make it through one complete date this year.

"Sean." Given the look on his very expressive face, I have a feeling I should have stayed in the back instead of seeing Mrs. Michaels and her Pomeranian out.

"Sawyer. I know you're about to close up, but . . . well, I'm just going to come out and say it. The League and some very chipper lady named Miranda sent me to check in with you. I've become your official LoveVine point person."

For a moment, I forgot that he's part of Landry's gossip—I mean, 'community information network'—group.

"Man, you get that I'm doing this under duress, right?" I quietly remind him, hoping Belinda is out of earshot.

"Well, there's also the familial expectation and the charitable commitment you made. Double whammy. And we appreciate your time and efforts, of course. We also would appreciate a timely response to the questionnaire you were sent so the selection committee can finalize their contestant choices."

"How many candidates could there possibly be? Just choose the most well-rounded, sane applicants." I shrug.

I've avoided the email they sent for the last few days. The thought of my mom and several others scouring the information trying to find the right woman for me to date induces a fair amount of guilt. And panic.

The idea of a ringer has never sounded better.

"Look man, I'm going to level with you. You can either fill it out or they can guess and choose based on their own preferences. I heard them consider putting a question about the results of the ladies' last medical checkup on there. And there was something about freckles and their association with higher rates of melanoma. It was getting *genetic*, Fletch. So fill out the damn form." He whistles to Sammy and heads toward the door.

He's nearly out the door when he turns around, "Oh, actually, I also need more of that special dog food for Sammy. We ran out and had to use the regular stuff while we were away this weekend. His farts have been making my eyes water. A kid ran away screaming as we walked in here."

I move to the storage area to get his dog food. While hefting the bag back to the waiting area, I tell myself it's great that Sean's the go-between. At least he's levelheaded and will hopefully help me avoid the worst of this event. Maybe he can even work *with* me.

"I'll fill out the questionnaire," I tell him, transferring the bag

FALLING FOR THE BACHELOR

into his arms. "But if you're my point person for this insanity, it means you advocate for me too. We're a team. Got it? If I'm stuck in this bullshit—even if it's for a good cause—you're going to help me make it bearable."

"Fair enough. But there are some things I *can't* tell you."

"But if they don't specifically tell you it's off-limits, it's fair game. And if there are things *I* tell you I don't want you sharing, same rules apply."

"Done." He juggles the bag of food to one side and holds out one closed hand for a fist bump. "For what it's worth, I think this will be good for you. This town has a way of helping you find the path you're meant to be on—even if you don't want them to."

With him helping with whatever he can, and a fake contestant, maybe.

The public dating and scheming will likely have me shame-sweating through every event. But if I could get a friend, someone I'm comfortable around and enjoy spending time with to do this with me, to end up with, no real feelings or obligations to uphold, I think I could handle it. Someone like Liv. But *not* her because . . . Well, lots of reasons—her brothers, our families being friends, my current dating hang-ups, her recent divorce. Even if it wasn't real, it would still complicate things because our families wouldn't know it was all pretend.

But with the ideal ringer *and* Sean on my side, how bad could it really be?

———

THE FIRST QUESTION on the form reads, *Do you have any kinks we need to know about?*

The first fucking question.

First—why do kinks get top billing?

Second—are there kinks they *don't* need to find out about? What makes a kink "need to know" worthy? I almost wish I had a

43

truly depraved one. As it is, a little role-playing and dirty talk is about as adventurous as I've ever gotten. Kinky, adventurous sex requires the kind of trust I haven't much experienced.

The girlfriends I've had since college have been a various mix of sweet, fun, and fiery. Each bringing new horrors and disastrous outings. I legitimately thought I was jinxed.

So I let my friends set me up.

I no longer do blind dates or setups.

I've never dated anyone for longer than three weeks. Ever.

My brother, who's serving our country and is typically only in the States for a couple of months per year, has longer-lasting, better relationships. Cole thinks I'm either too picky or genuinely bad with women. I asked him if he'd want a relationship with a woman who believed unicorns actually existed. Or that the earth was flat. Or who smacked the shit out of a server at a restaurant when she thought the girl was leaving me her number instead of the bill.

His response was, "Where the fuck are you finding these women, bro? You have a thing for the crazy ones or what?"

That's how I came to the conclusion that the chances of finding someone I'd want a relationship with, who was cool with my very limited free time but was still smart and fun, was highly unlikely.

So I should have predicted that letting The League set me up with Chloe Caldwell—now Chloe Daniels—was risky. Her husband, Hayden, still glares at me when I run into them around town, even though our dates were huge failures. Which he is fully aware of considering he sabotaged at least one of them.

While the outings with Chloe didn't end in epic disaster like many past dates, it did land me in this current predicament— being in the spotlight of the biggest, most over-the-top blind date setup imaginable.

Had they interfered in my dates? Yes. Was I still angry about it? No. I don't approve of most of their tactics, but I understood their reasoning.

The bigger question is if their interference was the reason I stopped trying to meet someone again.

The answer is no. And Stella is fully aware.

She recommended I treat LoveVine like immersion therapy. She believes my past dates have been miserable because *I* was miserable. Then she said something about putting positive love juju out into the world so it'll manifest . . . No idea what that means but she had me confused enough to nod along.

But after glancing over some of the questions on this form, I'm legitimately worried about what kind of women The League and Vine members will find.

Within minutes of submitting the form, I get a phone call from Stella.

"Sawyer, I just received your email and took a quick glance at it. Can't wait to really dig in! I'm currently helping Jane field some candidates and found a potential contestant with a few interesting hobbies and skills. She scuba dives. You know what that means, right?"

No, and I don't think I want to.

She doesn't bother waiting for me to answer. "She's skilled at breath control. If you're into that. It's not specified on the form you filled out, though it would fit into the kinks and other sexual preferences questions. So I thought it best to double-check in case you forgot because you left some of those questions blank. And some answers say 'no' even though they were not 'yes' or 'no' questions."

I have no words. No words at all.

"So . . . are you?" she asks again.

I consider hanging up, then she says. "Oh. You're holding your breath right now, aren't you? I'll mark you down as 'enjoys breath play.' Thanks love." She hangs up before I can respond.

Great. My mom's going to read that.

While Stella finds someone who wants me to choke her, I'm going to work on finding the right person to help me with this mess.

What if I gave it half a chance? Or even five percent of a chance, and if no one sparks an "I want you to have my babies and grow old with me" feeling, I can at least say I gave it a shot. Which will ease my guilt-ridden mind for misleading everyone involved. Though I suspect this guilt will dissipate before the end of the first night, and I'll be left with a "fuck this, I don't care, I need out" stance.

Liv was right. A planned, fake romance is the exact out I need to keep feelings from being hurt and negate any false hope. It will also ensure I don't get the quiet, sad look of disapproval from my mom if she found out I bailed.

And if she finds out you rigged the contest?

She won't. And even if she does, the charity gets their money, and everyone got to witness the humiliation of having our towns find me a girlfriend. But at least I won't have had to legitimately pursue all those women. I'll have a partner, a buffer, a lady to fake fall in love with.

With that in mind, I spend an hour painstakingly cultivating a list of potential candidates. Specifically, candidates who are not my best friend's gorgeous little sister.

The first person who comes to mind who might be willing to help me out and loves drama is Jenny. However, she's kept her distance ever since she followed me into the men's washroom at Taps one night, telling me she knows I want her. I didn't. I wanted to piss. I might have snapped at her, threatening to report her stalker tendencies to Sheriff Alex.

Then there's Adriana. She's sweet but there's no attraction there. It's almost comical how much we aren't in sync, even in conversation, but it could still work for that very reason. Unfortunately, she *cannot* keep a secret.

Hannah would be torturous to spend time with, but the all-expenses-paid vacation would have her on board.

From Vaughn, there's Jana. But she's not into serious relationships, and people would question her sudden interest.

Jessica is single and may have already applied to be a contestant. She's a basket case, and the perfect example of someone I likely would have ended up with a few years ago. I cross her off the list.

Sheryl-Anne is hilarious and fun, but she's fourteen years my senior and used to babysit me.

I'm scraping the bottom of the barrel after six ill-advised options.

I pause, tapping my pen in frustration. Seeing my lack of options written out is putting me into a bit of a mental tailspin.

There's one name I haven't written down yet. Resigned to my potential fate without securing a ringer, I sigh and add the name of the woman I've been trying to avoid thinking about.

Liv is fun, smart, gorgeous. I'm unsure if her offer is still valid or if asking her to do this is wise. There are many factors to consider . . . her brothers, who will have thoughts—possibly loud, violent thoughts. And our moms would get serious ideas.

Oh. And after seeing her the other night, touching the soft waves of her deep auburn hair, her pretty, dainty fingers laced in mine . . . I've discovered that I'm intensely, unavoidably attracted to Olivia Vaughn.

Which means I'm completely fucked.

CHAPTER
SEVEN

OLIVIA

Not only did I suddenly get an invitation to apply for LoveVine from The League event organizers, but The Vine also announced my official return to Vaughn over the weekend. They glossed over my "heartbreaking divorce" enough to draw immense interest in the lack of details.

Drew and I, while only a year apart in age, were in vastly different social circles in high school. So we didn't get together until we reconnected in college, but when the town found out, they were thrilled. Our wedding was a huge Vaughn event, so our divorce will likely be met with a similarly intense but opposite reaction.

People are already taking sides, asking questions, jumping to conclusions. And since Drew stayed in San Francisco, I get to experience the brunt of it firsthand.

I've got a cap on so I can hopefully traipse undisturbed down Juniper Street, one of the older roads within our adorable downtown community.

As I skirt around a couple of sidewalk bistro tables, I nearly crash into Mr. Gillespie.

"Don't think the hat is fooling anyone, Ms. Vaughn—or is it

Ms. Kipperson? Did you ever change your last name? Hope not, given the nature of your return to town."

"Hi, Mr. G." He hates when I call him that, but I can tell by his tone I'm in for a prickly conversation, so I might as well get my digs in while my spirits are still high.

"So you're divorced, huh? You look fine. Miranda wanted to circle the wagons, figuring you were all distraught over losing your chance at happiness and child bearing. That you were wallowing in heartbreak and self-pity."

Oof. Poking at my inability to find happiness *and* my ticking biological clock. Good one.

He taps his cane against the pavement when I take too long to answer.

"Nope. I can still bear children. Look at these birthing hips . . . I'm simply ripe for fertilizing." I give one hip a hearty, open-handed smack.

"Don't get nasty with me, young lady."

"Well, see, you answered your own question by calling me *'young* lady.' I still have plenty of chances to reel in my next potential impregnator. Heck, I could still head down to Rocky's or The Hole anytime I want and pick up a young, impressionable, tipsy hunk of a man to put a baby in me. Doesn't have to be smart or anything, as long as he has the sperm I'm needing. Right?"

"I see you still have all your snark."

"Wouldn't want to disappoint. People seem to love it."

He snorts. "So, Ms. Vaughn, I'm hearing some speculation about the details of your divorce. Some even say they heard it straight from the source, but I decided to do some fact-checking. Some of the stuff floating around this town tends to be complete horseshit at least half the time."

That's probably true. And it was only a matter of time before rumors started flying. "What have you heard?"

"Your marriage ended because you are the jealous, controlling type. They're saying you demanded that Drew stop training female clients, but complained he wasn't bringing in enough income to support the big family you desired and you required someone who would keep you in a certain lifestyle. Then there was stuff about when you'd have kids, who he could spend time with, you spending all his money, and how you gave up on your marriage at the first sign of trouble . . ."

He trails off and my jaw drops.

Having lived here most of my life, I'm fairly used to the way things work. People talk about *everything*. And when someone clams up, shock and awe is a reliable tactic to get them to open up.

You got me, Mr. G. I am in awe of this absolute bullshit.

The problem is, there's just enough twisted nuggets of truth in there to reveal that the agreement Drew and I made about keeping the circumstances of our separation and divorce private have been breached.

Because, yes, I did have an issue with his female clients. Not because most of his clients were women. It was that some of those women would send him inappropriate messages and pictures, asking to meet up with him outside of the gym, which he allowed to continue. Oh, and then there was the little issue I had with how he was fucking some of them.

This is why you don't marry the fuckboy. You play with him and then walk away.

"Well, what a fun and interesting twist on the dissolution of our marriage. Sorry to disappoint those wanting to feel sorry for Drew, but it wasn't that he wasn't contributing financially to our household or that he had female clients. It was because he was screwing those clients." I clasp my hands over my heart. "Isn't marriage grand? If they still want to think of Drew as some kind of incredible, panty-melting catch, they are free to chase him."

Mr. Gillespie is wholly focused on me, leaning on his cane as he assesses me.

With a dash more sarcasm, I add. "Hard to believe I let him get away, right? Hold on, let me try to drum up some post-divorce regret." I close my eyes as if in deep thought. After a few seconds, I straighten my spine and open my eyes. "Nope. No regrets. Other than marrying him in the first place."

With my sweetest "eat shit" smile firmly in place, a hint of regret niggles at me for letting the brutal truth spew from my mouth. I stand still, breathing heavily, wondering if poor Mr. Gillespie felt the heat of my scornful words even though they weren't meant for him.

He harrumphs, seemingly unperturbed, giving me a nod. "Wondered if it was something of the sort. Little prick. Never liked him."

I let out a breath and suck in my lips to keep from grinning. "You don't like anyone, Mr. G.," I remind him.

"True. Don't mind kids sometimes. They're honest and real, and I appreciate that about them. Even when they're being shits."

I nod, accepting his rationalization.

"You might want to clear things up then. The Kippersons are spreading some embellished stories to gain favor for their son. People have been saying you're hiding out here, trying to get your life together but floundering, waiting until Drew takes you back."

The rage-fire that's been simmering in my veins explodes as I let loose a dark, depraved laugh.

"Who's saying that? I want names."

He ignores my question. "That's not to say everyone believes it, Ms. Vaughn. I wanted to find out for myself. But some are prone to believing whatever they hear. Thought you deserved to know."

With how enmeshed my former in-laws are with the members of Town Council and other prominent residents, I imagine this rumor had to have originated with them. Otherwise they would have quashed it by now. Which means this information likely came from Drew finally telling his parents. Maybe because they found out the divorce was final? Drew didn't want to tell them, thinking we'd fix things and get back together. And I sure as hell wasn't going to have a heart-to-heart with them.

But it makes sense Drew would spout off about this and try to come out as the victim. He's a petty bitch who would, without pause, turn his back on our agreement—much like he did with our vows.

My phone dings in my bag, and I groan, wondering if the questions and 'friendly check-ins' from nosy Nellies have already begun.

"I appreciate the heads-up and will make sure to straighten this all out." And hopefully prevent as much of this crap as possible from ending up in The Vine.

"Very good. And if Drew wasn't the love of your life, the man you won't ever get over—as they're saying—you might want to make it clear you've moved on from that fool. I've got a grandson who's a few years younger than you. He mostly plays online games and makes videos with his Star Wars replicas, but he'd take you out if I told him to."

Biting the inside of my cheek to keep from laughing, I take a moment to pull together a response. "Thanks, Mr. Gillespie, but I think I might want to aim for a man who is a bit more established, ready for something serious, and not living with several of his gamer buddies."

"Very well. But you might want to be quick about it," he says, continuing on his path down the double-wide sidewalk. "The Vine has already been putting out feelers to write up a clarification to the announcement they made the other day."

Fucking great.

With a parting lift of his cane, he takes off. He stops to give some love to a dog who's tied to a bicycle rack as he waits for his owner. The old man is an ornery bastard to almost everyone, but he sure loves dogs. If I had brought my pooch with me today, our conversation wouldn't have had such a rough start. Maybe. But I have a walk-through for my new condo and that might be too much for her.

My phone vibrates in my pocket, and I sigh before checking the screen. An unknown number. Ugh. That doesn't bode well.

UNKNOWN: Offer accepted. If your half-serious ringer offer is still on the table, I accept. I need a partner for this, and I'll do whatever it takes to make the madness less excruciating.

Sawyer Fletcher has my number?

I probably had his number at one point too, but it's been years since I've used it so maybe it didn't make the last contacts purge? Or he's gotten a new number.

I wonder if he changed it after The League decided they wanted him for the next Bachelor and he thought this was the best way to avoid them. I chuckle to myself and head into Grind for an afternoon caffeine boost.

The question I have to ask myself is if I can do this—help Sawyer by pretending we have a connection building while everyone watches us "fall" for each other.

It's not as if it would be a hardship to spend time with him, but this situation could complicate things. Especially since he's the kind of handsome that draws every woman's eye. He's almost too likeable, too sweet, but then he has this quiet, intense sexiness to him, which almost guarantees a lip-biting moment every time I see him.

Even when I was younger, in a bad place after dad died and nice guys were not on my radar, Sawyer still had an alluring appeal. But it's been a train of thought I'd easily diverted or ignored for years because I was with Drew.

Since I'm single again, there's no denying he's insanely attractive—maybe even more so now than when he was in his early twenties.

That should make this easier, more believable, right?

But afterward, then what? We go back to being friendly, bumping into each other around town, and teaming up to trounce everyone else during our usual round of charades when his family visits during Christmas?

On the other hand, doing this together might bring us closer as friends. And it has the added benefit of ensuring the town understands I'm moving on. I don't wait on men, let alone pine away hoping they take me back. Do these people even know me? Maybe not as well as they once did. But they also always thought of Drew as this amazing man. One they think I couldn't keep.

I'm not petty enough to intentionally leak all the details about our shitty marriage. Though my outburst with Mr. G. isn't a shining example of that. Thankfully, he's not typically the sort to get involved in gossip, but he *is* the sort to investigate matters for himself.

Either way, I'm going to rise above and show them I'm not guilty of being the crazy, controlling, pathetic ex-wife Drew and his family portrayed me as. And I'm definitely not over here waiting on his cheating ass.

I'm moving on.

Starting with LoveVine.

But first, I'd need to get the word out that I'm interested in Sawyer. That I've always been attracted to him, and now I can have my chance.

It's easier for people to believe something that has a grain of truth to it, right? Especially if I'm not even sure which part is the lie.

CHAPTER
EIGHT
SAWYER

"Here's your list of preplanned dates and outings The Vine have planned for all Vaughn events. The backside are the Landry-based events. And I want to remind you all group dates are live, ticketed events, and take place at Rocky's Tavern."

The Vaughn events far outnumber the Landry ones. But what jumps out the most are the date activity details.

"Let us know if there are any scheduling conflicts, and we'll try our best to . . ." Sean seems to grapple for words. "Well, honestly, I was told it's all pretty well set in stone since it was a mad rush to rebook all this to venues in Vaughn, and the production crew has a tight schedule."

I hand the list back to him. "Sean, no. It's all ridiculous. Did you look at these?"

"Hiking with your dog? Did you see that one? Nice and normal."

"Pretty sure it's the only one."

"Romantic chef's table dinner?"

"We're supposed to feed each other blindfolded and describe what we taste and feel."

"*Hot.*"

"Sean," I warn.

"These dates are set, most will be fully filmed unless they're in the wilderness—like the hiking one. The organization and planning behind this has been huge. We had over twenty members of both town planning committees meeting three times a week for months. We've made it fun, interactive, and sexy. Well . . . mostly. I had no part in the boys' night out at the shooting range one. I mean, it's *boys'* night . . . I think they're trying to push you into determining if the woman you've chosen gets along with your friends. But at the shooting range? And with preset questions, each of your friends will have to 'test' the lady? It'll go poorly. But that's not until you get to the last two ladies."

Whoever I do this with will have to be someone I truly get along with. Someone capable of coming through all this crap with ease and grace. Someone my mom and the committee will believe I like.

I can't avoid it anymore. I need Olivia Vaughn.

My attraction to her won't be a problem. I'll make sure of it.

I think I'd be more concerned for my well-being if I *wasn't* attracted to her. But it doesn't mean I'll act on it or be anything other than appreciative of her help.

In a few months, once the show is over and the town moves on to some other drama or event, we go back to being friends.

Ignoring Sean as he attempts to explain the validity of the pottery/*Ghost* reenactment date, I slip my phone out of my pocket and send her a text.

ME: Offer accepted. If your half-serious ringer offer is still on the table, I accept. I need a partner for this, and I'll do whatever it takes to make the madness less excruciating.

OLIVIA: Ooh, intrigue! Something happened didn't it? You'll need to fill me in later. I'm definitely in. I think this arrange-

ment will work out nicely for both of us since my divorce seems to be a popular topic around town lately.

OLIVIA: Anyway, I'm off to bait the hook.
ME: What?

OLIVIA: It's a fishing term. I know you fish—my brothers have talked about what a stickler you are for proper fishing etiquette.

A few times a year, I go fishing with Cole, my dad, and Jaxon, sometimes Olivia's other brothers too. Fishing requires patience, tranquility, and best of all . . . quiet—something I don't get much of at my clinic or while in town.

Hiking and fishing are my go-to winding down hobbies. Usually I do them alone or with close friends, but I haven't taken a woman in a long time. Not since the incident with Deidra. She's still no longer welcome in Sonoma Valley State Park, and I was finally taken off their shit list in the last couple of years.

ME: Are we going fishing? Is that part of your plan?
ME: And speaking of your brothers, what are we going to tell them? Jaxon is bound to give me shit, Brody will probably have his officers surveil me, but Jensen has impulse control issues and at least twenty pounds on me.

OLIVIA: It's getting too cold to fish. I meant bait the hook as in hint that I'm interested in participating, or maybe mention how I saw you the other day. That you're looking hot, and I can't believe you require any help finding a girl-friend. Someone already sent me an application, but I want to lay some groundwork to make sure the right people are pushing for me to be a contestant.

She thinks I'm hot?

That's just what she would say to feign interest, moron. Don't get all fucked in the head about this before it even starts.

OLIVIA: And let me handle my brothers.
ME: You sure about this? You know what you're signing up for?
OLIVIA: I'm sure. It might be a bit weird at first, but I think we can make it fun. It also has the added benefit of solving both our problems. I'll text you once it's a done deal.

See? It'll be fine. Good, even. We won't have to do much more than flirt and hold hands.

Though holding her hand the other night got way more fucking heated than I expected. The simple act of tracing a finger down her impossibly soft, creamy skin, created a hot current that spread from my hand straight to my dick.

That particular part of me is going to have to sit the fuck out for a couple of months. He's not invited to this event.

I'll keep touching to a minimum. We'll set boundaries. All I have to do is get in her space, lean down and whisper in her ear, look at her like I want her. That should be more than convincing.

She's simply doing me a favor while scoring a vacation and solving her town gossip problems. That's it.

CHAPTER
NINE

OLIVIA

"Marco!" I yell as I let myself into my mom's house.

"Polo!" The faint response arises from the back of the house.

I head to the back porch since she's likely out watering her flowers and tending to her garden.

She's kneeling in front of her pea plants, picking tiny weeds from around the base of the trellis. I've barely reached the bottom porch step when Daisy, my part shepherd, part mixed breed, charges from around the side of the house, straight toward me. I give her some love before heading over to my mom.

"Got you an iced coffee from Grind," I tell her, holding it up.

"Oh, thanks, honey! Did they put a shot of—"

"Vanilla syrup? Of course." I bend down, kiss her cheek, and hand her the drink. I kneel next to her, Daisy cuddling up to my side. "What else do you have to do out here? Want me to grab the watering can?"

"This is the last of it. Jensen installed an underground sprinkler system this spring, so watering isn't as much of a chore."

"Sounds fancy. Do you hate it?" I ask. She's old school about most things, but particularly when it comes to her garden and reading. She's strictly rain barrels and paperbacks.

She chuckles. "Not as much as I thought I would, actually. It's been perfect to do the lawn and some of the harder to reach beans at the back of the plot. I couldn't say no to Jensen anyway. Once he gets something in his mind, he doesn't let it go."

"He's always had you wrapped around his finger, Mom."

"You all have your special ways of getting what you want from me, make no mistake."

"What's mine?"

She takes a long, pointed sip from her coffee. "Considerate surprises," she says with a knowing wink.

I narrow my gaze at her. She's right. I enjoy doing things for people, so what? "I don't always have ulterior motives."

"You don't, honey. I'm only teasing." She takes another sip of her coffee. "Please don't stop bringing me coffee."

"I have some news though."

"Oh, so this is a 'soften the blow' coffee? Thought it tasted extra sweet."

I roll my eyes. "I was grabbing coffee and knew you'd want one. But if it also softens the blow, then so be it." She raises her brows at me, waiting. "I signed a lease today. I'll be moving into my new place this weekend."

She heaves out a breath. "Oh thank goodness."

"Mom!"

"Not that I don't love having you, sweetheart. But your brothers have been stopping by more to check on you, and they tend to find new projects every time they're here. It's exasperating—sweet, but exasperating." She takes another sip, pausing for a moment as if she's unsure if she should speak the rest of what's on her mind. "And . . . I also think it will be good for you to have your own place. You need a fresh start. How are you supposed to move on, meet people, build a new, better life if you're living with your mom and your brothers stop by every day to snoop and pry?"

"Right? Did they work out a schedule or something? They even find me when I'm not here."

"Well, that's just life in Vaughn, but I wouldn't put it past them. Where did they track you down?"

"Jaxon found me at Food Truck Friday."

Mom takes off her gloves, starting to stand. I give her a hand up, and she says, "If it helps any, he's there most Fridays, so it might not have been about you."

We move to the covered back porch, and I prepare to dangle the bait. "He said as much." We both stand. "Guess who else was there?"

She drops down into one of the lounger chairs, and I do the same.

"Who?" she asks after taking off her wide-brimmed sun hat.

I clear my throat. "Sawyer Fletcher."

Her drink freezes halfway to her mouth, and I wonder if she heard the nervous tension in my voice.

"Oh? Was he alone?"

"Yeah. He was supposed to meet up with Jaxon and Anders, but Anders was late, as usual, and then Jaxon had to take off. So we . . . talked."

A delighted grin takes over her face as she diverts her gaze. "That sounds nice. Did you hear he's our bachelor for the Love-Vine dating show Vaughn is cohosting?"

"Yes, I did. Someone sent me a contestant application, if you can believe it." One of her brows quirks, and I continue. "Honestly, I think he's nervous about the whole thing. He's had a rough go of dating recently."

"Mmm, yes. Poor thing. He's definitely husband material, though, don't you think?" Her eyes search mine.

"I wouldn't know, Mom. I recently gave mine the boot.

Clearly, I don't have an eye for what makes a man good 'husband material'."

"Oh, honey. Drew wasn't for you." She rubs my arm briefly and then pulls me onto her lounger for a side hug. It brings me both comfort and tears. "I think you've known that for a while though. Sometimes young feelings can appear bigger, better than they actually are. We all make mistakes and you fixed yours. He's gone, you're home and starting over. What's that song . . . 'Next, please'?"

I sniffle through a laugh. "Thank U, Next."

"Right. That's the one." She squeezes me tighter. "It's okay not to get it right the first time, honey. I didn't either."

"What? Daddy wasn't your first husband?" It's a good thing I'm lying down.

"Oh, no. That's not what I meant. He was my first, and only, husband. But I was engaged to another man before your Daddy. He was . . . Well, Pete was a prick. I liked the bad boys when I was young too—you got that from me—and he happened to have a motorcycle and a bad attitude. I was only too happy to be the girl he chose to spend his time with."

"Did Daddy steal you away?"

"Well, Pete and I were on one of our 'breaks.' I was pissed because he drank himself stupid, and sometimes his eyes and hands had a tendency of roaming. He explained that he'd do what he wanted, when he wanted. Then I'd make a fuss and leave him, only to sometimes get tangled up again. Your dad had been witness to our relationship over the months." She's staring into the distance, a tender smile on her lips. "One night at a party, Pete was groveling, trying to get me to take him back again, go home with him. I said no, but Pete wasn't the best at listening. Ethan came right over, threw an arm around my shoulders, and told him to piss off, that I was with him and he was my ride home."

Tears fall from my eyes, my heart full of the love I know grew from that moment.

I lean in closer, waiting for what happened next.

"So I shoved his arm off me, and told both boys I didn't need a guy to claim me, walk me home, or crawl into my bed. They either earned my time and attention or they could find some other girl to put up with their egotistical bullshit."

My head rears back. "Mom! That's"—I burst into laughter, tears falling harder—"amazing. Oh my god. What did Dad do?"

"He took it surprisingly well. He waited for Pete to leave, then asked if he could follow me to make sure I got home safely. When I glared at him, he even offered to stay several paces behind me." Her eyes are shining as she says, "He walked me home, right by my side. Then came to visit me every day for a week before I agreed to a date. After that I knew he was it for me. He was the man in the future I'd always imagined."

It's a while before I can speak, telling her the words I've been holding back for so long.

"I didn't have that with Drew. I saw *a future*—the fun we'd have, what it would be like to live with him, starting our new jobs. But . . . shit. I never saw us getting through the tough times. Or having a family. I had no idea what kind of dad he'd be. He never truly wanted kids but would always say he did to make his mom happy. The year after we married, he admitted he preferred his life the way it was too much. And I'm kind of thankful we didn't ever try for kids. I never really saw our future being more than what we were in college."

I let out a deep sigh, glancing over at my mom, needing to know what she's thinking.

"I know, honey."

Relief and sorrow hit me in equal measures. "Why didn't you tell me then, Mom? Geez." I elbow her and manage a lopsided smile. "Could have saved us all the stupid, sexist jokes and those family dinners he'd ditch out on early. Oh and the cost of the wedding. We spent a small fortune to have it in the baseball stadium he wanted. Though the divorce cost more."

"I wasn't sure until you got out of your honeymoon phase and seemed lost. You didn't seem to know where your relationship was going or if you were happy."

"Yeah. It only got worse. I promise not to be that stupid again."

"You learned a lot from your mistake. You've gotten rid of your Pete, now it's time for an Ethan. And I think this time, you'll see what you want a lot more clearly. This next man is going to take you by surprise."

"Let's hope so. If I ever bring home a Pete again, you'll tell me, right?"

"You'll know, baby. But yeah, I'll accidentally forget his name and call him Pete. He'll think I'm a forgetful old lady, but you'll realize it was intentional." She winks at me.

"Brazen. I like it."

Suddenly, letting my mom believe I'm falling for Sawyer makes my chest tighten with guilt.

She wants you to find the guy, that one exceptional man. The one you can imagine your whole future with.

"Do you think you're ready to get out there and date again? Or have you been?"

"I've seen a couple of guys since Drew. Nobody that had me picturing any kind of serious future."

"If you're having trouble weeding out the respectable men from the Drews, I'd be more than happy to put out word. Actually, Jane and I were talking about wanting to set you up just last week. But with you interviewing and still getting settled here, I told her you might not be ready."

"I'm very ready. I'm home, I have a townhouse, and I think I'm going to get the position on the birthing unit at Vaughn Valley Medical Center. So I'm open to finding a good man to spend time with. Maybe we could set up a *Hometown Honey Love-*

Vine event for me like the town did for Sawyer?" I waggle my eyes at her.

"I think it's such a fun idea, even to get out there and spend time with potential love interests. And Sawyer chose such a wonderful charity to support. I don't think he even realizes how many women applied."

"I bet. I couldn't believe Sawyer agreed to participate though. The man could get any woman he wanted, all he has to do is put himself out there. I mean, growing up, I always had a bit of a thing for him. I was distracted by all the wrong boys, but I still had eyes. At the time, though, the older guy with the devastating dimples wasn't ever really an option for me. Jaxon would have flipped, and it never would have worked given we were both living in different cities going to college. I mean, I'm probably not even his type. He's always kept his romantic life fairly quiet, so who knows." I duck my head down, a real blush rising to my cheeks remembering his comment about being vocal in the bedroom. "I'm sure the organizers will put together a great event and find someone perfect for him. Even the short amount of time I've put myself out into the dating world has been rough, but this whole LoveVine thing sounds kind of fun though."

A slow smile pulls at my mother's lips. "It does, doesn't it?"

And just like that, I'm in.

CHAPTER
TEN
SAWYER

Pulling up to the address I was given the other day, I find a cute townhouse with a short, wide front yard, a stack of flattened boxes leaning against the front railing.

Did she have help moving?

The front door opens before I can give it anymore thought. Liv's head peeks out, her natural reddish-brown hair I've always been fascinated by twisted up into a bun. She waves a hand in a shooing motion.

Huh? I thought she wanted me to come over so we could discuss our game plan?

She points down the road and then at her eyes, exaggeratedly looking around.

Oh shit. She told me to park down the road so none of the neighbors spot my car outside of her place. It's the reason we're meeting at her new place and not mine. I live by two League members and there's no way someone wouldn't notice Liv driving through town and winding up at my house. Cursing, I put my car back in drive and park down a few blocks.

Ball cap in position, I take the alleys to get to her place. When

I reach her yard, I check for Daisy. I've only met her dog a few times, so I'm not sure how she'll react to me.

"Get in here!" Liv whisper-yells from the screen door.

Feeling like a criminal, I glance around, making sure no one is watching before I jog across her yard.

She cracks the door, holding it open. I brush past her, turning sideways but still grazing her hip. Fighting the desire to peer down at her ass as she closes the door behind me, I move into her empty dining room.

"Sorry about the place. I don't have any big furniture yet. I'll be accumulating it slowly. Hope you don't mind eating pizza on the floor."

"That's how I prefer to eat pizza. Unless Karl is around, he's well trained but can't say no to pizza." It was one of the first foods he managed to snatch out of my hand when I first got him. He's a gorgeous Australian shepherd, but as a rescue from a failed adoption, he required a lot of training. Now the only times he acts up is when it involves his favorite foods and cats.

"Well, your pizza is safe since neither of our pups are here tonight."

"Where's Daisy?" I ask.

"At my mom's. I still have some cleaning and painting to do and didn't want her to accidentally get into anything."

Liv is still avoiding my gaze and keeps flitting around while I take in her new place. She's wiped her hands on her jean shorts at least twice. Is she just nervous about getting caught? Wanting to take back her offer?

"Did you order me one with pineapple?" I tease, hoping to distract her.

Her eyes finally lift to mine, her mouth twitching as she fights a smile. "Out," she says, pointing to the door.

"That was a test and you passed. Now give me the pepperoni."

She grimaces. "I ordered you a veggie pizza. You're typically super healthy, so I thought you'd prefer it to a big, greasy, cheesy pepperoni pizza." Her shrug almost seems natural, but her sparkling hazel eyes betray her.

"Liar. I might generally make healthier choices, but not when it concerns pizza." I scoff before muttering, "Veggie pizza," with obvious disdain.

I lead the way to the living room where she has napkins, plates, and two pizza boxes waiting.

"Let me guess . . . the other pizza is cheese?"

"Nope. *Extra* cheese," she answers, a proud smirk lifting the corners of her plush lips. I shake my head, mostly to clear it of my thoughts about her mouth.

"You have no furniture, barely look moved in, but I can almost guarantee you have at least three kinds of cheese in your fridge."

She frowns, hands coming up to those curvy hips. "You think you know my cheese habits?"

"I used to regularly eat out of your family's fridge. So yeah, I know your cheese habits."

Liv scrunches up her nose, dropping her hands. "Fine. I technically have four kinds of cheese in there." She drops down by one of the place settings. "But one is a cream cheese spread, and I don't think that counts."

"Cream cheese is still cheese. It's even in the name," I inform her while joining her on the floor.

She shoves a box at me. "Eat your pizza."

I pop the top and inhale. Pizza isn't a regular occurrence in my diet, and I'm currently reconsidering my stance. Grabbing a slice, I fold it lengthwise with one hand before shoving half of it into my mouth.

"Shit, that's delicious," I mumble.

When I glance up after taking another giant bite, Liv's got a slice with strings of cheese falling from the sides held up to her mouth, but she's not eating. She's watching me.

We stare at each other, me chewing, her gaze skimming along

my face with irises that appear a more intense green as they lock on my hat.

She bites her lip before reaching over and plucking it from my head.

Swallowing my bite, I ask, "Was my hat offending you?"

"Yes. I mean, no. It's so . . ." She sets it down, sliding it away. "You'll get it dirty."

Her creamy cheeks turn pink as she goes back to her pizza.

Women are confusing as hell. I'm beginning to think I'm the reason they act all nutty and my dating life is shit. I can't even eat pizza with a friend anymore without it getting weird.

"Let's talk about how this is going to work. We need a plan for how to act, what to expect, and our predetermined encounters outside of the events," she suggests.

"Right. Well, I have the basic schedule and theme for each date. Let's decide which ones I'll be sure to choose you for, what days we'll have our encounters, and then each week, we'll debrief and modify things if we need to."

"That works. Should we come up with a code word for if either of us gets uncomfortable?"

"Uncomfortable how? Like if I want you to interrupt and save me from another contestant? Actually, that's a genius idea. How about 'cheese?'"

"Okay, first, that word is too commonplace in my vocabulary to be used as a code word. Second, I didn't mean it as a 'rescue me from the clutches of other women' type of code word. But if you don't want to wear the whistle I got you, then we can definitely use the code word for that too."

Laughing, I grab another slice of pizza. "Good to know. So if you didn't mean it like that, how did you mean it?"

"Well, in case things get uncomfortable between the two of us. Like if one of us is faking a little too well, getting too close, touching too much, going in for a kiss, and one of us wants to pull back. We can use the code word to let the other person know to dial it back a bit."

"Olivia . . ." I push my plate away and shift so I'm fully facing her. "I would never do anything to make you uncomfortable. So if it gets to be too much, I definitely want you to be direct and tell me."

"We'll be in front of everyone, so we can't just say, 'Hey, can you nix all the touching' or 'What's your tongue doing in my mouth?' We're *supposed* to want to be all over each other. Which is why I think a code word would be best."

I roughly swipe at my forehead, not liking where this is headed. I don't want to make her uneasy. "Will touching you make you uncomfortable? I want to know where the lines are."

"No, touching won't make me uncomfortable."

"Okay . . . Well, help me understand because I don't want to feel like an asshole every time I approach you because I don't know if I'm doing something wrong."

She drops her head into her hands and groans, muttering something.

I reach over, touching her wrist, coaxing it away from her face. "Want to try that again but using real words?"

Her eyes turned darker, more hazel—no longer the playful green they were five minutes ago.

"I wasn't asking because *I* would be uncomfortable. I was asking because I can be a bit touchy-feely and wasn't sure if it would be okay with you. If we have a code word, then you can signal when you want me to step back or if I've gone too far."

Oh.

Ohhh.

"Liv, that's not an issue. Unless you plan to stick your hand down my pants in front of everyone, there won't be any problems with you touching me."

"So an ass grab during the first group date is totally acceptable?"

FALLING FOR THE BACHELOR

With a grin, I grab another slice of pizza. "Let's maybe wait until the second group date for an ass grab. But if you can't wait, you can cop a feel on my way out tonight."

"I might hold you to that," she says, picking her pizza back up. "What else should we be prepared for?"

"They are going to want us to talk about our past relationships. Sean said to have something prepared to say about why I'm still single at thirty-two years old."

"I'd like to think they'd phrase it more tactfully, but it's doubtful. So what did you decide you'll tell all of us, and the thousands of people witnessing these arranged dates?"

"That I haven't found the right woman for me yet, but I'm eager to meet her."

"Oh, great answer. What's the real one?" She's sitting with legs bent and her chin propped on one knee, curiosity lighting up her face.

"That *is* the real answer."

"Nope. There's more," she says with such confidence, I'm sweating a little.

"Yeah, I guess there is."

"Plus, you *do not* seem eager to meet anyone. Otherwise, you'd have been more open to this whole thing instead of panicking and looking for a way out."

"I didn't panic." I totally panicked. Still am. We are only days away from the first event.

"Mm-hmm."

"Why are *you* doing this? You mentioned this situation solving both our problems. But you're newly single and could be out there dating for real."

"At first I merely offered to help you out. Honestly, I thought it might be kind of fun. Prearranged outings, a sly game of pretend, finding out what our kooky towns have in store for some of the singles in the community."

"It'll be entertaining for everyone who *isn't* a participant."

"I plan to have a great time, thank you very much."

"But then?"

"What?"

"You said 'at first'. What changed?"

"Oh. Well Drew, or maybe his family, has been spreading some misinformation about why we got divorced. I found out the details the other day."

"Shit. Was it bad?"

"Yeah. Apparently once I've fixed my controlling, gold-digging tendencies, I'm hoping Drew will take me back. Until then, I'll be here, on some kind of marriage time-out, pining and thinking about what I did wrong."

"Drew has money?" I ask, thoroughly confused.

"*Thank you!*" she says, pointing at me with her pizza. "No, I paid most of the bills, including his tuition payments for a degree he never finished. He spent more money than he made, so I ended up taking up all the slack and then having to foot the bill for the divorce too. I think I get to be a bit pissy about that."

"He wasn't helping with the expenses?" What a piece of shit.

She sighs. "That wasn't even one of the main reasons our marriage didn't work."

"What was?" I ask, desperately curious.

"It's a long, shitty story."

"I have some of those too."

"Do they have anything to do with why you've given up on dating? I'd even go as far as to say you're *scared*."

"I'm not scared of dating." I wouldn't use the term "scared." I have a legitimate reason to exercise extreme caution. "I don't have the time or energy to be in a relationship right now, and I definitely don't want to date anyone while the whole country watches."

"Hate to break it to you but that last part is still happening."

"But it won't be real. We know each other and can fake a great date."

"Guess we're going to find out."

I narrow my gaze at her. "Is this your way of avoiding my questions about what really happened with your ex?"

Liv pokes a finger into my shoulder, saying, "You are a smart man. Already several steps up from previous boyfriends."

"If you're using Drew as a baseline for relationship expectations, I'm about to blow you away." My tone exudes playful confidence, but I'm dead serious. If Drew has been taking her for granted for years, I'm at least going to show her how a real man would treat the woman in his life.

"Guess we'll find that out too," she sasses.

I grin, asking her again, "So why are you doing this?"

"I'm hoping the idea of coming home and eagerly chasing after a missed opportunity with an old crush will squash any notions that I'm still pining for my ex. The whole 'second chance at love' really gets those matchmaker hearts all aflutter."

"An old crush, huh?" My knee bumps hers.

"That's what I've led my mom to believe, yes. She always thought I had a thing for you. Or maybe she always hoped? But I wasn't your type and you weren't mine. Unless you had a dirt bike or motorcycle I didn't know about or became very into competitive sports when you went away to college?"

"Nope. I stuck to education while in school. And I like my brain and limbs to be fully functional."

The quiet giggle I'm sometimes able to coax out of her creates a simmering warmth inside me. Which keeps me from asking her why she thinks she wasn't my type.

"I think my mom wants me to start trying again. Be happy. I assume she also enjoys the process of finding the right woman for me. But the problem is, if I find a woman who truly makes me happy, doesn't fuck me over or test my sanity—someone who has me thinking about her nonstop—I'd probably be tempted to wife her up. But it's never happened and I don't have the heart to tell my mom it'll likely never happen. Finding anything other than a mediocre connection and companionship is aiming high given my track record."

"We both deserve better than 'mediocre,' Sawyer. For now, though, I'm hoping this convinces everyone I'm not all torn up over Dickhead Drew." She rolls her eyes, a resigned smile on her face. "Even if it doesn't, it will still be good dating practice. For both of us. Getting taken out on a proper date will be a nice change."

"Had some improper ones?" I ask, hoping to lighten the stormy expression on her face.

"Maybe." She shrugs. "I made a few attempts after the divorce went through. Figured it would be valuable for me to build some confidence and mentally and emotionally put an end to my failed marriage. I realized quickly though that I prefer what Jaxon refers to with disdain as 'relationship sex.'"

What I think Liv doesn't know about her brother is that he's actually mostly talk.

"Well, if it makes you feel any better, I haven't had a 'proper date' in a long time either. Mostly by choice, but the ones before that weren't all that proper either."

"Oh." Her eyebrows raise in surprise. "Is that part of the reason you weren't on board with this? You want to keep your relationships . . . um, *improper*?" My face scrunches up in confusion, losing track of what euphemism we are using the term 'improper' for. "You know . . . hookups?" she clarifies.

"Oh. No, that's—shit. That's not what I meant at all. I just don't want to get back out there yet. I'm busy and . . . well, there's a few reasons. But the very public spectacle this show is going to be makes the idea of dating even less appealing."

"Right. Much too public for the vocal bedroom activities you enjoy."

I nearly choke on a bite of my pizza, and she ends up slapping a hand on my back. The moment I catch my breath again, I look over at her and am treated to flaming cheeks and eyes full of amusement with a hint of uncertainty.

"Were you waiting to bring that up again?"

"Maybe."

"Well played. I almost died."

"You're fine, you big baby. Plus, I heard you like a little light choking."

Fucking hell. Who else did Stella tell? "Where did you hear that?" I ask, my voice still hoarse from the pizza going down the wrong way.

"My mom was talking to yours, and it might have come up . . ."

"Well, fuck. That information went even more sideways than I expected."

"Don't worry. I didn't ask any questions." I give her a small appreciative smile. "I didn't want it to taint all the different scenarios I imagined for how this particular rumor was created."

I knew her staying quiet was too much to hope for. "Stella had asked—"

Her hand lifts up to cover my mouth. "Don't ruin it with common sense and logical explanations." Her eyes go wide before she removes her hand. "Sorry. I didn't mean to cover your mouth. Was that too . . . *sexual* for you?"

She peeks up at me through her lashes, biting down on her pouty lower lip before exploding into a fit of laughter.

This brat is about to get it.

I swipe her pizza and toss it on to her plate before kneeling and moving into her space. She leans back, her bent leg dropping to the floor, unintentionally making more room for me. I'm hovering over her, hands planted beside her hips, noses almost touching.

My hand covers her mouth. "I don't know, Liv, do *you* think it's too sexual."

Heat flares in her eyes, and I know I fucked up. She's practically under me, breathing heavy and arching into me. I'm seconds from fucking my friend's little sister, and I've never felt more out of control. Never wanted anyone more than this sassy woman with the incredible curves, mesmerizing eyes, and sunset-colored hair I want to run my hands through.

She's so fucking gorgeous, and the more she talks, the more I want to devour every word from those sexy lips.

I remove my hand so she can answer and I can hopefully calm the hell down.

"I think I might need our code word and a list of your kinks so there's no more surprises." Her voice is teasing and edgy, almost as if she's unaffected. But her eyes tell a different story. They are dark, curious, blazing.

Shit. If she wants me back . . . We. Are. Fucked.

"Pineapple."

"Huh?" she says, tipping her head.

"Pineapple can be our code word for when you tease me but can't take the consequences."

Her mouth drops open in a scoff as she rolls her eyes. I want to grab her hips, haul her tightly against me, and thrust my tongue into her mouth.

Instead, I retreat and sit my ass back down on her floor.

"So Tuesday night I'll be pleasantly surprised to see you and will make my way to you if we're given time to mingle. When Garrett Caldwell was part of Landry's last town matchmaking attempt, they had him do a quick three minute date with each contestant as a get-to-know-you thing. Want to plan ours out?"

She nods, but there's something in her gaze I can't quite decipher.

We go over a few details of what things to discuss and how we can make sure the audience notices interest brewing between us. I ask her to do some recon work with the other contestants after she meets them.

After cleaning up the remnants of dinner, she asks, "Do you

have time to meet up again on Wednesday? To debrief before Thursday's solo date."

She gives me a small smile in return before turning away. "Wednesday works. Same time?"

Putting my hat back on, I nod, not trusting myself not to say something stupid or do anything other than agree and get the hell out of here. I haven't totally fucked up yet, so it's only a matter of time.

When we get to the back door, she pats my arm and says, "See you at the big event, buddy."

"Uhh, yeah. Sure. See you there, friend," I reply, infusing as much mocking awkwardness as I can muster.

She covers her face with her hands, muffling a garbled groan.

"What the heck was that? Hands down that was the most awkward goodbye you've ever given me." I'm not sure which is worse, this or the sexual tension from earlier.

"I know. Sorry. I suddenly got weirded out about how to act around you when it's just us since things will be different when we're at the event."

"We could simply say bye or a fist bump or maybe—if you insist—a high five. Though I'm not a high fiver usually, so it might feel as awkward."

"Yeah. That works. But then I was thinking about how we'd end a date or I'd accept a rose—"

"Daisy," I correct with a grin.

"Right. I'd accept a daisy and we'd fist-bump? That doesn't exactly convey romance."

She's not wrong. "We'd hug. We've hugged, haven't we?" I think back to holidays, birthdays . . .

"I don't think we have."

I know for a fact I've hugged every other member of her family. Never her. Did I do it intentionally?

She snaps me out of my thoughts by saying, "We should practice."

"Practice what?" I ask, but I already know.

"Hugging. What if our first hug goes as horribly as the bro-pat I just gave you? The crowd will outwardly cringe as hard as I did on the inside. We want them cheering for us."

"Fine. Bring it in. We got this," I tell her with confidence I don't have.

My hands go to her hips automatically pulling her closer. She stiffens against me but then lays her hands on top of my forearms to steady herself. Stepping closer, I tighten my grip for a moment before flattening my palms and letting them slide into the dip of her waist, up her ribs, and wrapping around her back in a loose hold.

I gaze down, waiting for her reaction, her next move. I don't have to wait long before her hands move from their spot on my arms, up to my biceps before shifting over to my chest. Her soft palms flutter there, making my pecs twitch involuntarily.

When my breath stalls, she glances up, gliding her palms upward, creating an unpredictable arousing friction against my nipples.

Wasn't expecting that. Fuck. I'm getting hard, and there's no way she's not going to notice if this hug lasts more than a few seconds.

She finally wraps her arms around my neck, stretching on to her toes, pressing even tighter to me—and my unwanted erection.

Her cheek rests on my shoulder, and my arms tighten around her.

"Told you we had this. Anything else you want to practice—"

Knock, knock, knock.

We jump apart like we're sixteen and our parents caught us making out.

She puts a hand on my chest and leans backward so she can peer through the kitchen to the front door but keep me out of sight.

"Livvie, open up. I've got a shit ton of paint stuff to bring in."

"Shit, it's my brother," she whispers.

"Which one?" I ask because her twin brothers sound exactly the same. If it's Jaxon, we could maybe tell him the truth, and he might be okay with it.

"Jensen."

"Fuck."

"Yeah. You sneak out of the back yard. I'll keep him in the living room until you've had time to clear the alley." She places both hands on my chest, this time pushing instead of exploring. "See you Tuesday."

She closes the door, and I watch her rush through the kitchen, shouting that she's coming.

Don't think dirty thoughts. Don't.

I jog out of the backyard with a boner and a feeling that Liv becoming a fake contestant who I pretend to fall in love with will end up being either the best thing that's happened to me in a long time, or my ruin.

And that's saying a lot because I've dated women who have done some pretty fucked-up shit.

CHAPTER
ELEVEN

SAWYER

My palms are sweating, and my dress shirt keeps trying to strangle me. Miranda ushered me straight into one of the back offices to wait until the start of the event. They want my reaction to the contestants to be real, which means I can't catch a glimpse until they're presented.

"There are a few ladies you've already met, and some I know this town is going to be rooting for. Good thing we are letting them choose some of the solo dates."

My eyes cut to our mayor, but she's already talking to one of the bar's staff members as she prepares for our entrance.

"What was that, Miranda? The audience chooses the individual dates?" This was not in the details I received.

"We are calling them 'solo dates.' No audience, no other contestants, not even the organizers will be in attendance. Only the two of you—and the cameraman, and likely Sean, of course."

"Yeah, sounds romantic. But what was that about the solo dates not being of my choosing?"

"Oh, we thought it would be fun and would encourage audience engagement and enthusiasm if they were able to vote for one or two of your solo dates."

Shit. The walls around our plan start to shake. Like a strong breeze threatening to tumble the delicate house of cards we've built.

"Miranda, that wasn't the deal. What's the point if I don't get to choose who I want to spend time with?" I try to reason with her. "The solo date time is limited, and I'm going to need it to determine which contestant is the one I want to explore a long-term relationship with at the end of this."

Hopefully, it's a solid enough argument to get her to reconsider letting the audience choose some of my dates.

"You still get to decide who gets a daisy, Sawyer. This gives you the opportunity to spend some precious one-on-one time with one of the participants you maybe haven't had the chance to connect with yet. Or a woman they think would be a decent match. Or make pretty babies with. Hard to say with this town." Her tinkling laughter echoes through the room.

Well, this is going to fuck our plans right up. I can't go on random dates with random women. I scratch my thigh through my slacks. They are super rough and itchy. The sweating isn't helping either.

Shit, I think I'm breaking out in hives.

Sean strides into the room, amusement shining in his eyes. The man was supposed to be my point man, prepping me for this.

"Time to head out there," he says to me, tipping his head to the door. "They'll introduce you, and then each lady will greet you as Miranda and Stella provide some details about them. Make sure you're paying attention."

A member of the production crew flags Miranda down from the end of the hallway.

"Oh, I'm already supposed to be up there!" Miranda rushes off to join the man wearing a headset, a low hum of excitement emanating from her.

I follow, sending Sean a glare as I pass. "A heads-up about the audience-chosen solo dates would have been nice, Wentholt."

He walks ahead of me, the hallway too narrow for us to walk side by side what with his ridiculous shoulder width. I've been meaning to ask what deltoid workouts he does, but that day won't be today. I need to focus and try not to fuck anything up.

"That was one of those 'they specifically told me not to tell you' things."

"Why?" I ask.

"They thought you'd fight it. And said something about how you might shy away from the whole experience, and go with safe choices."

I frown, wondering if they could have predicted what Liv and I have planned.

No. There's no way.

But it does mean, now more than ever, we'll have to work harder to sell our relationship. Maybe the audience will choose her anyway.

———

THE CONTESTANTS ARE BROUGHT OUT, one by one. The producers have placed me to greet each woman after she's announced, a brief introduction made including their names, age, height, job, and an interesting fact about them. I'm to stand at the cocktail-height table on the stage as our chipper hosts talk about each candidate. When Miranda and Stella are done with their spiel, the participant walks over and stands with me. I get several hugs, some kisses on the cheek, and a few handshakes. We are supposed to speak for a few minutes, the microphones at the table picking up our stilted conversation. It's painful. I talk to people daily, I'm a people person almost as much as an animal person. But this is something else altogether.

My heart is pounding, and I barely remember any of the women, none of the details. I've lost track of how many contestants I've met.

Some seemed almost as nervous as I probably looked, and it eased my mind a little. Until the cheers, laughter, or comments from the audience would trickle in and I remembered how many people were witnessing our small talk.

When Miranda says Olivia's name, I tune out everything else and pay attention as she appears on stage in a stunning, deep purple dress, her auburn hair flowing in long waves, those hazel eyes appearing especially big and bright in her flawless face. She turns to me, and my gaze flickers to the coral-tinted lips I want to touch. And taste. I wonder when my curiosity, this craving I seem to suddenly have, will be satisfied. When we'll share a kiss for the show. Maybe it'll be enough.

She walks toward me when her introduction is done. Her gaze lifts to lock with mine, and she gives me a wide, nervous smile. I grin back with a wink, trying to boost her confidence and communicate that we've got this.

Her hands find my biceps when she reaches me. She surprises me with a kiss on the cheek, and I take the opportunity to whisper, "You look amazing." Liv pulls back to lock eyes with me and whispers, "You too. You're supposed to act surprised, remember?" I laugh because she's right. I was distracted.

We sit down, and I decide to break the ice, hopefully catering to the audience a little to get Olivia in their favor. "So, for those who aren't aware, I've known Olivia since we were kids. Our families are close, and her brother is one of my best friends."

"*Ex*-best friend, Fletcher," a harsh voice from the audience declares.

My gaze searches the crowd, but the person I'm expecting to find is hidden in the mass of attendees. She told her brothers, right?

If she had, wouldn't Jaxon have confronted you about this? Questioned you? Told you to immediately back the fuck off?

But rational thought had no room to process this since frustration and panic taking up every square inch of space in my mind for the last week.

"I was the annoying preteen who would try to hang out with all the boys when Sawyer came over," she says, shrugging at the people observing us.

"And now they are all huge men who will probably beat my ass for taking you on a date. Especially after I admit to everyone that you grew into a beautiful woman I never thought I'd have a shot with." Cooing erupts from the audience, but I keep my eyes on Liv.

"You still don't have a shot, Fletch." Jaxon calls from somewhere left of the stage. "Especially once Jensen gets here. Should be quite the show . . . dating, dinner, and our vet getting decked."

My best friend has the audience's rapt attention. If it appears the Vaughn family is against Liv and I being together, this could all backfire.

Harper steps out from behind the bar. "Actually, I heard Jensen's squad was called out to an emergency involving Gracie." A few gasps of concern for the sweet but clumsy Gracelyn Parker buzz through the crowd.

Jaxon speaks up again, a grin on his face. "Apparently, she's fine—as fine as Gracie can be with all the shit she seems to get into." The audience chuckles. "But I doubt my brother will make it here anytime soon. Plus, he doesn't have a ticket."

"You didn't tell them you were a contestant?" I ask, but it's not really a question at this point.

She grimaces at me. "With my brothers, it's better to ask for forgiveness than permission. Plus, I'm an adult—a single female adult who wants to explore a potential spark with the boy I grew up with who turned into a total *stud*." Her eyes sparkle as she teases me again with that awful nickname. "I'd be stupid not to, right ladies?" she asks the spectators. The shouts, hoots, and comments she gets in return have me shaking my head as I stare at her. She's good at this.

Liv and I prepped for our short 'first meeting' conversation the other night, so we decided to make this part of the show a casual conversation about our hobbies and career aspirations. But we get offtrack when Liv encourages me to talk about my partnership with the Humane Society.

She leans in, a charged tingle spreading up my arm as she rests her hand on mine, and suggests I bring some of the animals who need adopting or fostering to the next show. Miranda interjects with excitement, offering to give me a section of time preshow for some 'pet love' each week.

There's a signal from the production crew that we've gone well over our time slot, and Miranda brings a close to my time with Liv. I meet one other contestant, making a total of twelve before dinner is announced.

Seating is assigned for each participant. Sadly, Liv isn't anywhere near me. I can't help the frown etching its way onto my face. My eyes seek hers as she finds her spot. She grimaces, presumable realizing she won't be able to get closer to me and I'll have to simply make it through.

I start to relax when the women sitting on either side of me don't require me to be an active participant in conversation. They take care of all the talking. Takes the pressure off but does necessitate a lot of listening when I'm already preoccupied and overwhelmed.

Between all the questions and distractions, I've barely eaten dinner when Stella approaches me, greeting the ladies as she passes them. "Sawyer, a word?"

She steers me away from the long table. "Stella, something wrong?"

"I wanted to remind you that ten daisies are in the back office waiting for you. Please mark down your choices and give them to Sean. We will announce the contestants coming back next week and the two ladies who will not be moving forward."

"I'll give the list to Sean."

"Very good. Oh and there's another daisy—the one covered in glitter, with the pink ribbon. That's the flower given to your solo date."

"I think I already know who that will be."

"That's lovely, dear. However, tonight the audience will choose your solo date. Gets everyone more invested right from the beginning."

Fuck.

Fuck fuck fuck.

"While our attendees are finishing their dinner and ordering more drinks, they will be given the opportunity to vote on who they'd like to see you go on your first date with. For this first show, that woman will also automatically move on to next week." I guess it leaves one less person I have to randomly choose. "So you go on back to the office and make your list. Oh and in case the lady who is chosen for your solo date is someone you have on your list to eliminate, you may want to have a backup." She pats my arm. "You have ten minutes."

Jesus. If I was doing this for real, that would be a tight timeline.

I walk away, my eyes catching Liv's as I pass her. She gives me a coy wave, and I can't tell if it's for me or for the viewers, but it's cute. Sensing something's off, she juts her chin up in silent question. With a tiny, almost imperceptible shake of my head, I jog down the stage stairs and head to the back office.

Sean is already in the room when I open the door. Thankfully, he hands me a list of the contestants with their basic information and tells me to circle the ones I want to keep.

I quickly circle ten random names, making sure Liv's in there, and absently hand it back to Sean. He doesn't take it right away, so I glare at him. He's staring at me as if assessing me for any indication of what I'm thinking.

After a few moments, his intense gaze remains in place, but he snags the paper and walks away.

A few minutes later, he comes to get me, tipping his head toward the door without a word.

He's quiet the whole way to the stage.

"What?" I ask, unable to bear more tension in an already tense situation.

"Nope. I'm not saying a damn word."

"Why not?"

He shakes his head, a sly smile creeping onto his face.

A few beats later, he laughs and must decide against keeping quiet. "Man. You think you've got this all figured out, don't you?"

"I don't know what you're talking about."

He laughs again. "Fletcher, you don't think they've accounted for every possibility? My best advice: hang on tight and go along for the ride. Because whatever you have planned to escape this dramatic matchmaking attempt unscathed isn't going to work. But I'm *really* looking forward to seeing it play out."

Miranda calls me to the stage, and I'm left wondering whose side Sean is on.

CHAPTER
TWELVE
OLIVIA

The contestants stay together in the staff room of Rocky's when we are not on stage. Some ladies are already friends, some have gotten into arguments. Like a few others, I have mostly been keeping to myself until we're on stage or participating in our group activities.

All twelve of us are brought out and lined up, waiting for Sawyer to decide the ten ladies who will be back next week.

He climbs to the stage, his thighs stretching the material of his dress pants. Why does he have to be hot? It makes this a little more challenging. Though, easier in some ways too.

The first thing they reveal is who was voted to be his first solo date. The disappointment at not being chosen surprises me. Fiona is given the sparkling first date flower, and if it wasn't for the momentary downward twist of his lips when her name is announced, I'd have thought he was genuinely happy about it. His bright smile spreads wide across his handsome face when Fiona jumps and squeals in excitement.

Once he delivers the glittery flower to her and she accepts it, he continues to call out the ladies' names, all of whom hug him and beam as they walk back.

As he gives the ninth woman her flower, a smirk I can't tamp down pulls at my mouth when his gaze darts to me in anticipation. He left me for last, and given the glint in his eyes, he did it on purpose.

My name leaves his lips, and I put extra sway in my hips as I move toward him to get my flower. But I don't wear heels often and the jaunty walk puts me off-kilter.

I trip.

This is what I get for trying to be sexy. When Sara strutted over to him, hugged him, and halfway back to her place in line, did this graceful spin to give him another beaming smile, I actually thought I'd be able to do something just as titillating.

I was wrong.

Falling flat on my face after trying to shimmy over to him—not so sexy.

But here he is, catching me and pulling me into him, his hands gripping my waist, mine plastered to his chest.

After a moment, I peer up at him to find a curious look on his face. He dips down so his mouth is at my ear. "You do that on purpose, Liv?" he whispers, and the audience murmurs at his heroic action.

I give him a quick shake of my head and an embarrassed smile. "Thanks for catching me. It would have been a hard one to live down. *'Olivia Vaughn throws herself at the feet of our Hometown Hottie, Sawyer Fletcher. It's clear she's been out of the dating game for a while, and we have to wonder if he'll be keeping her in the running.'*"

Sawyer is quiet, pursing his lip to keep from laughing, but the crowd doesn't hold back. My gaze lands on the microphone he's holding. It picked up everything I just said.

I'm still in Sawyer's arms when a deep voice shouts, "What the fuck, Fletcher!" from somewhere near the bar area.

Everyone turns to stare at my brother. He's still in his station wear from the firehouse and probably came straight here after helping Gracie.

"*Oh*, I love how they added Vaughn boy drama! This reality show couldn't be more perfect." Fran from the bakeshop pipes up.

Technically, my contestant status was to remain a secret until after the first show. Only producers and organizers were aware of who were chosen as participants, and they kept a tight lid on all show details. Though, giving my brothers a heads-up might have prevented this situation.

Miranda scrambles over to snatch the microphone from Sawyer's hand. "Jensen Vaughn, as much as we enjoy your handsome face, you do not have a ticket, nor do you have the right to disrupt this event. Your sister can decide on her own who she wants to date. You may discuss this in private at another time. Could someone please escort Mr. Vaughn out?" She glares at the bar staff, but they skillfully avoid eye contact.

My brother is a tank, so I don't blame them. By the way his shoulders are set, face smug as he leans against the bar in stubborn defiance, he's not moving unless someone forcibly removes him.

A throat clears and someone grumbles.

Sean steps out, making his way across the room. "Since when did I become The League bouncer?" he asks no one in particular.

I don't want those two to fight. There would be casualties.

I hold out my hand for the microphone, and Miranda promptly hands it over. "Jensen, the moment you start interfering in my dating life is the moment you invite me to do the same. I love you, but mind your business and get out of here."

He glares at me. I glare back.

"Or maybe some of the single women here wouldn't mind redirecting their attention to another bachelor in the room. Ladies"—I address the crowd—"this is Jensen. He's a thirty-two-year-old local firefighting hero." Murmurs go through the crowd as they ogle my nosy brother. A few women have risen from their chairs and are slyly making their way toward him at the bar.

"He's a Leo, allergic to cats, likes his food spicy and his women spicier. He might appear to be the grumpier twin brother, but I think he just needs the love of a good—" I trail off as he backs up toward the door, hands raised in defeat as some of the women reach him.

He shouts, "Well played, Livvie," before turning and storming out. Sean follows him outside.

The crowd's attention turns expectantly back to us as I pluck the flower from Sawyer's fingers and say, "No take backs."

CHAPTER
THIRTEEN
OLIVIA

Rapping at the back door brings a smile to my face. I bite my lips between my teeth and get myself together for who's on the other side of the door.

Sawyer and I decided debriefing after group and solo dates would be necessary to stay on top of our plan. Especially with the rules changing at the whims of the organizers.

I open the door, but one glance at our Hometown Hottie leaning heavily on the doorframe, and I'm unable to keep in the laugh from bubbling up.

The frown on his face is too adorable.

I grab his arm and yank him into the house, giving the neighboring houses and alley a quick inspection.

Before I've even finished closing the door, I ask, "How was your date?"

"Don't," he practically growls.

"Want to talk about it?" I ask through a grimace.

He makes his way over to my new sofa. "Not particularly." His palms glide over the new chestnut-brown leather. "Nice couch."

I follow his lead and sit beside him, allowing him to get comfortable before asking, "So you *don't* want to talk about smashing the clay to smithereens, or accidentally choking on her hair, or dumping the pitcher of water in her lap, or how the kiln exploded your—well, honestly I have no idea what it was you made—or about how the Vaughn Fire Department had to send their rescue squad and the truck to inspect the studio?"

My brother was on the truck and kept Sawyer's "creation" as a souvenir.

"*You watched it?*" His tone is incredulous, and his eyes carry an accusatory look of betrayal.

They were supposed to reenact the pottery scene from *Ghost*. There's no way I was missing it.

"Of course. You think the other contestants weren't viewing it? Hell no. We have to study this. Me more than anyone. We're a team, and we need to come across as the strongest couple." I tilt my head and lower my voice to soften the blow of my next comment. "Though, I don't think it'll be a problem because tonight's date was—"

"A travesty? I'm aware." He drops his head into his hands and groans.

"Honestly, I think you dodged a bullet. Some people are saying she was only on the show to get more content for her social accounts. She got her followers to vote for her online the other night. Her thing is postmortems on first dates—especially if they end in a one-night stand."

"There was zero chance of that ever happening. Talking to her was painful. I'm sure she still has plenty to post about though. And now I know why she was trying so hard even after how horrible the evening went. At the end there . . ."

"Where you palmed her face so she couldn't lay one on you? That got big reactions over here as we watched."

"'We'?"

I have no idea how he's going to feel about this. "Our moms, Ellie, and Harper got together to catch your date night live stream."

"Great." He scrubs a hand over his face. "What did my mom think?"

"She kept herself in check much better than the rest of us. Which was impressive because your date provided some solid entertainment. But she also seemed a little . . . I don't know. Concerned? Guilty? Maybe because she helped choose Fiona?"

"Her name was Fiona? I thought it was Flora."

"Yeah, I'm aware. When they did the post-date interviews, she mentioned thinking it was a cute nickname you'd given her because of her perfume until she heard you use it with the cameraman."

"Ah fuck. So I looked like a total asshole. I'm pretty sure I did all the things someone would do if they wanted to completely ruin a first date. I guess I'll keep that in mind for any of the contestants I want to get rid of. Might as well go full asshole." His hands go up to cover his face as he mumbles, "I knew this would happen."

"What exactly *did* happen out there, Fletch?" I should start calling him Sawyer to get used to it, but using his last name like my brothers tended to has always allowed for a degree of separation between us. And it made sense back when he was twenty and I was freshly sixteen with braces, driving a Honda Civic nearly the same age as I was. For this fake love match situation we have going, using his first name would be more personal. And sound better when we're in front of half the town every week.

"What happened is what always happens," he mutters.

What does *that* mean?

"For the first thirty minutes, I thought you were doing it on purpose—tanking the date. But we hadn't discussed that as a strategy."

"It wasn't intentional." His frown deepens.

"Were you nervous? Or maybe you . . . took something?" His eyes cut to me, dark and broody. "Kidding. You didn't seem at all like yourself, and honestly, it was hard to watch."

He holds a fist up to his forehead, letting out a frustrated breath. "Look, how about we make a plan to ensure all other dates are with you. That should prevent any future disasters."

Is he saying this only happens with other women on dates? "Oh. Okay. So this has to do with being with a woman you are sexually attracted to?"

"What? No. It's the date—any dates, all dates, whether I like her or not. Most of the time, we don't even get far enough into the evening to get to know each other before it all goes to hell. But with you, it wouldn't be real, so it might not end as badly."

"That's your plan? We can't have you only ever date me for the rest of this matchmaking event. Especially since we know some of the solo dates will be chosen by the audience."

"I don't know if I can do it again." He's twitching slightly. "But I'm up for another suggestion. Maybe you could give me a small push down the stairs or something, then one of your brothers could fill in for me like you threatened the other night, and this can be over. Easy out."

I slide closer, placing my hand on his warm, broad shoulders. My fingers explore the tense muscles in soothing, involuntary strokes.

"Sorry, Fletch, I'm not pushing you down the stairs. Though, I won't rule it out completely. I'll wait and see what you do to me during our first outing." His response is a broken-sounding groan. My hand slides down his back as his head drops down, arms dangling over his thighs. "I'm teasing. Our fake date will be fine, this will be over in a couple months, and you'll have helped raise a ton of money for the Humane Society."

He nods. "Yeah. And I doubt anyone is going to want to set me up again after this, so that's a bonus."

The misery emanating from him makes me want to climb into his lap and wrap myself around him. I settle for rubbing my hand along his corded back. "What's really going on, Sawyer?"

After a while, in a hushed tone, he mumbles, "I've had a lot of bad dates."

"Okay . . ."

"Not *normal* bad—epic failures. Then I'd decide to stop dating for a while, but eventually I end up trying again, and it just kept getting worse."

I nod, waiting for more details.

"It's stupid, and I'm possibly psyching myself out, but I feel like the most unlucky fuckup when it involves dating, love, relationships, all of it." His hands cover his face, muffling his voice when he says, "And I just want to open my clinic, run the shelter, play squash with the guys, and be happy for a while before even thinking about dating again."

"Wait." I grip him in alarm. "You guys play squash? Jaxon told me you all play basketball."

"We do that too sometimes."

"Do you wear the goggles? Anyone ever get nutted? That would be brutal . . . I imagine. If the tiny, hard ball hit one of my tits at high speed, I'd go down like a European footballer—with flare and hysterics."

Sawyer straightens under my touch. Dropping his hands from his face, his head snaps to me. "What?" His eyes dart down to my boobs, and I grin. "No one's been nutted—Liv, I'm trying to be serious here." But his mouth twitches as he stares back down at his hands.

Trying to bring him out of his broody funk, I keep going. "Nutting *is* serious. As is a tit hit."

"Christ." He throws himself against the back of the couch, staring up at the ceiling. The laugh coming out of him starts out rough and aggressive, like he's unsure whether to laugh or scream.

He shifts to face me, scanning my face to gauge my reaction.

"You don't believe me. You don't believe I'm astonishingly unlucky in love."

I hold up my hands. "No, I do. Especially after seeing you with Fiona." He winces, so I put my hands back on him, giving his forearm a supportive squeeze. "Is that why you didn't want to be The Stud—I mean, Hometown Hottie?"

One side of his boyishly handsome face quirks into a near grin before twisting back into a frown. "Yeah. It's been a nightmare. Thinking about all the ways my dates could go wrong in front of both towns? I couldn't imagine anything less appealing. So I politely—emphatically—turned them down when they approached me about it. In Stella's mind, it only confirmed that I needed someone to step in to help. She was aware of the details of my last few dates."

I want the details *so* bad, but the distress on his face, the panic in his eyes, and the tension in his body make me hold back. "How can I make this better for you?"

He glances over at me, his face softening. When his fingers graze over my knuckles to wrap around my hand, my breath catches. Those deep blue eyes flicker from our hands to my face, landing on my mouth.

"I'm not sure what else we can do, honestly. I'm in this, no turning back."

He gives me a half-hearted grin, and I hate that he'll have to answer questions about this trainwreck of a date, that people will be talking about it for a long while. Everything he secretly worried about going wrong is happening.

"You're not alone in believing you're unlucky in love. A past filled with awful exes and complete dating failures can definitely mess with your head." I take a breath and unload one of my deepest secrets. "My ex-husband originally fucked me thinking— hoping—I was someone else."

His head snaps over to me again. "What?"

"He had partied much harder than I had that night and thought I was his buddy's ex he'd always had a thing for. They'd recently broken up, and he thought this was his shot. She was more of a true redhead, but when you're high, apparently I'm close enough." I shrug.

"He told you this?"

"Not exactly. When he didn't text or call after, I figured it was a one-night thing. Which I was fine with. But after talking to him at another party a couple weeks later, I realized he didn't know we'd had sex. He explained he didn't remember that night very well. My feelings were hurt, but he turned on the charm. He wanted to hang out, asked if maybe I'd give him another chance for a night neither of us would forget." He snorts at the cheesy, douchebag line. At the time, I was a young, emotionally unstable fool, and I fell for those words. "Turns out he *did* remember that night but not the same way I did. A friend of his accidentally outed him at our wedding while he was reminiscing about old times. The rest of his speech was very sweet though."

"He said that during a speech?" he nearly shouts.

My head tips back as I laugh. "No. Thankfully it was later on when we were making our rounds. Still sucked though." I had added it to the many other red flags I'd hidden away in my mind.

"I hate that he hurt you. How did you end up with such a dick? And how did your brothers not find out and interfere?" He's still playing with my hand, and I can't drag my eyes from the long, strong fingers tracing mine, his thumb swiping over the pale pink polish of each nail.

I blow out a breath. "I did not make smart decisions about boys in college. Dad had passed unexpectedly, and I was miserable, trying to fill a void, acting out in ways I hadn't when I was younger. But I eventually learned how to look through the bullshit better. And you'll learn from this too. You might have to get out of your own head first though. I'm sure your next date will go well. Especially if it's with me. I'm going to knock your socks off. Best fake date ever."

The grin he's trying to hide by keeping his head tipped down has his dimple popping. "Well, there's no way it could be worse. So you're at a bit of an unfair advantage."

"Hmm, maybe. But it'll break your unlucky streak."

"That doesn't seem possible. Even if I have the potential for a good date, now if it's not her messing it up, it's me."

I try to think of something to help, some way to argue, but without knowing what's happened, my mind is drawing a blank.

"Would sharing another Drew story help? I've got a few doozies."

One of his hands moves to his forehead, giving it a quick swipe. His head rises up, one eyebrow arched in challenge. "Your ex was a dick. I always thought that. And while you might have me beat in the worst ex area, I'm pretty sure I have you beat in the bad dates department."

I straighten my spine, pursing my lips. Game on.

"Prove it."

"What?" he asks, his hands stilling.

"We each share a shitty relationship or dating story until the other concedes."

I remove myself from his hold and sit cross-legged to face him. He looks uncertain but curious. I give his shoulder a shake. "Come on. It'll be therapeutic for both of us."

With a growing smile, he drapes an arm over the back of the couch.

"What've you got, Liv?"

"One guy in college asked me to give him a hand job."

Sawyer shrugs. "Most guys are pretty fond of those."

"I wasn't done. We were in the theatre."

"I feel like there's still more," he says, catching on.

"We were at a play his ex-girlfriend had a starring role in. He wanted to record me jerking him off with her voice in the background. To this day, I still don't know if it was for his own personal use or if he planned to send it to her."

He grimaces. "I hope you left."

"Eventually. First I pretended to be into it, undid his pants seductively—though looking back, I was being a bit aggressive—and then dumped my ice-cold soda right on his crotch."

He smirks at me. "Nice."

"Your turn."

"Hmm, where to start?" He leans against the couch, propping his head up on his hand. "I dated a girl so gullible, one of the lacrosse guys convinced her she'd broken up with me and *they* were dating. I found them fucking in *my* dorm room. The asshole was my roommate."

"*What*?" I gape at him. "Wow. Have you checked in on this girl? There's no way she's out there living life and totally fine. Were you aware of how gullible she was?"

"Are we going to have this many follow-up questions after every story? If so, this might take all night."

"I'm fully willing to devote the time." I have a feeling I'm going to have *a lot* of questions for him if this is the direction all his stories are going.

The amusement on his face seems to be chasing away the anxiety present a few minutes ago. But the way he's looking at me, all soft, curious, and *interested*, is making me squirm.

"Yes, I was aware she was gullible. But not *that* gullible."

"I hope she at least gave great head."

He chuckles, running a hand through his hair. "At that time in my life, a blowjob was hard to screw up too badly."

"Yikes. That was a no." My cheeks hurt from grinning so hard.

He adjusts his position, bringing one bent leg up onto the couch, leaving the other planted on the floor. He's fully facing me as he says, "No more about Lana. Your turn."

I tip my head to the side, deciding which awful college dating story to share. "One guy showed up to our date with another woman. His schedule was apparently *super* complicated, and he got the times wrong. He suggested we go with it, see where the night ended."

"Ballsy."

"Yep."

"I dated a woman who got a kick out of public urination. She'd been arrested four times for it. I was with her for the last arrest, which was when I found out this was a 'thing' for her. I was shocked as shit."

"*What*? That's awful," I say on a laugh.

He's still smiling, his warm eyes appraising me while I think of another story.

"Drew shit his pants during a dinner date," I tell him. Sawyer tilts his head, waiting for the rest of the story. "We had to leave immediately—he wouldn't even clean up or go to the washroom. Left some, uh, residue. It was mortifying. He was coming off this cleanse he'd tried to convince me to do with him, and his body had reacted—violently. When we got outside, I laughed so hard. Like couldn't breathe. He was furious, and ended up driving away without me. I had to call an Uber and found myself locked out of the bedroom when I got home, but I wouldn't change a single second of my reaction."

A mix of emotions sweep across his face. "Fucker," he mutters. "Okay, um, no shit stories for me, thankfully. But I did take a girlfriend on a hike through Sonoma Valley State Park. She was leaving food out for the wildlife throughout our hike. I had no idea until we were about an hour in. A park ranger stopped us, questioning what he'd seen her doing. We were issued a hefty fine, and then she gave him lip, running around, dumping all the 'animal treats' out like a crazy person, and we both ended up getting banned for a year."

Tilting my head, I bring a finger up to my chin. "So, if you had to describe your type . . ."

"Apparently my type usually ends up being batshit crazy."

I laugh and wave him off. "You've just found some weirdos. We all have. But I mean honestly, the math is on your side. You've met and spent time with more than your fair share, so in terms of probability, it should be somewhat smooth sailing from this point."

"That would be nice, but recent events have me doubting your math."

I grab both sides of his face, the scruff along his jaw bristling against my palms. "Forget about tonight's date. That wasn't bad luck, it was past experience-induced panic." His eyes search mine, and before he can disagree, I reluctantly release him. "My turn. I've had some pretty bad dates, and Drew has done *a lot* of stupid shit. But I have a feeling you might have me beat in terms of sheer numbers. So I'm going big—the worst story."

"You want to go straight to our worst story? Quality over quantity?"

"If you're game."

He shifts around, the tension in his shoulders building again. "You first."

I inhale deeply. "Drew tried to talk me into an open marriage after I found out he was cheating on me."

He frowns, anger simmering in his eyes. "Jesus. What an asshole."

"Yep. After I filed for divorce, he admitted he fucked up but didn't want to fail at another thing. His baseball career dreams didn't pan out, he never finished college, and now a divorce too? I think he was finally forced to realize he wasn't doing as well as he led people to believe."

Sawyer's hand lifts to my face, gently taking my chin between his thumb and fingers. "I didn't know any of that. If I had . . ."

"Most people don't know. Not even my brothers. Only Ellie and my mom—and now you."

"So what you're saying is, I'm going to have to fuck him up on behalf of all of us?"

I roll my eyes. Planting my hand on his chest, I shove him lightly. "Be serious. No one needs beating up. He was never the guy who was going to be my *everything man*—the man who'd cherish me, the one I'd envisioned standing beside me during the best or worst days of my life. He was never *the* man, *my* man, period. We pushed to make a future together that was never meant to be."

"He still should have treated you better. Guys like that piss me off. They somehow convince incredible women to be with them, take it for granted, and fuck it all up because they can't keep their dick in their pants? Makes no fucking sense. If they're in love, how can they even *see* other women?"

"Some men aren't meant for monogamy. Or they don't care enough to ever prioritize someone else's needs or wants before their own. Emotional connections and sex don't always go hand in hand for some people. Young as I was when Drew and I got together, I hadn't quite figured that out yet. And I didn't care enough. He was what I was looking for at the time. By the time I saw him for who he was, I naively thought it might still work out." I shrug. "I was an idiot."

His hand grips my knee, giving it a sympathetic shake. "You don't get to blame yourself for his mistakes. Especially not around me. So cut it out."

The deep timber of his stern tone creates a flutter of chaotic sensations. With as close as we're sitting and the secrets we're sharing, I feel vulnerable—practically naked. Telling this man I've known most of my life that I fucked up, chose wrong, was disregarded, cheated on, and loved in all the wrong ways has the sharp sting of failure returning. It doesn't seem to matter how many times I tell myself it wasn't my fault or how often I've heard it from Ellie and my mom.

"Fine. It's your turn anyway. What relationship travesty do you have that beats wasting most of my twenties with a cheating manwhore who lives life like an irresponsible, faultless teenager, who tells his wife he prefers to fuck her when she's drunk, and would sometimes bark like a dog when he screwed me from behind?"

"What?"

"Yeah. He thought doggy-style was a primal act, and he'd get so into it he'd sometimes bark at me. Not as an obnoxious joke." I quirk my brows at him. "Figured I'd sprinkle that tidbit in at the end there to firmly push me into the lead. You ever had anyone bark at you during sex?"

He grimaces, looking down at where his hand still rests on my knee.

"Nope. Jesus. You win. The fact that he could do that to you, that you had to put up with his bullshit, far outweighs anything I had to put up with for the few days or weeks I was with someone."

"No, come on. You can't concede because you feel bad about my shitty marriage and messed up sex life."

"Liv, you win." He holds his hands up.

My face twists in mock derision. "I'm not sure there are any real winners in this game."

He laughs, a warm, playful smile transforming his previously solemn face. "That's true."

My lower lip pops out in an exaggerated pout. "You're not going to tell me, are you?"

He props his elbow back on the top of the couch, resting his head on his closed fist. For a few moments, he's quiet, contemplative.

He lifts his hand, thumb grazing my puffed out lip before he jerks it back, sighing.

"Not tonight, Liv," he says, his tone flat and resigned. "Looking back on it, my worst story isn't so bad. It's stupid and embarrassing. Let's save that tale for another night. Maybe I'll save it for after our date, if it goes well. Because you never know . . . our evening together could become my worst date story."

I scoff, taking a second to study his face, his neatly trimmed scruff, full lips, and thick, dark lashes. "Impossible."

Up close, he's a mixture of rough and soft, warm colors and bright eyes.

He shifts, clearing his throat. Worried he's caught me staring, I bring my gaze back to his. The warmth and intensity from minutes ago has been replaced with resolute detachment.

"A date with me will make a whole new man out of you, Fletcher. I think you simply need the right woman to put an end to your unlucky streak. Your luck is bound to turn around with me at your side."

He nods, but the look he gives me confirms that his walls are back up. Which might be for the best. We should both be careful, especially given our situation.

The whole reason we're sitting here is because I offered to help him avoid the messiness of a relationship—specifically when it's arranged by the nosy residents of our towns and involves dating ten women at once.

Which means any thoughts of Sawyer as anything other than a friend—my brother's *best friend*—needs to stop. Something that was never an issue until recently.

Probably because I've never been single around him before now. Meaning there's nothing stopping me from leaning forward and stealing a kiss from his unavoidably tempting lips.

Except Sawyer. And maybe my resolve to never fall for another perpetual bachelor. Because even if Sawyer is nothing like Drew, he's still resistant to serious commitment.

I think everyone in town knows the lady-bit-stirring man sitting in front of me would be the perfect boyfriend. He's exactly the kind of husband material I hadn't given enough thought to when I was younger.

A muffled beeping resounds from somewhere near us.

"Shit. That's my emergency line." He digs his phone out of his pocket, reading the screen. "The clinic is on-call for all emergencies tonight, and we have a dog with a throat obstruction." He stands, and I follow him to the back door. "Sorry. We'll talk more later?" he asks.

I nod, still in a bit of a daze as he slips out the door.

A while after Sawyer leaves to save a dog's life, I realize the problem isn't only that Sawyer's too busy with his career. It's not because his bar for women is set too high. He's not overly picky, a player, or averse to commitment.

No.

The reason Sawyer Fletcher doesn't want to be in a relationship is because he's scared of dating. And I plan to change that.

CHAPTER
FOURTEEN
SAWYER

MOM: The next date will go much better, honey. Don't get caught up in the first tiny blip.

Blip? I stumbled through that date like a drunk racing through a haunted house.

ME: Mom. It was a complete disaster. I wasn't being dramatic when I told you this was a bad idea.

MOM: Today's group date will be better. Promise.
MOM: Oh and you never told me who your top picks were after the first night.

I don't even know that I noticed much about any of the women. It was a blur of people, names, and information.

ME: Nothing much to report yet, Mom. I'd tell you if there was.

MOM: Oh, okay. Want to know who my top picks are?

ME: Mom . . .

MOM: First, I want you to know I wasn't the one who approved Fiona as a contestant. But there are a few others I did help choose that I think you will appreciate spending time with. And one in particular who I think is perfect for you. I've always wondered if one day you two would be in the same place at the same time and bam! Magic. Romance. Burning for each other.

ME: Have you been rewatching Bridgerton?

MOM: Don't pretend you didn't like it. Even your father is voluntarily watching it with me this second time around.

ME: There's no magic or burning yet, Mom. I've got to head to Rocky's though. See you there.

MOM: Oh, I'm sure Sean will fill you in as well, but Fiona has pulled out of the show. Given her recently discovered social media content, I'd consider it a mutual decision, so please don't blame yourself.

I can't say I'm surprised, but I still take some responsibility.

MOM: Also, we had her delete the unkind posts about your date. It's been taken care of. Love you. See you soon.

Okay, guilt officially eased.

I shove the solo date from my mind, refusing to let it mess with me, and focus on tonight's group event instead.

Not long after I arrive at the bar, Miranda calls me up early to do my presentation on the animals we are attempting to find foster and forever homes for. Our mayor with a flare for the dramatics then takes the stage once more and gushes about how I saved her dog last week. It was her bulldog who had the obstruction, and I was thankfully able to remove the torn piece of ball he was chewing on with an endoscope.

She hailed me the "Hometown Hottie *Hero*" and brought Bruce up on stage to thank me with lots of slobbery kisses. I hate to admit it, but his affection was much preferred to the female variety I'll be exposed to all too soon.

Sean has approached me twice and advised that I chill the fuck out. But I can't. Because along with the rest of the audience, I found out tonight's group event is a competition. The winner of the pool tournament will accompany me on a solo date this week.

Which means, if Liv doesn't win, I'm going on another date with one of these women in a few days.

I pay close attention to the ladies' reactions to Stella's and Miranda's recap of my date, which they attempt to gloss over. Most haven't said anything or reacted any differently, even though they must have seen the footage. These women should be heading for the exit without a single glance back.

Tonight my goal is to learn more about them. But it's like when a cat knows you're not a cat person and zeros in on you. When you play hard to get with cats, it can attract more of their attention. They'll follow you, rub against you, get your scent. In my case, these women have watched from afar, approached, touched my arms, shoulders, chest, circled me like I'm their new toy.

Not all of them though. While some women are more forward, others are more contemplative and subtle. Another thing which became more obvious as I observed the group—the organizers have no idea what my type might be.

Abbie, Jaclyn, and Marie are all brunettes, with Marie being the shortest, curviest of that group. Abbie and Marie seem to have hit it off with Liv, but Jaclyn is a bit more abrasive and has said—for everyone to hear—she's not here to make friends. Marie pointed out this isn't actually a reality TV show, and that one of her closest friends is already a contestant so she should stop being so dramatic. Liv and I looked at each other and then quickly away so we wouldn't laugh.

While the contestants wander between pool tables, regularly stopping by to talk to me, Liv, Abbie, and Marie have grouped together, laughing, helping and cheering each other on as they line up their shots. I even saw Liv encourage Abbie—the timid one of the group—to chat me up after she lost her round of pool. She mouthed, *Be nice*, as Abbie started in my direction.

When am I not nice? I'm going to assume she means for me to be extra nice because her friend is nervous. Has she forgotten how fucking anxious this whole thing makes me? Why would she send her friend over here since disaster could strike or I could have some kind of nervous breakdown?

The last of the participants are circulating the stage, not inter-acting with anyone in particular. Velora, Raine, Sara, and Isla vary from sandy to platinum blond. Both Raine and Isla are very quiet and closed off. I'm surprised they wanted to be contestants because they don't seem comfortable with the cameras and audience.

Velora and Sara, on the other hand, are in their element. Extroverted and loving the attention, they are naturals. Particu-larly Velora, who flirts shamelessly and is happy to keep the conversation flowing, mostly about her. But it saves me from filling in any awkward silences.

There seems to be a dichotomy happening in the group of women though. The kinds of cliques and dynamics I don't fully understand. Liv appears to fit in well with most of them. Except Velora. I don't know if anyone else has noticed, but it's pretty clear the two women don't like each other. If I had to guess, it's because Liv is a gorgeous auburn-haired beauty, and Velora is used to being the most attractive woman in any room she's in. Over the years, I've run into Velora a few times during my visits to Vaughn. She's flirted, but it's never lead to anything. She's not my type—at all. And I can't help but wonder if my mom selected her, and if so, why.

I manage to talk to Raine for a few minutes without incident, before she's called away to face off against Marie. I leave the cocktail tables, which Miranda has insisted we call "conversation tables" and choose a spot off to the side of the pool tables.

There's a cheer from the audience as one of the ladies makes a tricky shot. There are a few more rounds to go and Liv is still in the running, but I have no idea who will end up winning.

Liv glances around, her face perking up when she spots me. Casually, she makes her way over to me to stand at my side facing the pool tables. Her arm brushes against mine, a sly grin on her face. For the first time tonight, I can take a full breath.

"So, anyone you want me to let win?"

Thankfully, there are only mics at the pool tables and conversation tables, so we can talk freely as long as no one else approaches.

"Don't even joke. I hope you have some kind of inner pool shark hidden among your many talents because I need you to win."

She turns to me, wincing slightly. "I don't want you to freak out, but saying I'm fairly average at pool would be a gross exaggeration. And Jaclyn might be much, much more than average. If I had to put money down, I'd bet on her."

"Shit," I mumble.

Her hand on my bicep draws me out of my panic spiral. "It'll be fine. The next group event, you'll surely be able to choose your own date. Hopefully. Has Sean not told you anything yet?"

I switch my focus to the man in question. He's leaning against the bar, holding Sadie in his arms. When he dips down to kiss her neck, I turn back to Liv. "Nope. He says he can't reveal the activities in advance."

The hand which was previously gripping my bicep moves up

to my shoulder, slowly, seductively. My gaze trails from where her hand is caressing, down her arm, and up to her eyes.

"You were frowning and acting all grumpy, which isn't quite the look of rapt infatuation we're going for here. Think you can try to smile at me?"

My lips twist into a half smirk. I've given all of these women some kind of smile tonight, but Liv always draws out the kind that sink in, that cramp your cheeks, the ones I feel I should hide so no one figures us out. But we are supposed to be in this together though, so smiling at her as if we have a secret, like she lights me up, is probably a good idea.

She leans into me, so I wrap my arm around her, setting my hand on the small of her back. "With dimples, please," she whispers.

A relaxed laugh bubbles from my throat. My other arm slides around her as I lean down, bringing my mouth next to her ear. My hand brushes through her hair, pushing it off her shoulder. "You always get the dimples, Liv."

The murmurs behind me draw my attention back to the stage and the people surrounding us. I pull back but leave my hand on Liv's back, my fingers shifting down until they sweep across the top of her ass.

There's a faint blush to her cheeks and a gleam in her eyes I can't place. My gaze shifts to fixate on the plush lip she's biting on.

A hand lands on my shoulder, startling us both.

My head snaps to my left, where Velora is standing, pool cue in hand. She doesn't acknowledge Liv, her focus is solely on me. "Sawyer, would you mind helping me break? I've never done it before and I'm up next." Liv expertly covers an eye roll with a long, pronounced blink. Another grin tugs at the corner of my mouth. Liv's hand slides down my arm as she steps back, but my fingers curl around her waist, not wanting her to move. Her eyes smile at me as she gives an imperceptive shake of her head, telling me our time is up.

"Sure, Valorie."

"*Velora*," she corrects with a touch of venom in her tone.

"Right, sorry. *Velora*." I motion for her to lead the way, but before I follow, I turn back at Liv and wink.

She has her knuckles shoved against her mouth, laughing silently.

I walk away from Liv with a grin on my face that lasts the rest of the night. Well, not quite. The moment Liv loses to Jaclyn, my smile fades.

Sean ended up telling me later the cameras caught my reaction to Jaclyn winning. It was replayed several times on the screen at Rocky's after the ladies and I left and the attendees stayed to discuss, drink, and rewatch the disappointment on my face.

Holding up one of the eight flowers given out tonight, Liv mouthed, *Sorry*, before she left with Ellie.

She thinks I'm disappointed I have to spend the evening with Jaclyn, trying not to fuck it up too badly. And while I'm *not* happy about it, in that moment, I don't think that's what I was most disappointed about.

CHAPTER
FIFTEEN

OLIVIA

"You seem . . . off," Ellie tells me, waving a fork in my face.

I pluck the utensil from her fingers and take a bite of the coffee cake she ordered. I've already had a Danish and a tart, but Dani makes the absolute best baked treats in town. She only opened this second location of Baked Delights less than a year ago, but it's already a hit—as evidenced by how much money I spend here weekly.

"Nope. I'm totally fine. Busy with my new job, delivering all those cute babies, helping new moms, and getting settled back into Vaughn life. Lots of changes lately."

"Mm-hmm, sure. The 'totally fine' sold it." She rolls her eyes. "Don't pretend you haven't been craving those changes. You love being back home, doing your own thing, working at the hospital." Her eyes narrow, lips pursing.

Oh goodie, she's going to guess what's going on with me, and I'm going to crumble, unable to withhold the details of why I'm acting like a nervous, amped-up weirdo.

"Is Drew still causing problems? Wouldn't put it past that asshat."

I grin, loving that pregnancy has added some spice to Ellie's usually calm, pacifying demeanour. "No. I mean, other than him trying to gain sympathy from his parents by making me the fall guy for our crappy marriage and initiating the spread of all kinds of rumors about how desperate and regretful I am."

She grimaces. "Those rumors have stopped, if it helps at all. The Kippersons have been very quiet lately too. Know anything about that?"

"I might have sent Drew an email demanding he tell his parents the real reason I divorced him, and that I would rather eat raw fish while bathing in pig crap every day than ever be his wife, girlfriend, or casual acquaintance ever again."

My best friend shudders in disgust at the ultimate taste and smell sensory nightmare I've conjured.

"Graphic, but appropriate. At least LoveVine has the town well distracted, so you'll likely get a slight reprieve from all the chatter."

I hum in agreement, forcing a smile.

"Oh. Ohhh. This is about Sawyer? About his next solo date?"

"Everything is fine with Sawyer."

"He's dating other women, and you want it to be only you, right?" She continues guessing. "That must be hard."

I put her fork back on the plate, not looking at her.

"The show is going fine." Other than Sawyer not being able to always choose his own dates and me not being able to help him.

"Are you sure? You seemed fine when we watched the first date. Though, it went horribly, poor guy." She leans forward, glancing around at the other tables conspicuously. "I have to tell you . . . I was skeptical about you joining this thing, but observing you two, there's definitely a spark, and I'm crazy excited. I couldn't be more invested in this whole dating show thing. I almost intentionally tripped Raine at the market the other day because she hugged Sawyer a bit too long after accepting her flower."

I groan and put a hand up to my face.

"I don't think you have anything to worry about though. I mean, the man *stares* at you during group dates, tracking you like a predator does his prey. And it's super hot. I know something is happening, and you have divulged almost no details. I understand we couldn't talk much because your mom and Jane were sitting right there as we watched Sawyer's solo date. But it's just us now, so spill."

"It's not real," I blurt, immediately covering my mouth. "Shit," I mumble through my fingers.

"What?"

"Ellie . . ."

Her head gives a small, confused shake. "What's not real, Liv?"

I glance around, making sure no one is eavesdropping as I lower my voice and let Ellie in on the secret that's been eating at me. The feelings that have been burning inside me—the ones that are supposed to stay pretend.

"All of it. Sawyer never wanted to be part of LoveVine, to go on any dates, to find a girlfriend. He got suckered into it. He was going to bail, but then realized he'd be raising a lot of money for rescue animals and shelters and caved." Stella was also holding something over him, but I still haven't gotten that story out of Sawyer.

Ellie leaves her side of the booth and squishes into mine. "Olivia Renee Vaughn," she whisper-yells at me. "You've been keeping secrets? Big secrets." She motions for me to continue.

"I suggested he use a ringer and then accidentally offered to be said ringer." Maybe "accidentally" isn't the right word, but I can't think of a reasonable explanation for why I would have intentionally offered to pretend to fall in love with him in a very public dating type setting. Thus: accident.

My best friend flashes me her most impatient expression—a mix of desperation, excitement, and frustration. "I have no idea what that means. What's a ringer? You're killing me here, Livvie."

"A ringer, as in an imposter. He needed someone to pretend to be a participant, to ensure they'd win and he wouldn't have to actually choose someone to have a real relationship with."

Her eyebrows jump up to her hairline. "So you became the fake contestant—the 'ringer'?"

"Yes."

"I should have known," she whispers to herself. I don't think she's hearing me at all, her mind is going, piecing it all together. "You were being way too cool about all of this at first. You hate showy couple-y things, and you don't share. Meekly sitting back while the man you like goes out with a bunch of women? Not a chance. Remember the guy in college you were seeing who said he had a thing for a sorority girl and wanted to find out if you two were exclusive? You walked away and never looked back because any guy who was considering anyone else when he had you wasn't worth your time. You dropped him like the badass bitch you are."

"Ellie. This is serious. You can't say anything or act like you know."

"Fine, yes, of course. But I have *a lot* of questions." She scooches in further. "Because there is no chance what I saw was all fake."

Moving around her, I take a huge bite of coffee cake in hopes of boosting my spirits. Or at the very least, raising my blood sugar levels to give me the impression that my spirits are lifted.

She swipes the fork from me and chucks it over her shoulder. It flies through the air at least ten feet away before hitting a chair and crashing to the floor.

Okay then.

Ellie's intense blue eyes lock on me. "Can you at least tell me you offered because you secretly like him and saw an opportunity to figure out if he could ever return your feelings?"

Now she's just making me feel bad.

"Honestly, I don't even know anymore." I sigh, scanning the

bakery again, making sure no one is within hearing range. "At the time I suggested the ringer, I had no real intention of fulfilling the role. But before I knew it, the offer flew from my mouth. I don't know why."

She grins at me, and laughs excitedly. "I do."

Here we go.

"What did he say when you offered to be his ringer?"

"Not much. He was surprised and a little uncomfortable. A few days later he realized he was kind of stuck and texted me asking if I was still up for helping him. And after those rumors about my failed marriage started circulating, I definitely was."

She slaps the table, shouting, "Out with the old dick, in with Sawyer's dick."

"Shh! Ellie! Christ."

"It's fine, no one is around. Well, except Mr. Dodson, but he can't hear worth a damn and doesn't like to be interrupted once he commences his weekly pie binge." She spares him a quick glance before waving a dismissive hand in his direction and turning back to me. "Now try telling me again that none of what I've seen between the two of you is real."

"I'm supposed to be helping him through this, pretending to fall in love. He chooses me for most of the dates—if the organizers allow him to actually choose them at some point—and I'm given the final daisy. This way a girlfriend isn't forced on him, the attendees are entertained and happy, the Landry Life League members are appeased, Vaughn Town Council got to help organize and host an exciting new town event, and The Vine is producing and has the online platform required. As a bonus, the town sees that I've moved on with their hottest bachelor, and everyone who has been running their mouths about me being a simpering ex-wife hanger-on can fuck right off. Everyone wins."

She nods, eyebrows raised as she considers this.

"So you're pretending so that everyone wins?"

"Yes. That's all it's supposed to be."

"So you don't really like him? You haven't had a thing for him for years as your mom and his believe? The way they tell it, there's always been something there, and now you're both able to give into it. The romantic in me loves that, but you were in a distinct bad boy phase in your late teens, and Sawyer was no bad boy. As your best friend, I know we both thought he was hot, but you didn't harbor a secret crush on him. Unless you withheld that, in which case, I will be supremely offended and will storm my emotional ass out of here."

I sigh and debate admitting something which could end up crushing me.

Because falling for Sawyer Fletcher is dangerous. My heart wasn't ever at risk with any of my exes. With Sawyer, everything is different.

Instead, I give her the truth that doesn't confuse me or put my heart at risk.

"It's not that I never noticed Sawyer. I have. I definitely have. I liked him but he wasn't what I thought I wanted until it was too late. By then, I was married to a dickhead and was trying hard to make it work."

"And now?" she asks.

"Now I'm part of a town effort to set him up with his ideal match. And I agreed to help him avoid those matchmaking efforts by being his ringer. Am I attracted to him? Yeah, sure, who isn't?"

"Me."

"You're disgustingly happily married. Doesn't count."

"True." She taps her pointer finger to her chin. "So let's see if I have this right. Your plan is to continue being his ringer while ignoring your hot, rip-his-clothes-off, have-his-babies feelings? Sounds fun. I will be getting Harper to sneak me into all the events from now on. I refuse to miss a single minute of you two dancing around whatever is truly going on between you."

I knew she was going to give me shit about this.

I cross my arms. "Pregnancy makes you sassy. And I'm not sure I like it."

"You do," she says with a wink. "Okay so have you two planned when your first kiss is going to be? That's usually a big moment, and if you make it super sweet, it will absolutely win you over with the audience."

Sighing, I humor Ellie by talking strategy with her for the next twenty minutes. Her expressed disappointment in our lack of sufficiently planned 'falling in love' moments is punctuated by long yawns.

"All right, let's call your husband to pick you up."

"This baby-growing thing is taking more out of me than I thought." She looks at her phone. "Ugh. It's only 8:30 p.m. Are we meeting at your mom's place tomorrow night to watch Sawyer's date?"

"Yep. Should be a blast."

"Olivia?" Her voice is soft, serious.

"Yeah, sleepy mama?"

"It's okay if you fall in love with Sawyer for real. Even if you weren't supposed to. Because love doesn't always wait until you're ready."

After Liam picks up Ellie, I walk home. I can't help but wonder if falling for the man I'm only supposed to *pretend* to fall for is either exactly right or profoundly stupid.

CHAPTER
SIXTEEN
SAWYER

I 've officially moved most of my belongings into my new house in Vaughn. It's about a ten minute walk to Liv's house, which has made our meetups much easier than before.

Jaxon drops a box onto the floor, eyeing the open floor plan. My favorite part of the house is the living room with the wood-burning fireplace, tons of space above the mantel for a mounted TV, and built-in bookshelves on either side. The big furniture has already been moved in, thanks to Jaxon, Anders, and even Jensen, who showed up to help but as usual hasn't said much.

My best friend turns to me and says, "So you and Liv, huh?" His arms are crossed, as he sizes me up. At six foot two, I've got a couple inches on him, but he's quick and scrappy. If he does come at me, it wouldn't be the first time. This time would be serious though. Messing around with his sister without even talking to him would earn me a few jabs.

"Yeah."

"You going to choose her or is this all a game to you? Just toy with the women, get to taste test some pussy, then go back to not wanting a relationship?"

Ah, shit. "Jax, don't act as if you suddenly don't know me. It's not like that. I didn't even want to do this, remember?"

"You don't seem too torn up about it. You've got a date with Jaclyn tonight, don't you?"

I throw out my hands in frustration. "I committed to this stupid thing, and it includes going on some dates. In case you missed the last one, it's not going overly well."

"And one of the women you're hoping to pursue is Liv?"

"Yes. We just . . . that night at Horton Beach, we talked. She's ready to move on from her asshole ex."

Jaxon glares at me, and his identical twin brother wanders in from the kitchen with a bag of almonds, snacking while he listens to us.

"Her moving on I'm fine with. You dating her and a bunch of other women—that I'm *not* fine with."

"That's funny because you were all pro-Hometown Hottie, buying tickets, telling me to adjust my expectations and go for it. Suddenly Liv is interested in doing the same thing—with me—and you're all bent out of shape?"

"I'll be bending *you* out of shape if you don't tell me what exactly is going on between you and my sister."

Jensen chimes in, "*Our* sister." He shoves an entire handful of almonds into his mouth, his face unreadable.

"Liv said she talked to you. So why are you asking me?"

"Because Liv is allowed to find a rebound. She deserves to have some fun. Using this dating contest as a way for her to get back out there? Sure, fine. But mom seems to think she's not only in it for a few fun dates. She thinks Liv applied because she's got a thing for you and has for a while." He steps closer, his hands pulling at his neck.

I'm at a loss for words because I have no idea what's true anymore.

After several tense minutes, Jensen says, "I think what Jaxon is trying to say is if Liv is interested in you, wants a relationship with you, we're going to need you to tread carefully. If you're not going to end up with her at the end of this, don't lead her on. You're dating other women, and she has to witness all of that. She's already had one fucker treat her like crap. That shit's not happening to her again."

"I wouldn't do that. You know that. We've been friends since before we even liked girls."

"Which is why we wanted to level with you. Don't string Liv along. Tell her you care about her, you'll take her on a date because you're friends and want her to get the most out of this experience, but there's nothing else between you."

"Didn't seem like it the other night," Jaxon adds, his voice deceptively quiet but full of violence.

"There *is* something between us," I admit.

There's a few things between us, but I can't tell them all of it.

"Sometimes I hate that mom is always fucking right," Jensen says, closing the bag of nuts and heading back into the kitchen.

"Since fucking when?" Jaxon asks me.

"It's . . . recent."

"I knew I shouldn't have left you two together at the beach."

My jaw grinds at the implication that he can't trust me to be alone with his sister.

"Would it be so bad if your sister and I ended up together? Because, I have to tell you, she's my top pick." Even if this weren't fake, she'd be my top pick. "And not just because she's beautiful, and fun, and smart. Everything about her is fucking amazing. So *I* need to know if us being together is going to be a problem for you."

Growing up, I knew not to even look at my best friend's little sister. Back then, it wasn't a problem. But now? I want to do a hell of a lot more than look, and he knows it.

"Well, fuck." He crosses his arms across his chest and levels me with a serious expression I rarely see cross his face. "Obviously, I don't think you're an asshole or anything, but that doesn't mean I want you boning my sister."

"I'm not 'boning' anyone."

Yet.

I shove that thought down to overanalyze later.

"Yeah, and when you do, it'll likely be either my sister or someone else in that contest, which I'm sure Olivia will have some feelings about. Those aren't ideal options, Fletch."

"I'm not fucking any contestants."

"Maybe not yet, but the whole situation is a cesspool of shitty consequences waiting to happen. If you had a sister, would you want to watch her try to compete with a bunch of other women for some asshole's attention?"

Staring at my feet, I admit, "No."

"Add to the fact that the asshole is your best friend *and* his dating track record is almost as bad as mine? Worse in many ways, actually. It's a goddamn mess."

"You think I'm bad for Liv." I'm not asking him, but reiterating what he's trying to tell me.

He crosses his arms, exhaling loudly. "I think she's vulnerable right now. And I think you didn't want to date, let alone have a girlfriend." He's right, I didn't. Girlfriends are serious, and that has always led to serious disasters. "That doesn't bode well for her, no matter how much you might care about her. So when it doesn't work out or things get screwed up—as they tend to with you—or you hurt her, it's going to fuck up a lot of other relationships, not just yours."

Reading between the lines, the anger leaves me. My hand creeps up to rub my forehead as I consider how much this could affect my friendship with my best friend. Not to mention my mom's relationship with *her* best friend—Olivia's mom.

"What am I supposed to do, then, Jax? I'm not kicking her off, and I'm absolutely going on at least one date with her. Did you tell her she couldn't do the show? That she couldn't date me?"

"No, I wouldn't dare. She'd have my balls."

That makes me laugh. "All right, then, what are you wanting me to do here, man?"

"Treat her with respect, don't lead her on, and watch your fucking hands. Don't think we haven't noticed she's the only one you touch like she's already yours. If you aren't willing to commit, you need to step back. Let her find someone else."

Not fucking likely.

I'm familiar with the kinds of idiots Jaxon would set her up with, and they wouldn't keep her interested, wouldn't be good enough. Jaxon simply wants her with someone he can keep under his thumb and fuck up if necessary.

But I have no claim on Liv, no right to say a damn thing about who she dates. And that grates a whole hell of a lot more than it should.

"You done with the big brother speech?"

"For now. If this gets serious—not just a few dates at an event our town put together for shits and giggles—we'll be having another chat."

I nod at him, clamping my lips closed against the urge to tell him the truth, because I can't. Not if I want the rest of the events to go smoothly.

We finish with the last few boxes, and the guys help me mount the TV. Unloading everything from Jaxon's truck took a bit longer than I thought, so I'm running behind. I'm stopping by Liv's house to chat about the group date and get a little pep talk before my date.

I thank the guys, grab my keys and head out right behind them.

Jensen turns around before I even make it down the steps. "Break her heart, I break your ribs. Got it, Fletch?"

Always a man of much fewer words than his brother. Still very effective.

"Yeah, man."

"Good." He pats my arm, almost knocking me off the steps. "She'll be watching your date with what's-her-name tonight. Her, Mom, and Ellie watch it online together. Don't fuck up."

More pressure. That'll help.

I get in my car, questioning what makes me more nervous— the date itself or the idea of Liv witnessing it.

CHAPTER
SEVENTEEN
OLIVIA

S awyer lets himself in the back door as I'm cutting the brownies into squares. Glancing behind me, I take him in. He's dressed for his date with Jaclyn. Grey slacks stretch against his thick upper thighs, a belt accentuating his narrow hips, and a crisp white shirt with the cuffs rolled up, roped forearms on display. Dressed-up Sawyer looks good. Really good.

His hair doesn't appear to have any product but still match his usual style, longer on the top, falling in soft waves to his brows. The sides and back are a bit shorter but still curl slightly around his ears and the nape of his neck. Sawyer oozes that dreamy boy-next-door vibe. It makes me want to sneak through his window in the middle of the night and surprise him.

I'm allowed to fantasize as long as I don't act on them. At least until I determine if those fantasies are welcome.

"Hey, Stud, you all ready? Want some sugar to give you a boost for tonight?"

He raises his eyebrows, taking a peek into the pan as Daisy charges in. Sawyer leans down and gives her some love. My attention-seeking pup soaks it up, happily sitting at his feet. His fingers still rubbing her ears, he says, "Nah, I shouldn't. Sugar in the evenings wrecks me. They smell great though."

I hold up a square with a glare, using it to point at him. "Liar. You don't even like chocolate."

His mouth opens but nothing comes out. I tilt my head, waiting for some kind of response. Finally, he says, "I was being polite. They do smell good, even if chocolate isn't my favorite. And I was being honest about not having sugar in the evenings. Can't handle it." His face scrunches up. "Wait, if you knew I didn't like chocolate, why did you offer?"

"I was being polite." I laugh and shove the gooey chocolate square into my mouth. "I made them for the ladies. Your mom does not have your weird disdain for chocolate. But this is also a reminder to be yourself tonight," I say with a mouth full of brownie, smiling at the end, teeth coated in the deliciousness.

He grins and reaches for my face. I freeze when his thumb strokes across my bottom lip. I study his face as he brings his finger under my chin and his thumb moves to the center of my lip, pulling it down. Those midnight eyes are locked on my mouth, and then he licks his own bottom lip. I inhale sharply, my whole body heating up.

"I don't know when I last felt like myself on a date," he admits.

Against all thought—all reason—my tongue pops out and swipes across his thumb. He takes a step closer, his thumb pulling my lip farther down, as a rough sound leaves his throat.

Oh my god. Was that a groan?

Sawyer releases my face suddenly and steps back.

Shit. Oh shit. My thighs rub together, trying to ease the ache —the throbbing need that creeps up every time we get close. At our group date when his hand was on my back, fingers in my hair, lips at my ear, I almost collapsed against him with a whimper of desperation.

Slowly he sucks his thumb into his mouth. "You had chocolate."

I lean against the counter, hands gripping the edge, not sure if my legs will give out or if I'll grab another brownie and smear it all over my body to get the same treatment.

"Thanks," I croak.

"Living room?" he asks, motioning in that direction. Daisy takes off first, heading toward her toys.

I nod and lead the way. Heat still burns through me, and I swear his eyes are searing a path down my back. When I glance behind me, he's following but his eyes are cast down—at my ass. He keeps staring the whole way to the living room, without a clue that I've caught him.

This is going to complicate everything. Ellie is right. There's no way we'll be able to ignore this.

Fine . . . there's no way *I* will be able to ignore this.

"Can you do me a favor?"

Absolutely. Drop your pants.

I give myself a mental shake. "Maybe. What's the favor?"

"I'm going to need you to step up your buffer game."

"My buffer game?" I ask, confused.

"Last group date, the moment any of the women got knocked out of the competition, they used that as an excuse to switch their attention from pool to me. And some of them are handsy. You were casually chalking your cue stick, not even noticing. We need to kick things up a notch. Especially during and after our one-on-one date—if I ever get a chance to finally take you out. Which means you're probably going to have to appear a little jealous, pull me away, stay close to me . . . That kind of thing. I'm going to need you all over me." He smooths a hand down his chest seductively.

It's not easy to make me blush, but this man is making me tingly all over. "First, I can't be your full-time bodyguard. These women want you to choose them, woo them, take them on a romantic getaway. They are going to flirt, touch, whatever, and yeah, it's gross, but to be fair, they think you're interested in them and are hoping their affections will be returned. I can't hop in and toss them off you. I have no right to do that, and I would come off as crazy and jealous, which isn't going to help me win anyone over, that's for sure." And it would also only serve in confirming the rumors Drew and his family have been spreading about me.

He leans back, propping an ankle on his knee. "You might have a point about it looking bad if you kept all the women away from me. But can you still stay close? I feel better when you're next to me." His eyes meet mine, sweet sincerity shining through.

"I can do that. But remember, you're supposed to be into me too, so you should also be seeking *me* out." He already does to some extent, but we need to make it more obvious.

"Got it." He slides over, wrapping his arm around me and pulling until I'm crushed against him. "You won't be able to shake me." I try for a chastising frown, but it's impossible to even pretend to be upset when he's being so adorable.

"Second, to kick things up a notch, how about we have an encounter this weekend? We could bump into each other getting coffee at Grind? Or head to Hewlett Park and have a fire, a few sneaky drinks, let our dogs meet each other?"

"Let's do coffee this weekend, stick close during our group date, go on a romantic, hopefully incident-free solo date, and then Hewlett Park next weekend."

"You'll be sick of me by the end of this."

"I won't," he assures me, his eyes dipping back to my mouth. I raise my hand to swipe at it, wondering if I still have chocolate there.

Okay, we're doing this. The town will recognize we're getting closer when they spot us together. Sawyer said he hasn't seen anyone else around, he's been too busy with the move and clinic.

"Should we talk about the other contestants? I mean, if we're going to let everyone know that there's something between us, they are going to have thoughts and feelings. They might even try to get the same time with you outside of the show."

"Yeah, it might become awkward during group dates."

"There's already tension, so this will amp it up. And I want to make sure no one's feelings get hurt. None of the women remaining have had much time with you, and no solo dates. So no one's *in love* or anything yet." I avert my gaze, uncomfortable.

He nods, his eyes still intense, face unreadable.

"But the candidates still might have their hopes up. And some of them are in this for similar reasons as me. Marie and Raine are both post-breakup, a string of shitty men in the rearview mirror. And Abbie recently ended an engagement because her fiancé's family asked to have her virginity medically proven—which can't even be accurately assessed given some women don't have intact hymens for a variety of reasons, even if they *are* virgins. Not that Abbie was one. Her fiancé might have been a virgin and his family might have had certain religious or cultural preferences, but they had no right to demand that of her. That doctor was a 'family friend' too. Creepy."

The image Abbie's story conjures makes me shudder, and Sawyer holds me tighter.

"After that, she went on a sexual self-discovery. She's ready to settle down but wants to find the kind of man who can ignite both physical and emotional passion. I truly hope she ends up with someone great. And who fucks like a beast."

Sawyer's eyes widen, laughing so sharply he winds up in a coughing fit.

I put my hand on his chest and ask if he's okay.

"Jesus. That was so, so much more about Abbie than I ever needed to know. I thought she was shy and timid."

"That's not common knowledge, so you're going to have to keep it to yourself."

"Who on earth would I tell any of that to?" He looks baffled. "Actually, Sean would eat that shit up, and then get his fiancée involved, and it would be a whole thing."

He's not wrong.

"My point is these ladies have their own hang-ups and feelings. So be nice, but don't give them too much false hope. Because you're supposed to be falling hard for me. And if you're drooling over say . . . the golden, exotic-looking goddess-slash-haggard witch, for example, our moms and the audience may think you're into *her*, and could even work behind the scenes to get you two together. And that's not what you want, right?"

His forehead screws up in confusion. "First, I don't drool. I make a fool of myself while simultaneously attracting all the wrong kinds of women. Second—haggard witch?"

"Velora is horrible, and the next time they seat me next to her, I'm switching spots. I don't care if Miranda glares at me for the rest of the night." My lip curls as I add, "And she's exactly the kind of woman who would burn your life down around you, so watch yourself."

"I can't tell if you're being jealous or protective, but I'm liking it." He settles us deeper into the couch cushion. "I'll also agree she's a bit intense."

There's one more thing we haven't brought up again since the show started that needs to be said. Or maybe I need convincing.

"Also, I want to make sure you know that if at any point you find yourself clicking with someone or wanting to pursue a relationship, you just have to tell me. I mean, your date with Jaclyn could be amazing, or maybe you'll get to talking with Marie and feel something. As you get more comfortable and dating one of them doesn't seem as impossible or nerve-racking, you never know. And I don't want to stand in anyone's way."

He leans forward and turns to face me. He braces one arm next to my shoulder on the back of the couch, the other he places on the outside of my thigh.

"Not going to happen."

"You don't know that."

His face is serious, focused, his jaw clenched tight.

"That first night, when they introduced the contestants, you're the only one I even noticed. I search for you every chance I get. My attention isn't on them, it's on you."

I'm holding my breath and don't know why.

There's a sound in the background. Something draws Sawyer's attention away from me.

"Liv? I think that's your phone."

Shit, he's right.

I'm equal parts disappointed and relieved.

I pull my phone out of my back pocket and my mom's face fills the screen.

Showing Sawyer, I ask, "Do you mind if I grab this quick?"

He shakes his head and shifts away slightly—enough for it to be intentional.

"Hi, Mom."

"Hi, honey. I wanted to let you know that we can't watch Sawyer's date at my place. Jensen was installing the new air conditioning unit, and something happened with the electrical panel. Some kind of a fuse situation. Can we meet at your place?"

"Of course. But my TV isn't mounted, it's still on the floor. So bring some extra pillows since it's more comfortable to watch it lying down there."

Sawyer makes a disgruntled noise as he gets up and walks over to the TV.

My mom has no issue with a floor watching party and goes over the things she's bringing. Sawyer wanders back over and tilts his head toward the back of the house, holding his phone up with the time. He has to go. Because he has a date.

My mom is still talking about what Sawyer's mom thinks about his next date and the activity for this evening when he leans down toward me.

Mind blanking, body still, expectant, he whispers in my ear, "I'm going to mount your TV this weekend." *You can mount anything you want.* "Wish me luck. I'll text you later to arrange our meetups."

"Liv?"

"Huh? Sorry, Mom. What were you saying?"

Sawyer pulls back and I mouth, *Good luck.*

"Everything okay?" my mom asks. "I called your name three times."

"Sorry. Distracted."

I watch Sawyer's ass as he leaves my house to meet Jaclyn for their date night.

CHAPTER
EIGHTEEN
OLIVIA

SAWYER: Did you watch?

ME: I did . . .

Tonight's date was salsa dancing, and it was supposed to be followed by a romantic picnic in Town Center Park. Things were going well until Jaclyn tried to take things PG-13 with the cameras still live streaming their every move.

ME: You okay? How's Jaclyn?

SAWYER: Not great. She has a sprained ankle and a nasty bump on her head. She's being checked out at the hospital.

ME: Oh good. I was hoping it wasn't as bad as it looked.
ME: It didn't look too bad. But she screamed SO loudly, and then we weren't sure if the red on the glass door was her lipstick or blood.

SAWYER: It was lipstick. Her makeup was all over the door. I squashed her like a bug, Liv.

I suck a breath through my clenched teeth. He's not wrong.

I'm tempted to invite him over to talk, but we can't risk him sneaking over too often. Still, I need to hear his voice. Maybe I should—

My phone rings. I answer before the second ring.

"Hey, gorgeous."

A grin works its way onto my face. "Hey, Stud. How are you holding up?"

"I feel fucking terrible," he grumbles. "We're at the hospital waiting to see if she has a concussion. If anyone asks, you had an urgent veterinary question about Daisy."

"Done. Though while we're on the topic of bugs, I wouldn't say no to you checking her for botflies next time you're over. I saw a video online and can't unsee it. So. Nasty." I shudder.

With a soft laugh, he says, "I can do that."

"So, I have to ask . . . What happened with the door situation exactly?"

He sighs and I can practically see him rubbing those fingers along his forehead. "As I was carrying her out to the EMS truck, she was talking about how it's too bad our date was cut short and that maybe after she gets her ankle checked, I could go back to her place to finish the evening. Then her hand wandered."

I cringe. "Oof. That's bold."

His voice is terse as he continues. "She pinched my nipple, Liv. I almost dropped her, tripped, and sent us flying into the glass door of the dance studio. And now she may have a concussion."

"It was an accident, Sawyer. One that was not your fault. Which you could have explained in the post-date interview. All you said was you hoped she was okay. I would have preferred the unfiltered version. Much, *much* more interesting."

Sawyer's voice lowers to a rough whisper. "I wasn't going to say she was inappropriately tweaking my nipples on camera. Or that she twisted her ankle because our feet got tangled from her getting too close. She was practically rubbing up on my dick."

We all gagged as that horror unfolded on our screen. All I could think about was if it was working . . . if he was hard. Hard for someone else.

My mom grabbed my hand at one point, and I made sure to fix my face into a neutral but attentive expression.

"Ugh. Fine. You shouldn't have said any of that on camera. Next time just use the whistle I got you."

He covers his laugh with a cough.

"Just be glad you get all the heinous details afterward."

It was crickets over here for two full minutes when Sawyer and Jaclyn hit the glass. We were all stunned. And I knew Sawyer would be beating himself up.

"I live for the heinous details." A text comes in as we're talking. I pull the phone away from my ear and see that it's Jane. "Oh, and if you haven't yet, you might want to update your mom. She seemed a little . . . unsettled."

Shocked and concerned is a better description, but that information will not help him right now.

"I planned to call her in a bit. I wanted to check in with you first."

Ripples of giddiness crashed through my chest.

"Okay. Well, how about we meet at Grind tomorrow morning and try to do some damage control. You can hold the door open for me, incident free and everything."

I grimace second-guessing the teasing while he's still upset.

"Too soon, gorgeous." His tone is light and playful.

Wait, did he just call me gorgeous again?

"Sorry. Did I at least get a smile?" I ask.

He hums as if he's thinking about it. "Yes . . . But you didn't get the dimples."

I sigh loudly. "Understandable."

There's some chatter in the background as he talks to someone.

"Sorry. That was the nurse. The doctor should be in soon."

"Okay. Let me know how it goes."

"I will." He clears his throat. "Are we still good for tomorrow?" he asks.

"Absolutely. I'll be at Grind at 10:30 a.m. But you should show up a bit later."

"I'll be there. But um . . ." He hesitates. "Maybe bring a helmet. There seems to be a high risk of physical harm for women in my presence.

I tsk at him. "I won't need one. Tonight's date was better than the last one, so I think that's solid progress." Even though an ambulance was required, there were still a fewer number of incidents throughout the date. Progress. "Get ready for the best preplanned, pretend encounter, fake date you've ever been on."

"Can't wait." His voice is lighter, and I hope I had something to do with it. "Night, Liv."

Now I just have to make sure tomorrow goes perfectly.

CHAPTER
NINETEEN
SAWYER

"You mind if I sit with you?" I ask Liv, aware that she already spotted me while I was ordering.

"Oh, hi, Sawyer. I don't mind at all. Have a seat."

I drop into the chair across from her, placing my black coffee on the small corner table directly in front of the window.

"Smart." I nod pointedly at the window, understanding that she chose this spot so people who walked by could see us together.

"Thank you." She grins at me and takes another sip of her frothy drink.

It's quiet for a few beats, almost too quiet. Usually Grind is bustling—chatter, clinking of dishes, coffee-making machines whirring and frothing as they do. I scan the handful of tables near us for spectators.

Several pairs of eyes dart away.

"So . . . black coffee? Were you afraid anything too adventurous would be risky today? Like if you got a shot of vanilla or some almond milk in there, bad things would happen? Like maybe you'd enjoy your caffeine today?"

"You going to be this sassy the entire coffee date to try to distract me from thinking about the impending date doom?"

"Yep," she responds, tapping her coffee mug to mine.

God she's cute. "For your information, I do prefer it black. Everything else tastes a bit too much like dessert."

"I know. I've seen you order coffee before. But I thought maybe you needed to get out of your head a little."

I'm not sure that's possible, but I'm willing to let her try.

"Say something funny," she demands under her breath, her gaze darting behind me.

"Putting me on the spot a bit here, Liv," I murmur back.

She widens her eyes at me expectantly.

Fuck. Fine. "Um, flatworms fence with their penises."

"What?"

"They're hermaphroditic, and the 'loser' of the battle ends up pregnant, while the other one continues to battle other flatworms until it also gets pregnant," I explain.

There's laughter in her eyes as she asks, "That was the first thing to come to your mind?"

"I have a weird, filthy mind," I admit. She chuckles, and her hands play with her coffee mug.

I reach across with one hand and pull her fingers away. I lay my palm on top of hers on the table for a few seconds. She's staring at our hands, the bottom lip I couldn't keep from touching the other night is tucked firmly beneath her teeth.

Her hazel eyes meet mine, a little more of the vibrant green in them today. Then they dart over past my shoulder again. She mouths, *Sally.*

The youngest of the hair stylists at our local salon is sweet, animated, and endlessly curious. She's also Drew's cousin.

"Incoming," Liv says, her gaze averted.

I shift our hands, threading our fingers, giving hers a quick squeeze as Sally makes it to our table.

"Olivia!" She bends down to give Liv a side hug. "I was wondering when I'd finally run into you."

"Hi, hon. Yeah, sorry. Been busy."

The young woman's eyes cut to me. "I can see that. Hi, Sawyer."

"Hi, Sally." I flash her a brief smile.

"I meant I was busy with the move, and I started at Vaughn Valley Medical Center last week."

"That's really great, Olivia. Though, I have to admit, it's slightly less exciting than your new boyfriend here. Wait, did I miss a show? Did you two have a date?"

I answer, hopefully taking some of the pressure off Liv. "No, we haven't had a chance for a solo date on the show yet. But we ran into each other while grabbing coffee and figured we'd keep each other company."

Liv's eyes don't leave mine as she explains. "Sawyer's been a friend of my family for a long time. But with us both being single and recently moving back to town, things started falling into place."

Out of the corner of my eye, I try to gauge Sally's reaction.

"Right . . ." Her smile widens. "Well, I should probably head back to my friends. Treat her well, Dr. Fletcher. She's a keeper."

I grin at her, then examine Liv. Our hands are still clasped together, so I rub my thumb over her wrist in soft, slow strokes. When did holding hands become sexy?

"Yeah, she's pretty damn amazing, isn't she?"

Liv's soft smile and the color of her cheeks distract me from questioning if she grasps how serious I am.

Sally leans down to give Liv a parting hug before heading to the table where her friends are waiting.

We definitely have an audience now, which is what we wanted. But snippets of conversation filter back to our table and it's not all about LoveVine. There's also several poorly hushed comments about Liv's divorce.

When we take our leave, the air is thicker around us, tensions are high. The things I want to say will have to remain unsaid until we're alone.

I open the door for Liv and pretend for an instant to close it on her. She shoves me out through the door first, but I turn around, wrapping my arms around her waist and spinning to put her in front of me. I keep my arms around her as I guide her out to the sidewalk, maneuvering her to the inside.

Once we get in front of the shop window, I switch to holding her hand. We walk about a block before I move us over, stopping once we reach the bookstore. I walk her backward until she's up against the brick siding.

"How long have you been having to put up with all the shit Drew's been telling everyone?" I figured some of the residents would be checking on her, but if they've been fed lies, they might be bringing some hurtful assumptions to whatever conversation they've had.

"Meh. It's been fine." She moves to keep walking. A low, impatient hum resonates from my chest as I press a hand to the brick, caging her in.

She rolls her eyes, but when she brings them back to me they're shining with mischief.

"You're frowning again. People are going to think we're arguing."

"I don't give a shit what people think." Fuck. I'm losing sight of the entire point of this outing. "Plus no one can see my face right now anyway."

"I can and I want my smile. With dimples."

My cheek trembles with the effort not to beam at her, not to give her everything she asks for.

"After you answer my question."

"Fine. It started when everyone found out I was back for good. For those who have been persistent, I've been telling them whatever they've been hearing is nonsense rumors. But for the rude assholes, I've been adding a 'thank you for your concern. I'm so glad you asked because I've been meaning to make sure everyone knows exactly how me deciding to leave my marriage is no one's fucking business.'"

"That's my girl." I bring a hand to her face, my thumb on her soft, pouty lower lip I can't seem to stay away from.

"More chocolate?" she whispers.

"No chocolate," I murmur. Then I give her the grin she wants —the one that's all hers.

Those gorgeous eyes dip to my mouth, and her own widens to match mine.

"Liv." She's still staring at my lips, and her hand has crept up to hold on to my shirt right at the top of my jeans. The bell above the bookstore door rings, but we ignore it.

"Sawyer . . ." Her voice is low and raspy, filled with desire, and it has my stomach tightening. "How far are we taking this today?"

I close my eyes briefly to try to keep her soft lips, pretty hair, the dip in her shirt, and the snug fit of her jeans from messing with my head.

She glances across the street to where the dance studio is. "Miranda, Amina, and Daria are watching us from JoJo's."

My hand is still on her face, and her tongue peeks out to moisten her lips. "Hmm. Well, Daria is part of the Town Council, and I believe Amina helps with The Vine. This would probably be a prime opportunity to ensure everyone knows I'm into you—that you're it for me."

She takes a few beats to respond. But then her hands move to my chest, and she steps into me. "And how do you suggest we do that?" I zero in on her mouth, and slowly let out the breath I was holding. "You going to kiss me or what, Fletch?"

I shouldn't. Not with where my mind's at. This won't be a chaste kiss on the side of her mouth. If I get a taste of her, I'm going all in.

She's my best friend's little sister. She's just doing me a favor. We're friends, that's it.

So why is she all I fucking think about?

Because she scrambles my fucking brain. She must, because this is such a bad idea. If things get complicated, our families will be upset, friendships will become strained.

I'm supposed to be focusing on my career and the new business. Relationships are hard enough, but opening a new clinic at the same time, with my focus and priorities split—it wouldn't be fair to either of us. Plus, Liv's only recently started dating again. What if I'm simply the easy choice, a rebound?

I tear my gaze from her mouth to peer into her eyes. They're dark, searching, heated.

"Fuck it," I murmur inches from her lips.

I latch onto her sweet, fat lip, devouring her mouth. She tastes like her caramel-flavored coffee and something else—something fucking delicious that's all her.

Keeping my right hand planted against the side of the building, I pull her closer to me with the other. My hand splayed over the flare of her hip. Her fingers bite into my chest as I tilt my head and deepen the kiss. My tongue sweeps into her mouth, desperate for more of her.

She moans, a sound I want to hear over and fucking over again. The last of my reserve snaps, my hand leaving the brick and going directly to her plump, perky ass. Moving my mouth desperately against hers, a smile curves against her lips as her hands delve into my hair.

Slow the fuck down. This is supposed to be a chaste, fake kiss, I tell myself.

Do I listen? Fuck no.

Plastering herself to my chest, she nips my lip, earning a desperate grunt from me.

My hand goes rogue, gripping the back of her thigh. She slides it up the outside of my leg with ease. I lean into her as she hooks

144

her leg around me, bringing her center in direct contact with my thigh.

The sexy roundness of her ass, the wide flare of her hips, her skilled mouth moving against mine, and now her pussy pressing into me . . . I fucking *need* her. I'm hard as stone, punching against my fly, wanting to lift her and put her hot pussy exactly where it belongs.

But I can't do that, she's not mine. My body doesn't know that though. I practically shake with the need to rock her against me, make her come on my thigh.

Shouting from across the street infiltrates the bubble surrounding us.

Liv pulls back but I don't, I can't seem to move. Our noses are still touching, breathing the same air coming out in sharp pants.

This kiss was real. There's no way around it. The only problem is that it's cheapened by the fact that it was initiated because of this damn show.

"No! You can't—Sawyer Fletcher, unhand that contestant!" Without turning around, quick footsteps rush over to us as we separate.

"I think they noticed," Liv whispers, her eyes dark and hazy as they lift to meet mine.

I'm slow to grin, still focusing on calming my shit down.

Liv's palms retreat, and I brace to face off against Miranda and her Town Council entourage.

Turning, I greet her. "Good morning, Mayor Tisdale."

"Don't you dare have your first kiss—especially a kiss like *that* —with a contestant outside of an event night!" she scolds, closing in on us. "Good grief, did you even read the contract?"

No, not really. Liv's eyes widen at me briefly before she shakes her head. Guess she didn't either.

"You'll need to have a redo on your solo date—if you choose her next week, that is. I also want to remind you that you've consented to giving the other remaining women a chance to get to know them all, so we need you to see that through. For your own benefit as well. Stella has enlightened me about some of your dating history, and I will not have any of those kinds of relationship catastrophes on my conscience, so I'm going to need you to trust this process and give it a real shot." Her eyes dart nervously to Liv, as she realized she was telling me to not lock myself into a relationship with one woman and said woman is standing right there. "Oh gosh. Not that I don't want him to choose you, sweetheart, you know I love you to bits. Had I known sooner you were interested in dating again and had your eye on our dashing veterinarian, which I totally understand"—she winks—"I'd have set you two up immediately. But it's only fair to finish this show with good intentions, open minds, and open hearts."

"Just got a little carried away, Miranda. Sorry. Sawyer will be seeing this through to the end. We ran into each other at Grind and chatted a bit about how this is a tricky situation with other people involved. The two of us have been friends for a long time, so we were both wanting to explore if there was more there."

I slip a hand around her back, gripping low on her hip, pulling only enough to keep her firm against me, covering my reaction to her, hoping it settles down soon.

But her ass against my dick isn't helping at all. I twitch against her, and her quiet gasp is the only indication that she felt it. Shit.

"Well, I think it's safe to say you've got enough chemistry to light the whole town ablaze. Lord, we thought you two were going to get to it right here in front of the bookstore."

"We will be sure to save any further explorations for our date night. I'm sure the next group event will finally be one where I get to choose my solo date for the week?"

"That might be the plan. You'll find out in a few days." She smiles warmly at me before shifting her focus to Liv. Then back to me.

"Stella was right. The woman befuddles me, always two steps ahead. Teaming up with her has been enlightening."

Her words give me pause. "Stella was right about what?"

With a wide smile and a dismissive wave, Miranda ignores my question. "No more sidewalk foreplay. Save it for the cameras, but keep it a bit more PG-13. And read those contracts—there are rules, you know."

Liv and I track Miranda as she crosses the street, back to where her friends are in front of JoJo's Dance and Pilates Studio.

I step back away from Liv, and thank god the bulge in my pants is no longer as pronounced. Then Liv turns around and gawks directly at it. Fuck. Can't catch break.

She glances up at me, and a faint blush colors her cheeks.

"Mission accomplished," I mumble under my breath.

I hold out a hand, and she examines it, then awkwardly slaps it like I was asking for a low five. I chuckle and it seems to break through whatever trance she was in.

Holding my hand out again, I say, "I was actually thinking we could hold hands for the walk home."

"Oh, are we walking home together?" I nod, a grin on my face as I turn toward her. Those wheels are spinning, but I'm a bit too happy about how our fake date went—especially the ending—to let my own mind go to all the places I'm sure hers is.

Because the truth is, our kiss was fucking amazing. The part of me that's been holding back, drawing lines, not letting myself think about how soft her skin is, how addictive her scent is—that part knew exactly what kissing her would be like. It wouldn't be fake because what I feel for Liv isn't fake. And I don't have a clue what the hell to do about it.

She slips her hand into mine, and I thread our fingers together.

"And when we get to your place, I'm mounting your TV. And hanging the curtain rods too. I saw you had your ladder out, but I can probably reach without it."

She gives my hand a squeeze.

"Having a fake boyfriend is kind of nice, Fletch." She leans into me, glancing up with those enticingly warm eyes. "What do you know about tile?"

I grin at her. "Putting me to work, huh?" Little does she know that I'm more than happy to have her put me to work all day.

We reach the end of Main Street, and all talk of how we'll spend the rest of the afternoon stops when Mr. Gillespie appears from around the corner.

"Sawyer Fletcher, welcome back to Vaughn. Seems our two new residents have rekindled their young love."

"Rekindled? We just started seeing each other, Mr. Gillespie," Liv tells him, slightly confused.

"Oh, come on. As if you didn't have a thing back in college. He was over at your house all the time. An older, handsome college boy? I may be old, but I remember what it's like to be young and frisky."

I hold in my chuckle, but Liv lets hers out. "Mr. G., we were never like that. He was off to college before I even started dating."

"That's what holidays at home are for."

"Nope, sorry, Mr. G. Liv's telling the truth." I slip an arm around her, meeting her eyes, which have a bit more green in them once more. "We were only friends. This, uh, whole Love-Vine thing is what brought us together. We've both returned to Vaughn in a place where we might have a chance at something."

"Ah, yes, I wondered about that. Been watching, of course. The whole town is. I'm rooting for our Olivia here, but some of the residents are hoping Velora catches your eye. Her mother is on Town Council, you know."

"I didn't actually, I'm not up-to-date on Town Council or Vaughn happenings yet. I'll be sure to get better acquainted since I'm a resident again." Mr. Gillespie takes town news and events very seriously, always has. But since his wife passed, it's become a bigger part of his life, a way to fill the hole his late wife left.

"You do that." He turns to Liv. "I can already tell this one's much better for you than the last one." His gaze cuts back to me, his cane pointing at me threateningly. "Treat her better than Drew did. Got it?"

"Yes, sir."

And the growly old man strides away, cane clicking alongside him, I question if I can keep such a promise. Because somehow, disaster always seems to strike my relationships in a way there's no coming back from.

But I'm not sure I can stay away from Liv anymore.

CHAPTER
TWENTY
SAWYER

W e made it through this week's group date much like the last—with too little Liv and way too much of everyone else. I'm starting to wonder if I'm being irrational or if Stella and Miranda are keeping us apart on purpose.

I can't even fucking *sit* where I want to.

Or date who I want to.

As they rolled out the poker tables for the group competition, my plans to take Liv out for a date were crushed. She has a sweet, expressive face, and pale, easily flushed skin. Her poker face is nonexistent, and she has a marked disdain for card games. She's a board game girl.

She shot me a grimace, and twenty minutes later was the first participant eliminated from the poker tournament. She was so furious, it was cute. She left the table in a huff and plunked down next to me at the 'observation table'.

I stretched my arm out across the back of her chair, making contact with her bare shoulders. Her competitive nature had her begrudgingly asking questions about terms and strategies as we observed the ladies play. Leaning into her, I whispered explanations in her ear, drawing lazy lines along the slope of her neck.

She sucked in a breath as goose bumps broke out all over her skin. When I nip at her earlobe after answering another of her questions, she gasped. Squirming in her seat, her hand shifted to my thigh, climbing higher as she leaned in to me.

"Sawyer—"

Her soft, desire-laced tone was cut short as another contestant crashed in on our limited private time together.

It wasn't until later, during the daisy ceremony, that I found out the winner of the tournament, and this week's solo date, was Marie.

And now the poor woman is sitting across from me, no doubt eating as awkwardly as I am.

"I think there's cardamom in it?" she guesses as we try to identify the spices and flavours of the dish the chef made specifically for us.

We're at an upscale restaurant located at one of the vineyards on the northern edge of Landry. I've been here before but the meal the chef has created for us consists of all original dishes crafted for a LoveVine romantic chef's table dinner.

"Uh, thyme?" I guess.

Someone tsks. Not sure who. Because I can't *see.*

It's a *blindfolded* chef's table dinner.

And I hate it. All of it. But I'm trying to be a good date. I can do this. I don't even care about the food. As long as they don't accidentally feed me coconut, everything should be fine. I'll make it through this date—eat some fancy food, and make polite, engaging conversation so Marie feels heard and respected. Then I plan to go home to Karl, who likely convinced my mom to feed him one of each kind of dog treat I have, and call Liv for our usual post-date debrief.

"Feed her another bite, Sawyer," Stella cues.

I pick up my fork and stab my plate until I think I've snagged something. Then gently bring it over to where she sits across from me.

This is such a fucking terrible idea.

I push the fork closer to her, and she yelps. "That's my cheek."

Fuck. "Sorry." At least I didn't get her eye. Again.

"No. I-I can do it. Just . . ." She swipes the fork from my hand. "Mm-hmm," she murmurs as she chews. "Yes, braised lamb with a mint cardamom sauce."

"Correct," the chef booms from the busy kitchen behind us.

How the hell did she know all of this?

And cardamom has made it on my spice shit list.

Attempting to wash the flavor from my mouth, I find my glass empty. I hold it up and turn, hoping to ask our server for a refill.

"*Oomph!*"

Shit. I hit him with my elbow. "Sorry, man. Um, could I get another drink, please?" I wait until his fingers grip the glass before letting go.

Somehow the glass smashes to the floor anyway.

Come. Fucking. *On.*

There's a flash and sizzle sound that has my head whipping in the opposite direction.

"Shit! Cover it, Jimmy!"

Having never worked in a restaurant before, I had no idea how chaotic it is in the kitchen.

"Here," a peppy voice says, and suddenly a hot, crispy piece of food is being lodged into my nostril.

Brussel sprouts. Hard to confuse that aroma.

Bringing the napkin up to my face, I wipe the remnants away.

"*Get it under control!*" comes a roaring shout.

A piercing alarm blares around us, our table is bumped, instructions are bellowed.

Fuck. This. Shit.

I tear off my blindfold and absolute chaos surrounds us. Flames kiss the ceiling of the kitchen, acrid smoke billowing above, creeping toward us at an alarming rate. The kitchen staff tries to put it out at the source, but it's gotten too big, too wild. Our production crew is trying to step in to help, others are covering their faces and escaping to the front of the restaurant. Hopefully to get everyone out.

Marie still has her blindfold on while she clutches the table in a white-knuckled grip. Jesus. I reach across and yank the silky material off her face.

"We're getting out of here," I tell her.

"Sawyer! Marie! Evacuate," Stella shouts from the emergency exit doorway. "The guys at the fire station are on their way."

Everyone is scrambling, and I make sure they all head in the right direction, since some appear confused and startled.

Marie and I are about ten feet from the exit when the sprinkler system goes off, drenching everyone and everything in seconds.

By the time the Landry Fire Department arrives, consisting of mostly volunteer firefighters, Marie is crying, Stella has half The League calling everyone's friends and family, and the camera crew has regrouped and continues filming.

Once the fire is out and the damage is being assessed, Stella brings me over to Marie, having taken over for Sean as the host of tonight's date. Sean decided he needed the week off to be with his fiancée because she has fall break at the school where she works. He mentioned she's not going to "impregnate herself," and that's when I hung up.

"We will begin with Marie's post-date interview. Obviously, you'll want to include your thoughts or feelings about these unfortunate circumstances. However, I'd appreciate if you could make sure at least half of your interview time was spent discussing how the date was fairing before it was lit on fire." Stella waves down the camera and audio guys, who shift from getting footage of the fire crew, and make their way back to our huge fail of a date.

"Actually, Stella, I'd appreciate a moment with Sawyer alone before we do the interview."

Stella's gaze jumps to me before returning to Marie. She gives us both a tight smile before directing the production crew to the fire chief, who recently arrived on scene.

Marie turns to me, blowing out a long breath.

"That was crazy," she says, her voice holding a slight tremor.

"Yeah. Don't think I'm cut out for a restaurant kitchen. Guess I'll stick with puppies and kittens." I shrug, smiling lightheartedly at her.

"Sawyer . . ."

Here it comes.

"For a minute I really thought you were messing up some of the dates on purpose. Spilling drinks on contestants during group dates, mixing up names. But then there were also wardrobe malfunctions, lost items, equipment failure, and some mild food poisoning."

"Those things happen on these kinds of shows. You put enough people together and shit happens," I explain, hoping to brush off her observations and get this night wrapped.

"And your date nights? How do you explain those? Or tonight?"

Nothing I say is going to change her mind, and while I hate the implication of what she's saying . . . She's not exactly wrong. And I'm not about to try to convince her otherwise.

"Shit luck. It's the only explanation I've got, Marie."

She studies me for a beat. "Yeah. Well, your shit luck has cost me two dresses now"—she pinches the smudged, waterlogged fabric of the second dress I've had a hand in ruining during a LoveVine event—"and my dignity."

My jaw clenches.

"Listen, there's been some talk among the ladies about how you're bad at dating, or shy, maybe have a small dick, who knows —which is why you needed this show to help find you a girlfriend even though you're the seemingly charming, good-looking, intellectual type." She pauses, lowering her voice. "But I'm thinking now that you're actually cursed. And I do not need this kind of bad juju in my life."

I rake my fingers through my hair. Another candidate withdrawing from the show after a date gone wrong. I can't do these fucking dates anymore. This here—a scorched kitchen—that's the line.

Nodding at her, I tell her I understand and ask that she leaves those details out of her interview. I don't need anyone else getting it into their head that I'm somehow causing this, intentionally or not.

By the time I leave Landry, it's after 11:00 p.m., and all I want to do is go to Liv's, watch her make her gross cheesy snacks, and have her help me shake off this whole damn night.

But she's working tonight.

The minute I get home, Karl takes one sniff of me and then retreats back to his dog bed. Before heading into the shower, I pull out my phone and check if Liv responded to the text I sent her earlier.

ME: Don't watch tonight's show.

LIV: What happened?

ME: She tried to fuck my nostril with a brussel sprout, I forked her in the eye (it was thankfully covered by the blindfold), and the restaurant went up in flames.

LIV: Shut. Up.
LIV: Is everyone okay? I haven't heard anything about an influx of ER patients or a fire. Tell me you're okay.

ME: A couple of the kitchen staff were treated on-site for second degree burns, but otherwise everyone is fine.

LIV: Including you, right?

Her concern washes away every shitty thought, every negative feeling.

ME: Yes.
ME: We're down another contestant though. Marie believes me to be cursed. She made some good points, Liv. Then she hissed at me, crossed herself and fled with Lenny, the camera guy.

LIV: That's a little dramatic. Do you need some talking down? We can FaceTime in about an hour. Though, after the night you've had, I understand if you're not planning on staying up.

ME: It's a date. One hour. I'll need about four showers to get the smoke smell off me anyway.

LIV: K. I'm not wearing makeup and I might have to eat while we chat. I've helped deliver two babies already, and I just started three hours ago. Had a dad faint—on the mom. Trust me, after hearing the full story, you won't feel quite so bad about your botched date.

ME: Doubtful. Unless he fell, knocked over her calming lavender scented candle, lit half the room on fire, and then farted loudly while a firefighter carried him to safety.

LIV: Did you fart on a firefighter? Who? Do I know him? Was it Jensen?

ME: What? No! I was just trying to—you know what? Never mind.

She sends me approximately eighteen laughing emojis followed by a single wind emoji.

I put the phone down and turn on the shower. Before stepping in, the screen light up again.

LIV: You're not cursed, Stud. You're simply going out with boring women who are ridiculously judgmental, need to brush up on their fire safety, have weak ankles, and a questionable code of ethics.

The fact that she thinks it could still be everyone else and not me—the common denominator in this dating fuckery—is sweet.

And her sweetness is the prize I'm going to claim next week during the group date, because there's no fucking way I'm going on a solo date with anyone but her from this point on.

Fuck everyone else.

Because if I don't get another taste of her soon, another reason to get close, put my hands on her and calm the overwhelming need I've been denying, I'm going to start sneaking over to her house for an entirely different reason.

CHAPTER
TWENTY-ONE

OLIVIA

I've spent the last week thinking about *the* kiss. My vibrator's battery has been tested to its limits. God, the things I would have let him do to me on that sidewalk. I could have stuck my hand down his pants while sucking on his neck, relishing the scrape of the scruff at the edge of his jaw before coming hard on his thigh.

The fact that I've fallen so deeply into Sawyer Fletcher isn't as surprising as I once would have thought. My seventeen-year-old self was an absolute moron for not chasing after him. I could have locked him down years ago. But I wasn't ready for him yet.

Plus, there was one time, before dating Drew, that I ogled Sawyer like the solid hunk of delicious man meat he is. Just *one* time. And Jaxon got all up in my face about it. I told him he was crazy. I was semi-dating a boy in my senior class then, but let me tell you, he couldn't kiss worth a damn in comparison. Then again, compared to Sawyer, all my past experiences were subpar in the kissing department.

And if that was what he brought to a pretend kiss . . . I can't even imagine how all the other aspects of a physical relationship with Sawyer would compare.

But every part of me is screaming that our kiss was *not* pretend. It wasn't for show.

It was everything.

To me anyway.

I thought our public kiss would be slow, sweet, somewhat chaste. Last a few seconds. Maybe a few lingering pecks before we continued down the street, popping into stores or wandering through town.

Nope. I was so aroused, we were basically fucking with our clothes on.

And now I have to sit through another group competition with my thighs squeezed together, attempting to focus on the wine tasting game—not Sawyer's mouth.

Abbie, Raine, Sara, Velora, and myself are the last contestants. Whoever gets the daisy tonight automatically makes it to next week, and Sawyer has to choose someone else to eliminate.

The problem is that while I drink wine readily, I'm no expert. Red, white, rosé, dry, sweet, fruity, oaky, and smells a bit like feet are the only describing factors I can contribute to wine talk. So hazarding a guess about which red wine is which out of six different varietals—nope.

Harper has tried helping me from the bar area when I searched her out in desperation. But Sean's been watching me like a hawk, as if he knows I'll do anything to win.

But I don't win.

Velora does. I swear someone helped her because she seemed far too confident from the start. Thankfully, Velora's win means she has secured her spot for next week, *not* that she has won a date with Sawyer.

During dinner, there was a small hiccup that's adding some lingering tension to the final portion of our evening.

Sara decided to be a bit of a diva, throwing a fit when Sawyer came to sit with me after she tried to pull him down next to her. Later she tripped on stage and he didn't see, so someone else helped her up. She has been embarrassed and sullen for the last thirty minutes.

With Sara still in a foul mood, we all steer clear of her as we take our places for the elimination ceremony. Giving Sawyer a wide, reassuring smile, I stand on my mark.

As Sawyer steps forward to call his first choice, so does Sara.

What fresh hell now?

"I have something I need to say before we continue with the ceremony." She waits dramatically. "Unfortunately, I can't in good conscience remain on LoveVine pursuing a relationship with Sawyer Fletcher." She turns and faces him directly. "Sawyer, I cannot accept your daisy."

I fight a shocked laugh—because, hello! Presumptuous!—and study Sawyer's reaction to this declaration. His eyebrows twitch slightly as he tries to keep his expression even. But the press of his lips gives him away.

All he does is nod, and Sara sweeps off the stage.

Miranda and Stella make a few comments and promise to get an interview with Sara afterward, which will be posted to The Vine's website.

Sawyer moves on to presenting the winning flower to Velora, and my blood boils as she hugs him, kissing his cheek—so close to his mouth, if it weren't for him swiftly turning his head, she would have planted one on him.

Couldn't he have tossed the flower at her and walked away?

The rational part of me understands he was being polite and isn't interested—in *any* of us—but I stand by my idea that flower throwing would have been better.

I'm not typically a jealous woman. But this contest is fucking with me. I wasn't even overly possessive over Drew, and he was my husband.

Yet here I am, filled with rage because the man I'm only supposed to be pretending to fall for is spending time with other women, and it isn't pretend to me anymore.

After this stupid show, would I want to be with Sawyer for real? Yes. Absolutely, yes. More than anything, I want to find out if he fucks half as good as he kisses.

I don't even know what he thought of our kiss or if he felt the same things I did. I've been avoiding talking about it, even if it's constantly on my mind.

And I'm not sure where that leaves us. Because he made it clear from the start he doesn't want a relationship.

So I stifle the feelings I have no right to express and wait for him to call my name. When he does, something inside me shifts. Because this time, Sawyer finally gets to choose his own date, and he's holding the special solo date flower.

"Liv, will you accept this daisy and be my date?" He's supposed to say, "Be my date *this week*," but he leaves it out, and I'm pretty sure it was intentional.

"I'd love to," I tell him.

And then his hand cups my cheek, and he pulls me in. Sawyer kisses me—a soft, swift claiming—and I nearly melt at his feet.

I'm in a daze as he calls the other contestants, unable to keep my eyes off of him, unable to hear a word being said.

The show wraps up, and audience members mill about for a while. Once most have left, I make my way back out front, hoping Sawyer is still here.

It only takes me a few seconds to spot him. He's across the room talking to Abbie, and I wonder if he'll want me to interrupt. As if he can feel me watching, he grabs the back of his neck like he's working out a kink, turning slightly and smiling at me—with dimples—mouthing, *Hi.*

Fuck. That smile turns me into a useless puddle of want.

I wink in return, and when he turns back to Abbie, I catch my lip between my teeth, tempering my wanton grin, and treat myself to one quick glance at his ass.

"I'm glad you applied to be a participant, Olivia." I startle, Sawyer's mom sidling up beside me.

I glimpse back at Sawyer briefly before saying, "I, um, I'm glad I applied too."

"I always had a feeling about you two, but the timing was never right. And with the way he's been about relationships lately, I tried not to get my hopes up when Lilah mentioned you were moving back to town. Actually, for a moment, we were worried this contest might be an obstacle to you two finding each other."

She and my mom had talked about the two of us? Maybe that's why my mom seemed a bit smug when I brought up Sawyer and the show.

"Sometimes these things don't happen until we're ready for them. Other times, they happen when we least expect it," she adds, her eyes darting to her son, who has been taken aside by Velora. When she looks back at me, her smile widens. "I think he wants you to go over there," she says with a knowing smirk almost exactly like her son's.

I turn my attention back to Sawyer, and she's right. He's staring at me, a plea in his eyes. Right. Buffer.

"I guess I should go stake my claim, huh?"

"I think he looks more like he wants you to save him. Velora is the worst." With a laugh, I give her a quick hug. God I love this woman.

The click of my heels on the hardwood floor of Rocky's alerts Sawyer of my approach. He blindly reaches for me, pulling me into him.

With his arm wrapped firmly around me, he peers down at me. I tip my chin up to meet his gaze.

"You're not leaving yet, are you?" he asks.

"Not yet."

"Was Ellie here? I didn't see her."

"No, she planned to but Liam said she fell asleep immediately after dinner. It's common for this part of her pregnancy, but she's going to be pissed when she wakes up." He laughs, his eyes never leaving mine. "Did I tell you she got to have her first prenatal appointment on Monday? And then I ran into Chloe Daniels. Hayden and his daughter go to every prenatal appointment with her. It's the cutest. Chloe asked about you just to rile Hayden up so he'd stop being so delicate with her during . . . you know." I wink at him as he swipes a hand down his face, trying to cover his reaction. Making him smile might be one of my favorite things, mostly because I get to see those dimples.

A voice cuts in. "You're a midwife? Huh."

Sawyer rubs my back in small, calming circles. I completely forgot Velora was here and have no doubt she's about to say something awful.

"I would want a doctor to deliver my babies, in a hospital with everything I could need—including medical professionals." She places a hand on her chest, drawing attention to the massive amounts of cleavage she's got on display. It's a nice rack, I'll give her that. If I had it, I'd probably flaunt it too. "Not that your prenatal care would be ineffective, just personal preference," Velora says. "I'd want only the best for my babies, and glorified nurses wouldn't be my first choice."

This bitch.

I take back the nice things I thought about her tits.

"There are actually many benefits to choosing midwifery for prenatal care," Sawyer tells her, giving me a soft smile. "Nurses tend to deliver more babies than doctors. And midwives in particular are known for being better in tune with the mother's needs and wants, providing more options, lowering the chances of C-section—"

"Oh, I would *want* a C-section. We wouldn't want a baby permanently damaging anything down there, right, Sawyer?" Her voice turns sultry, and I simply stare at her like she's cracked.

Sawyer holds up a hand in defence. "Not my body, not my choice, Velora. But even still, I can't imagine how your choice of child delivery method would have anything to do with me." He looks at me, and his wide eyes say, *Change the subject. I'd rather talk about* anything *else.*

"What is it you do again, Velora?" I ask, aware that steering the conversation so she gets to talk about herself is an easy redirect.

"I provide online and in-person, one-on-one life coaching for those who struggle with health, life balance, and career challenges."

"Wow, and you were able to do that with no experience, education, or professional credentials? Impressive," I snark, but it goes unnoticed by Velora.

"Well, I hate to brag, but yes, my career came very easy to me," she brags, tossing her hair over her shoulder. "People want to emanate my style and success."

"Gag me," I mumble.

"What was that?" she asks.

Sawyer turns his head toward me and whispers, "Kinky," out of the side of his mouth.

I lock down my amusement and respond with, "Nothing. That's great, Velora. If you don't mind, I promised Sawyer's mom I'd bring him over. She needs help with something."

"Oh, well, I'll be heading out soon. Want me to wait? Or maybe we can arrange to meet for a coffee after work? With you being spotted around town with some contestants"—she gives me a pointed glare—"I'd love if we could connect more outside of this whole thing." She waves around at the stage and event setup, acting like it's an inconvenience instead of the showy production she thrives off of.

"I'm not actually meeting with anyone from the show. I ran into Liv at Grind, and we ended up talking for a bit."

"Well, why don't we run into each other tomorrow for lunch at Fork'd? Or are you still working out of the Landry clinic some days? I could meet you there instead."

"Um, no, Dr. Erlandson has mostly taken over the clinic in

Landry with a bit of help from my dad. I'm here full time." Sawyer's hand is still hovering at the small of my back, grazing across my hip every so often. Velora's eyes narrow a hair.

"Great. I'll meet you at 12:30 p.m. then," she practically purrs, stepping closer on Sawyer's other side. He shifts closer to me, almost stepping on my toes.

"Um, as much as I love the food at Fork'd"—ha! The food, not the chance to spend time with her—"Miranda read me the riot act about spending time with contestants outside of date nights—intentionally or unintentionally—for the remainder of the show's run. It's, and I quote, 'strictly prohibited,' which I apparently should have known from reading the contract we all signed."

"Oh." Her face falls, leaving behind an ugly sneer. I mean, she's still perfect and gorgeous, but that expression wasn't quite so perfect, and it might have been my favorite Velora moment mostly because it was real. "I'll just have to keep an eye out for you around town then. I'm sure we'll cross paths soon."

Lightning fast, she kisses his cheek and sashays away.

"That kind of sounded like a threat, didn't it?" he asks me.

"Sure did." I wipe her gross kiss off his cheek, trying not to make eye contact while my hand is on his face. Not sure I could take the intensity of his deep blue gaze right now.

"So does my mom really need me?"

"No, but like her son, she suggested I step up my buffering efforts."

He laughs. "She told you to save me?"

I hum in agreement as he turns me into him so we're facing each other, both of his arms around me now. "She's a great mom."

"The best."

"All right, love birds, time to clear out. My staff needs to take down the rest of this section," Harper says while pushing some chairs out of the way. "I've got a babysitter who charges me out the nose if I'm even two minutes late."

"Hugh," Jane calls, signalling to her husband. "Come over and help Harper with those tables, honey. She's got her little one to get home to. Sawyer can help stack the extra chairs."

When Hugh Fletcher approaches, he gives his son an affectionate smack on the back. "Sawyer, this group date was slightly less painful to watch. The wine definitely helped."

"Thanks, Dad," he grumbles. "You're not even the one up there with everyone observing your every move."

"Sorry, champ. I would absolutely hate that. I'm not sure how they talked you into this crap." His wife gives him a playful smack on the arm.

"Probably about the same way Mom talked you into coming to it," Sawyer responds.

"I very much doubt that, son." Hugh Fletcher gives his wife's butt a jaunty slap that has me chuckling into my hand.

"Jesus," he says on a groan. "All right, I'm going to stack chairs and pretend large portions of this night never happened—particularly this last part. Liv, want me to walk you out to your car?"

Suddenly worried what will happen if we're alone, I say, "Actually, I planned to stick around and help Harper. She's dropping me at home after. But thanks. I'll see you this weekend for our date . . . handsome." I walk my fingers up his bicep.

Ugh. Flirting in front of his parents apparently turns me into a fool.

"All right, *gorgeous*. See you then." He boops me on the nose, an amused smile playing at his lips.

As he walks away, he turns and stares back at me with a gleam in his eyes that hints at the shit he's going to give me about this later.

Sawyer and his parents help Max store the tables and chairs. I retreat to the kitchen to grab the clean glassware Harper says needs to be put away before we can leave. I return as Sawyer's delectable ass disappears through the wooden double doors of Rocky's.

"He wants to bang you."

I frown at my friend who's restocking beer.

"Stop. There are several contestants left, and it's not like I'm even a—" Oh god, I almost told her this wasn't real, that I'm not a real candidate.

She shakes her head, a crooked smile on her face. "I'm not sure what's going on between you and him or this whole damn show, but you're in deep."

I cover my face with my hands and let out a frustrated breath.

"I think I might be a little bit fucked."

She slings an arm around my shoulders. "Yeah. But maybe not in a bad way."

And she's right. Maybe this is going to be the start of something. After our date night—if he doesn't freak, if I can convince him he's not unlucky in love, and that luck doesn't matter when you're with someone you care about—I'm going to tell him I want him to choose me for real.

CHAPTER
TWENTY-TWO

SAWYER

I'm nervous. Really fucking nervous. Because to me, unlike the other dates, this one means something. And the fact that we'll be out on a trail and anything could happen to her has me twitching.

"Hey. You okay?" Liv asks, easing her hand up my arm and then back down again in agonizingly brief contact.

With her hands on me, I'm definitely okay. "Yeah. I'm glad you're here. Did you just arrive? I didn't hear you."

"Yeah, you looked lost in thought. They wanted to mic me but I asked if I could check on you first. As a heads-up, I think Sean is still getting them to film the pre-date footage and your mic is probably on."

She's reminding me we can't talk freely, but that she's concerned about me.

"Want me to watch Daisy while you get mic'd?" I ask.

"Sure. That'd be great." She hands over the teal-colored leash, still assessing me.

Hesitating, she takes a couple steps toward the EMS truck, which now remains on high-alert during all of my dates. She pauses before she reaches the audio guy and hurries back toward me, getting in my space, hands gripping the sleeves of my flannel jacket. The pounding in my chest picks up as she tips her head up, rising on her toes before slowly capturing my mouth with hers. I freeze momentarily, enjoying the aggressive way she's taken charge of the kiss before wrapping my arms around her.

I groan in surprise as she opens the kiss, her tongue sliding against my bottom lip. She sucks gently, letting her lips brush against mine.

She moves to my jaw, leaving a trail of hot kisses until she gets to my ear. I find the underside of her jaw and inhale her delicious warm honey scent before sucking there, inexplicably wanting to mark her.

"There," she says in a hushed tone against my ear. My heart hammers so loudly, I'm sure the mic is picking it up. "Was that what you were worried about? The kiss is out of the way and now we can just go for a walk. Us and the dogs, and our ridiculous tagalong, Sean." Her eyes bore into mine with a sweet kind of intensity. "You with me, Sawyer?"

"Yeah, Liv. I'm with you." She leans back, but I keep her held tight against me. "You're something, you know that?" Something I want a whole hell of a lot more of.

She bites her lip and grabs the bill of my cap. "I like you in hats," she whispers before her sweet, soft lips touch mine once more, leaving me wishing more than anything that we were alone.

Liv spins out of my arms and heads over to get her mic. And I can't tear my eyes away from her. She's in a warm puffer vest, jeans that fit like a second skin over her perky ass, and a pair of dark brown hiking boots. My date looks like the sexiest hiker I've ever laid eyes on. Her outfit isn't meant to tantalize, her smile not intending to turn me on. And yet, I can't help imagining unzipping her vest, peeling off those hip-hugging jeans.

If I can't snap out of this, the very obvious bulge in my pants is going to be the talk of the town after people watch this latest date night episode.

Tonight is the only solo date that's technically outside of both Landry and Vaughn. We're in a regional park on the outskirts of Vaughn, going on a hike with Karl and Daisy in tow, their leashes tangling as they play.

Sean is the only one with us today, since the camera crew weren't on board for trekking through the mountain trails. Which means he's the cameraman and host. If it weren't for his heavy feet, we'd barely be able to tell he's following behind us.

We make it to a lookout point where the crew planned for us to stop for a rest and some snacks they put together for us.

"Should we take a break?" I ask as Liv moves to stand beside me. I whisper, "I feel like kissing you again, and I don't want to wait until we finish this whole trail loop."

Her giggle rings out among the trees. Karl and Daisy go to her, curious what's got her laughing.

"I'm sweaty," she warns, moving toward the edge of the lookout area.

I spin her around, drawing her into me. The dogs wander around us, wrapping us up.

"I don't care. I've had to watch that ass for the last half hour, and I need to taste you." The words tumble from my mouth as her hands smooth over my chest.

Her face flushes as she whispers, "We're wearing mics, Sawyer."

With her hands on me, my awareness of anything else is shot. "Shit. Your brothers are going to beat my ass."

"You'll have an easier time convincing me to kiss you if you don't mention my brothers right before."

"Fair enough. How about I talk more about how much I want to peel these damn leggings off you and lick every—"

Her hand covers my mouth as she gasps, *Sawyer!* in a way I

know she wants to shout, but can't because of the mics. I grin against her palm before giving it a kiss and pulling back.

"They can edit it out," I assure her.

"Um, luckily this one isn't live because we don't have great internet access in the mountains, but you're trusting the members of The League and The Vine to cut the naughty bit out of the date. I can pretty much guarantee it's not going to happen," Sean tells us from behind the camera. "But for future reference, we only edit the pre and post-date testimonials."

Fuck. I knew it, but I'm too focused on her, too far gone to care that Sean is even there, let alone that other people are watching. In fact, I *can't* think about that.

"Great. You can back off now, Sean, and give us a minute." I swoop down, murmuring against her lips, "Tell me this is real for you. Tell me it's not just me."

She takes a breath, nodding before looping her arms around my neck. "It's not just you, Sawyer."

I pick her up, grinning as her squeal turns into soft laughter. "Will you accept my daisy, Olivia Vaughn?"

"We aren't even finished our date." Her tone is chastising but the beaming smile on her face tells me she likes that I asked her early.

"There are no rules to say I have to wait, gorgeous."

She's quiet for a moment, a mischievous glint in her eyes. "Can I think about it?"

I put her down with an exaggerated frown. "Guess I'll have to convince you some more." My hands delve into her messy bun as I go in for another kiss. This one is deeper. She opens up to me, her tongue sliding across mine, letting loose a submissive moan as she melts into me.

Pulling back, I take a few more sips from her juicy lips. I brush my lips gently across hers, and ask, "Still thinking?"

Her breath flutters across my mouth on a sigh. "No thinking happened at all. Flower me, Stud."

I carefully remove the flower from the backpack I've been carrying, and present it to her.

"The first solo date night flower has been presented to Liv Vaughn—a top contender for the heart of Vaughn's newest veterinarian, the previously love-evasive, Sawyer Fletcher. Tune in next week for the last group date to find out which contestants will be bringing him home to meet their families." Sean shoves the camera into the equipment bag slung over his shoulder with a satisfied huff. "That's a wrap. So are we turning around and heading back down or is it closer to finish the loop? I've got a fiancée at home who I'd like to plan my own date night out with."

Liv laughs, still clutching my arm, still leaning against me. "Sean, aren't we finishing the rest of our hike . . . the rest of our date? You're supposed to film—"

"Come on, you two. Don't try to bullshit me. You think I haven't noticed what's going on here?" He points between Liv and me.

Shit. What does he suspect is happening?

"What are you talking about, man?" I ask, trying to remain calm.

"You two."

"What about us?" Liv asks him.

"Did you forget I've been on almost all your dates?" He's staring at me, a half smile creeping up on his face. "I've seen you with the other women. This is the first date I've felt like an intrusive third wheel. I mean, it was awkward during the others, but only because I was extremely uncomfortable by how badly the date was going and the sheer number of injuries and fuckups. This one was different."

Liv and I share a knowing look. Not one bad thing has happened on this date. In fact, I've never been happier, more energized, or confident that this date was exactly what I needed— that *Liv* is exactly *who* I need.

"You did it. Curse broken," she whispers low so Sean can't hear.

"*You* did this, Liv." I walk her backward until her back meets the tree in front of me.

My hands tighten around her waist as I kiss her again. I can't fucking get enough. This isn't just *want*. Not merely attraction. It's *need*. I can't remember the last time I liked someone this much, craved her as if she's my next breath of air after being submerged deep underwater for far too long.

The thought of her body touching me, fusing with mine, over-shadows every other thought.

I reach around and disconnect her mic. She does the same for me, unsure if anyone is listening, if it could still be recorded.

"See? Aren't you glad I stopped filming?" Sean calls from somewhere behind us. "I'll take Daisy and Karl, bring them down. The team can hang out with them while we wait for you two. Don't get arrested for indecent exposure. The police chief might be a good friend, but since that's his sister you're all over, I have a feeling your ass will end up in county jail. If that happens, they'll want me there to film it—which would interrupt my Sadie time. So don't do anything stupid."

"Sean," I say, my voice rough.

"Fine. Yeah, got it. You want me to fuck off. See you next week, lovers." He takes the leashes from us, and I turn back to Liv.

His footsteps fade away as I kiss down her neck. She smells sweet, like the best kind of treat—one I'd gladly binge on for as long as she'd let me.

"You smell so fucking good I want to lick you. Fuck, Liv, I want to do a lot of things to you." Slowly I unzip her vest.

She gulps, the pulse in her neck fluttering.

"Let me touch you. Just for a little while. Let me make you come."

"Shouldn't we . . ." My hands slip under her shirt, and my

caresses along the smooth skin of her narrow waist, up her rib cage, to the undersides of her breast make her pause. "Talk about all of this?"

"We'll talk, I promise. I want to talk, but first I want to feel you gush all over my hand. I want your moans in my ear. I want to swallow your cries and feel you go limp against me."

"Oh fuck. You really are a dirty talker."

"Yeah, gorgeous. But if you still want to talk right now, it'll be to tell me what you like. All I want to hear from these pretty lips is how I can make you feel good."

I swipe a thumb across her nipple, finding it beaded and ready for my mouth. Not here though. No chance I'm letting anyone else see her sweet, bare tits.

As my mouth takes hers again, I eagerly slip a hand down to unbutton her jeans. She hums in anticipation against my lips, tilting her hips toward me.

"I'll get there. Anticipation is half the fun," I tell her.

"Not when you haven't had someone else's hands on you in months," she says, grabbing my forearm and shoving my hand down exactly where she wants it.

I chuckle as I trace the edge of her panties. I wasn't expecting the plain cotton—no lace or satin—and I love it.

It's been a long time since I've been with someone, but I don't tell her that because it would spark a discussion I don't plan on having until after I've felt her pulse against my fingers.

She's wet—so wet I slip through her bare folds with ease. I use my booted foot to kick her legs farther apart, granting me better access.

My control is hanging on by a thread as I slide two fingers up and down her slit. I dip into her entrance, and her grip on me tightens, fingertips digging into my shoulders. Lightly circling the swollen bead at the apex of her thighs, I relish the moan escaping her lips.

Her head drops back, falling to the trunk of the tree. "Sawyer . . ."

Her long, delicate neck calls to me. I run my lips up her smooth skin, nipping as I get to her jaw. "Tell me, gorgeous. Do you like it when I tease you like this"—I circle her clit again, this time with a little more pressure—"or like this?" I flick my fingers up and down.

She makes a garbled sound in the back of her throat, and I grin into her neck.

It feels good to finally be doing something right. To bring this beautiful woman the pleasure she deserves. I can't go back to the life I had before her.

Fuck pretending. That was never going to work.

Her hands dig into my hair, her grip intensifying.

"Answer me, Liv, or I'll stop." I look past her, down the trail to make sure no one is coming up.

She tilts her head to meet my gaze, and those lusty hazel eyes connect with mine for a moment before lowering to my mouth. "Circle. But faster." I move my fingers as she suggests and watch her hooded eyes. "Just like that."

Our lips meet, and she switches from sucking on my bottom lip to mumbling, "Yes," and, "Oh god," into my mouth.

My balls are drawn up tight, ready to bust. She's the culmination of every temptation I've ever faced in one endearing, curvy package.

I change the angle and enter her in one smooth motion, hooking my fingers, rubbing them against her front wall, finding the spot that'll make her go off.

My palm presses against her clit, still circling, not as fast but with more pressure. She jerks against me as I press into her exactly where she needs it. Her legs shake and I lean closer, making sure she stays upright.

"Sawyer . . . I'm c—" She doesn't have a chance to finish telling me what I already know. She clenches around my fingers,

AMY ALVES

her sex rippling around me in waves. So tight, so wet. Fuck, I want to be somewhere a hell of a lot more private with her. My cock throbs, and I tell myself I can take care of it the minute I'm home. Just thinking about this moment.

I ease my fingers out of her, lightly sliding along her core in slow strokes, milking the rest of her orgasm out of her.

Kissing along her collarbone as her breathing evens out, her hands find my face and lift it up. Her bright, adoring gaze meets mine. "Best. Date. Ever," she mutters softly.

"Yeah? If you'd have asked me yesterday, I would have told you I was certain I'd fuck it up somehow. Since I seemed to avoid that this long, I figured I'd reach for something I've wanted for a really fucking long time."

"Finger-fucking a woman against a tree?" she asks playfully, her hands on my chest, her tiny fingers toying with the buttons of my flannel.

"Finger-fucking *you*. And getting to taste you." I slide my hand out of her pants and bring my fingers to my mouth, her flavor invading my senses as I suck her release off of me.

"Oh shit. Why is that so hot? I need more . . ." She arches into my hardness, and I groan, grabbing her hips and holding them in place as I grind against her lower abdomen.

"I'll give you anything you want," I promise, ready to strip her down and fuck her raw.

"Sawyer . . . We still have to hike back." I kiss her softly and she moans. Breaking away, she's still somewhat breathless as she says, "Then do our post-date testimonials. People are waiting for us."

"Fuck."

Her hand goes to my belt. "I can—"

My hand covers hers. "I want that. Badly." Now that I'm starting to think a little more clearly, the likelihood of someone coming to find us becoming more apparent, I add, "But I don't want us to get caught, especially with you on your knees."

"I never said I'd be getting on my knees, Fletcher."

"Oh, you'd be on your knees, gorgeous. I want to see those hazel eyes light up fiery green as my cock hits those soft lips."

She gapes at me.

"Yeah. You'd open your beautiful mouth just like this."

An amused smirk forms right before her tongue darts out to lick the lips I want wrapped around me.

"Dirty. So dirty," she mumbles while tracing the top edge of my jeans with her fingertips. "Tonight? My place?"

"Your place," I confirm, pressing in for one more taste of her.

Breaking away, I reach down and get her jeans zipped back up before guiding us back down the trail to the parking lot.

The team approaches us, but we excuse ourselves to use the park washrooms to clean up before letting them drag us over for post-date testimonials.

"Olivia we'll record your testimonial first. Unless . . . you look a little flushed from the hike. Do you need some water? A few minutes to cool down?"

Badly smothering a choked laugh earns me an elbow to the ribs from the woman with the post-orgasm glow beside me.

"I'm fine but thank you. Barely worked up a sweat. In fact, I was left somewhat unsatisfied with the intensity of the hike. I think I'll need something a bit more physically demanding next time."

My head whips over to her. *Unsatisfied?* The instant need to show her exactly how satisfied I could make her with some privacy and a rock-free, horizontal surface has blood pumping right back to my lower regions. As they lead her away, she turns back to me, sending me a teasing wink.

Everything about her is such a fucking turn-on, and I have no idea if I'll ever be able to turn it off.

A teenager appears in front of me with Daisy and Karl in tow. She holds the leashes up. "Mrs. Shaw from school said I could earn some of my volunteer hours by helping with this event, but I refuse to pick up dog crap. Your dog took a massive dump over by the EMS truck. Some guy took a picture and said something about how it's the perfect metaphor for your dates."

She glowers at me expectantly, but I simply take the leashes from her and hope she stops talking.

"You know, because you basically crapped the bed on all your dates so far. Loads of people are pitying you, saying you're nervous with the whole town watching you, but Mrs. Langerham from The Vine hinted that she's working on an article about you being love-jinxed because your last few relationships have been a shit show."

Fucking great. I have no idea which of my past dates Bernice Langerham would have contacted, but there's not a single one that wouldn't be readily able to share a horrendously embarrassing story.

The girl shrugs and dashes off, passing Liv.

I spot Jaxon sitting in the back of the medical truck and decide to get this next conversation over with.

"Good hike?" he asks.

"Pretty good." I try to hide my grin by turning around to pick up after my dog.

"Yeah? Is that why Sean told us not to go looking for you guys?"

I hitch a shoulder. It's better to say nothing than to put my foot in my mouth.

He hops down onto the gravel, and he's about to lay into me. "You two been seeing each other outside of the show?"

I blow out a breath and face him, nodding.

His eyes narrow. "It's serious?"

"We haven't fully discussed it yet, but yeah, it feels like it could be."

He's quiet for a minute, kicking at the gravel under his feet. "You still going to continue with the show? If it's serious, I can't imagine Livvie being okay with it."

Avoiding his gaze, I clear my throat, preparing for what I have to tell him. "Man, there's something I have to tell you about the show."

His brows draw together. "What? You torn between more than one contestant? Are you only in it for the money? I mean, for your charity. Because you did make it clear you didn't want to date, and suddenly you're getting serious with my sister. You knew she was off-limits, but you still encouraged her to do this, didn't you?"

Before I can answer him, soft fingers wrap around my fist, extracting Daisy's leash from my clenched hand.

"Thanks for watching her. They are ready for you if you're done being grilled by my most obnoxious brother." Her tone is directed at Jaxon, but her eyes are on me.

Jaxon steps back and leans against the truck, hands held up.

I kiss Liv on the cheek, whispering, "See you tonight," in her ear.

"Drinks, Fletch," my friend demands.

"Busy tonight. Tomorrow?" I ask.

"Yeah. Text me with a time as soon as you're done gushing about how you finally managed to get through a date without incident. Though, I'm sure it had more to do with Olivia than you."

"It was all her, buddy. I'm glad she came." Olivia chokes on a sharp inhale as I jog over to my interview.

"That better not have meant what I fucking think it did, Fletcher," he shouts at me.

I laugh. He's probably going to put me on my ass at some point tonight, but the bright blush on Liv's cheeks made it worth it. She'll probably put me on my ass too, though I'm hoping it's so she can climb on top of me.

CHAPTER
TWENTY-THREE

OLIVIA

"Against a tree!" Ellie shrieks while flopping against the back of her chair.

I nod emphatically, trying to rein in the smile I haven't been able to wipe off my face for hours.

"I'm texting Liam right now to tell him we need to try getting freaky in a forest. Though, we'd probably want to bring some bug spray. Oh! Maybe we could bring one of those bug nets and hang it from a tree, then we can be insect-free. And maybe a mat or sleeping bag? And some kind of portable hand-washing station? Now that I think about it, your boyfriend was standing right next to your brother with your sex juices all over his hand." She shoves her hand in my face in an unnecessary reenactment.

"Ellie, no. Stop. Never again." I grimace, mentally shoving the image from my mind. "And he took care of his hand . . . kind of."

Her forehead wrinkles, confusion marring her sweet, golden face. "What does that mean?"

"He, um . . ." I don't think I can tell her.

"Used some leaves?" she guesses. "No, wait. That seems really ineffective."

"He didn't use leaves."

"Did he use his sock and then discard it?" I shake my head. She'll never guess. "Does he carry around hand sanitizer? Because that's smart. I love a man who plans ahead for hygiene."

I laugh. As a highly germ-conscious person, she *would* love that. I think Liam's penchant for impeccable personal hygiene was what first attracted her to him.

"You're going to hate it," I tell her.

"Ugh. Did he wipe it on the front of his shirt?" She gags lightly.

"He sucked it off his fingers."

The memory of him savouring my taste is etched into my mind. My walls clench in anticipation of more.

Her eyes bug out of her face. "Ohhh . . ." Gulping she adds, "That's . . . Honestly, I'm not sure how I feel about that. Kind of sexy, kind of gross. Because that definitely didn't get it clean enough that I'd be willing to shake his hand without knowing I'd have secondhand touched your coochie."

"I'm going to blissfully ignore any notion of secondhand coochie being out there in the world of non-handwashers. Thankfully, we were able to clean ourselves up in the park washrooms."

A whoosh of air leaves her. "Oh good." She pouts at me. "I don't think I'm meant for spontaneous forest sex."

I'm not the type to fool around in public, let alone a hiking trail, but I've also never come harder in my life. I'm pretty sure it had little to do with the possibility of getting caught. I knew Sean would redirect anyone coming up the trail. It had everything to do with Sawyer's mouth on me, his hands exploring, his body claiming mine even with our clothes on.

Pursing my lips to keep from giggling, I agree, "Maybe not. But you won't know unless you try. I highly recommend it."

"I bet you do. So, I'm guessing this means things are getting serious? Real?"

"Yes." I confess. "I think . . ."

"You two are *so* into each other. What's there to think about?"

"Well, he's coming over in a bit to talk. And finish what we started on our hike."

She squeals excitedly. "Well, I'll make sure to be long gone by then." Her expression morphs into one of concern as she holds a hand up, stopping herself. "Wait. I thought contestants weren't allowed to 'consort' outside of show events?"

I throw her some side eye.

"Right, sorry, I got caught up in the rules. Which are clearly ignoring because love knows no bounds."

Rolling my eyes, I tell her, "Well, we aren't flaunting it. We're keeping it a secret because it's none of the town's business and would probably screw up the show, which could put the donations raised for the Humane Society at risk."

"What will happen with the show though? He still has to go on more dates, right? Are you going to be cool with this? Is he? Knowing Sawyer, he's not going to like misleading someone and their whole family."

I gnaw on my lip, wishing I had an answer. It's a shitty situation. But the producers can't seriously think Sawyer would fall equally for multiple women at the same time until the very last day of the show. Ellie's right, we need to come up with a way to mitigate as much collateral damage as possible.

"We'll develop a plan tonight. We can't shut the show down. People have tickets, venues have been booked, arrangements made. But we might be able to do something else instead."

"So you got all hot and heavy in the mountains, and you think when he gets here, you'll be chatting about work-arounds and LoveVine event alternatives? Really?"

If he doesn't kiss me the minute he walks in my door, I might cry.

"Point made. We'll probably back burner the problem-solving convo." I jump up from the chair. "Now, I hate to give you the boot, but I didn't exactly plan for sexy activities during the hiking date. So I'm going to go dig out my sexy lingerie, shave my legs, tidy up my lady bits, and anxiously wait for him to show up."

"Attagirl! Go tame your lady garden. Make sure to call me later. I'm going to need details," she says while making her way to the door. "Oh, and you should probably be aware that somehow your mom knows Sawyer has been coming over here, so you might want to make sure no one sees him sneaking in tonight."

Christ on a cracker. How the hell does my mom know everything? At least Miranda hasn't found out yet, otherwise it would be everywhere.

Wait. Why didn't she say anything to me?

She turns the doorknob, and without even turning around, says, "Wear the navy lace bralette set with the cheeky sheer bottoms. It's fire." With a quick wave, she saunters over to her vehicle.

We may have gone on a sexy lingerie shopping spree after Drew and I had separated and I decided to start dating again. Most of those beauties haven't seen the outside of my panty drawer yet.

Grabbing the navy set, I send Sawyer a text, ignoring the quivering nerves that have set in.

ME: My mom somehow knows you've been sneaking over. So you might want to keep an eye out in case someone notices you tonight. Miranda can't find out.

SAWYER: Sorry. That might have been my fault, actually.
SAWYER: I told my mom we've been spending time together between events. She wanted to talk about the contestants and break down the qualities and long-term relationship potential of each. There were a lot of questions, and I had to give her something.

ME: What did you tell her?

SAWYER: I talked about you, and she pieced it together that we've been seeing each other outside of the show.

ME: Who else did you talk about? I imagine she wanted the whole run down.

SAWYER: There's no one else to talk about, Liv. I made that clear. There's only you.

I'm so far out of my element here that excitement bubbles up inside of me at the thought that I wasn't the only one with those first tingles of awareness, of attraction.

SAWYER: I'll be there in thirty. Then I can show you the many things I've been fantasizing about doing to you all afternoon.

ME: Hints?

SAWYER: I want to lay you out on your couch, peel those sexy leggings off your delectable body, bury my face between your thighs, slip my tongue into your sweetness, and make a meal of you.

Sweet heavenly creator of filthy, pussy-loving mouths. That's so much more than a hint.

Having never sexted, I'm at a disadvantage. Like I should do some research first. But I don't have time for that.

ME: Yes, please.
ME: Also . . . I hope one of those fantasies includes riding the hell out of your face.

I hold my breath as I await his response.

SAWYER: It sure as hell is.
SAWYER: Fuck, Liv. You've got me so hard.
SAWYER: 15 minutes.

Shit. What happened to thirty minutes?

SAWYER: Nevermind. I'm already walking over. 10 minutes.

I drop the phone and jump into the shower.

CHAPTER
TWENTY-FOUR

OLIVIA

I haven't even gotten dressed before an urgent rapping sounds from the back door.

"Just a minute!" I shout as I stumble putting on the sexy panties I hope he immediately rips from my body.

Last time I had sex? Several months ago.

Last time I had sex that mattered, that I craved and presented infinite possibilities? Much, much longer.

Throwing on a simple, thin T-shirt dress, I scurry down the hall only to stop at the entrance to the kitchen and calm my shit down.

On unsteady legs, I stride coolly to the door, opening it a crack.

I try and fail at not letting my eyes eat him up. They linger on his wide shoulders encased in a simple crewneck black tee clinging for dear life to the alluring curves of his traps and deltoids.

God I am such a shoulder whore.

"The Vine posted about some creepy dude in a black T-shirt skulking around alleys with a giant boner." I glance around him to the yard. "You see anyone? Because I have to admit I'm intrigued if the last part is true."

He grins wickedly, stepping into my space, his hands immediately grabbing my hips and maneuvering me inside. "You're about to find out."

The door slams behind him, his hands and eyes never leaving me. Oh, he kicked it closed. This is the kind of intensity I was desperate for.

"Fuck first, talk later?" he asks before his head dips, our mouths brushing, nipping as he awaits my response.

God, yes. But I have to be smart about this. I need to make sure we're not making a huge mistake.

"I think we should at least talk about what this means. Is it only convenient, casual fucking while we're on the show? Or do we have feelings for each other, want to date and build something serious?"

I'm yanked closer, my breasts crushed against his chest, his hands sliding down to cup my ass.

I glance up into those navy blue eyes, his long lashes tipping down as his gaze flickers to my mouth, then back to meeting my gaze.

"This has nothing to do with convenience. We have feelings for each other, we're good together. That's all I know right now. Let's take this one step at a time."

My hands roam along the tops of his shoulders and I nearly moan simply from the feel of him.

"You worried it's going to fall apart? That your bad luck will strike again?"

He wraps his arms around me, keeping us locked together. "I don't know anymore. Everything always feels right with you. Like my luck can't ever be bad as long as I'm with you. And that might have me more worried than most of my tragic dates ever have."

I take his hat off and run my fingers through his hair, something I've wanted to do for a long time. It's surprisingly soft, and I love the way he's let it grow out a little.

The strands of thick hair curl into my fingers, earning a low, suppressed moan.

"I won't break, and you've known my brand of crazy for years. I don't think you're in for any surprises with me. If we get a flat tire, we make out in the truck until we want to change it. If one of us takes a tumble, the other will do the catching. Whatever crazy surprises life throws at us, we tackle together. Even if it means standing up to this whole damn town."

His eyes soften as they dart between mine. "How are you so damn perfect and I've only just realized it?"

I shrug innocently. "First, it would have been weird if you realized it back when I was a lanky teenager. Second, my brother would have found a reason to throw your ass in jail if you'd made a move on me. You should have seen what he did to that skater guy I dated freshman year in college. But Blake had been arrested before and could hold his own. You, however . . ."

A rough sound leaves his throat. "That smart fucking mouth."

My hands wander down to his chest, raking my nails down his pecs. "I bet your jail husband's name would have been Ivan. He'd have been Russian mafia, covered in rose tattoos—one for every life he regrets taking—and would have loved being the little spoon when you cuddled at night. Hot."

He bends, grabs the backs of my thighs underneath my dress, and lifts me. My legs wrap around his middle, a giggle leaving me.

"No more talking." He kisses me again and I lean into him. "Jail husband. Christ," he mutters between kisses.

He sets me down on the island counter.

Pulling back, he braces himself against the island, hands on either side of my hips. "Lift up your dress and let me see you."

I remove my hands from his neck and clutch the hem of the simple, sage-green dress, slowly pulling it up.

His growl of impatience has me smiling and moving slower. He's going to be very fun to play with.

Once the skirt is pulled up to my waist, I lean back against the counter and ogle him.

"You put those on for me?" he says, his eyes never straying from the blue lace barely concealing the area eagerly awaiting his touch.

Instead of answering, I wait for him to meet my gaze. When those blue eyes dart up to mine, my tongue trails over my bottom lip before I nod.

"Take this off." He pinches the dress pooled at my hips. "I want to see it all."

"I want *you* to take it off me," I say.

He steps closer, leaning so close, his jeans roughly brush the sensitive skin of my inner thighs. I peek down to appreciate the contrast between my near nakedness to his fully clothed body. Those jeans are doing a poor job containing his erection. It's banging on the door, demanding release. And staring at his impressive package all I can think is, *Same, big guy, same.*

His wide hands grip my hips and slide me toward him, making sure we're fully lined up. Finally breaking out of my dick trance, my chin tilts up to look into his handsome face.

Those skilled fingers move under my dress. Chills race up and down my ribs. I have to fight arching into his every touch.

"Arms, babe."

I move my hands from his biceps and raise them. Instead of pulling at the fabric of my dress, he smooths his palms all the way up, letting the material catch on his wrists so it follows the path his hands take up my arms.

This is how I want to get undressed every night for the rest of my life.

Rest of my life?

Shit. I really need to—

Sawyer's mouth is on my chest, kissing along the edge of the lace that dips into a deep V. My hands are still caught up in the dress he hasn't finished removing, keeping them trapped.

"You're going to undo me, Liv. Fuck. All this sexy lace covering your pretty tits. Where the hell do I even start?"

"Wherever you want, Stud. But make sure you take off your shirt first. And pants. I want to see you too."

"Not until I make you come at least once, or I'll be too tempted to fuck you hard and much too fast. I want to play a little first."

Well, all right, then.

He sucks at my nipple through the delicate material covering it. One of my hands immediately threads through his hair, my insides clenching. I'm so wet, I'm unsure if my pretty panties will be salvageable after this.

I tip my head back. In a rough voice filled with need, I say, "Then make me come."

He groans against my breast, pulling me to the edge of the island in one hard yank.

"Stay there," he demands before lowering down to his knees.

Oh god, yes.

He tosses my dress aside and hitches my legs onto his shoulders. My sexy new panties are wrenched aside, and he drags a thumb through my slick heat. There's a fleeting thought about if I'm too hot, too wet, too desperate for him, but those pass the instant he breaches my entrance.

His finger disappears inside me, and it's everything I need yet not even close to enough at the same time. I gasp, shifting my hips for more, and his molten eyes flicker up to my face.

Gently, he strokes my clit in slow circles, and another finger joins the first. The moment those fingers curl up inside me, I release a loud moan.

"Sawyer . . ."

"Patience. I'm taking my time, and there's not a damn thing you can do about it, gorgeous."

"I haven't had sex in a really long time. I'm going to need you to fuck me with some part of you. Now."

He surges forward, yanking my underwear farther still, and absolutely devours my pussy. Throwing my head back, I whimper, using my legs to pull him in as close as possible.

The arms I'm using to brace myself against the counter behind me buckle. Sawyer's tongue swipes in lavish strokes against my clit before sucking it into his mouth.

The breath in my lungs stalls, the simmering need searing every nerve ending until heat soars down my lower abdomen through my core, down my quivering legs.

My back arches, and a whimper leaves my lips. My body hitches upright, almost violently, as I explode. Euphoria washes over me in waves as the fucktastic man between my legs gives a few final swirls of his tongue in what was irrefutably the best oral sex I've ever experienced.

Should it be like this our first time? This can't be normal.

"What the fuck did your mouth just do?" I ask, still panting.

He grins up at me, still between my legs. Like the crazy-hot sex fiend he apparently is, he licks his lips wickedly slow before answering, "That was my appetizer. It was even better than I imagined, Liv. You're even better than I ever imagined. And I'm going to greedily accept everything you give me."

Goddamn. Take whatever you want, sir.

"Did you just call me sir?" he asks.

I bite my lip, too deliriously incredible to be embarrassed. "Not intentionally. It was an inside thought, but my brain isn't exactly in full control at the moment."

"I think you're going to enjoy letting me be in control for a bit longer."

"Yes, sir." A cheeky grin spreads across my face.

He picks me up off the counter, and I wrap myself around him, not caring that I'm likely making a mess of his shirt.

"While I *really* like you calling me sir, tonight I'd rather hear you scream my name while my cock fills you up."

Oh fuck. Hell yes.

"Since that hasn't happened yet, I'll stick to sir," I sass.

A quick slap has my ass tingling and my insides rippling. I'm laughing as he moves us to the bedroom, the one he hasn't seen yet but finds instinctually.

I'm dropped onto the bed with a bounce. His gaze is a soft caress as it travels down my chest to my lace-covered center. The rumble of approval released from his chest makes my cheeks bloom with heat.

Those night-sky eyes slowly inch up to meet mine again. There's heat and desperation in them. Without thought, my hands tear at his shirt. He helps by reaching back and grabbing the neck and tossing it off with a quick pull.

I uncover a wide chest dusted with hair and twitching in response to his movements. Or maybe in anticipation. Sawyer is all man, and the way he's filled out since the last time I saw him shirtless has tingles erupting in my lower belly.

I dip my gaze to his tight, tapered waist and abs. I want to lick all the way down to the head of the dick trying to bust out of his pants.

After I pop the button on his jeans, I run my thumb over the tip jutting out at me. He blows out a harsh breath, mesmerized by my hands.

Seconds into touching him through the soft material standing between my hand and his hardness, the rest of his clothing disappears in a few jerky moves.

He settles over me again, and all I can think is, *His cock is what dreams are made of.*

I hold back a giggle that dissipates as the heat of his long length burns against my thigh. My gaze drops, trying to take in as much of him as I can.

He's so fucking sexy, all I can do is rub my thighs together and hope he doesn't make me wait too long. Sawyer seems to be the "tease and torture until both participants eventually scream out their orgasms" type.

My breathing is mere shallow pants, hands wandering, following the hard planes of his shoulders, to spread against the taut curves of his pecs. His chest meets mine, interrupting my exploration. Hungry lips suck at my neck, breathe into my hair. Shivers break out all over, my eyes roll up into my head.

Skilled lips and a scruffy beard on my neck are weaknesses I hope I never overcome.

He moves down to my chest. "God, these are fucking amazing," he murmurs as he nuzzles the side of my breast. "I want to say I'm going to last long enough to come on them, but once I get inside your pussy, feel you squeeze around me, I'm not going to want to pull out." His hand moves casually up my inner thigh.

My body flares with heat. Fuck. He's going to talk like this the whole time, isn't he? They say to watch out for the quiet ones.

My core quivers, and my back arches on a slight gasp. He lifts up, and his hand eases my leg outward, opening me up. He hums deeply, stroking himself twice before lining himself up.

Wider still, my legs move up his sides, and I pull him closer.

When our eyes meet, there's a flash of hesitancy.

"You weren't kidding about the dirty talking. And I have to admit I've been really damn curious about the comment you made at the beach."

His eyes brighten as he grins, notching himself at my entrance. "Yeah?"

"I've wanted to find out for myself exactly what you meant. I haven't been able to get the brainy, puppy-saving, dirty-talking vet I grew up with out of my head or my dreams." The sex dreams I've had since we started this have been revealing in too many ways.

His eyes bore into mine right before he bends the arms holding him up and kisses the breath right out of me.

While he moves a hand up to my thigh, squeezing it before sliding it down to my ass. He exhales loudly, his shoulders suddenly tense.

The air between us shifts, and the hurried desperation from earlier left little time for nerves or thoughts. But slowing down, taking our time to look and taste and touch, his thoughts must be running wild.

"Sawyer?"

He hums in response, still running his hands over me, deep in thought. One tilt of my hips and he'd be inside me, no more thinking necessary.

"You okay? We can slow down or stop—"

He bends to suck my nipple into his mouth. I yelp and then moan.

"No, babe. We sure as fuck are not stopping."

I tug at his hair, bringing him up for a kiss. Pulling back, I say, "You're nervous. I can feel it."

"The last time was . . . disastrous. I want to make this really fucking good. For both of us, so I needed a moment. I want you a little too much, Liv."

"Me too."

"I know." His rumbly voice taunts my nipple, so close my grip tightens in his hair. "I can feel how wet and ready you are." His jaw locks, teeth grinding. "There's not a chance in hell I'm letting all that bad luck shit stop me from having you."

My pussy spasms. Can you orgasm from words alone? I think I might have.

He advances, capturing my mouth and entering me in one quick thrust. I gasp and press even closer, needing the feel of him on my breasts, my stomach, keeping him between my legs.

"Fuck." He groans, dark and needy.

Undulating under him, encouraging him to move so this ache can finally be sated, his mouth leaves mine on another curse.

"You'll wait until I've had my fill of you."

"You are completely filling me, handsome. Time to move."

"So sassy." He pulls out, barely, his hips snapping right back, deeper this time. An indecent moan leaves me.

"Like that," I say breathily.

He powers into me, one hand still exploring. I have no idea how he has any control over where his hands are going—I certainly don't. Mine are randomly roving, blindly taking in every part of Sawyer Fletcher.

Our hips move in tandem, grinding, finding our rhythm, skin sliding against skin. A deep, husky moan echoes through my bedroom. "Your pussy is my new favorite place, Liv. *Fuck.*" His fingers tighten, curling into my ass.

The thinking part of my brain is nothing but background noise and ignored whispers. Pleasure and wish fulfillment taking up the forefront of all my thoughts. Yet, somewhere in the back of my mind, I wonder if I can finally be his good luck girlfriend.

Because Sawyer is exactly the kind of man I've always imagined ending up with. The kind of man who would love me back with passion, loyalty, and exuberance. And I don't want anything to stop us from having that either.

A sharp, dangerous pull at my tummy tells me I've fallen for this man. His eyes sear into mine as one of his hands reaches up to pluck at my nipple, already picking up on how sensitive they are, how that move from those fingers makes my walls spasm. He must feel it as he grins, slowing down and changing the angle until I'm squirming and chanting his name in utter shock.

This perfect fucking man who has given up on love, found and can reach that *deep* spot within me. The pleasure so great, the ecstasy it brings has my release roaring through me—legs clenching, pussy pulsing, tears prickling my eyes.

Because he's found more than that deep spot of pleasure. He's burrowed his way deep into every intimate aspect of my being.

"There it is." His grin widens. "God, you're beautiful when you come."

The sweat on his brow, the tightness around that grin, the look of determined concentration and awe in his eyes. He's holding back, and I won't be having any of that.

I'm not usually one to talk much in the bedroom, but I've recently realized how much I enjoy it.

"Come inside me." The grin drops, and his hips hitch slightly before pounding harder into me. "I want to see you let go. I want to hear you as you lose yourself inside me."

"Fuck. Me." He mumbles on a groan. "I'm trying to last here, Liv. That mouth of yours is going to destroy me."

"I don't want you to last. I want you to give in. Take what you want. Give us both what we want."

A fire dancing in his eyes is the only warning I get. He leans back, grabs my hips and slams into me. My clit sparks back to life, sensitive yet eager as his pelvis smacks mine.

As my legs start shaking again, the pressure building, he draws me up to him. Sitting back on his heels, without severing our connection, he lifts me onto him so I'm straddling his lap. He pumps me up and down, grinding me onto him every time he bottoms out. We're wrapped around each other as he bounces me on him.

I suck on his neck and desperately dig my fingertips into his back.

"Fuck, Liv. I'm—" A long, low groan fills the room, vibrating through my chest, imprinting itself on my heart, my body.

He twitches inside me, and I moan along with him. He moves my hips to grind the top of my swollen, sensitive slit against him and my orgasm hits in slow, strong waves. He drops his head to my shoulder and curses into the crook of my neck.

Holding me tight against him, he whispers, "How the hell did I get this lucky?"

CHAPTER
TWENTY-FIVE
OLIVIA

Waking with Sawyer's hand between my thighs was a significant improvement to the annoying blast of my phone's scheduled alarm.

I'm still panting, happy hormones blazing through me when I say, "Miranda is going to be *so* pissed we've been keeping our 'overnight dates' a secret." It's only been a couple of overnights so far, but the more time we spend together the more I want him around. MIranda is bound to find out eventually.

He half groans, half chuckles. "Please don't mention any of the Town Council members while I'm still inside you."

"Miranda has great legs and a can-do spirit. You could do worse."

He shifts as if he's going to move, but then sighs and leans back into me. I squeeze around him, and his head snaps up, a grin on his handsome face.

"Trust me, I've done much worse."

"Ew. How about we not discuss your questionable past sexual experiences while you're still inside me?"

"You started this, gorgeous. I was just resting here, trying not to crush you."

"Crush me? These hips were made to take all you've got," I thrust upward.

He glances down with a devilish smirk. "They sure as hell are." Gripping them, he slides out of me.

We shuffle our way to the bathroom, me trying not to drip on the floor, when it hits me.

"We didn't use a condom. Again." I always roll my eyes at people who get into these situations, and I've become that woman. The one who was too overcome with need and passion to give protection a single freaking thought. Dammit.

"Do you want to use them? You mentioned you have an IUD." He snakes a hand through his hair, the deliriously sexy glances he was sending me evaporating with that one single thought. "And we're both clean. If you want, I can show you the results . . . they tested me after—" He stops himself.

I tilt my head at him in curiosity. "Me too. I got a full checkup after—" I stop, wide eyes looking coyly up at him.

His forehead scrunches. "After what?"

"Sucks to be left hanging like that, right?" I give him a toothy smile.

"We exchanging stories again, gorgeous?"

"While we shower?" I offer.

"Hell, yes. You wet all over, rubbing against me, washing those sweet tits? I'll tell you whatever you want."

I grin and move to the shower, Sawyer trailing so closely behind me, his front is nearly plastered to my backside. I bend to turn the water on, and he's right there, hands all over my ass.

Stepping in, I hand him the loofah and body wash. "You can soap me while you talk." I've been dying to find out what happened to him. I mean, he's hot in bed—like "out of this world, ten out of ten, pesky thoughts of moving him in" kind of hot. Maybe things got out of hand in the bedroom? They were caught in public? Did her hooha spontaneously combust? Role-playing took a turn? Broken cervix? Accidental anal?

My mind has come up with many scenarios as the cause of his last relationship catastrophe, which put him off dating indefinitely.

I'm kind of hoping it's just plain old bad sex or terrible dates and nothing too jarring.

A few bad dates is one thing, but when all you've experienced for years is cringe-worthy ones and an endless stream of alarming women, that's a kick to the balls.

The loofah is full of suds, traveling down the center of my chest, lingering as it lavishes each breast. "I've told you about some of the incidents before but they only got worse the harder I tried. The League sabotaging a few dates was a drop in the bucket."

"You said you were just getting back to dating again after a bad relationship, right?" I probe.

"Many bad relationships. Some weren't even relationships because they didn't get that far."

I frown sympathetically, letting my fingers dance along his biceps. "Dating sucks."

"I was on a couple of dating apps a few years back and thought this one woman I had been chatting with for weeks had stood me up on our first date and ghosted me. Turned out she died."

My jaw drops and my hands stop. Instead of looking me in the eyes, he keeps them down, trained on the loofah as it caresses my body.

Words fail me as he continues. "The morning of the day we were supposed to meet up for drinks, she went rock climbing about an hour north of Vaughn and fell."

"Shit. Wow. That's awful. Sawyer . . ."

"I know it's not my fault or anything, but that was after months of shitty dates and sketchy meetups. I even had one lady pickpocket me." He sighs, his hands slowing but never breaking contact. "So I got off all the dating apps and decided I'd meet someone organically.

I did, and it ended with me in the hospital, and my ex and her family doing a bad job of keeping the details of our breakup a secret."

I press myself to him, wrapping my arms around his neck. "I am here for you for whatever this is, and I'm hoping you're not still too torn up over it that you'll be offended by whatever my reaction might be." I wince dramatically, earning a small smile from him.

"It was only traumatic for me because it involved my dick. It's embarrassing, and I think if we wanted to keep the sexiness alive so early on in our relationship, it's a story we should skip."

"Nope." I wiggle, slippery skin rubbing against hard muscles. "I need to know. You are aware of all my past trauma, let me help you unload yours."

A frown pulls at his mouth, a soft hesitation darkens his eyes. "Last year I dated a woman who, I'll admit, was a little young and very eager. She wasn't my usual type, but I thought that might be a positive thing. And I tried. I really did."

"Oh god, here's where it gets good. You smashed her with your big dick."

"No. It was the other way around. She destroyed my dick. Unintentionally, but my dick was harmed in the making of a breakup avoidance surprise."

I glance down, wondering if I missed anything while I was studying the silky ridges of his very sturdy cock.

Nope. He's down there poking at me, looking extra rideable.

"The staring isn't helping."

I shrug. "He seems to like it."

"Do you want to kiss him better or should I finish my story first."

I tilt my head back up, grinning at him. "Proceed."

"So we were seeing each other fairly casually—nothing serious, a date night here and there. She wanted something more serious. I told her I didn't want a girlfriend, I preferred to keep things casual, and she took it badly. To be honest, we didn't click, and spending time with her was exhausting."

"How was she exhausting? Like in the bedroom? She was too much for you?"

"No. I can keep up in the bedroom." He smacks my ass, and I bite down on a moan. "She was endlessly chatty, needy, and used baby talk regularly."

I grimace.

"Yeah. But she took me pulling back as a sign she should double down on her efforts to take our relationship to the next level." He pauses. "She ended up planning a surprise break and enter, snuck into my bed, naked, and climbed on me while I was sleeping."

"Oh my god. Did you think she was an intruder and throw her off you?"

"Um . . . no. She was, uh, doing things to me that made me less objectionable."

Men.

"Did you know it was her?"

"I didn't know what was going on at all. I was half asleep—I'm a deep sleeper. Part of me probably assumed it was her at some point. Who else would come into my house and lube me up? But I was later asked about pressing charges since she broke in and touched my dick."

I make a face at him. "Gross."

"I tried to warn you." His arms pull me closer, his length a hot brand across my abdomen.

"Fine. So how did your dick get maimed?"

"There was no maiming—thankfully. Just a terrible, burning, allergic reaction to the coconut oil she decided to use all over me because it 'smelled nice.'"

"Noooo!" I gasp. "I knew you were allergic to coconut if you ingested it, but not that it would react on your skin."

"Yeah. She was also aware but apparently didn't make the connection until later."

I soothingly run my fingers through his damp hair. In a soft, placating voice, I say, "That must have burned like a bitch, babe."

He laughs. "That's not even the worst part."

I pull back, drawing his averted gaze back to me.

"It got in my mouth."

"Shit. How did it get—" I cut myself off from finishing that question. The answer will only make me jealous, and I hate feeling like that. It's not something I've been overly familiar with because it required that I have deep, delicate, heavy feelings for a man.

"That shit was all over the place. When the burn woke me up, my airways had already started closing up. She freaked out, wasn't able to help much, but did call an ambulance." He sighs loudly. "Your brother was on-call."

My hand slaps over my mouth, and I mumble, "Oh no," through my fingers. "Did he laugh at you before or after helping you?"

He quirks his head to the side. "Somewhere in between."

"Sounds about right."

"That's not even the end of it."

"How on earth could there be more?"

"Because Kylee was still covered in coconut oil, Jaxon thankfully didn't allow her to ride with me and ordered her to shower before visiting at the hospital. She got into an accident on the way there."

I hiss inadvertently. "That's . . ."

"Super fucking unlucky? Yeah."

"She was okay though?"

"Yes. Shit, if she had been seriously injured, I might've never dated again."

"You haven't since though, right?"

"I thought a break was wise." His hands skim down my spine.

"What happened after my brother took you to the hospital?"

"I was admitted for a while, then released. Kylee and I spoke, and I asked that we not say anything about this to anyone. I still had a nasty rash on my dick, a newly ingrained fear of coconut, sex, and women, and an embarrassing sex story to keep secret in a small town."

He's joking, but the severe timber of his voice gives away his distress.

"Stella found out anyway?"

"Guess so. She either found out months after the fact or she kept it to herself for a long while, waiting for an opportune moment."

She's not that bad. I didn't think. I'd only met her a handful of times before the show.

"She held it over you?"

He grumbles. "Not exactly. But she did use it as justification to meddle in my personal life."

My hand wanders from his chest to the hardness between us. "And he's all better too?"

He grunts in answer.

"Want me to kiss it better?"

"Not gonna turn that down."

I stroke him, drawing an uneven inhale from his chest.

His arms reach out, easing me down to my knees. Moving back, he makes sure I'm out of the stream of water, which I appreciate but hadn't even thought about. My eyes have been on his twitching dick.

Definitely no indication of a horrible run-in with an overeager coconut oil enthusiast.

Hands grasp the wet tangles of my hair as he feeds me his length. I swirl my tongue around the tip before dipping lower and licking from the base back up to the crown. A grin pulls at my lips as his hand leaves my hair and slaps against the slick shower wall.

Taking him into my mouth, I ease over him until he reaches the back of my throat, making my eyes water.

"Ah, fuck, Liv. Of course you'd give mind-blowing head."

Slowly I slide my hand along the underside of his length and continue exploring until I find the seam that runs from the balls drawing tighter to his backside. I press along, back and forth, peering up at him. His gaze is dark and hard. Like he's holding back from pumping violently into my mouth.

If his dick weren't in my mouth, I'd be grinning. If his bad dating luck returned, choking on his big dick wouldn't be the worst way for that to happen.

"You like that, babe? Your mouth teasing me, your eyes shining up at me with satisfaction."

I hum in agreement. I do like it. A lot.

I've never been a fan of face-fucking, but if Sawyer were to take control, he'd do it in a way that would make me feel desirable. He'd talk to me in his deep timber, using those dirty words, and make me nearly beg him to fuck my mouth.

I swallow around him, and he groans, his eyes going hazy for a beat before focusing back down on me.

"Do that again," he demands.

When I swallow again, his voice rumbles, "Good girl."

My belly flutters with his praise as I hollow out my cheeks, sucking him harder, swirling my tongue around the sensitive tip. How do I reconcile the quiet, private guy with the man grumbling sexy praise with his cock in my mouth?

"Oh fuck. I'm gonna come." He groans. "You want it down your throat or on your tits, gorgeous?"

I nearly choke on his cock. And it wouldn't have been from bad luck, it would have been the thigh-quivering effect his words have on me.

This man has the dirtiest mouth.

I take as much of him into my mouth as I can without cutting off my air supply and then moan around him in answer. He leans forward, body arching over me, one hand planted on the shower wall behind me and the other gripping the back of my head.

I tug gently on his balls, and he jolts, letting loose a long moan. His hot release fills the back of my throat.

"Swallow it. Every drop," he commands.

He keeps his eyes on me, and I do as I'm told. When I pull away, I give him a few more licks to make sure I've gotten it all.

"That mouth of yours is going to damn near kill me."

Right back at you.

Drawing me back up to my feet, he holds me against his chest.

"Hopefully not. I promise to stay away from coconut. I like your dick too much to see it get hurt again."

The sound he makes is part moan, part laugh.

"Too soon?" I ask, scrunching my nose in hesitation.

"Nah. I think I'm getting over it."

"Because of me, right? And my trauma-healing mouth?"

He scoops me up, stepping out of the shower. "Something like that," he answers.

I'm still soaking wet when he lays me on the bed. The sheets will dry but I'm not sure other parts of me ever will as long as he's around and deliciously naked.

"Now open your legs and let me see what sucking my cock did to you."

Yeah . . . growly dirty talkers are definitely my weakness.

CHAPTER
TWENTY-SIX
SAWYER

There's not a cloud in the sky today, but the fall chill in the evening air requires another layer for those of us accustomed to the warmer California temperatures.

I wound up in Landry tonight since Liv got a call that one of her patients went into labor earlier today. I might not see her until tomorrow, and I'm not a fan.

I'm not sure when it happened—when I became addicted to her. My hands in her soft auburn waves, the dip of her waist as I pull her into me, her petal-soft lips trailing my neck. I need it, all of it. Can't get enough.

This is the first night we are spending away from each other since our date. It's only been a week, and I have no idea how we haven't been caught yet.

And that should worry me, but it doesn't.

It's not lost on me that for the first time in years, I've found someone I want to keep—something real, surpassing the deep-seated expectation and doubt I've carried.

It has me questioning everything. Am I unlucky in love or have I just been waiting for her?

I smile into my beer, spilling a few drops as I'm jostled by the person taking a seat on the stool next to me at the bar.

Setting my pint down, I turn toward the man beside me.

"Taps looks good, doesn't it?" Sean says, running his hands over the bar top. "Missed you at the grand opening. Reopening? Whatever it's called. It's been packed in here all week. Lauren and Sadie already broke one of the new lighting fixtures when they tried dancing on a table. It was awesome."

I shake my head at him, and flag down the bartender.

He orders a beer and juts his chin at me. "So you didn't ask to meet up to shoot the shit about our friends or my lovely wife." One of his eyebrows lifts. "This have anything to do with your solo date with Olivia?"

"It does."

"You don't want to continue with the show anymore," he guesses. "Not because you don't want to do the show, but because you already found your woman."

My fingers knead into my forehead before swiping into my hair. "Something like that."

"You still have a group event, solo dates, and Meet-the-Family nights. You're close to the end. I'm sure at this stage it's normal to already have a front-runner."

"She's more than a front runner, Sean. She wasn't supposed to be, not really, but here we fucking are, and I don't know what to do." I push away from the bar top, taking a swig of my cool drink. "I don't want to pretend anymore."

"Anymore?" he asks, much too casually. His shit-eating grin tells me he's being intentionally obtuse. The asshole has probably known I've been faking my way through this whole damn thing from the start.

I put my beer down. "Cut the shit. Liv and I are a thing, and I can't figure out how to get out of this damn show without letting anyone down or costing the Humane Society any of the charity proceeds."

He pauses before answering. "Bro, I get that you're done. But people want to see you choose her. They want to witness the emotions, the uncertainty transform into determination, the hope. All that chemistry and drama unfolding right in front of them. Shit, even I love it, and I already know how it's going to end."

"Then ask Stella and Miranda if we can skip to the final ceremony. They can even film a family episode of us at the Vaughn residence."

"They already have that planned. You are not giving The League or Vaughn Town Council anything they don't already have scheduled. They won't go for it."

Shit. He's right. Why did I even bother asking. Liv has been avoiding talking about the show, both of us unsure what to do.

"Fine. I committed to this, I'll see it through. But understand that I won't be very cooperative with my other dates."

"Not my business. I'm essentially your handler. I make sure you attend the events, and I listen to you gripe. I'm not your boss, and I don't make the rules. If I were you, I wouldn't do a damn thing to fuck up something real with a great woman. So you do what you gotta do, man."

Begrudgingly, I nod. I knew Sean couldn't let me off the hook, but I hoped he'd have a better solution.

"Does Stella know?"

"Know what?" he asks.

"*Know*," I emphasize.

"She isn't keeping after-hours tabs on you, if that's what you mean. But I'm not sure about Miranda or the rest of the organizers. Hell, even some of the contestant's families have been intensely involved. Which is why—never mind."

"Why what?"

"You'll find out at the group date."

"That sounds super awesome." The edgy tone to my sarcasm

makes him grimace. "Thanks, man." The clap I land on his back is a not-so-subtle *fuck you*.

"Sorry. Really. It's not so bad, but . . . it's basically the opposite of what you brought me here to ask for. I can't give you details, but I can tell you they added another date night."

"What the fuck, Sean!"

"It's to make up for the women you drove away in the first few weeks."

"I didn't drive anyone away." I scoff. "That shit simply happens around me. Or used to."

"Either way, less women in the show meant fewer dates and ceremonies."

Yeah, and I was very much hoping they would cut the schedule down. No such luck apparently.

"Fine. I'll take Liv out again on a solo date. I'm sure you guys have something crazy planned for our date night, but at least we'll get to do it together."

I check my phone for messages from her, wondering if the birth is going well or if she's in for a long night. With no new notifications, I glance back up at Sean. His expression tells me I'm not going to like whatever these changes are.

"You going to tell me what your expression means?"

He sighs. "Wish I could, man. All I can suggest is that if you have a chance, maybe it would help to quietly tell the other contestants your heart has already chosen. And you don't want to screw the Humane Society out of the donations from the last few weeks even though you've already found love." A ridiculous grin spread across his face. "This way they know the score. Done."

"I'm not saying all of that. Liv and I have something, but it's a bit early to be talking about love."

"Oh? How long have you known her for? How long have you been interested in her?" I glare at him. So fucking invasive. "Years, right? Feels big, kind of scary, like she's infiltrated the air you breathe?"

My feelings for Liv have changed over the years. I've been attracted to her for a long time. Yeah, years. She's always been sexy as hell but completely off-limits. This woman—my best friend's little sister—with an ass and hips meant for worshipping and all this incredible hair I wanted to grip in my fist, dreamed about spilling over my thighs.

How the hell *wasn't* I supposed to notice.

She's sweet, funny, and mind-obliteratingly sexy. And every day I spend in her presence makes it so much harder to think of it ever ending. Is this how love feels or are these big, intense emotions about the show and how badly this could all go wrong?

"Shit," I mumble.

He smirks, taking a final pull from his glass. "Well, I'll let you chew on that. See you tomorrow, Fletcher."

CHAPTER
TWENTY-SEVEN
OLIVIA

Harper drops extra cheesy nachos on the table between Ellie and me.

"Well, well, well. Seems like Olivia has some news to share." Harper taunts as she plops down onto the cushy booth seat beside me.

"I delivered Kendra's baby girl late last night. Active labor lasted nearly twenty-four hours, but mama and baby are doing well."

The Vine already shared the details this morning, so this is my way of not-so-slyly switch the subject away from what she's implying. Which might make me an evasive friend, but I have girlfriend responsibilities now.

Wait.

Am I Sawyer's girlfriend?

How has that not been brought up at all yet? Maybe because realistically it's not like I can publicly be his girlfriend yet. We're not even supposed to be seeing each other until the show is over.

"Olivia Vaughn, you've had sex, and since my downstairs fun bits haven't felt, seen, or caught wind of a decent dick in years, I'm going to need some details."

Ellie snorts, gives her a sympathetic frown, and then redirects her laser focus to me.

We might need to stop meeting here early on LoveVine event nights.

Ellie rolls her eyes, then points at my uncontainable grin with a nacho chip. "We all know who's giving you the kind of D to put *that* look on your face."

Harper turns to glare at me. "You told her before I brought your over-cheesed nachos?"

"First, they are not over-cheesed. There should always be a higher cheese to chip ratio. So they are perfect. Second, I have not yet told Ellie the details about whatever orgasmic glow you two think you can see."

She bounces in her seat, anxiously awaiting, rocking the booth.

"So you and Sawyer finally got naked," she says through clenched teeth, eyeing the tables around us.

Does she think people are spying on us and able to read lips?

She leans forward. "You two are together. Like *together, together*. Have you been from the beginning? Either way, Max owes me money." Her head turns and she shouts, "Max!"

I smother her face with both hands.

"Harper! You can't collect yet because you can't tell anyone. We aren't supposed to be together until after the final show in a couple of weeks," I tell her. She attempts to talk again, but I've still got my hands on her face. "Nod if you understand how important it is to keep this to yourself."

She nods, removing my hands, and waiting exactly one second before asking questions.

"Who initiated? Does the show have official overnight dates? Do you have to sign special consent forms for that? Tell us about the sex because, girl, your man is one hot mystery."

"All I'll say is, I've dated some guys with impressive reputations, but they've got nothing on Sawyer."

Harper waggles her eyebrows. "It's always the quiet ones."

"Oh, he's *not* quiet. Not in all the ways that count anyway." I grin at them as Harper's jaw drops.

The audio guy calls me over but Harper begs me to stay and give her all the juicy details.

"Sorry ladies, contestant duty calls," I say, sliding out from the booth.

My feet carry me a little faster, away from my friends' increasingly lewd comments. A few more weeks left of this show and then no more secrets. No more uncertainty.

TAKING in the scene before me, I can almost guarantee this evening's group activity was Sean's brain child. And I'm grateful.

I'm stepping into some coveralls next to the other three ladies with confidence since I've got this event in the bag.

We're using the outdoor patio and forested space behind Rocky's for a paintball target competition. Should we have gone to an outdoor paintball field? Possibly, but Paint It Up on the outskirts of Vaughn didn't want this many spectators and people were promised a live show.

Instead, Town Council, Rocky's Tavern staff, and an assortment of volunteers banded together to create a makeshift course and target practice area.

They had to shut down trails, block off the neighboring businesses. All so four women could compete for the interest of our town's most eligible bachelor.

And it might give me a bit of sick satisfaction considering I've already accomplished this task.

I also plan on winning this competition. Specifically, I'm going to wipe the floor with Velora, no holding back. She put her hands *all* over Sawyer during their one-on-one time at the start of tonight's show. And then she talked about her family and how excited they are to meet him, and how she was hoping they could have some alone time afterward, biting her lip at him all coy-like.

Not happening.

Then she kissed his cheek, so close to the edge of his mouth, my soul left my body and circled her, plotting her demise. She even had the gall to wink after.

The atmosphere has changed for group dates. It's tense, desperate. And I'm not unaffected.

I'm stuck pretending and I hate it. Ellie was right—I'm not cut out for sharing, and if a guy's looking elsewhere when he's got me, fuck that. But it's an impossible situation when we're here because Sawyer is supposed to show interest in the other women.

After my separation, I promised to never waste my time on any man who doesn't have the same sense of loyalty and devotion I bring into a relationship. I want a man whose gaze never lingers, who gives his mind, heart, and body to the woman he loves and only her, forever.

This show is hurting my heart and messing with my head.

Today's not the day for letting those insecurities bubble up. The audience members are all crowded on the patio, waiting for us to begin. My expression sobers as I make my way through to the back gate where a table is set up with our gear.

Sawyer is standing off to the side with Miranda, Stella, and his mom. He catches sight of me and grins, mouthing, *You got this.*

I've only gone paintballing with him once, and only because my brothers insisted on it as a family outing. I got annihilated and took it a little personally. That weekend, when I returned to college, I joined a paintball league. Next time my brothers and I were all together, I suggested we give paintball another try. I dominated that game. Well, other than Brody. He's an armed forces vet and the current chief of police, so he has some serious skills.

"Maybe Sawyer can show me how to hold this?" Velora asks, peeking back toward him and the organizers.

"We actually have someone from the Vaughn Paintball League here to go over the safety and technical aspects. Police Chief Brody? Where did you go?" Miranda shouts into the audience area.

Ah shit. Really?

My oldest brother jogs over and swipes the Airsoft gun from my hands. "Thanks, Livvie. How about you throw your goggles on and be my target?"

"Pass, asshat."

I get a half smile from him before he moves to face us, the spectators raptly listening behind us.

After his spiel, we all take turns with bull's-eye targets. A couple of the women ask Sawyer to go first to show us how it's done, and I chime in. I want to see him shoot.

He lines himself up and takes his shots. He's decent. Good, even.

But I'm better.

After I take my three shots, I turn to catch him ogling me. He licks his lower lip, eyes dark with heat. I shoulder past Velora, knocking her back a step as she moves to take her shots.

I settle next to Sawyer and Miranda to observe the rest of my opponents.

"That was way hotter than I expected it to be," he whispers to me.

"Which part?" I ask.

"Every. Damn. Part." His voice holds a hint of a growl. "Your impressive skills, your determination, and especially the fiery edge of competitiveness."

I smirk. He likes that I'm getting feisty, fighting for him.

Miranda announces that the top two shooters move on to the final challenge where they've set up a mini paintball course with hay bales, large tubes, and inflatable obstacles in the clearing between the patio and the forest backing this entire side of town.

Velora and I end up in the final round. They've created a type of elimination game. If you hit your opponent, you gain a point, then both players return to their starting places as a new round begins. The player with the most points by the final whistle, wins.

Craning my neck, I find Sawyer, who appears a mix of amused and worried. My wide, cocky smile has him shaking his head. *Be nice*, he mouths.

Velora steps up next to me and, without sparing me a glance, says, "Look, we both know I'm better suited for Sawyer." After a beat, she turns to appraise me, leaving no doubt she finds me lacking. "You've had your date and now it's my turn. Don't expect him to settle for less after he's had me."

My gaze flicks back to Sawyer, who watches us. I suck my cheeks in and try to find a calming breath.

Nope, not working.

Looking out into the field instead of her self-satisfied face, I tell her, "You don't stand a chance," with an even, confident tone.

"I don't care about this game, Olivia." She waggles her fingers at the course. "Win or lose, I'm going on a date with Sawyer. You might have temporarily caught his eye, but I'm leaving here with him tonight."

"Over my dead fucking body, you fun-sucking twat," I spew at her.

Twat, Liv? Really? You've called her way *worse in your head a million times, but that's what you're going with right now?*

"Ladies. You. Are. Mic'd," Miranda growls through clenched teeth, appearing behind us.

Oops. I forgot they had mic'd us so everyone could hear us while we're on the course.

Oh well, it'll make for a better show. This is what the people want, right? Seeing us fighting. Experiencing our unguarded sides and true emotions.

A hand finds my back and slides over to squeeze my hip. "Everything okay over here?" Velora and I continue glaring at each other. Sawyer's hand smooths soothingly over my hip. "I think Jaxon is waving you two over for your starting positions."

Miranda leads Velora over and I go to follow, but Sawyer's hand wraps around my wrist.

"You going to behave?"

My eyebrows lift in challenge.

"Jaxon still has a scar on his elbow from when you surprise attacked him and he fell down the ravine."

"Taught them to stop underestimating me."

The dimple in his cheek pops with his lopsided smile. "It sure did." His eyes flash to the course where Velora and my brother are waiting.

"Worried?" I scoff. "You should be," I murmur darkly. Easy prey makes for a boring game, but I think I'll toy with her for a bit.

He leans into me, pressing his lips to my ear. "The number of times you hit her before the final whistle is the number of times I make you come tonight."

Heat drops into my belly, and my breath stalls.

I stalk off to the course with a whole hell of a lot of enticement.

EXCESSIVE HITS almost cost me my daisy.

Apparently, hitting Velora with six paintballs after the initial one where she shrieked in surrender was considered "unsportsmanlike conduct."

Technically, in this game, you are only supposed to hit your opponent once to win the round. However, no such rule was stated before we began. My stupid brother pointed out that since I'm an experienced paintball player, I should have been aware of this rule.

Whose side is he on? He'll be paying for his comment some-time soon.

Ignoring him, I argued that her murder-scream triggered my fight or flight response.

"As the winner of tonight's group date competition, Olivia has secured her spot for next week's family meet and greet. It's been decided for this last solo date, one of the remaining ladies will be given a final chance at their own one-on-one time with our Hottie," Stella announces, nodding at Miranda before stepping back from the microphone. She glances at Sawyer briefly, a hint of concern on her face.

What? I thought the winner of the competition got the solo date tonight.

Sawyer calls me up for my winning flower. As I accept, I whis-per, "Ten," against Sawyer's bristly cheek, dragging my lips slowly back across the side of his mouth as I withdraw from his arms.

Before I'm able to slip away, planning out how I was going to spread those orgasms all night long, accepting that I probably wouldn't be able to walk tomorrow, Sawyer draws me back into him.

"Only four of those were legal hits, baby. Nice try though."

"Don't I get anything extra for coming out squeaky clean? Not a drop on me." I spread my hands, gesturing at my coveralls, smiling wide.

"It won't be the case for long. I'll be painting you with my come later."

I gape at him, stepping back with my flower clutched to my heaving chest.

Damn him and his hot-as-fuck words.

Sawyer gives out the rest of the flowers, choosing to eliminate Abbie. Earlier today she told me she would be approaching Sawyer about not keeping her for the family night if he wasn't serious about getting to know her better. She considers meeting her family serious since they live hours away, are retired, and would not understand this kind of dating situation.

Stella and Miranda take the microphone from Sawyer and begin their usual wrap-up, including announcing the details of the next solo date.

"This week the solo date will be voted on by the audience." Our quirky mayor clears her throat as a poll is displayed on the screen at the front of the room. "It will take place tonight after the show. Unfortunately, the venue of this date is not capable of hosting all of us, so it will be filmed on location. Be sure to check The Vine's website when you get home to watch the live stream in one hour. Otherwise, the recorded episode will be posted there tomorrow. Sawyer and his date will—"

A frown works its way into my forehead as I tune Miranda out, wondering how Velora knew there would be a date tonight when the rest of us didn't.

"—at the Bradford Inn & Resort Spa for a night of luxurious and sexy pampering," her voice breaks through the thoughts running wild in my mind. "They'll be rubbed, scrubbed, and treated to an herbal aphrodisiac bathing experience." Several *oohs* and a few snickers echo through the audience.

"You have five minutes to vote while we take a short break."

So Sawyer and one of these ladies are going to get semi-naked together while being sensually massaged, and then share an erotic bath? Gee, that sounds awesome.

I get a hike for my solo date while this contestant gets a clothing-optional seductive spa night?

Then again, I also got some finger-banging action on said hike, so I shouldn't be complaining.

There's this part of me that, while previously accepting of continuing on with the show, is suddenly much less accepting. Not because I don't trust Sawyer, but because I don't want the impression that, for even a moment, he's not mine.

None of the candidates say a word, but Velora shoots me a smug grin. Minutes later, Miranda steps back up to the microphone.

"We are pleased to announce the contestant with the highest votes this evening, and about to be whisked away to a romantic evening at our local inn is . . ." Miranda pauses for dramatic effect. "Velora Afferton."

Velora was already walking forward. She knew she'd win.

Goddammit. I bet she worked some kind of bullshit with the Town Council to get this date. Miranda has already walked off the stage, only Stella remains, and she's staring right at me. With a quick breath, she tips her head toward Velora, rolls her eyes, and sends me a sympathetic smile.

Sawyer cranes back to glance for me as he's herded offstage. I keep my expression neutral and wish we could have spoken last night. He was called away to an emergency at the clinic and slept at his own house afterward.

I have so many questions—ones I didn't know I had until tonight. Until I realized what it would mean to watch the man I love be fawned over and feign interest in other women.

How long is this date?

Will my brother be attending again for emergency medical purposes, and if so, would he be willing to beaverblock Velora's dubious sexual intents?

Are their spa treatments in the same room?

How will Sawyer react to a beautiful woman coming on to him all night?

Why wasn't I better prepared for this?

Without Sawyer here to guide me out of this question spiral, I numbly descend the stairs of the stage, ignoring the victorious smirk on Velora's face as she strides out of Rocky's with her arm hooked through my man's.

I avert my gaze, finding my mom and two best friends waiting for me across the bar. They likely already planned our date-watching night.

The problem is that I don't think I'm going to be able to witness this next date.

And by the expressions on the faces of the three ladies before me, they're pretty hesitant about it too.

CHAPTER
TWENTY-EIGHT
SAWYER

I fucking hate this. But I'm smiling, following instructions, and doing my best not to walk out the door. The growing guilt that arose because I'm required to play along, giving my date the impression I'm interested, is gnawing at me. The least I can do is try to be as pleasant as possible.

"You wouldn't mind, would you, Sawyer?"

My attention snaps back to my "date," not acknowledging that she was even talking to me. Doing a shit job of this so far.

Her toe nails are still being painted whereas my foot treatment was over a while ago. The manager, who had booked everything, suggested we have this one service be together so Lenny could get some live stream footage of us talking and getting pedicures. Since we're fully dressed and five feet from each other, I relented. The couples massage, however, I turned down.

How the hell am I going to even pretend to court the remaining contestants without feeling like a cheating asshole? I can barely drum up so much as a smile at them anymore. I only want to see Liv. I only want to touch Liv.

I'm so sick of this bullshit.

Earlier during the paintball competition, I was only allowed to participate in target practice, meaning I was able to stick close to Liv—whose impressive paintball skills was more of a turn-on than I would have ever guessed—without having to interact as much with anyone else.

Which worked out well because I had no plan. Liv and I were supposed to see each other last night, but I was called in for an emergency since it was my clinic's rotation for after-hours calls. Normally I don't have an issue with providing on-call care two nights a week. But suddenly it's a heavier obligation. One that takes me away from Liv.

Or maybe it's that my time is hardly my own anymore.

But now I want to hire another vet part-time to ease my workload, and that wasn't something I was planning for years yet.

Once the show is over, maybe it'll be different again. Maybe I won't be resentful about not getting enough time with my girlfriend. If that's what she is. Shit. We haven't even talked about it, and here I am on a pseudo-date with a woman who seems to have it out for her.

"Sawyer?"

Fuck! I did it again.

"Sorry, what were you saying?"

"I was asking if you wouldn't mind driving me home after this? My polish won't be dry, so I was thinking you could drop me off? It'll give us a chance to talk more. Since they had us in different rooms for our massages and steam baths," she explains, her tone terse, "we haven't had a lot of time together."

I glower at the cameraman to intercede since we aren't supposed to spend time together outside of the show. He gives me nothing.

"Um, yeah, of course I can drop you off."

And I will be forcing the cameraman to come with us. Which means riding along for an uncomfortable five minutes of me trying to dodge Velora's wandering hands while keeping us on the road.

"Hey." Fingertips find my hand and remove it from where I'm scrubbing my forehead. "You're going to rub your skin clean off."

Most of the time I don't even notice I'm doing it. Often I'm too lost in my thoughts.

"So . . ." she drags the word out. "I had a really great time. An evening at the spa was exactly what we both needed. And look, we both made it to the end happy and healthy." Her tone is teasing, her smile wide as she twirls with her arms extended, showing her excitement at making it to the end of the date unscathed.

Goddamn. Now women are merely hoping to be able to withstand a night out with me?

"It's a sign."

Fingers thread through mine and my body locks up. We're holding hands.

Will Liv be okay with this? We talked about what I would have to do to pretend, and this was part of it. But things are different now. It's not pretend between her and I, but it's still very much pretend with Velora.

She leans over the space separating our massage chairs, hand locked with mine. Her other hand creeps toward my arm to squeeze my bicep like she does every time she gets near.

If I don't put a stop to this, Jaxon is going to remove my balls from my body. And I wouldn't blame him. Thinking about Liv being out with someone else—touching, flirting—I'd be fuming. And he knows his sister is watching this.

"I think we should talk after this," I whisper, hoping the mics don't pick it up.

Her eyes search mine, her lashes fluttering as she whispers back, "Okay."

I give her hand a squeeze to hopefully ease the transition of me pulling away. She settles back into her chair, sending me a dim smile.

We leave the spa shortly after, cutting through the lobby, and waving at the manager on our way out.

"Wait!" The lady scurries around from behind the front counter, stopping us. "A viewer has graciously offered to pay for a cozy overnight stay for you two, should you choose to extend your visit and your date."

What the . . .

"That sounds lovely!" Velora steps forward, beaming. "I think we could use the room to have this talk you wanted to have. In private." Her gaze flickers to the camera, ducking her head as if she just remembered we were being filmed.

I hold in my sigh and hope like hell I can manage to get out of this without telling anyone to fuck off.

CHAPTER
TWENTY-NINE

OLIVIA

"What presumptuous horndog paid for a room for Velora to get laid in? Jesus." Harper slaps a hand to the side of her face and leans in closer to the television. Sawyer seems to be chewing his words before letting them loose. "I have to admit though, this makes for great reality TV. If you weren't personally involved, this would be working for me."

Jane's chuckles turn into a shush as her son steps forward to address Mrs. Bradford.

"That's very generous, Mrs. Bradford, but I don't think it would be appropriate."

"It's just a room, Sawyer," Velora coos, snuggling into him. Her hand settles on his chest, and he glances down at her with a soft expression I can't decipher.

He's been so kind, quietly accepting of her flirtations, but discreetly moving away from her groping attempts. And I've been a wreck this whole time and have hidden it poorly. Jane has held my hand several times throughout the evening, almost as if she's apologizing for what I'm having to witness.

"We can talk, *not talk*." She gazes up at my man dreamily, the innuendo clear to all of us. When he hesitates, she adds, "Or watch a movie, play games, hang out. It would feel wrong to turn down this opportunity when we're trying to get to know each other better. Overnight dates are crucial in determining compatibility, don't you think?"

A long, silent pause stretches as we all collectively hold our breath, awaiting Sawyer's response.

"I'm saving myself for marriage," he says.

I snort. Full-on snort at the ridiculousness of his statement.

"What?" The pitch of Velora's tone reaches a squeaky octave, and her eyebrows shoot up so far her forehead almost wrinkles.

"Oh my god," I mutter through the fingers I've pressed against my face.

Sawyer's jaw tics right before he pulls her aside, likely hoping the camera crew would give them some privacy.

Thankfully the cameraman does not.

"I made it clear to the organizers of the show there would be no overnight dates, nudity, partial nudity, or sexual activity of any kind with any of the contestants. This includes events where the central theme predominantly features any of those activities."

I grin, unable to tear my eyes away from this insanity. Sawyer was smart to include those stipulations because the ladies would have had him at least partially undressed plenty of times by now.

"Being in a bedroom together doesn't mean we're going to have sex, Sawyer. There are plenty of other things two consenting adults could fill their time with. Even if one of those adults is holding out for marriage." Her gaze narrows as if she doesn't quite believe him but isn't willing to call him out.

He clears his throat, staring at his feet.

"Oh, Sawyer," his mom mumbles.

"Did you know he was saving himself?" my mom asks her.

Jane tsks at her, brows mashed together, giving her a look that says, *Don't be an idiot.*

"Do you think he's saying that so he doesn't have to outright reject her?" Ellie asks.

"No idea, but if he's trying to politely shut her down, I'm very curious how that's going to go over," Harper says.

A dark, scarred part of my mind wonders how far he'll take this. And if maybe now that he's more confident, he'll want to casually date.

"That's tempting, Velora." Sawyers words hit me like free-falling rocks.

Is it? *Is it?!*

He places his hand on her elbow, and she steps closer, leaning into him. "But I think it's best we end the evening here and I drive you home."

Disappointment and frustration flash across her face, but she's quick to brush it off. "Well then, the date's not quite over, is it?"

She hooks her arm through his, leading him outside.

Before they get in the vehicle, the crew leads each of them away to answer a few questions about the date. One of the questions they ask Sawyer is if he is pleased his last two dates ended without incident. They suggested that perhaps the dates went well because him and his date clicked. That maybe he's found something special in both Velora and me.

I gasp at the statement because . . . they're right.

There was speculation about why there was no kiss with Velora yet. And when Sawyer answered with, "Some things are meant to be private," I started to feel really stupid. Because maybe he did want to kiss her—in private. Or at the very least, he might think he should for the show.

Looks like I got what I wanted though. Sawyer doesn't seem nervous about dating anymore. He may not have wanted a girl-friend when he started this show, but now he may be considering his options.

And I don't know where this leaves us.

I *do* know that I need to get some answers from Sawyer. Because there's no way I'm going to let myself get into another situation where I look the other way or settle for whatever the guy I've chosen to attach myself to is willing to give me.

Never again.

Because the man you're in love with has a unique kind of power.

The power to heal, embolden, lavish with heady promises, but also the power to destroy your heart. And the man I give that kind of power to needs to deserve it.

CHAPTER
THIRTY

OLIVIA

SAWYER: It should have been you with me tonight. I hated that it wasn't.

My day has been full of new patient exams but I can't get his text messages from last night out of my head. I'm torn between regret at not answering his calls after his night with Velora and telling him he's an idiot.

Because after I let that sweet text go unanswered—because I was *asleep*—he sent me another one.

SAWYER: At least it was a disaster-free date. Think of all the time we'll save not having to rehash the gory details? We should celebrate my dating success! I definitely have some ideas how.

At least it was another disaster-free date?
Maybe I'm being sensitive but is he boasting about the success of his date to the woman he's fucking? Like we're buddies? I dare him to try to say this shit to Jaxon—I've already received many texts from him. I'm sure Sawyer has too.

I mean, his mom looked at me with such pity, it might have stirred up a bit of self-pity too.

But that's on me. I need to shake it off and remember this has been hard for him. And we set no expectations or boundaries. He made me no promises.

ME: Hey. Sorry I didn't answer last night. I was all talked out after watching the show with the ladies.
ME: And yes, looks like your bad luck has turned around. Now you can go on all the dates you want.

I frown, groan, and then drop my head to the staff room table with a thud. Passive aggressive texts are not my thing. Why am I being weird about this? I knew what I was getting into.

Except you fell in love with him and everything changed.

SAWYER: And I know exactly who I want to go on all those dates with. What are you doing tonight?

ME: Well, I was thinking about staying home with my vibrator since I was owed four orgasms last night and my guy didn't deliver.

A choked laugh explodes out of me as those dots come and go a few times.

SAWYER: I definitely haven't forgotten that I owe you orgasms.
SAWYER: And I hope this is an invite because it sounds more fun than anything I had planned.

ME: What did you have planned?

SAWYER: How about you join me and find out?

ME: We need to talk too, Sawyer.

SAWYER: I know.
SAWYER: Meet me at Kenzie Trail parking lot at 5pm? I'll drive us to our date.

And when I leave work, a nervous kind of excitement builds at finding out what Sawyer has planned for us considering we can't let anyone in Vaughn or Landry see us. Sneaking around sounds kind of hot.

Do we even really need to talk?

Yes, Olivia!

Because I have firm boundaries, and they definitely don't mesh with him dating other women *or* being vague as fuck about what kind of relationship we have. And I hope like hell that won't push him away.

Truth is, if I'm looking for a man worth keeping, he should want to be kept.

THE CRICKETS CHIRPING their last mating call before fall slips away into winter here in Sonoma County provides a jaunty serenade while I make my way to Sawyer's car. It's a peaceful evening, full of possibilities and hope.

Soundlessly I open his passenger door and slide into the seat.

"Hi," I say.

His smile stretches wide right before he reaches for me. Those large hands capture my face, bringing my mouth to his. Every thought leaves my head as those skilled lips move against mine.

Fuck. I'm so fucked.

His tongue swipes in to taste, torment. This man knows exactly where I want that tongue.

I pull away. "We can't have sex in this parking lot."

He chuckles. "I'll admit I may have gotten carried away. But be honest. If I told you to take your panties off, recline your seat, and let me play with your pussy, you'd be wet and ready for me."

"Joke's on you. I'm already wet and ready," I tell him, voice raspy with want.

"Jesus, Liv. Now I really do want to fuck you in this parking lot."

"You promised me a date, and we need to talk. If we mess around, we may never—"

"I also promised you four orgasms. And that promise came first. Just like you will."

Am I willing to let our much-needed conversation get derailed by sexy promises?

"Sawyer . . ."

"Lean back, baby. Let me touch you."

Ah shit. He's using his rumbly, sexy voice that makes the bottom drop out of my libido, letting it flood my entire body.

I lean back and shimmy my panties down. He stops my hand before they get to my knees.

Leaning over me, he says, "Leave them there. I want to see you looking indecent with your panties around your thighs as my fingers work your clit."

Heat blazes through my limbs, heading straight to where his fingers are brushing up my thigh. I'm unable to do anything but desperately whimper.

"You're a constant temptation. Took all I had to keep my hands off you during the show. I can't go a single fucking day without wanting you."

A wisp of unease slithers through my wanton thoughts as I wonder what this means for us. Because it's the same for me.

We *really* need to talk.

But then he reaches the apex of my thighs, easing over the triangle of hair in a near caress before delving lower.

I grip his forearm, tipping my head back on a moan, his

fingers slipping over my clit to my entrance and then back again. He teases around my swollen bud, not quite making contact. I squirm, crying out in frustration, lifting my hips.

"Patience. I'll give you what you need."

I relax back down, and he moves away from my clit, his fingers barely entering me.

"Now open your pretty mouth and tell me what you want me to do, how you want to come."

"I want you to deliver on the orgasms you owe me," I say, partially breathless.

He withdraws his hand. "Try again. Tell me."

Shit. I'm not vocal during sex. And I realize it's so much harder when he's doing naughty things to me.

I try again, without sass. "I-I want your fingers inside me . . . pushing against that perfect spot. I need you to make me come all over your hand."

"Good girl." His fingers thrust hard, curling up inside me. How the actual fuck is he getting this wonderful angle in this position?

His wrist wrenches hard, fucking me so good the car is shaking. He shifts his upper body until he's hovering over me and kisses me, mumbling hot words against my mouth.

"So hot."

"Yeah, squeeze my fingers."

He bites and pulls at my lower lip, and my legs shake.

"I want this pussy strangling my dick, gorgeous."

"Soak my hand."

"Come for me."

Oh shit. My body clenches, burns, following his sexy commands. I gasp into his mouth as I pulse around him, unable to do a single damn thing other than shudder.

I pant against his mouth as I ride the wave of pleasure.

"Mmm . . . that's a good start." I barely recognize my own voice. "Unzip those pants."

Still on an orgasm high, I attack his mouth with renewed vigor, trailing my hands down his chest to the large bulge in his pants.

He returns my kiss, smiling through parts of it, before capturing my hand.

"'Fraid not, gorgeous." He brings my hand up, kissing the tips of my fingers. "That was just for you. I can wait until after our date." He brings my hand back down and places a soft kiss on my lips. "Besides, I still owe you three more orgasms."

"What if I offered my mouth and promised it would only take three minutes."

"I think at this point, with your panties still around your knees, your release all over my hand, and your 'fuck me' eyes, I'd be lucky to last thirty seconds. So if you could let me preserve my dignity, I'd—"

With one hand down his pants, I undo them with the other. I push him back into his own seat and palm his dick through his ridiculously soft, stretchy boxer briefs.

"Fuck. You don't play fair," he tells me, voice hoarse.

"I don't like playing games. I want what I want."

"And you want my cock?"

"Yep." I take him out and stroke him from base to crown, squeezing lightly at the top. He groans.

I lean over and take him into my mouth, swirling the tip with my tongue like he's my favorite flavor of lollipop.

This man beats out a lollipop any day.

His hands move to my hair, fingers gathering the strands from the sides of my face and neck. Once he has it all in his fist, he tightens his hold, pulling firmly but gently to shift the angle so he can have a better view.

He groans. "You taking my cock like that is one of the hottest things I've ever seen." He practically growls when I hollow out my cheeks, sucking him harder. "I love your mouth on me."

I hum in agreement, pussy clenching in response to his groan.

His head drops back against the head rest, and I fight not to stop and smile around him.

"Shit," he barks out. But this one isn't a sexy outburst. I pause.

"Baby, someone's pulling into the lot. You're going to have to stop."

I come off him with an audible pop. We *cannot* be caught together, let alone messing around in his car.

I slink back into my seat hoping they didn't spot me as they came up behind us.

Sawyer tucks himself back into his pants while stealing a glance in the rearview mirror. "Ah, hell. That's going to complicate our night." His hand rises to worry his forehead before slipping through his hair, his wry laugh filling the interior of his car.

I turn to peer in the side mirror.

The car pulls up directly behind us—patrol lights blazing.

"No!" I gasp. "Oh no. Oh shit. This is bad. So bad."

"It'll be fine, Liv. He knows I'm into you, that we're on the show, dating. He'll understand why I'd want to sneak away with you."

A stream of foul words spew out, poorly trapped against the hands I pressed over my face.

"Don't freak out. It'll be fine."

"Sawyer. He's going to know what we were doing," I hiss, slouching farther down in my seat. "You are *so* getting locked up."

The slam of a car door startles us. The side mirror reveals my brother strolling toward us.

"That would make for a shitty date night," Sawyer says.

"Don't joke. And don't bait him," I whisper.

"Fine, I'll be good. But you might want to pull up your panties."

My eyes fly to my legs where my black panties still circle my knees. "*Oh my god!*"

I snatch them from their incriminating location and shove

them up my thighs, out of sight below the thin skirt of my floral dress.

Sawyer pinches the material between two fingers, rubbing it. "This is pretty, by the way." His eyes dip down my body and then back up to my face. "Light blue looks amazing on you. Especially with your hair."

"You cannot seriously be hitting on me right before my brother—"

Two loud raps at the window has me clutching my chest.

With the press of a button, Sawyer rolls down the window, casually nodding to my brother.

Brody places two hands on the roof of the car, leaning over. Ignoring Sawyer, he glares directly at me. "Livvie."

"Brody. What are you doing out here?"

He doesn't answer. After a thorough visual assessment, he switches his focus to Sawyer.

I hold my breath so long sparkles appear on the edges of my vision.

"Breathe, Liv," Sawyer tells me, sliding his hand over mine, linking our fingers together.

"He's not saying anything. I can't take this. He knows exactly how to rile me up," I whisper to Sawyer.

"What are you two doing out here? Together. Sitting in the parking lot," he finally says.

"None of your damn business, Brody." Oh good, I got my shit together long enough to tell my brother off. Now I pay the consequences. Brody doesn't respond well to being challenged.

Dammit Liv!

He sighs. "So this is a thing now? You two?"

"Yes," Sawyer and I say together.

"That a problem, Brody?"

"That's Chief Vaughn to you right now, Fletch," he practically growls.

His radio goes off, and he takes a moment to respond in some kind of cop code.

Afterward he turns to stare at the trail on the other side of where we parked.

"That show has this town acting stupid as hell. Do you know how many times you've been reported for lurking in back alleys, Fletcher?" People saw him and reported him? I grimace. "Or the reported sightings of you at other contestants' homes because it was breaking the rules—*contest* rules, not the law. And I'd have to pretend I didn't know you were actually over at Liv's. Or that you were on-call for an emergency or even out with Jaxon, because it was just easier to take their complaints down and get them the fuck off the phone." I'm already on edge, and his frustrated sigh is unbearably loud. "People are calling into *emergency services* about a fucking low-budget, dramatic-as-shit, matchmaking, local dating show. And now you two are out here necking or whatever the fuck? No."

My brother steps back from the door. "Step out of the vehicle, Fletcher."

I grasp the edges of my seat. Oh shit, he's really going to arrest him.

Sawyer throws me a quick, reassuring grin before stepping out. I move to open my door and get out too.

"You stay in the vehicle, Livvie," he calls as he leads Sawyer to the rear of the vehicle. I stick my tongue out at him like I did as a kid, even if he can't see me. He brings out the worst in me sometimes.

The guys talk for a few minutes before Brody slaps Sawyer on the shoulder roughly and rounds the patrol car.

As Sawyer gets back into the car, I'm ready with a million questions.

"He grilled me a bit, warned me to keep things better under wraps, told me he's thrilled about us, and then wished us well on our date."

My eyes narrow on him as he pulls out of our parking spot. "Bullshit."

"Yep. But I didn't get arrested, did I?" His smile is pure male satisfaction.

CHAPTER
THIRTY-ONE

SAWYER

A squeal cuts through the boisterous clatter around us. "Did you see that? I'm kicking your ass, Fletcher."

I fight my grin as I take her in. She's finishing up her "strike dance," rolling those hips in a way entirely too sexy since we're in a bowling alley and I can't touch her the way I want to.

I drove us forty minutes away to the nearest bowling alley not located in close proximity to Vaughn or Landry.

The first half of the drive was a bit tense and filled with many questions, all of which I did my best to evade. She texted her brother only to get brushed off by him as well.

Which is fine by me. I'd rather keep that conversation private anyhow. Her brother is protective, and I appreciate it. What I don't appreciate is him assuming I'm some kind of player who's going to hurt his baby sister.

My overzealous bowling companion races back to me and wraps her arms around my neck. "Strike," she whispers against my lips.

Her competitive nature has always caught my attention— during family game nights, even hanging out with her brothers when we were all teenagers. I've met plenty of other women who were competitive, aggressive, loved a challenge. I've never thought much of it—until now. It does something to me. Something that makes me want to cut this date short and take her home.

Because yeah . . . I like it.

"We only have a couple frames left. You're down by fifty points, *gorgeous*."

I wrap my arms around her. "You're going to steal the game and the cute nickname I use? I see how it is."

"So I'm not allowed to use any sweet nicknames for you? You've already got Liv. No one else uses that name. Everyone has called me Livvie since I was a kid."

I incline my head toward her. "And that's why I call you Liv. You are definitely not the girl I once knew. You're a woman and the culmination of my every wet dream. I'll stick with 'Liv' and 'gorgeous'. Sometimes 'babe' or 'baby.'"

She moves closer, fingers moving into my hair. Her cheeks, rosy with excitement, flush even deeper. "You took all the good ones."

"I can make some suggestions . . ."

She laughs before placing a sweet, lingering kiss to my lips. "I bet you can."

I step away but not before sliding my hands down to grip her butt through her sexy-ass dress. Her curvy booty has been swaying and bending in front of me all night.

I'm fucking her from behind tonight.

"You going to bowl, sweetknees?"

I spin around to glare at her. "No."

"Want me to bowl for you? Try to get your score so you can break one hundred?"

This goddamn woman. I'm gonna be slapping that ass tonight too.

"I meant the nickname, Liv. That's a hell no."

"Hmm . . ." she hums with a sweet, mischievous smile on her beautiful face.

She can call me whatever she wants, and I'm still going to hang on her every damn word. I turn and grab a ball, leaving her to think of more silly nicknames.

"Fine. I'll stick with stud. I mean, it's fitting. I'd let you breed me any day."

My first ball flies down the lane. Straight into the gutter.

I keep my back to her for a moment. When I turn around, she's standing there with both hands covering her mouth, shoulders shaking.

My hands are on my hips, waiting for her to get herself together.

She schools her face, clapping twice—intense, encouraging claps. "Good try, Stud. You got this next one."

But all I can think about is breeding her. I think I might officially have a kink worth mentioning on Stella's ridiculous bachelor form.

I groan and turn to the ball return area, choosing the color Liv uses for every turn.

"Great choice, Stud Muffin!"

My shoulders hunch in as I mentally gather all the strength I have to not turn around and ensure her mouth is too busy to tease me any more.

Gripping the ball, I tell myself I'll finally get a strike.

I feel it on the release.

Gutter ball.

Fucking dammit! Why? Was I always this bad at bowling?

Turning, I have no idea what I'm in for. Her lips are pinched shut, wide eyes watering from trying not to blink.

"Nothing to say, gorgeous?"

She shakes her head, biting down on those sweet lips.

I focus on my last ball, holding it with fierce determination. I've been enjoying how much fun Liv is having wiping the floor with me. But I have to at least break one hundred. Hell, even the preteen kid beside us has one-thirty and he still has several frames left.

Liv is cheering behind me and talking about my butt. Grinning, I take my shot.

It skips right over our lane.

Into the next lane.

And then lodges itself into the wall at the end of our section.

Into. The. Wall.

Gasps ring out through the lanes my ball blew through to embed itself in the structure of the building.

"Of fucking course," I mutter.

It gets eerily quiet.

Except for one sound.

Snorting laughter coming from directly behind me.

Liv is bent over, hands holding her stomach as she laughs unbidden at the damage I've inflicted on this unsuspecting bowling alley. She looks up at me, tears streaming down her face while mine likely displays something close to horror.

And that's when she drops to the ground, not a sound coming from her as she waves her hands around.

Slowly I walk over to her. She clutches at me and manages to get out, "Can't breathe. Your ball . . . in the . . . I can't—" around gasping inhales.

Two employees, and what looks to be a manager, are rushing over to our lane. Expressions of concern wash over their shocked anger when they spot Liv on the floor.

"Is she okay?" they ask.

"Pretty sure she's not." My droll tone only makes her crack up more.

Their faces harden once more. They must realize she's laughing and not having some kind of episode.

Eventually I have to haul her up. She leans against me, covering her mouth as the manager reams us out.

I offer to cover the costs of repairs and Liv pulls out her phone. I figure she's going to jot down his information, or she's maybe getting a call.

Nope. She's taking pictures of the damage. Of me. Of management standing in front of me, pissed.

"That better be for documentation purposes, Liv."

"Mm-hmm, sure."

"Liv."

"Memories, Stud. Memories."

Her eyes lift to the top of my head. My hair is probably standing on end from the number of times I've raked my hands through it. She lifts her phone and takes one more photo of me, cutting off the chuckle escaping her.

They kick us out after I give them all my information. We are officially banned.

Another place I'm banned from after a date gone wrong. Maybe my bad luck streak isn't over.

I open the passenger door for Liv, but instead of dropping into the seat, she reaches up on her tiptoes and kisses the hell out of me.

Pulling back, her beautiful hazel eyes slowly flutter open. "Best date ever."

The tightness in my chest eases and fills with an unexpected warmth. This woman is infiltrating the dark places I've kept blocked off for years. The parts I keep private. Because sharing those parts means that when it all goes to hell, nothing is left untouched.

But I can't seem to stay detached when it comes to her.

CHAPTER
THIRTY-TWO

SAWYER

W e sneak in through the back door of her house, even though people have noticed my visits. She suggested we go to my place since she hasn't seen it yet, but I'm not sure I should have anyone over there until the end of the show—and until we figure out what we're doing here.

One thing Brody made very clear to me is that I need to be all-in with her. He said when Olivia loves, it's with everything she has to give. And if I'm not going to be the first man in her life to live up to that and exceed her every expectation, I should walk away.

Before physically walking away is no longer an option for me.

With a few succinct details highlighting the proposed destruction of several of my vital body parts, he slapped me on the shoulder and told me to make sure Liv had a nice time.

It might not have been a romantic date, but I will make sure the rest of our evening is more than "nice" for her. Probably not what he had in mind.

The instant we're through the door, my hands are all over her.

Her body is irresistibly perfect in my hands. Sweet and perky breasts, lusciously curvy bottom. "Why can't I get enough of you? You make it impossible," I mumble, dropping my head to kiss her neck, taking in her honeyed scent. She drops her head to the side, exposing more of her to me, her delicate collarbone waiting for my teeth.

Her knees wobble, and she holds tighter to my shoulders. I hug her closer, taking on her weight so she can let go as I feast on her.

"You already know all my spots." She sighs, gliding her fingers through my hair as I move to the other side of her neck, nipping at the spot under her ear.

"I do?" Grinning, I gently rub the scruff of my face down the length of her neck to the peek of cleavage at the vee of her dress.

She hums in agreement while I slip the cardigan off her shoulders, letting it drop to the kitchen floor. She guides my head back to her mouth right as my fingers find the zipper of her dress.

The straps fall off her shoulders, exposing beautiful rosy nipples tightening into hard buds.

"Fucking knew it," I murmur, brushing my thumb against her nipple. "No bra."

Giggling, she explores the planes of my back before gripping my T-shirt in her tiny fist and pushing it up.

We're undressed within seconds. I follow the top edge of her lacy thong to her lower back. My palms meet the firm, round cheeks of her bare ass, and I groan, having waited all night to have this ass in my hands.

"Bed or table?" My voice is gruff, direct.

Her eyes flicker to the table. She bites her lip, her hands moving to my front, right along the band of the briefs.

I slap her ass and grit my teeth at the feel of her against my palm.

She yelps, her face flushing.

"Choose, gorgeous. I need to be inside you."

Her fingers slip under the band she's been toying with. "Bed," she answers.

"Up," I demand, gripping the backs of her thighs, lifting her. Not missing a beat, she wraps her legs around me and presses her core against my throbbing length.

I move toward the hallway, each rasp of her tight nipples against my pecs eliciting a groan from me. Her gaze finds mine, her hands cradling the back of my head. Those eyes light up green, and her mouth moves toward me.

Suddenly she pulls back, eyes rounded, forehead scrunched. What could she possibly be thinking about that's not about her skin on mine, my hard thrusts as she comes, my mouth working her slick heat?

"We forgot to talk first again."

Her hooded eyes drop down to my mouth, then meet my gaze again.

"Do you want to stop to talk?" I ask, slowing to a stop just outside her bedroom.

"Or we could stick with our sex first, talk second tradition?"

"It's a tradition now, huh?" I take the final steps to the door, adjusting my grip on her so my fingers spread to reach the edges of her panties.

"Just go with it," she says against my lips.

I kick the door open, and in three strides, reach her bed. Kneeling onto it, I lay us down, covering her smaller frame with my much larger one, my hips sandwiched between her soft thighs.

Her eyes dip down my chest, to my abs and lower. Taking my hands out from under her back, I bring them to her sides, pressing along her ribs.

I move my hands down to the flare of her hips. "The shape of you . . . every time I feel these hips, I want to grab on tight and fuck you hard."

"That would make our dinner dates the talk of the town," she sasses while squirming beneath me. Giving me shit while rocking against me.

"Turn around." She looks up at me, and even in the dark, the excitement shimmers in her eyes. I sit back on my heels, giving her space to flip over. "On all fours."

She does as she's told, and I watch every movement with hunger. Her ass pops up and sways in front of me. Her thong putting those plump cheeks on display. She tilts her hips up, shifting wider to give me a view of her lace-covered pussy.

Licking my lips, I move my hands to squeeze her, my thumbs pulling her wider apart.

When she gives me another little shimmy, I glance up, and her head is turned back to me, watching, waiting.

Leaning down, I groan against the flesh of her cheek, giving it a quick bite. It drives her wild when I give her ass the attention it deserves, which is fortunate because I'm fucking obsessed.

My thumb finds her center and strokes over the fabric I've been fighting the urge to tear from her skin. Instead, I ease the lace barrier down her thighs.

Returning my attention to her backside, I bring one hand back and let it fly. The sharp sound echoes through the room, followed by her gasp.

"For the life of me, gorgeous, I can't remember which of your comments or sass that was for, but I know I owe you a few of those."

"I didn't—"

"Or maybe I just wanted to see your ass turn pink while I drive into you."

She hums and arches her back when my fingers find her soaking entrance. Teasing her, I circle her swollen bud before thrusting into her with two fingers.

She clenches around me, groaning and moving her hips toward me.

"Want more, baby?" I ask.

"You. I want *you*. Jesus . . ." she trails off.

I remove my fingers, swiping the arousal on my cock to mix with the precum leaking from the tip.

Lining myself up, I drag the head up and down through her folds. She pushes back impatiently, mumbling something.

"What did you say?" I ask.

She whimpers.

"Tell me."

"I said, 'just get in me!'"

I grin before doing just that. Thrusting through her heat, I bottom out, my heartbeat booming in my ears.

My voice is deep and rough as I ask, "That what you needed, babe?"

"Yes. God, yes." She bites her lips closed, blocking her sounds from reaching me.

"Open up your pretty mouth and let me hear you. I want to hear what my cock does to you."

She does, adding, "Holy shit, Sawyer."

Huffing out a tortured breath, I drag out of her a few inches only to dive right back in. My hands circle the small of her waist, keeping her firmly in my grasp. I'm losing all control of myself.

I owe her three more orgasms, but now that I'm inside of her, I don't know if I can deliver on them all before blowing my load inside her.

She feels so fucking good. Every inch of her walls gripping me. Her sexy sounds filling me up. My hips pumping as I stare at where we're connected. Her sweet arousal coating me.

I spread those cheeks wider and groan at the wetness soaking my dick. "Being inside you bare is the best fucking thing I've ever felt. Never want to stop."

"Don't stop," she rambles breathlessly.

My hands tighten, digging into her softness. I pull her into me with each thrust, my balls slapping against her clit.

"Yes . . ." she moans.

I smack each ass cheek in quick succession, watching them shake as my handprints light up on her smooth skin.

"This first one is going to be hard and fast. You feel too damn good," I warn.

"I'm close. I'm so close." Her fingers reach under us to rub herself. I release one hip to flick her hand away.

"That's mine. When you come, it'll be my dick, my fingers, my voice that makes you cream all over me. Got it?"

I use three fingers, thrumming side to side. Changing my angle, I grind into her with short strokes until she tightens all around me, and that telling sound rips from the back of her throat.

There it is.

Her release tips me over the edge, and I hold her shaking body tight to me as I empty into her.

I shudder, filling her up, but feeling too fucking relaxed to leave her warmth and the delicious aftershocks of her own orgasm. I need a bit, but then I'm going to paint her ass with my come as I promised the other day.

Massaging my hands over her waist, hips, and ass, I show my appreciation for the body that drives me wild.

She collapses against the mattress, and my dick immediately misses the cozy bliss it was all wrapped up in.

"That's only one. I still owe you two more, gorgeous." I place kisses along her spine from the divots of her lower back all the way to her neck.

She flips over and smiles up at me. "Well, you made quite the mess of me." Her fingers trail through her slit, lifting to show me. My gaze darts down to see my come leaking out of her. My previously softening cock is half-hard again.

"Let's get in the shower and clean you up."

"You better be planning to dirty me up again in there," she

says, tracing the line down my abs, watching as I harden again beneath her touch.

I scoop her into my arms. "You bet your ass I am."

Her throaty chuckle as I carry her into the walk-in shower thoroughly detracts from thinking about the conversation we'll need to have once she gets all her orgasms.

CHAPTER
THIRTY-THREE
OLIVIA

The morning after our late night of endless sex shenanigans —which did in fact include Sawyer leaving his mark *all* over me—requires coffee and carbs. I hand Sawyer his black coffee and gingerly sit on the stool beside him.

He grins at my wince before bringing the coffee to his wickedly skilled mouth.

"Proud of the fact I can't sit right, Stud?"

His grin widens as he silently puts down his mug and spins me on the stool to face him.

"Talk time?" he asks. I nod, and he sits up a little straighter. "It's the last few weeks of the show, and things are going to get complicated. We need to figure out how to get through the rest of this without pissing anyone off or fucking it up."

"Your last date went well." I try for an excited expression but am doubtful if I've pulled it off. "I'm sure the rest will too."

"If I could, I'd demand we do the final ceremony tomorrow. But I might have an idea of how to make sure no one's feelings get hurt and everyone still gets what they want."

"What the other two contestants want is *you*," I point out.

"I'll be talking to them before the family dates. I can explain that I've already made my choice but want to follow through on my obligations to the show."

"Do you think it will affect the way they conduct themselves afterward?" I ask.

He tips his head to the side, his mouth downturned. "Maybe?"

"Okay. So the plan is to try to talk to them first so they don't get their hopes up but to do it in a way that doesn't make things obvious and uncomfortable for the rest of the show. Pfft. Easy."

He scrubs both hands down his face. "Uh-huh. I should plan out a speech or something."

A lighthearted laugh leaves my lips. "Good luck with that."

"I'll make Sean help me since he suggested it."

Sean already knows? Did Sawyer tell him?

"And . . . where does this plan leave us—you and me?"

I watch his Adam's apple as he swallows down a large gulp of coffee. He clears his throat. "Where do you want it to leave us?" he asks, turning my question around on me.

I want him to tell me we are a given. That I'm his and he's mine. To verify everything I've been feeling but too nervous to say out loud.

Warily he observes me for a few tense seconds before I remember that I need to say something. Might as well get right to the point.

"First I'd like to know what we are, what *you* want us to be. And not just right now, but also after the show is over."

His jaw tightens as he sets down his coffee before bringing his eyes back to my face. "We're . . . us. We're together, having fun— in a variety of ways. If you want a specific label, I don't have one at the moment. I think for now, let's just be us. But in secret for a few more weeks until the show is over."

"And after that? Am I your girlfriend? Are we working toward something serious? Because I'm ready. I didn't think I would be, and I've never truly opened myself up enough to make it work . . . until now. So I need to know if this is what you want too" He inhales, his shoulders tensing up. "Or I need you to tell me if this is simply a bit of fun for you. If I'm your warm-up before you officially dive back into the dating pool again."

His breath leaves him in a torrent of air.

"All I wanted was to keep things simple for a while." Both of his hands rake through his hair. "You of all people know how my relationships go, Liv. I didn't want a girlfriend. Not yet."

Crushed. Breath-stealing disappointment. Confusion.

Why did we bother then? Why did he start this with me?

"I'm—" he clears his throat. "I'm not sure I'm ready to make anything official yet. What if it messes everything up? What if I—"

"What if it doesn't?" I ask, my voice a broken whisper.

His fingers move to his forehead. "I like you, Liv. *Really* fucking like you. For longer than I care to admit, I thought you were gorgeous but completely off-limits. When I first saw you after you moved back—at the beach the day you offered to help me with LoveVine—I knew I was fucked." His smile is sinfully crooked, but his eyes are lined with worry. He leans closer and slowly runs his fingers through my hair. "I wanted to get a handful of this incredible hair in my grip while you took me into your beautiful mouth. I had thoughts, Liv, so many thoughts." His fingers leave the tips of my hair and caress down my back. "Sweet, funny, and mind-obliteratingly sexy. You're a fucking dream. One I'm not sure I deserve."

I stare, the faint remnants of butterflies churning in my gut, but I remind myself this isn't what I want. Well, it's not the *only* thing I want. Because I'm already in love with him, and he's merely in lust with me.

Clearing my throat, I clarify, "So you want to be friends with benefits? Fuck buddies?"

"No. I have feelings for you, Liv. So many fucking feelings."
Then tell me. Tell me how you feel, what you want! He lets out an exasperated groan. "You're making it sound—"

"Like we'd enjoy each other sexually without expectations of real romantic feelings or commitment? Isn't that what you're asking for?"

"No." His voice deepens, firm and full of conviction. But his gaze is cast downward.

"No? Well, will we be seeing other people while we 'keep things simple'? What happens if one of us finds someone else who wants more? This all stops? Because I guarantee the man I'll want to be in a relationship with won't be wanting other women. Because men who bask in the affections of other women aren't worth keeping."

"Liv . . ."

"You asked what I wanted. And we seem to want different things, so I have questions."

"Fuck," he mumbles. "I don't want to see other people, or to be fuck buddies, or any of that. But I don't know if I'm able to give you what you want. I *do* know that I don't want anything else with anyone else. So I can promise that won't be an issue."

"Exclusive fuck buddies, then." I hate myself a bit for the snark creeping into my tone. But I don't play nicely when I'm hurt.

He drops his chin to his chest and sighs in defeat. "You know that's not what we are. Once we can actually be seen together, and there are no more contestants or group dates or the whole town watching . . ." Gentle fingers cup my chin, his thumb brushing in soothing strokes. "I think getting through the insanity of this show first is the safest choice."

Safest?

My brows lift. "The whole town is *always* watching, Sawyer."
His jaw clenches. "Are you saying you need more time to decide?"

"It's not about deciding. I wasn't ready for a woman like you, Liv. You're a game changer."

The air stalls in my chest. That almost sounds like a confession.

Say it. He needs to be aware of your boundaries.

"Sawyer, if you're unsure, if you think this is too much for you, then maybe we dial it back." I'm shaking inside, hoping he disagrees and tells me that's not what he wants.

His shoulders droop. "What does that mean, Liv?"

"We press pause on us. Take a step back. I don't want to be getting deeper into this if you don't know what you want or how you feel. And the show will only complicate that."

My breathing is shallow as I wait for him to respond. Reaching up, I ease his fingers away from his forehead, like I usually do when he's stressed and tries to rub it raw. And I wonder if I'm doing the right thing.

I'm pulled firmly against his chest. "No." His heart hammers against my ear. "I don't want to press pause. And I'm not unsure how I feel about you."

A sigh of relief rushes from my lips. "Good," I whisper into his shirt.

"Can we . . ." He chews on his words a moment. "I'd like to keep things as they are for now. Once the show is over, we'll have more time and freedom to be us, to take things further. Can we talk more then?"

I meet his troubled eyes and reluctantly nod. He takes hold of my chin, tipping my face up for a sweet kiss that begins to ease the distress churning inside me.

"I'm going to make you a grilled cheese sandwich—triple cheese—and then we'll take Daisy to pick up my vehicle, I'll grab Karl, and we'll all go for a hike, okay?"

This sneaking around isn't all it's cracked up to be. We'll have to go somewhere quiet and hope we don't run into anyone.

Someone seeing us all cozy together would throw another wrench into our complicated situation with the show.

Sometimes I wish the show were real. That I'd have entered as a real contestant because then, when he chose me at the end, it wouldn't be to get out of this stupid matchmaking game. It would be to let everyone know he wants to be with me, call me his girlfriend, and build something special with me.

CHAPTER
THIRTY-FOUR
OLIVIA

The savory aroma of my mom's spicy sausage rigatoni permeates the whole house, even out on the back patio where I've escaped for some quiet before my *date* arrives.

Mom decided to make Sawyer's favorite, serving it with extra cheesy garlic bread for me, and plenty of wine. At his first Meet-the-Family night with Raine, he was served brisket and a vast assortment of fancy sides. My mom decided to lean into comfort food, which had my enthusiastic approval.

I take a minute to enjoy my glass of wine and the calming effects of the cool evening air before the chaos begins. While also trying not to focus on the ways this could flop. Sawyer's probably fretting enough about that for the both of us. I'm more worried about my brothers.

Jaxon had no qualms about being here tonight. In fact, he seemed a little too eager. As did his surprise—uninvited—guest Anders, who's been over for dinner fairly regularly over the years but was stopped within three feet of the door by Stella and Miranda. The women are here in a "behind the scenes" capacity, acting as hosts in Sean's absence after he was called out for a semitruck emergency. And at that moment, I was grateful. We don't need anymore participants in our dinner. Especially my brother's nosy, drama-loving friends.

Brody and Jensen have been cagey though, not big on having our family dinner broadcast for the whole town—and other "online creepers" watching.

The door behind me creaks open, and a deep sigh resounds.

"You look nervous," Jensen observes as he takes a seat on the patio step beside me.

"We're getting close to the end. It's harder than I thought it would be," I admit quietly.

He nods, staring off toward the sunset painting the sky in a myriad of dusky, warm colors. "You told me you were just getting back out there, Livvie. That you wanted to prove to the nosy people in this town you weren't still into that asshole you never should have married."

He turns to me, awaiting my response, but I don't have one to satisfy him and I don't want to lie, so I keep my gaze locked on the sunset. Brody is usually the brother I confide in most. He might be quiet, serious, and surly, but he's a great listener.

"Sawyer wasn't supposed to let more happen, yet he told us pretty quickly into this whole thing that there was something more between you two. Now here we are, you introducing him to us like we haven't been friends for years. Then with Miranda and Stella showing up here, having some kind of secret meeting with Mom." He points behind him, lowering his voice. "And that weirdo, Lenny, is setting up to film the whole thing."

I smack him. "Don't call Lenny a weirdo."

"He touches things and then sniffs his hands immediately after. I also caught him rifling under mom's bathroom sink and using her body lotion." His thick brows quirk up at me.

I pull my lips back in an apologetic grimace. "Fine. *That's* weird. But it's only a couple of hours, then this will all be over."

"You're in love with him, so I very much doubt it."

My head snaps to the side to gape at my brother who tends to be the quiet one. "W-what?"

"You and him. Even before you met Drew, around Fletcher, you were always . . . I don't know. Soft? And now having to watch you two making eyes at each other like you do on the show might actually put me off mom's pasta. That jackoff better not ruin pasta for me. It's my main food group."

I squeeze my lips together, hiding my amusement. "What about burgers?"

"Don't try to change the subject. How serious is it between you two?"

That partially wipes the smile from my face. "You're awfully chatty today, big guy. You feeling okay?" I reach for his forehead.

He swats me away. "Olivia."

I avert my gaze. "Uh . . . it's serious. On my end anyway."

He sits up straighter, and his growing agitation is palpable as he shifts. I shouldn't have said a damn thing.

"It's not serious on his end?"

"Leave it, Jensen. Let's just get through this dinner."

"Fine, but I don't give a shit if Sawyer's basically family, if he hurts you, he's done. So tell me now what kind of dinner we're walking into."

"Why? You planning on asking him what his intentions are?"

"Yeah. It's what Dad would have done. He loved Fletch, but he'd have put up a front at first, grilled him a bit before patting him on the back and handing him a beer."

My nose tingles and eyes sting, wishing Dad were here. He'd have taken charge of this dinner, provided the perfect balance of stern and warmth.

"You can ask your questions, Jensen. Dad would have wanted that. And he'd have liked to see Sawyer squirm a little. Probably would have used 'the voice' on him." We both laugh at the memory of the booming voice Dad saved for special circumstances. Scared the shit out of all of us.

There's some commotion inside, Sawyer's deep voice resonating through the house. Jensen nudges my shoulder, tipping his head toward the door.

"Don't touch me with your dog-ball-hacking hands, sicko!" Jaxon shouts. "I heard you were running late because of a complication with neutering Mrs. Linden's Great Dane. Those are big balls, man."

A rough laugh echoes through the house. "No! Get away from me!" Through the door behind me, Sawyer chases Jaxon around the island with his hands outstretched.

"Him? You love *him*? You sure?" Jensen asks.

I sigh, smiling. "Yeah."

"How nice do you expect me to be?"

I put my arm around his shoulders. "Nice. But not too nice. It's what Dad would have wanted."

He stands and helps me up, a devious smile on his lips. "Deal."

"SO WE HEARD Raine's ex-boyfriend just about knocked you out at your last Meet-the-Family. Would you have fought him if her brother hadn't stepped in? Are you the kind of guy who fights for your woman?" Brody asks, having inside information about what happened after he was called to the scene.

Sawyer wasn't able to come over after because I was at the hospital, but I heard all about it—from multiple sources, all night long. He also messaged me immediately afterward giving me the rundown, telling me a bird fountain was destroyed, and Raine's ex was hauled away in cuffs. Which meant the evening ended early, and he hadn't been able to talk to her about not choosing her.

Another date disaster on the books, but Sawyer didn't seem

overly fazed by it, which was curious because it was quite the spectacle.

I prop my chin up on my fist, coolly watching my brothers turn on Sawyer.

In my defense, I tried to warn him that, while they usually fuck around together and talk about stupid shit without a care in the world, coming over as the man in my life for our first family dinner together would be a different situation.

He was *not* prepared.

"Those are two different questions, Brody. Would I have fought him? No. For several reasons." Sawyer puts his fork down, his second plate of rigatoni nearly empty. "Am I the kind of guy who would fight for *my* woman? Yes."

Okay, maybe he's a little prepared.

The spot in my chest that's been clenching tight shifts some more. This is like waiting in purgatory, hoping one day to find out my fate.

Yet, Sawyer and I are as close as we've ever been, probably more. He often holds me close, whispers both naughty and sweet things in my ear. We take turns choosing shows to watch while we cuddle on the couch, Daisy often joining us, Karl usually preferring the floor. And before he leaves, he kisses me like I'm the necessary breath of air you take before diving to the bottom of the deepest part of a pool.

But there are so many questions still between us. And I'm wondering if his fear of relationships will keep him from answering them.

And deep down I'm wondering if his fear of relationships will keep him from me too.

So I've agreed to give him time, but until he takes that next step, I have to be careful.

Brody's eyes dart to me before settling back on Sawyer.

"You haven't dated in a while, Fletch. Why is that?" Jensen asks next.

"Haven't found the right woman."

"Is Liv the right woman?" he returns.

"She's the perfect woman," Sawyer answers.

My face heats as his hand finds my knee under the table.

"And it took dating twelve women to realize that?" Jaxon asks, mouth half-full of food.

Oooh. Good one. I hide a smirk and turn, awaiting my man's response.

Sawyer's eyes narrow on his best friend. Jaxon shrugs in a way that tells Sawyer he's not acting the part of best friend right now, and he's going to have to get over it.

"No. I never wanted to date anyone. At all."

My head snaps toward him, the hair I smoothed into a sleek ponytail whipping me in the face.

"Oh?" my mom asks curiously. Until now, she hasn't chimed in during the onslaught of questions from my brothers.

"But then I was convinced to do this show, and I'm glad I did. Well, mostly. It's been a bumpy ride." He grins charmingly at my mom, and she practically melts, sympathy and adoration shining in her eyes.

It's quiet for a bit, nothing but the clatter of silverware against plates and the crunching of garlic bread.

Sawyer picks the cheese off his bread and puts it on my plate before finishing up the last of his pasta. I beam at him, savouring both the deliciousness of the cheese and his gesture.

"You love her, Fletch?"

Sawyer reclines in his chair, sweeping an arm to rest on the back of mine. I hold my breath, not expecting that question to come up.

"Jaxon . . . if I'm going to tell a woman I love her, I'd prefer to do so in private. And if I did, I sure as shit wouldn't tell you first."

He glares, offended. "I'm your best friend, asshole."

Lenny shushed him and mouths, *Language*.

"Not tonight. Right now, you're Liv's big brother. And that's the way it should be."

My brother nods before clearing his throat. "I have one last question, but I think it would be best to chat just the two of us."

Lenny is shaking his head and pointing at the table.

I'm sure it makes for a better show if everything is aired out in the open, creating increasingly tense dinner conversation. At this point, everyone watching probably sees this as a problematic family dinner and that it'll cause a rift between Sawyer and me. But this isn't too far off from how our usual dinners go. Cursing, shit-talking, and too much food.

I roll my eyes at my brother. "It's fine, Jaxon. just ask your question. That's part of what this night is about. Making sure everyone feels comfortable with what's happening between Sawyer and me," I tell him.

"I get you two have feelings for each other, but that's not what concerns me."

"No?" Jensen asks while my oldest brother grunts in disbelief.

"A couple weeks ago when we were out at Hewlett Park, we ran into Velora, and she seemed to think there was something between you two as well. I understand that's the nature of this process, but what's stopping you from choosing someone else, from taking everything Olivia has to offer for granted?" He barely pauses, not giving Sawyer enough time to do more than open his mouth. "The reality is that you might have similar feelings for someone else. Hell, you might even decide not to choose anyone at the end of this whole thing. Right?" He glances into the living room where Stella and Miranda sit, drinking wine off camera. Do they attend all the family dinners? "Can he do that?" Jaxon asks them.

They look at each other, a peculiar expression on Stella's face. They both nod, but it's slow, hesitant.

"Right. And Fletch, you've been telling me for months how you don't want a girlfriend. So where does that leave Liv?" His shoulders slump as he exhales roughly. "I'm not trying to be a jackass here, man. This is something that's been bugging me since you told me things were getting serious."

Sawyer's jaw tightens, nostrils flaring. He tears his eyes away from his best friend, seeming to be searching for words.

My mom attempts to defuse the situation. "Jaxon, maybe that's not fair—"

"No, it's fine, Mrs. Vaughn. It's a fair question." Sawyer peers back at me, lacing his fingers through mine. "It's a difficult one because there are other people's feelings at stake, and it's not fair to discuss it here instead of directly with those involved. I'll be talking to each woman personally about the future I'm hoping for."

"And have you spoken to Olivia?" This time it's my mom asking.

Sawyer turns to me, but I shift my gaze to my plate. His thumb moves over my palm, trying to comfort me without words.

"Liv and I have spoken. She knows my intentions." I glance up at him, not hiding my uncertainty.

"All right. That's good enough. For now, anyway," Jensen says, winking at me. "Let's grab the beers, head out back, and make Sawyer build the fire." He pushes away from the table.

I send him a grateful smile.

"Nuh-uh. All you shits at least clear the table," Brody barks at us. "Mom shouldn't be doing it all. Just because tonight's dinner was part of whatever the hell kind of whacked dating game the town's got going doesn't mean you should forget your fucking manners."

I smother a laugh while poor Lenny grimaces.

After clearing dinner, my brothers take Sawyer out to the backyard. But when I head out there five minutes later, my boyfriend—uh, man . . . friend? Nope. Man I'm seeing?—is soaked, and there's no evidence that they were anywhere near the fire pit.

Later on, once Sawyer gets the fire roaring, he plucks me up from my spot on the wooden bench and drops me into his lap.

Lenny leaves within thirty minutes since everyone seems to have quieted around the fire, too relaxed and comfortable to stir up anything exciting. Miranda and Stella follow shortly after.

"What happened?" I whisper into his ear, running a hand over his damp shirt.

"Your brothers and I had a private chat while Lenny stayed with you and your mom."

I lean my head against his shoulder, getting comfortable. "Did they get the Super Soakers out or what?"

"No. They sprayed me with the garden hose."

I snort into his neck. "What? Boys are so stupid. Why did they hose you?"

"I wouldn't answer the rest of their questions."

"Do I want to know?" I ask him.

"Nope."

"He wouldn't own up to what kind of relationship you two have when the cameras aren't rolling." Jaxon chimes in. "We're all pretty sure the touchy-feely crap we've all had to witness during the show is the tame version of what's going on. So we thought he might need to cool off a little tonight since that shit won't be happening here. He hasn't made a proper lady out of you, he doesn't get to fondle the goods in front of all of us."

My jaw drops. "Jaxon."

"He's not wrong," Jensen agrees, taking a sip of his beer.

"I know for a fact he's been staying at her house overnight, so *I* didn't need answers, but I did enjoy watching him cover his nips and yelling that they were going to snap off."

I peek down as Sawyer covers his pec with the hand not wrapped around me. My head tips back in an unladylike cackle.

His fingers dig into me as he tickles my sides. "Enjoyed that, did you?"

"Sorry, Stud. It was very honorable of you to try to maintain my virtue. But since we've had lots of sex, that ship has sailed."

A few shouts of outrage and disgust echo through the yard.

We stay up drinking and chatting until late into the night. I wind up nodding off in a camping chair Sawyer brought out from the garage. When it was time to leave, he scooped me up and carried me to his car without a peep from my brothers.

We end up at my house as usual, and he follows me in, slipping into bed with me. We don't talk, we don't do anything more than fall asleep holding each other.

When I wake up in the morning, he's already gone, but there's a cheese omelette waiting for me on the kitchen table with a note which reads, *Had to go in early, and you looked too cute to wake. Let's talk tonight after the last Meet-the-Family night.*

I take a huge bite of the savory eggs. Waking up without Sawyer is not how I'd hoped to start my day, but this sweet note and delicious breakfast is a close second.

THIRTY-FIVE
SAWYER

MOM: You're avoiding me.

S hit. Maybe I am. I hate keeping secrets from her—especially when she's aware I'm doing it.

MOM: I'm making a roast tomorrow. You can come over and fill me in on your last couple of date nights.

ME: Sorry, Mom. I'll be there tomorrow. I've just been busy and tired from work and all the show events.

MOM: Yes, I imagine it's exhausting pretending to be a thirty-two-year-old celibate.

Fuck, she's never going to let me live that down.

Sean appears in front of me, arms crossed. "You ready?"

I nod and send my mom one final message before embarking on another uncomfortable evening.

ME: Yep. And now your virginal son has his last Meet-the-

Family night to head off to. I'll call you later. Love you.

The producers have been trying to foster more excitement by having them all the same week, and it's been grueling.

Next week we'll have the ceremony so I can choose the remaining two contestants. Thankfully, there are no more group dates left. It's simply our individual preshow interviews and then handing out the daisies. After that I have a solo date with a contestant of my choice—I verified this. I've already decided Velora won't be moving on. My solo date with her made Liv uncomfortable, and I don't want to give her anything else to worry about.

I've had a few residents approach me about that date, and I imagine she's had as many approach her. A group of people even came into the clinic under the guise of spending some time with the shelter animals we've been treating. Instead, they grilled me and talked up their favorite remaining candidate all afternoon.

"Should we practice what I'm going to tell her again?"

"You've rehearsed it three times already. Please don't make me listen to it again. We had to send Lenny on a bogus errand to make sure he didn't hear or film any of it. And we need to keep it that way." He leans against the back fender of my vehicle. "So when you chat with Velora, be sure to stay off camera. Pull her aside, tell her, and then carry on with the night."

"Fine. I don't want to hurt anyone's feelings, but I'm done with all this. I mean, at this point, how many people know this is all bullshit? Brody said I've been reported going to Liv's house. And I'm almost certain Stella has known what Liv and I were up to from the start."

"Ah . . . you're finally confessing you got Liv to sign up as a contestant to bail you out of doing the show for real? Maybe skip those details in the Hometown Hottie Tells All or whatever the producers decide to call the post-show interview they'll want you and Liv to do."

"Nope. That's not fucking happening."

"But that's a yes to whatever fuckery you two cooked up at the start?"

I shrug, strangling the keys in my fist as we wait outside the grocery store for Lenny to grab whatever random item Sean told him we needed.

"Look, I know you're nervous, but soon you two will be free to be out in the open and all this will be over. The town and your mom will be content in the knowledge that they helped you find the love of your life." Something hitches in my chest. "Everyone will leave you alone, and you'll have enough leverage to duck out of any undesirable town event for at least a couple of years. But if you can't do this, if finishing the show is going to fuck things up for you—walk. Don't sacrifice your own happiness solely for the appeasement and entertainment of others."

I'd love nothing more than to walk. But I've come this far. "I'll spend some time with Velora's family, let her down gently, and then meet up with Liv to talk about the rest of the show. You might want to tell Stella how fucking obvious I'm going to be making it that I'm choosing Liv because I can't stay away from her, can't pretend I'm not completely in lov—"

Ah fuck. Sean was right. I'm so fucking in love with Liv, and I might accidentally let it slip during the show if I can't get my shit together.

Lenny jogs out of the store, hands over a bag, grabs his camera, and gets in the passenger seat. Sean gets in shortly after, and with a deep breath, I take my place behind the wheel. Before I've even pulled into the Afferton's driveway, Lenny's pointing a camera at me and giving me a live countdown.

Only two hours until I get to see Liv. Things have been tense lately, stuck in this situation, waiting. And if I'm being honest with myself, I think pulling away. Like she has to protect herself against me.

I've never been one to break hearts. I've fucked up plenty—my bad luck streak wasn't all on the women. But breaking a woman's heart means they'd have to truly love me, and I'm certain that hasn't been the case for most of my relationships. It never got that far.

Sneaking a peek at my phone, I'm disappointed when there are no notifications. Liv always sends some kind of "You won't embarrass yourself" confidence-bolstering text.

So this family meet-and-greet nightmare will have to wait for a moment while I check in with her.

ME: Meet at my place tonight?

LIV: Sawyer. You're live on your family date right now. You should NOT be texting me.

ME: You didn't answer my question.

LIV: Your place? I thought you didn't want to risk it.

ME: I want you at my place. Say 9:30pm? I put the key under the planter of azaleas my mom put on the front step.

It's marked as "read" but she doesn't respond.

LIV: Stop frowning, Stud. I'll be there.
LIV: I hear the Affertons are barbecuing, so fire will be involved. Steer clear of the grill, don't burn down the backyard, and it's all smooth sailing. But if anything happens, they have a large water feature you can seek refuge in. You got this.

I laugh, not because those are very real possible hazards, but because she cares enough, even when she's upset about our circumstances, to hope I don't make a fool of myself.

The car jostles violently. I look up, and Sean is waving his hands around, making sure to stay off-camera. He mouths, *What the hell are you doing?*

Right. Fuck.

"As I was saying . . . This is the last Meet-the-Family night, Sawyer. Do you know the Afferton family well?"

I focus on him instead of the camera pointed directly at me. "I see them around town regularly, and I know how involved Velora's mom, Katherine, is with the Town Council. But Velora and I were never in school together, ran in different circles. So this will be my first time at their house, meeting them in a personal capacity."

"Have you heard how her parents feel about her participation in this show? Do you expect there to be some resistance, or do you think you'll be welcomed inside with open arms?"

My brow wrinkles as I try not to glare at him. Plastering on a fake but dashing smile, I answer, "I'm hoping it's the latter. Better get in there and find out." I wink at the camera, grab the bottle of wine I brought, and escape the confines of the vehicle.

Sean follows closely behind, but Lenny hovers farther back, getting a wider shot of me approaching the front door.

"Wasn't trying to stir shit up. Simply planting a little doubt in case your chat with Velora has her or her family giving you the cold shoulder. Now people might think it has to do with their reservations about the show or the process."

I grunt at him, not wanting to acknowledge he might have a point.

I barely touch the doorbell before it flies open and Velora is there throwing herself at me.

Stepping back, I smile at her, holding up the bottle of wine as a physical buffer. "Velora. You sure you want to introduce me to your parents? I only bought one bottle of wine, and some tagalongs . . ." I tease, tipping my head toward Sean and the cameraman.

"Oh, stop. They already love you. I can't wait for you to get to know them better." She leads us into the house, her hand on my arm, which I slyly remove and place the wine bottle in.

Her pinched brows are the only indication she recognizes the distance I'm putting between us. "We have the back patio set up with refreshments and some light appetizers before dinner. They took down the spotlight aimed at your chair after some harsh negotiations, but you've been relegated to grilling the steaks tonight. Daddy says that'll be the real test anyway."

Guilt hammers at me. I can grill a steak with my eyes closed, but showing up at the house of a woman's parents under the false pretense of wanting to date their daughter is slimy. And letting Velora touch me and smiling at her as if I would ever return her affections . . . I can't do it.

Knowing Liv has to watch me be friendly with a woman who's constantly coming on to me hits like a punch to the gut.

I have to tell her now. I make eye contact with Sean, giving him a barely discernible shake of my head. His eyebrows go up in question. As we walk further into the house, I steer Velora into the office off the entryway, closing the French doors behind us.

Through the frosted glass, Lenny is standing in place, trying the handle without success. That'll have to be enough privacy.

Light streams in through the window behind Velora, casting a glow around her. It's bright and airy, with soft, soothing colors—a beautiful backdrop for an uncomfortable conversation. The sparkle of delight in her eyes and the soft giggle she releases as Lenny tries the door again makes me feel worse about what I'm about to say.

"Sawyer, we could probably have arranged some alone time later. While I'm definitely a fan of sneaking off for a private moment, my parents are expecting us outside, and—"

Sean calls for us once before hurriedly moving away from the door. He's speaking in the tone he uses when he's on camera.

"We need to talk for a minute before we head out there so we can both be on the same page. That okay?"

She steps closer. "Of course."

I stare down, running a hand through my hair. Velora slides both her hands up and down my arms, so I step back, letting her arms fall.

"I can't imagine how hard this must be for you. You've always been the reserved type, so to put you on display like this, especially when it comes to your love life . . . I don't want you to feel uncomfortable talking to me about anything. We're alone. Say whatever is on your mind."

She's gazing up at me adoringly, but something's not right about it.

Her eyes aren't hazel. They aren't warm with those bright specks of green that light up when she teases me, when she's turned on. These eyes don't look at me the same way. They're not Liv's.

"I appreciate that. And I'll need you to keep this conversation between the two of us, okay?" She quickly nods. Blowing out a tense breath, I continue. "This show has been especially difficult because I was more or less pressured into it." Her head jerks slightly. "I didn't want a girlfriend, a relationship, any of it. I moved back here to focus on my career. For a while, I had given up on finding someone. But then I did this show . . ."

Her hands move to my chest, a wide, sweet smile on her blood-red lips. Her heavily made-up eyelids blink in rapid succession at me. Are her fake eyelashes coming off? "And you found someone?"

A quiet acceptance has the cumbersome weight I've lugged around for weeks lifting off my shoulders. "Yeah, I did." A slow, sure grin pulls at my mouth.

Her head drops down in what I assume is disappointment, and I immediately switch to consoling her. Patting her back a couple of times, I say, "I know the timing is bad since we are about to have dinner with your parents, but I hope you understand why I thought it best to do this first."

She glances up, her hands moving to clutch at my shirt. Is she angry? I can't tell.

A clump of dark hair has fallen across her face, so I flick it out of the way to get a better look at her expression. "I'll be telling Raine as well so she knows I've made my choice."

"Are the producers having you go through with the rest of the planned events?"

"Yes, I need to see this through. But I wanted to warn you beforehand so you know how I feel, and that I've already chosen Li—"

With the strike speed of a viper, she's on me, attached to me. Her mouth on mine.

Velora is kissing me, and I have no fucking idea what the hell is going on. My hands wrap around her upper arms and abruptly remove her.

"There's been a serious misunderstanding here."

Her eyes blink up at me, mouth open, lipstick smeared.

Fuck, I probably have that shit on me. I swipe at my mouth, trying to get it off.

"What the hell was *that*, Velora?" Her shoulders droop in my grasp. I'm not letting go until I know she's not going to try shit like that again. "I was talking about Liv. It's been her since day one."

She tsks, pinching the bridge of her nose, tipping her head down.

"Velora?" I ask.

"I'm—I know, okay?"

"You know what?"

"You might have been talking about Olivia, think you love her, but you were supposed to give us all a fair chance. Spend time with all of us. You were right that you need to see the rest of this dating show through. That includes giving other women a chance, Sawyer."

Is that really how it works on other reality dating shows? The producers and contestants pressure the bachelor into giving women he's not interested in a fair shot? Taking them on dates, meeting their parents, kissing them . . . even if he has no intention of being with those women?

That's some bullshit.

"No. Velora, I'm done with pretending. I'll continue with the rest of the events but I don't want to encourage any unrealistic expectations. Would it have been better if I'd said nothing and out of the blue eliminated you next week?"

"You could've changed your mind. You've been so wrapped up in Olivia, following her around during group dates, sharing heated looks, touching her—you didn't even bother with the rest of us."

"I never planned to have anything real with any of you!" My voice is raised, and when Velora's eyes widen, I instantly regret it. All of it. What I said and how I said it. "Shit. Sorry. I meant I didn't want this, and Liv was my anchor. It was *me* who couldn't help falling for *her*. And I tried. I tried so damn hard. Because I didn't want to find my perfect woman. I knew either I'd fuck it up or someone else would." I throw my hands up. "And look at this shit show."

She frowns. "Sawyer, have you ever watched a reality TV show or a dating game show?"

Swiping a hand over my mouth, I answer, "No."

She sighs, long and loud. "They really chose the wrong guy for this. You're hot and charming—in your own way—so maybe that's why."

What did *that* mean?

"Look, that's how these shows go. It's dramatic and the process is questionable, but everyone is looking for that big romantic payoff at the end. They want to be twisted and turned as they watch each episode. They love it when the guy struggles with his decision. But the idea of having more than one love interest does occasionally anger some of the viewers who have a favorite or think he shouldn't be this conflicted. How you handle this is up to you." She points a finger, poking it into my chest. "And you'll likely get shit on either way. But the fact that you entered into this with no intention of finding love is *not* a secret I'd share with anyone else."

I think on this as she moves around me, placing her hand on the door handle.

"Come on, let's go have dinner with my folks. We'll keep things friendly, I'll divert as many questions as I can, then end it with a simple hug goodnight. Okay?"

I nod and grip the other door handle. We open it together, just as Sean and Lenny barge in the front door.

"Oh. There they are, ready to start dinner." Sean lets Lenny and his camera pass as the young man mutters, *Asshole*, under his breath.

We all walk together through the kitchen to the patio door.

Sean grabs my arm. "Lenny got your little chat on camera through the office window. Including the kiss. Just thought you should know."

Fuck.

Liv saw that.

And my mom . . . Everyone.

Even if I make it through this date without anyone getting hurt and nothing being destroyed, in reality, there's still one person who will be hurt. This time I managed to cause the destruction of a person—a relationship—without them even being present. The idea that this will hurt Liv hands down makes this the worst bad luck I've had yet.

The consequences of tonight's event may very well make the bit of bad luck I've had over the years seem like a cozy walk in the park.

CHAPTER
THIRTY-SIX
OLIVIA

S awyer . . . is telling her right now? Right before he meets
her parents? I thought he was going to wait until after the
dinner so she didn't act all weird and pouty?

"Oh. Did he just lock them in the office?" My mom speaks the
question the rest of us were thinking.

The cameraman tries to get in, prying at the French doors. He
gives up and goes outside.

What the hell is happening?

Sean appears on screen for a moment, a frown on his face,
before disappearing again.

Then through the front window of the house, we're shown the
inside of the office where Sawyer and Velora face each other. She
steps closer as he talks, running his hands through his hair.

"Harper is going to be pissed she missed this," Ellie states,
her mouth half-full of popcorn. "She hates Velora more than all of
us combined."

I stay quiet, not able to say anything in front of either of the
moms present.

Velora slides her hands up and down Sawyer's arms, in a
sweet, intimate gesture, which makes my jaw clench.

278

They talk for a while as Sean tries to get in front of the camera, speculating about their conversation and suggesting they go back in and try knocking again so the date can begin.

The cameraman stays, zooming in on the couple.

Suddenly Sawyer and Velora are embracing. Her head appears to be on his chest, his hand is on her back.

And then they're kissing.

They're *kissing*.

"What . . . ? Why did he . . ." I say, my cracked voice barely above a whisper.

Sean jumps in front of the camera and says something, but I don't hear it. I can't hear it.

"No way. That asshole," Ellie shrieks from beside me.

Jane stands up, but I don't dare look at her. Because she'll see it. She'll know.

I'm in love with her son, and he just broke something inside me. Something I swore I'd never allow within anyone's grasp—not after seeing my mom fall to pieces.

The future I want . . . ? The one I was supposed to see and plan with the man I'll spend forever with? Sawyer's the man I saw that with. He's always been this incredible possibility. A man I've always looked at and knew he'd make the best of husbands. The kind of husband you stare at and think about how fucking lucky you are that he chose you.

So what happens if you find that man and he doesn't choose you back?

Maybe I'll finally learn that everyone puts their own interests first.

That love only provides happiness when it's convenient for the other person, when it suits *their* desires.

Well, if the moment I decide to let in a man I could actually picture spending forever with, he doesn't choose me, there's only one solution.

I choose me. That's what I used to do. I walk away. I don't let anyone fuck with me, mess with my head. And I definitely don't let them break my heart.

"Liv?"

I turn to my mom, whose eyes are turned down at the corners, worry etched into her features.

"Hmm?"

"We turned it off honey, but you're still staring at the television."

"Sorry. I, um, I'm going to go home," I tell them.

"Sweetie, you're already home," Jane tells me.

"Oh, right. Sorry, all the drama was a lot for me tonight."

"Should we go?" Ellie's soft voice asks.

"I'll be leaving soon anyway," Sawyer's mom murmurs. "I have somewhere to be as soon as the show ends."

I don't. I'm not going anywhere, not anymore.

"Promise us you won't turn it back on," my mom requests.

"Don't worry. I don't think I'll be watching any more episodes," I assure her.

Her mouth twists. "Well, I think I'll stay anyway. I'll make some tea and we can—"

"Mom. I'm fine. This is what I signed up for, right?"

She collapses back onto the couch, so she's obviously not leaving anytime soon.

"I never—I guess I didn't think about the details. About what might happen when I encouraged you to go on the show." She tucks her shoulder-length hair, which she colors several shades lighter than mine, behind her ear. "When Stella asked, I figured I'd just see what you thought about Sawyer doing the show. Feel out if my instincts were right. I should have thought how hard it would be when he had to date other women." She frowns, tsking at herself. "I'm a shit mom for setting you up to get hurt."

"I approached *you* about the show, Mom. This isn't your fault. It's not anyone's fault. It's how this thing goes, right?"

Jane chimes in. "No. If there's blame to be laid on anyone, it's me. If anyone's the shit mom, it's me. I sent you the application, Olivia. Then I urged Lilah to cancel her plans with you and asked Sawyer to pick me up some food from the Horton Beach food trucks. It was *my* idea to send you the application and arrange for your encounter at the beach." The words come out in an exasperated ramble.

"Stop it, you two," Ellie chastises. "Did you see them from that first show? You were right, they are into each other. They have been from the beginning."

"Yeah, and then we shoved more women at him," Jane nearly shouts. "And I think we all know Miranda changed the rules so Sawyer was forced to go out with more of the contestants. And now look! He's been sucked in by that fake-boobed, perfect-skinned vagina trap of a woman."

I snort-cough so hard I accidentally spit on myself. *Vagina trap?* I store that gem of an insult away for later. I can't fully appreciate it right now.

"Vagina trap?" Leave it to my best friend to ask what the rest of us were dying to but I sure as shit couldn't vocalize.

"She's the human equivalent of a Venus flytrap. With her feminine parts." She waves a hand down there. "You know, her vagina."

Yep. That's exactly the explanation I was hoping for. Maybe I'll get Jane to keep talking so I can stay thoroughly distracted. Too distracted to think or feel or react about what happened with my non-boyfriend—the man I'm in love with, who kissed another woman under wildly confusing, suspicious circumstances.

"Regardless of how tonight's clandestine embrace happened" —why does that make it sound so much worse?—"I'll be talking to him," Jane asserts. "Just because he's on a dating show doesn't mean he should be intimate with several women at once. I did *not* raise him that way."

And that's when I remember the conversation we had about intimacy on the show. The first conversation, where we agreed that some small acts of physical intimacy would be necessary. And the last conversation, where he made promises of exclusivity.

And like a fool, I believed it. I never thought for a second I couldn't trust him. He's a great guy, one of the best guys I've known since before I even became seriously interested in the opposite sex.

Maybe this is why he didn't want to label anything or fully commit before the end of the show. Has something been between them the whole time or is it recent?

I don't let myself get in the middle of crap like this.

"Ellie's right. We may have nudged them, but it's only been about those two since day one," my mom tells Jane, her voice soft.

"It wasn't real," I tell them calmly.

"Oof. Shit's about to go sideways now . . ." Ellie mutters, settling deeper into the couch.

My mom's face contorts into a deep frown. "What?"

"I was helping Sawyer. He didn't want to do the show, and the town was giving me a hard time about Drew. I offered to be a fake contestant he could choose to go on dates with, pick as his girl-friend at the end." Jane settles on the couch next to my mom. "But I'm not sure it had ever been that simple. There were feel-ings from early on. Or maybe for years, I don't even know." I cover my mouth, breathing noisily through my nose. "And then we got closer, forced to be physically close, touching and flirting. We'd get together some nights and talk—about the show, ourselves, everything really."

Mom's wide eyes blink rapidly at me, gazing down, absorbing the news. Then she looks up at Jane and frowns. Sawyer's mom is slack-jawed, frozen in place, completely silent.

Turning back toward me, she asks, "You weren't interested in dating him? You were helping him avoid dating the women we chose for him?" Her words are slow, careful.

Jane is covering her mouth, a frown etched into her forehead. When she brings her gaze back to me, her eyes are filled with concern.

"Yes," I answer. "Kind of, but then everything changed."

"Baby girl. What were you two thinking?" Mom asks.

"I thought I was helping. I wanted to support him. But I think I also wanted to be around him." I turn to his mom. "He's had a hard time dating, and I'm a twenty-eight-year-old divorcée. So helping my handsome, single friend by being a fake contestant appeared to be a reasonably good idea at the time. But then I had to go and fall for your son. So hard. And I have no idea where we stand, what he's feeling."

Mom grabs my hand and pulls me down between them, both women wrapping their arms around me.

Jane speaks up. "And now I know why he's been avoiding me. But I think it had more to do with his very *real* feelings for you, Olivia. That son of mine, he's not too keen on being vocal about the big things, that's for sure."

"I think the rest of this conversation is going to require more wine," my mom announces. We all nod in agreement, Ellie offering to help and getting her own non-alcoholic beverage top-up.

"I don't know what exactly happened on the show today, Sawyer will have to answer for that. And while your relationship might have started off fake, there's not a doubt in my mind that he cares about you. He doesn't often talk about his relationships or girlfriends. But he brings you up almost without meaning to. He shuts down right away, not wanting to open that door given the situation he's in and my tendency to dig when something interests me. The quiet men in our family require persistence."

I nod numbly as the women around me continue to reassure, placate. I love them for it, but I also need some time to get my head straight.

Because the swoony, lovesick part of me has curled up in a

ball, holding tight to the love she found and wants to keep. But the part of me that's been cheated on, that's kept walls up for the last decade, warns that this could very well destroy me.

And that's when I know I can't keep doing this to myself.

Sticking to what we first agreed on—me being his ringer—might be what we need to return to.

So I'll tuck away all the hurt, the love, and the dreams of a future I'd already started building in my mind.

CHAPTER
THIRTY-SEVEN

SAWYER

When I pull up to my place after the friendly but thankfully short dinner I just sat through, my mom's vehicle is parked in front of my house.

That doesn't bode well for me. Especially with Liv coming over soon.

Unlocking the door, I say, "Mom? Where are you?"

"Here." I jump and drop my keys as she reveals herself from behind the front door, standing with arms crossed in front of the entryway closet.

"Jesus."

"Let's go sit," she suggests.

"Dad here?" I ask, hopeful.

"No. He didn't want any part of this until after I was done with you."

Done with me?

I lead the way to the kitchen and get us both a drink. Mom turns down the wine I offer, which is surprising. She settles for the sparkling flavored water I keep in the fridge for her.

"You watched the show."

"Not all of it. We shut it off after you two locked yourselves in a room and started kissing."

I take a long, deep breath. "That's not exactly what happened, Mom."

"Maybe. Maybe not. But I'm going to ask that you consider what it looked like. Do you have feelings for her or is it simply physical?"

I rake both hands through my hair, pulling in frustration. The hint of fire in her eyes tells me she's baiting me on purpose. And it's working.

"It's neither. It was a misunderstanding and I stopped it."

"It didn't look like a misunderstanding, Sawyer."

"It barely lasted two seconds, and then I moved her off me."

"Not what we saw, my boy. Though, I guess maybe Sean stepped in before we could see anything else." Fucking great. "But before that, you two looked very . . . intimate."

Trying to be a nice guy is for chumps. Lesson learned.

"I was trying to inform her I wasn't interested in her. Velora had other ideas. I was telling her about how I'd already chosen someone, and she pounced."

"You told her you were going to choose Olivia and then she kissed you?" Her head is quirked to the side, scepticism mixing with disappointment.

I think back to what I'd said to her. The speech I'd planned got tossed aside early on, leaving me to speak off-the-cuff.

I told her I was all-in with Liv.

Right?

Oh fuck. I'm not sure I did. I said I'd already found the woman I want but not who that woman was. She had to know though. It's always been Liv. Even when I told myself it was all pretend.

"Um. So I might have missed mentioning Liv's name specifically in my speech, but Velora had to know I wasn't talking about her and me. I may have flirted with the other contestants a little, turned up the charm a bit, but I never said anything to imply I was seriously interested or that they were who I wanted."

"You're technically not allowed to divulge that on camera anyway, Sawyer. The women are supposed to go solely off the connection they believe exists between you two." Her eye roll is a full body effort. "Good grief," she mutters.

I can't even imagine how bad it must have looked if Lenny caught the whole thing.

"Yeah, well, I screwed it up. Big fucking surprise."

"Sawyer Lance, watch your mouth. But yes, you did."

I'm so angry at myself, a slight tremor shakes my voice as I ask, "How did she take it?"

Hesitating, my mom's mouth turns down at the sides. "She was upset. We turned it off, but she kept staring at the screen."

Fuck. I check my watch and realize it's nearly 9:30 p.m. She'll be here any minute, and I'm not sure what the hell to say to her or how to make this right.

"And then she told us about your arrangement." She tilts her head at me expectantly.

This just keeps getting worse.

"Mom . . . I was either going to bail on the show or make a complete ass of myself. Both were less than ideal options. So Liv suggested I ask someone I knew and trusted to become a participant."

"So you lied to everyone and had Liv—your best friend's sister —become a fake contestant? What you two had wasn't real?"

"Is that what she told you? That we weren't real?" My voice is rough, desperate.

My mother doesn't answer. She waits, searching my face as if trying to see deep into my soul. Hell, maybe she can.

"She wasn't fake," I say through clenched teeth. "None of it has been fake for a long time."

Mom's tilted smile breaks through her previously flat expression. "I know. But I think she's questioning that. I'm going to guess you haven't been forthcoming about your feelings with your girlfriend."

I hesitate. "We're together, hopefully still are, but she's not technically my girlfriend. Not yet."

"You mean, because of the show?"

"Partly . . . I'm serious about her. Maybe too serious, and I'm not sure what to do with that." My fingers begin their disdainful attack on my forehead. "I don't want to fuck it up. I thought waiting until the show was over and then seeing how things went would be best. But honestly, I just don't know what the hell I'm doing."

"Oh, honey—"

Banging at the door interrupts us. As much as I'm hoping it's Liv, I can tell it's not. That knock doesn't belong to my dainty-fisted beauty—no matter how much anger or resentment she may have.

Mom follows behind me as I move toward the door.

I know who it is before I open it and brace for impact.

Jensen shoves me back mercilessly, slamming me into the wall. He points at me, "I warned you, didn't I?" My shirt is already in his fist.

"Jaxon's on a twelve-hour night shift, otherwise he'd be here too." I look down at my shirt to make sure there isn't a laser sight focused on me, courtesy of Liv's ex-special forces big brother.

So far so good. I'll take my ass-kicking though. I deserve it.

Jensen glances at my mom, who is hovering behind me. "Shit. Hi, Mrs. Fletcher."

"Hi, honey. You're off tonight?" she asks casually, like her son isn't about to be pummeled.

"Yeah. Was grabbing a beer with Brody, and Harper was there, fuming mad. Got the short version of what happened, so I thought I'd stop by for a chat. There was a disturbance at the bar, which Brody is handling, but he'll be by later for a friendly check-in too."

Liv's armed brother is stopping by late at night. Perfect.

"Oh. Well, don't let me stop your little visit."

Jensen's eyes flicker to me, narrowing with violent intent. With my mom here, he won't do anything and we both know it.

"What I have to say isn't exactly meant for polite company."

"Completely understand. You can take this 'conversation'"—she uses air quotes—"outside if you prefer. Safer that way anyway."

Is my mom advocating for Jensen to kick my ass?

"Mom. Really?"

She shrugs. "Best you two get this out of the way, so you can both move on."

A sinister, triumphant smile takes over Jensen's face. He moves to the side, sweeping out a beefy arm, gesturing for me to step outside.

Shit.

A phone rings, and Jensen reaches into his pocket, frowns and silences it. Turning back to me, he says, "Let's get to it, Fletch."

His phone rings again and he takes another look. Cursing, he answers it. "What's up?"

He listens for a minute, and I glance at my mom, who's on her phone too. She glances up, raises her brows much too innocently, and then tucks it away.

"No. We're just talking." Jensen glares at me but keeps talking to whoever is on the phone. He rolls his eyes while he listens. "He's fine. I haven't touched him."

After a few beats, he huffs. "Fine. I'll go, but he and I *are* going to have a conversation if he doesn't fix this."

His gaze fixes on me again as he hangs up, sliding his phone back into his pocket.

"Looks like my sister doesn't want us to talk yet. But I also don't think she wants to talk to you *at all*, so I'm sure I'll be back."

"That was Liv?" I ask him. "She was supposed to come over."

He snorts. "Yeah, that's not happening."

I'll go to her then.

"And you're not going over there either. Got me?"

I frown. Nope. "I'll leave that up to Liv."

My phone vibrates, and with my shit luck, I'm not sure I want to read any of my messages tonight.

I take it out and look anyway.

LIV: We need to talk, but not tonight. I'm upset, and I know we're not technically together in an official capacity, but it hurts all the same.

Because I knew I'd fuck it up! I mentally shout.

ME: I want to see you, Liv. To explain.

LIV: I can't, Sawyer. I want to be alone. I think I need to be alone for a while.

ME: No. I'm coming over.

LIV: Don't, Sawyer. We'll talk about the show another day. Good night.

I don't give a fuck about the show, so I sure as shit don't want to talk about that when I get to see her. I want to talk about *us*.

Looking away from my phone, my mom is at my side, her jacket in her hands, and she's staring at me. Seems like Jensen has already left.

"Give her some time, honey. And get some sleep, okay?"

I kiss her on the cheek and watch her leave.

By midnight, I'm done with waiting and this feeling churning inside me. So I get in my car and go to her.

I'm sitting in front of her house. Parked right out front because I don't fucking care anymore.

My feet carry me to her front door, and my heart beats in an anxious, angry rhythm. After knocking, I listen for her, wondering if she can even hear me, if she may be asleep.

I knock again, still not hearing anything. I prop my hands against the door jam and lean my head against the door.

"Liv," I say, voice raised enough to carry into the house but not enough to wake her neighbors. "Liv, come to the door. Please."

I knock again and keep at it until she says, "Sawyer, I told you to leave me alone."

"Open up, gorgeous. We need to talk."

The deadbolt unlocks, and the door opens a crack.

"Say what you need to and then please go. It's late."

"Can I come in?" I ask.

"Not tonight."

Shit. "Liv, it's not what it looked like."

She keeps her gaze down at my feet. "Yeah," she scoffs, "I've heard that before."

I tip her chin up at me. "It's true."

And then I take in her puffy eyes and red-rimmed nose. She's been home crying because of me. Because I'm a fuckup.

"Baby, she kissed me—not the other way around—but I'm so fucking sorry you had to see that."

"You kissed her back."

I frown. "No. I—"

"You didn't stop her or push her away. You let it happen. That's not what a guy who has feelings for someone else does. Not a guy I'd want to be with."

I should have watched the show on The Vine before coming over. "I *did* push her away, but I know it must have looked bad. I didn't think I was being inappropriate. *She* was inappropriate with *me*."

She laughs but it's clipped. "Maybe you think that because you don't have much experience with what it means to be a decent boyfriend," she throws at me.

Ouch. That one stings.

"If you enjoy that kind of attention and think it's appropriate to have private, sweet moments with other women who *clearly* want you, I think we may have identified one of the relationship problems you've had over the years. And it has nothing to do with luck."

She crosses her arms in front of her while I let her blow land. Her thinking I'm shitty boyfriend material hits deep.

You shouldn't have let her get close, touch you. Not even for the show.

I should have thought about how that would affect Liv.

Fuck this show for complicating the one truly good thing I've experience in a long time.

Having her is the only kind of luck I want for the rest of my life. Doesn't she know that?

She growls under her breath. "See? This is why I didn't want to talk tonight, Sawyer. I'm hurt and upset, and all of this is bringing up bad memories."

Of her relationship with Drew? She's comparing me to Drew.

I nod, swiping my tongue across my teeth, not sure what the hell else I can say.

"I'm fully invested in this, in you, in us. And you're still unsure."

"Liv, no. But there's so much going on right now, and I worry if we try to take things to the next level, it'll all go to hell." I rake my fingers through my hair, shame and desperation at war inside me. "In my experience, calling you my girlfriend is a guaranteed relationship grenade. All the fucked-up shit that always happens will start happening to us—to you. And I don't want that."

Maybe it'll take a few days, a few weeks, but it's every time.

She growls out her frustration. "So that's it? You're going to let your relationship issues, your 'curse', prevent you from ever having a real girlfriend? That's not a curse, Sawyer—it's self-sabotage."

"Liv, let's sit down and talk about this." She doesn't budge. Fine. I can stand here all night and try talking my way out of this mess if necessary. "I thought it would be best if we waited for the show to end. I needed us to get through all this first."

"And I needed a bit of security in knowing that the man I've fallen in love with feels the same way about me as he goes out with other women—even if they aren't real dates." It's everything I want to hear but not how I wanted to hear it.

"You don't have to worry about me with other women, Liv."

Her eyes bug out. "Are you kidding me? Look at where we are right now. What caused this."

I wonder what my conversation with Velora might have looked like on camera. From Lenny's position at the window, it probably seemed like we were embracing.

Fuck this show.

"Liv, I've been balancing on a very thin line to make sure no one's feelings get hurt—especially yours."

She peers up at me, eyes searching, wary.

"I've never given all of myself to someone, and I need to be sure the person I love is willing to take that leap with me. I don't want to hold back anymore, I want it all." She straightens, taking a heavy inhale. "What do *you* want, Sawyer?"

You.

But I'm afraid I can't keep her. She'll get hurt or things will end badly, and it'll be my fault.

"Listen, I know I'm just one option for you, and I—"

"You're not just an option, Liv. It's you. It's only you."

"Then I need you to tell me what we're doing without it hovering over us for weeks. I don't want to feel this way, Sawyer,

AMY ALVES

and I don't want to invest any more of myself if we're not going to work out or this isn't what you want."

I hesitate and she flinches with hurt.

She doesn't know she means so much to me that I'm fucking terrified.

Of fucking it up. Of losing her. Of not deserving her.

"Liv. I don't want to hurt you, and I hate that I have." Tears gather in her hazel eyes. I plant my hands on either side of the doorway, dropping my head down. "Deep down, I knew this would happen."

"Sawyer, listen, this is a sore spot for me. So if you're not ready, if you're not feeling the same, not ready to commit, I get it but I can't—"

I straighten, unable to make eye contact as I try to get a grip on myself. She's right to break things off before I hurt her any more than I already have. She doesn't trust me, trust that I'll put her first, that I'll be what she needs.

"No, you were right before." I was supposed to focus on my career. I wasn't supposed to fall for her. And I dragged her into my mess. "I should have let you take a step back like you wanted. This isn't fair to you."

She goes still.

I back out of her house and turn, pounding down the steps.

"Sawyer. What does that mean?" she shouts.

Opening my car door, I answer, "You don't deserve this. You deserve everything, not the bullshit relationship you'd have to settle for with me." The tightness in my chest seizes when those gorgeous eyes lift, filled with shock and so much hurt.

Fuck me.

She's still standing on her front steps when I drive off, and a part of me believes walking away from her is for the best.

The other part—the bigger part—is calling me an idiot. It's tempting me to go back and find how I can get her to forgive me for being a fuckup, and beg her to put up with all the inevitable

294

bumps in the road—the normal ones, not the ones placed in front of us by meddlesome townspeople with a penchant for drama.

My luck turned around in time for me to find a woman I want more than anything or anyone. But whatever good luck Liv brought my way would never have lasted, and I'd never have been able to keep her.

CHAPTER
THIRTY-EIGHT
OLIVIA

Normally the smell of coffee and bacon intermingling with the sweet decadence of fresh waffles would put me at ease. Which is why I thought meeting Ellie and Liam at the Kozy Kitchen Diner after their prenatal appointment would help settle me enough to celebrate their exciting news.

Instead my chest aches, my mind is wandering, and I feel twitchy being out in public. Other than work, I didn't leave my house for days after I told Sawyer I was ready to share every part of my life with him. Instead, he ripped my heart out and left me on my front steps.

People all around are staring, talking, and some are even approaching us.

Being part of LoveVine, I knew I'd garner some additional attention. But this is like being a local celebrity, and I hate it. I want to scream at them that we have real feelings, real problems, and that Velora isn't the problem between Sawyer and me—*he* is.

I helped out a friend who didn't want a girlfriend, was against dating in general. Then I fell in love with him like a moron and got my heart broken in the kind of completely devastating heart-break I haven't felt since I was a teenager.

My stomach churns, the threat of tears burning the backs of my eyes. See? This is why I don't want to talk or think about my situation.

I glare at the table of women next to us.

My mess of a love life isn't up for discussion.

Rationally, I realize that, as a contestant on a dating show, my love life kind of *is* up for discussion. The whole point is to stir drama, emotions, and uncertainty. Who will he choose? How does he feel? Are all the participants okay with the fact that he's interested in more than one woman or has there been some behind-the-scenes fighting?

Today the most obnoxious source of the meddling is coming from our own server. Other lunchgoers have been sending her over to eavesdrop and ask questions.

Ellie sighs and cranes her neck, searching for Kody, the owner of the diner, before turning her full attention to our server. "Listen, Lark, I'm going to ask that you stop trying to ask Olivia sneaky questions about the show. Every time you do I'll be answering with a fun pregnancy fact. Like, did you know that pregnant women are more susceptible to constipation, which can lead to hemorrhoids both inside and outside of the poop shoot? And when wiping, those suckers bleed like a bitch. I mean, they're essentially swollen, angry veins trying to escape the rock-solid demon poop trying to vacate the poor woman's bowels."

My sweet, graphically inappropriate hero.

I clamp my lips together and watch the young lady back away from our table with a disgusted sneer.

Ellie is not an aggressive person, so she must know I don't have it in me to drum up the sass or vitriol to ward them off today and stepped in.

Because the moment my walls crumbled and I fell from my "stay away from swoony men who could make you love them" perch, I put myself in this situation.

And I have to continue on, knowing I have the potential to

love in a way there's no coming back from. But if Sawyer doesn't want that, if he doesn't feel the same way, there's not a damn thing I can do about it.

"Sorry, Livvie. I didn't think grabbing lunch would be this much of a spectacle."

"It's fine. A hot bachelor choosing between multiple love interests is fascinating. Especially in Vaughn. We haven't seen this kind of all-encompassing, fabricated drama since Vaughn's Sexy Secret Valentine event years ago." Liam frowns and opens his mouth to say something, then shakes his head, keeping quiet. "Once the show is over, it'll die down."

The tension between Sawyer and me might not though. We'll have to talk. Especially since our families are so close. I have to keep my shit on lockdown. Bury those feelings.

I haven't heard from him or seen him in days. It's as if someone came and stole all the color from my life. Word of our front porch confrontation made its way quickly to my brothers and my mom. They check in, but I can't pretend to be okay in front of them like I need to, so I've been keeping to myself.

I tell myself I should be grateful we were only together a couple of months. Imagine how I'd feel if we were a year into this. Five years? Married?

Because I had imagined it.

No more cocky fuckboys, no bad boys, and no charming, man-of-your-dreams kinds of guys either.

Which I'm pretty sure will leave me celibate. And that's fine by me.

Because I'm not sure I'll ever rid my mind or heart of Sawyer Fletcher. Of how he smells and tastes, how he looks when he first wakes up, the way it feels to have him hold me.

Love is haunting.

My phone pings with a text, and I have to fight the urge to check it.

"You going to get that?" Ellie asks, gesturing with a forkful of lasagna.

It's likely either my mom, brothers, or *him*.

"Nope. I'm having lunch with you in celebration of your baby boy." I cup my hand around my mouth and whisper, "How soon will you be taking your husband to choose paint colors for the baby's room?"

"It's no secret, Olivia. She told me before our appointment today we'll be heading into the city to do some paint and decor shopping if we were able to find out the gender. She even borrowed Brody's pickup for it, so I'm preparing for a truckload of baby stuff."

I laugh, glancing back at Ellie.

"What? We need baby stuff, and I've waited five months for this day."

"You've only known about your little peanut for over three months, El," I point out.

She rolls her eyes. "I had a feeling before then."

Her husband snorts. "Baby, we weren't even trying. We figured if it happens, it happens. And boom. Pregnant."

Pushing back from the table, she grabs her crossbody bag off the hook on the side of the booth we're in.

"Don't ruin this for me. I'm excited. Let me buy all the things. And tacos. I want spicy chicken tacos."

Liam's brows shoot up before staring pointedly at the empty plate in front of his wife. Kody has a soft spot for kids and pregnant women, so instead of the lunch-sized portion, Ellie received a heaping full-sized lasagna. "But Els, you just had an entire—"

Cutting him off before he lands himself on her shit list all afternoon, I say, "Make sure to put some things on a baby registry so the rest of us have something to buy."

"We have an appointment in about an hour." She beams. "Which means, we should get going, babe."

Liam loops an arm around her and helps her slide out to stand.

"Oh shit," she whispers.

Worried, I glance over at Ellie, who is staring at the entry to the diner.

"Want us to stay a bit longer, Olivia?" Liam asks.

With his back to us, I don't immediately recognize the tall man in the baseball cap. On instinct, I almost take Liam up on his offer. Because that is not the ass of the man I've been avoiding all week.

The man who is headed straight for me is a different kind of ass.

"No, no. You two get going. I can handle him."

Ellie seems uncertain but lets Liam lead her outside.

My ex-husband stops in front of me.

"Olive," he says, greeting me with the nickname he's used since our first date.

Taking my cash out, I make eye contact with Lark a few tables down and flash her the money before setting it on the table.

"Drew. I hadn't heard you were in town." I fake a smile, not bothering to say it's good to see him—it isn't.

Spinning on my heels, I've barely taken more than three steps toward the door before he calls me again. "Olivia, come on. Hold up."

I look behind me, sigh, and then tip my head motioning for him to follow me outside.

Scanning the street, I walk directly to the Nissan truck his parents bought for him. Then he can leave when he's finished talking.

"You here visiting family?" I ask, trying to get the ball rolling.

"Yeah. Mom and Aunt Beth have been keeping me informed on what's been going on here." His tone holds a note of disapproval.

He disapproves of the way *I've* been living? That's rich.

"Liv, I hate to see you embarrassing yourself like this. I might have hurt you, but you're being unrealistic. My mom said you've been having a hard time on the dating show you signed up for. I've only been here for a few hours and I've had four people approach me about what my ex-wife has gotten herself into." He moves to place a comforting hand on my shoulder, but I shrug him off.

"I'm dating, Drew. Which is none of your business. I was ready to get out there but haven't dated in a while. Sawyer is . . . he's the ideal boyfriend—charming, smart, accomplished, reliable, hot as hell, with a biteable ass." I should know, I've definitely taken a nip at it. "Why wouldn't I have signed up for that?"

Drew scoffs, staring at me for a while before throwing his head back with a dark bark of a laugh. "You doing this to try to make me jealous?"

"No. I couldn't care less what you think. I decided to go after what I wanted. There's no embarrassment. Whether Sawyer and I end up together is absolutely none of your concern. Just like whether or not you're still fucking your clients is none of mine. Not anymore."

He rocks back on his heels, slyly looking around. "You promised not to share that information."

"And you promised to tell your parents the truth about why we divorced."

He rolls his eyes, shrugging one overly bulky shoulder. "Guys stray, Liv. It's how we are, how we're built."

No, you're just a bag of dicks.

"Being married doesn't mean the same thing to men as it does women," he explains like the prick he is. "There are advantages, sure. I thought of our marriage like a partnership, but it ended up being a prison. The kind of marriage you wanted didn't work for either of us."

"Well, congratulations, you escaped. Now, kindly fuck off."

"Fine. I just thought I'd come see you and let you know that if you were doing this for my benefit, to prove a point, you can stop. I still care about you, babe, and I think it's time we move on from all this bullshit."

I interlace my fingers, locking my hands together to keep from reaching for his throat.

"I *have* moved on, Drew. You haven't been more than a fleeting, annoying thought in months."

He grins, lowering his eyes for a quick, full-body appraisal. "You miss me," he declares with a wink.

God, he's the worst. How did I end up with this douche?

Clearing my throat to temper the screech that's waiting, I tell him, "Drew. Even if Sawyer doesn't choose me, even if I'm alone for years and no one ever loves me—I still wouldn't want to get within spitting distance of you."

And now I won't be able to stop thinking about spitting in his face . . .

He shakes his head. "Always so feisty. I'll admit, most of the time I find it attractive. But not being able to turn it into angry sex makes it less appealing and a lot more exhausting."

"I could see how caring about other people's feelings and being a decent human being *would be* exhausting for you."

His eyes darken as he moves in closer to me, his breath fanning down on my face as he says, "Hmm. I changed my mind. It's still hot. Your face flushes, bringing out a few more of those freckles you like to hide, your eyes brighten, your chest heaves. You look delicious, Olive."

I glare at him, reining in my temper. I do *not* need this shit today. He's so used to complimenting me, smooth talking me with his douchebag swagger. No. Not today. Not ever again.

"Back off, Drew." I push him away, and he holds up his hands, backing up a couple steps in compliance.

"Look, this is the last thing I'll say, and then I'll leave." His hands go in his pockets. "I don't think he's what you need. I've known him for years too, okay? And I've heard all the rumors too."

He doesn't know shit. But that doesn't matter.

"I still think you and I could make it work, babe. And I think if we sat down and figured out some realistic expectations and you chilled out a bit, we could be happy again."

"Drew. No. So much no. *Forever* no." My hair blows into my eyes as the breeze picks up. I fling it out of my face, letting out a frustrated growl. Even the air is fucking with me today. "I don't even *like* you anymore. And I am not into disgusting men who can't keep their dicks in their pants." Looking back, I shoulder a lot of the blame for that too. It's why I chose him. I was never *in love* with him, knew I'd never get too attached. So he's not the only one at fault for what came of our relationship.

His face tightens and he steps forward, using two fingers to remove another piece of hair. I smack his grabby hand away.

"No? But it's okay if your current boyfriend hits up other women?"

Well, damn. He's got me there. What can I even say? I can't tell him the show was fake. I can't tell him what we had turned out to be real and that Sawyer's kiss with Velora wasn't what it appeared to be because I'm still confused as hell about most of that.

"We're not in a committed relationship yet, Drew. That's the difference. Him and I are dating—in an unconventional way. And yeah, he might not choose me at the end. But the expectations have to be different when you date someone through a reality show."

He shrugs. "I'll be in town for the week. Think about what I said." He moves forward, my back pressing against the side of his truck, his arms caging me in. I try ducking under his arm, but he shifts, pinning me between him and the vehicle. "If things don't turn out with Sawyer, as I think most of us suspect, I'll be here for you."

I sneer at him in disgust, pushing against him. "Get off of—"

Before I can finish my ineffective beating of his grossly excessive pecs, he's ripped away.

Mouth flying open in shock, I watch as Sawyer slams Drew's face into the passenger window of his truck.

"You have zero right to touch her. Liv's made it clear she's done with your cheating ass, so you're going to leave her the fuck alone." Sawyer wrenches Drew's arm behind his back.

Oh god . . . If this wasn't about to escalate into a seriously ugly situation, I might take a moment to appreciate the visual.

"Fuck you, Fletcher. From what I've heard, you've been doing some sampling yourself. So don't pretend you're any better." He shoves against Sawyer's grip. "I think our girl here is secretly attracted to men who are attracted to other women."

Sawyer smashes his face into the glass again, busting my ex-husband's lip with a resounding crack.

"Stop it. Both of you." There are already people gathering on the sidewalk across the street. "Sawyer, let him go. Drew, if you make even one move toward either of us, I'm nutting you the first chance I get. Got it?" I ask them both.

Sawyer shoves off of Drew, who turns with undeniable fury shining in his eyes. Seething, Drew wipes a hand across his mouth, assessing the damage before spitting the remnants of blood in Sawyer's direction.

"Hey!" I shout, stepping closer, bringing his attention back to me. "I want to be clear. You're both idiots." I keep my tone low but unmistakably reprising. I stare each of them in the eye, lingering significantly longer on the inky blue depths of the only man to get past the walls I've kept around my heart.

I hold the tears at bay and set my shoulders. "I'm not willing to settle for anyone who doesn't love me, who isn't looking for forever, or who is too scared to even try. So you're both shit out of luck."

I turn and march away, leaving them both standing there like the fools they are.

"Olive, come on. I know you still want me," Drew shouts.

He's only saying this to rile Sawyer and spread more rumors, and it triggers my petty need for retaliation.

Without breaking my stride, I crane my neck toward him, my tone as intentionally loud as his. "Drew, your dick is smaller than average, your skill level never advanced beyond that of a freshman's first time, and the way you call out 'oh sweet mama' when you climax made me shudder in horror."

I made the last part up, but the rest is mostly true.

Drew's grumbled curses make me smile as I keep a furious pace back to my car. Sawyer calls my name, but I ignore both of them.

I'll be late getting back to work, but I feel stronger. Which is exactly what I'll need for the next elimination ceremony.

As I'm pulling out of my stall, I glance in the rearview mirror. Sawyer stands in the now empty space where Drew's truck was parked. Hands in his pockets, head dipped low, his shoulders sag in a defeated stance.

My breath catches when his head lifts, revealing a desolate gaze. A gaze that haunts me on my drive to the hospital.

My phone vibrates in my pocket as I walk up to the entrance doors. I blow out a breath and check the message.

SAWYER: The thought of disappointing you the same way he did is killing me, Liv.

My fingers tighten around the phone.

Sawyer technically didn't do anything wrong. We weren't officially together. But somehow it hurt more than what Drew did. It's like falling from the roof of your house versus falling off the front steps. They both hurt, but only one is potentially fatal.

ME: Don't. You weren't my boyfriend. You fucked a contestant and it ended badly, like I said it would. Now you're done and I get it. It's fine.

Ugh. Why would I say that? It's not *fine*, and now he knows it's not. Be indifferent, strong.

ME: I'm still willing to follow through with my part of our arrangement on LoveVine. Unless you've changed your mind . . . if that's what you're worried about.

SAWYER: It's not.

Those three dots come and go a few times, and I'm about to put my phone away when another message pops up.

SAWYER: Karl misses Daisy.

What? Really?

SAWYER: Maybe we can get them together soon? Because I feel the same.

ME: I'll let Daisy know you both miss her.

SAWYER: You know that's not what I meant, Liv. Though, I do miss her too.

SAWYER: I just . . . I want to explain.

I don't respond.

CHAPTER
THIRTY-NINE

SAWYER

A s a part of my daily self-loathing ritual, I stare at the messages Jaxon sent a few days ago. The messages I've been ignoring, like everything and everyone else.

Jaxon: What the fuck did you do?

Ruined fucking everything. That's what I did.

One of my neighbours told me he stopped by the house, banging on the door while I was out walking the trails with Karl.

I move to the front reception area, hearing the endless ringing of the phones. Thankfully, my receptionist has been successfully shutting down any non-veterinary care questions. It's been like this since the day after my night at the Affertons, and I'm over it. Even people from neighboring towns in Sonoma County who are viewing the show online are becoming increasingly involved.

It's insanity.

The producers didn't give me a flower to present to any of the women during the Meet-the-Family nights, so there's a lot of speculation about the next elimination ceremony. And with each passing day that I don't see or talk to Liv, things become that much more bleak.

In a couple of days, I'll be eliminating Raine. She wasn't who I planned on eliminating—I had already decided on Velora after the shit she pulled last week. But Raine asked if I could eliminate her since she's getting back together with her ex and figured it might look bad to have *another* contestant bail on me.

My phone buzzes, draining the little energy I have left today. It can only be a few people, and none of them are happy with me right now.

But I check it anyway in case it's the one person I actually want to hear from.

Jaxon: You want to hide away? Fine. I'm coming by your work. Clear your fucking schedule.

"Shit."

"What's that, Dr. Fletcher?" Julia, my receptionist asks.

"Jaxon Vaughn is coming in. Send him back to my office when he gets here, please."

She nods and then gets back to her confirmation calls.

Heading to my office, I work on finishing the notes from my morning patients, but my head's not in it. Minutes later, boots stomp down the hallway.

Jaxon barges in without so much as a knock or greeting, starting in on me immediately. "Mom says Liv's a wreck. She's trying to play it off like she knew what she was getting into, but you broke her damn heart, Fletch. And here's the part I don't get —you knew she was watching the show the other night, yet you still snuck off with Velora for some private fondling time?" He points a finger at me. "Fuck. No."

I tip back in my desk chair, holding up a hand as he moves to round the desk. "That's not how it went down, man. I swear. Have you seen the episode?"

His eye twitches. "Ainslee showed me."

I haven't been able to bring myself to watch it yet. Knowing how bad it looked from Liv's perspective would definitely add fuel to the fire of my self-destruction. Nothing I don't deserve though.

"There's an explanation, but it doesn't change the outcome." I stare him straight in the eyes. "I'd never cheat on Liv. It's not who I am. But the situation I'm in with the show fucked that all up. I was trying to do the right thing, and it got all jacked up." I throw my hands up, murmuring, "As fucking usual."

"What the hell happened, then, because what I saw with you and Velora in the office didn't look all that innocent, Fletch."

"Believe it or not, I was trying to keep something like this from happening." He crosses his arms, an unimpressed expression on his face. "I took Velora aside to explain that I was going all-in with Liv, that I was going to choose her. And then partway through my speech, she attacked me."

He tips his head back in surprise, but then his eyes narrow on me. "You better not be lying while trying to play the victim here. I'll beat your ass twice as hard."

He steps closer, pressing his hand onto the edge of my desk. "She was crying, man. I went by to check on her the next day, and she was crying. You know what that does to me. Went by yesterday too, and she still didn't look right."

I close my eyes, pressing my fingers into them. "I'm a fuckup, Jaxon. I don't know why I thought I'd actually be able to keep a woman I loved if I ever found her."

He throws his hands up. "What the fuck are you talking about? This is fixable. Velora made a move on you. We didn't get to see what happened after because Sean stepped in."

"I got her off me and told her I only want Liv. She was intent on shooting her shot, and didn't care who it hurt in the process." It stirs my rage some more every time I think about it.

He grimaces. "Did you tell Liv that?"

"Yes, but—"

"Once she's had time to think, she'll understand," he assures me. "But this will be the last time you make her cry. My sister has never once cried over a man breaking up with her, and it better not fucking happen again. You'll be the world's most perfect fucking boyfriend until she decides she's done with you." It's not a request, it's a warning.

He kicks my feet from under me and pushes the back of the chair with so much force, I'm flung backward. Sprawled on the floor, a gut-wrenching thought occurs to me.

"Wait. Does Liv think I don't want her?" I ask.

From under my desk, I can see his feet stop in the doorway.

"She said you walked away. That you gave up because you didn't want to commit to her."

A string of curses leaves me before I say, "I'm a goddamn idiot."

"Yep."

"I . . . I just needed some time to sort out my shit. I didn't want to lose her. She's invaded every part of me, and that's scary as fuck." At this moment, I'm glad I'm lying on the floor and don't have to look my best friend in the eye.

"Instead you broke her heart, made her cry because you were feeling fucking sorry for yourself?"

I scrub my hands over my face with a groan. He's rubbing my stupidity in my face, and I deserve it.

"Right, so you double fucked up." He walks back to the desk, peering over the top to where I am still laying on the floor. "This might be harder to fix than I thought."

"Why? You don't think I can get her to forgive me?"

"No, it's not that." He grimaces. "It's because you're a moronic chickenshit, and that'll have to change before you even try."

I drop my head back onto the ground. "That's fair."

The knock at the door has my head turning. "Dr. Fletcher?" She pauses, confused. "Mr. Vanson and Thor are here for their consultation."

She gets on tiptoe, searching for me behind the desk.

"Thanks, Julia."

She leaves but I still don't move.

"Get up. You look pathetic, and it's almost making me feel bad for you," Jaxon says, snapping his fingers at me.

I roll over and rise. Dusting myself off, I follow him out the door.

Confident in what I have to do, I send Sean a text.

ME: Set up a meeting with Stella and Miranda. We need to talk about the last few shows.

SEAN: On it. If it helps at all, I don't think they'll be surprised. Stella, in particular, feels bad.

ME: Let's use that to my advantage, then.

Hope flourishes inside me. I might be a disaster, but I'd give anything to have Liv bear it all with me, let me call her mine, love her with everything I have.

CHAPTER
FORTY

OLIVIA

"Five minutes, ladies! Sawyer is finishing up presenting the new furry additions to the shelter this week, and then we'll be getting started," Miranda tells us before slipping back through the curtain on stage.

I promised I'd do this, so here I am, waiting backstage until I'm called upon. There are only a few brief interviews and the ceremony tonight, no group date, dinner, activities, or anything else.

I've never been more anxious. Not even on the first night. Because I'll have to see Sawyer's sweet, nervous smile—the one I want to kiss right off his much too handsome face. I won't be able to keep from gawking at those broad shoulders that fill out a soft crewneck shirt a little too well. All those feelings, and I have no idea what he expects from me tonight, or even the rest of the show.

Barely able to get more than a few hours of sleep last night, a thought occurred to me . . .

Sawyer might kick me off the show. That might be what he wanted to talk to me about. He's done, and this could get intensely awkward, so why would he keep me around?

Why do you want to stick around?

I kept imagining how this evening might play out. But I can't think past getting through one day at a time, so I pushed this off and I'm completely unprepared.

"Liv? Olivia?"

Snapping out of my daze, I turn around as one of the stage-hands waves me over. I haven't been watching the screen back-stage because I couldn't handle Sawyer snuggling adorable little kitties.

Did the producers try to make him extra fucking sweet today to mess with me?

Unnecessary. My mind and heart are already fully messed up.

With shot nerves and shaky legs, me and the other two remaining women climb the stairs.

As my name is announced through the speakers, I keep my sights on the marked spot I'm supposed to stand on, avoiding eye contact with Sawyer.

Miranda's voice filters through the bar, but my heart is beating too loudly, breathing too difficult.

Scanning the crowd, there appear to be way more people than usual. What's the max capacity for this place? There are many familiar faces, including my mom, Ellie, Jaxon. Even Harper is out there, leaning against the bar. My eyes catch on movement to my left, and I realize too late that it's Sawyer. He's not standing where he normally does, and he's holding a very sparkly daisy.

He locks eyes with me and smiles lopsidedly. I force my gaze away, strengthening my resolve. I can do this. I can get through the rest of this show.

And it'll be easier next time, I tell myself.

But next time is the solo date, and it'll either be with me or the other contestant he chooses.

And then there's the final ceremony.

And a romantic weekend away in Tahoe.

Oh fuck. I clasp my hands together, fingernails digging into the flesh of my palm.

I can't do this.

CHAPTER
FORTY-ONE

SAWYER

I drove out to Landry to meet with Stella because she's in charge of ticket sales. She's also the reason I ended up doing the show in the first place. When I asked her to invite everyone who was supposed to attend the final daisy ceremony to tonight's show, her response was confusing, which was not unusual for her.

She gave me a sly smile, patted me on the arm, and typed something into her phone.

"I'll talk to Jensen and see if he can get me a meeting with the fire chief so we can get approved for the increased capacity. Or maybe I'll pop in for a surprise visit at the fire station." Her fingers came up to her lips as she giggled. "Chief Walker hates it when I do that, but I think we can make it work. And it'll make for a very dramatic evening," she commented.

"What will? The number of people?" I asked her evasively. Does she know what I have planned?

She stared at me for an uncomfortable amount of time. "I'm glad you came to your senses. This has been a long time in the making. I have to admit that I'm glad we're doing the next show in Landry. I'm not as familiar with Vaughn and the residents, so getting things done has been frustratingly less effective. Plus, spending all that time in the car going back and forth has cut into my Book Club reading time. And my butt has started to flatten from all the sitting." She turns to show me, and I step back.

Ignoring the rear end she's flashing me, my tone drops as I level with her. "Stella, I want to remind you that even if Liv doesn't take me back—" I freeze, but Stella is simply waiting for my response, not surprised in the least by this information. "I'm never doing anything like this again. You promised to keep from interfering in my love life from now on."

She grins. "I won't need to. As long as you don't mess up the final ceremony too badly."

I grind my teeth, keeping my jaw locked tight to prevent me from giving her what she would consider "lip."

Stella sighs wistfully. "Maybe one day we'll make it to the end of one of these matchmaking events."

My face softens. "Well, you're two for two with your bachelors finding love." I tilt my head. "Almost, anyway. I still have to convince my bachelorette I'm not a total lost cause."

"You will." With a curt nod and a sly wink, she left me sitting in the coffee shop.

The drive back to Vaughn felt longer than usual. Everything has this week. Because I had nothing to look forward to. I had work and the animals, and now I understand that's not enough. It's nowhere fucking near enough. Not now that I know what it's like to have Liv.

She won't talk to me, and my mom told me I need to stop showing up at her door or someone, probably Liv, will end up calling her brother to give me an official warning. No idea how she knew I was stopping by Liv's after work the last few days, but I'm sure that means she's not the only one.

I've fucked up enough, I don't need to add her brother arresting me to the list. I have one foolproof chance to get her to listen to what I have to say, to tell her exactly how I feel.

And being detained by the local PD means I won't be able to do that.

STARING at the flower I'll be giving out tonight—Liv's flower—I twirl it between my fingers.

My mom breezes into the office they set up for me before shows. "Liv is here. Lilah says she's trying to play it cool but she's a nervous wreck," she says before picking up the kitten I brought in today and giving it some love.

"Does Lilah know everything? That I went over there and made things worse?"

"You mean broke up with her daughter after she tried to tell you how she felt about you? Oh yeah. She's aware."

"Fuck. Great."

She raises her eyebrows at me.

"Sorry," I mumble. "Does Lilah also know I'm in love with her daughter?"

She silences her squeal with a firm hand over her mouth.

"Mom. Come on."

"Sorry, honey, just got excited." She clears her throat. "Lilah suspects you care for Olivia but ran away like a squeamish little boy."

I groan, kneading my temples. Cool. That's just perfect.

"Can you bring the box out and set it on the side of the stage for me?" I ask her

She puts the kitten in my arms and snags the box from the table. Kissing me on the cheek, she whispers, "Good luck, sweetheart. I'll stay close in case you need an intervention of some kind."

"Thanks for the confidence boost, Mom."

Her laughter follows behind her as she heads back to the event side of the bar.

A few minutes later Sean leans against the doorframe. "You're up. You want me to walk Scooter in?" He nods at the pup in the kennel.

"Yeah, that would be great, thanks. I'll take these two." I tuck the kittens against my chest and follow him out.

After I present the animals, Miranda and Stella recap the family dates with a few video snippets. I completely zone out, refusing to listen to all that shit a second time.

I finally managed to watch the episode with Velora, and once was enough. The angle made it seem much more intimate than it was, and it's clear I was stunned by the kiss but the camera was shoved away an instant before I ended it.

That particular scene plays on the screen right now, and I can't do anything but stare at the black stage floor.

When Miranda finally calls the women to the stage, my eyes shoot back up.

Liv's wearing a light blue dress that leaves one shoulder tantalizingly bare and fits snugly around her pert cleavage all the way to the fluttering hem high on her thighs.

Damn. I want to peel that dress off her slowly. Or maybe I'd leave it on and just slip my hands under her skirt and scrape my teeth over Liv's soft, delicate shoulder.

I look back up to her face, wanting to connect with those lively hazel eyes. But they're fixed on the crowd.

I move over to the side of the stage, taking the flower with me, and stand near the box my mom set out for me. When I glance up again, it's in time for Liv's striking irises to lock on me.

Miranda nods at me to begin.

"Last week was more challenging than I expected. Three family dinners, three lovely women, and plenty of surprises." I raise my eyebrows, blowing out a breath, earning me some chuckles from the crowd.

"But I don't think the recipient of this flower will be a surprise to anyone. The woman I hope to give this to was most definitely a surprise to *me*. The truth is, I had doubts about doing this show. I was nervous—really nervous—about all of it." I peer back at her and find her staring at her clasped hands. "But I'm not anymore because it brought me closer to you." I try to convey to her what I can't in public—that I'm not worried anymore. I'm not scared it will all go to hell. Because I've come to find that hell is forcing myself to live without her.

"Olivia Renee Vaughn." The use of her full name for the first time snags her attention.

In a hushed tone full of patience and sympathy, Stella asks her to step forward.

She stops a mere three feet from me. Her eyes burn into mine, unshed tears and pain flashing in their warm depths.

"Liv, will you accept this daisy?" Lifting her hand, I gently press the flower into it.

"Sawyer . . ."

A single tear streaks down her smooth cheek, brushed away with quick fingers.

"I can't." The crowd murmurs and my heart sinks. "I love you, and I can't keep pretending I don't."

Fuck yes!

Wait . . . why is she saying she can't then? Why is she crying?

"I thought I could finish this show, but I can't settle for less. I want everything. The whole relationship, the feelings, moving in together, date nights, getting married for all the right reasons this time, babies, all of it." She's ticking off each item on her fingers, and I watch them, wanting to kiss every digit, make every one of those dreams come true because they're my dreams now too.

The low hum of chatter around us quiets as she continues. "That you think a few silly accidents or bumps in the road could derail us means you don't feel the same way about me that I do about you. You don't want labels, you don't want to move forward, but I want it all. I dropped my guard and finally fell all the way in love, unable to hold back because it was exactly what

I'd been avoiding for years. That's how I knew, Sawyer. Because you felt so right . . . so perfectly dangerous."

Ah, fuck. She's killing me. Her tears, her unwillingness to see beyond my ridiculous concerns and know how fucking much I love her back. But I haven't given her any reason to believe otherwise and I hate that.

I wipe her tears away, holding her face between my hands, never wanting to let go.

"Baby, no, I—"

She takes hold of my wrists to move my hands away. She still clutches the flower, a small reminder that I still have a chance.

"I was committed to seeing this through, but I can't." She turns her head toward Miranda, who is standing off to the side of the podium behind me. "I can't do this show anymore."

"Oh. Oh dear. Um, well that's unexpected. Olivia, are you sure? Maybe you and Sawyer could take a minute backstage to talk?"

I'm floored, all the breath leaving my chest in a gusty exhale.

"Liv. Don't. I don't care about the show—"

She turns back to me, "I'm sorry, Sawyer. I love you, but I can't accept this daisy." She hands it back to me and flees the stage before I can get a single coherent word out.

CHAPTER
FORTY-TWO

SAWYER

I call for her but she doesn't turn.

I didn't expect her to walk off the stage. Be pissed off? Sure. Not make eye contact when she knows what those eyes do to me? Yep.

But bailing on the show and running off was not an option I had considered.

I deserve it but it still stings.

And now I have to figure out how to save this. All the things I wanted to say in private will have to be made very public.

Bringing the microphone back up to my mouth, I announce, "I'm a chickenshit." Her rushed steps falter. "Or I was one. I was hoping to correct that tonight. Because the truth is, Liv has every right to be upset with me. She saved me. She gave me hope, made me feel as if anything was possible. And I hurt her." The crowd quiets down. "After many *really* awful dating disasters and epic relationship fails, hope was not something I had a lot of. I figured even if I did find love, there's no way I'd be allowed to keep it. Something would happen, something would tear it all to shreds."

Stella is staring at me, her hands clutched to her chest, looking stricken.

"It's why I didn't want to do this show. I'm shit at dating and didn't want to make a fool of myself or anyone else. But then Olivia appeared and everything felt . . . right. Falling for her is easily the scariest thing I've ever done. And the best thing that's ever happened to me. Then I fucked it up like I knew I would. I felt things start to slip, and I walked away."

Liv sneaks away backstage, keeping her head ducked down.

"There were supposed to be two daisies tonight, but I have only one. I planned for only one woman. This daisy belongs to Liv. *I* belong to Liv."

From somewhere in the room comes, "Oh god . . . Is this just for the show, Sawyer? I can't tell what's real anymore." Her voice is clear through the mic attached to her, but I still don't see her.

"I've never been more real, more serious. I may not have wanted to do this show or call anyone my girlfriend. But I don't regret it. Though, I do wish I could go back to that first day, scoop you up, and ask if you'd be mine. No other dates, no cameras or interference. Just me and you. Forever just me and you."

"We already had one bachelor do that . . ." Stella chirps from the podium.

I chuckle, nodding. "And he had the right idea." Since Liv is somewhere listening, I try to draw her out. "Liv, please come up here so I can tell you how I feel about you while looking at your gorgeous face?"

"You're crazy if you think I'm coming back out there. There are at least double the number of people here tonight, and everyone is going to be staring while I blubber. That's a firm no, Stud."

I grin. "Then I'm coming to you. Where are you?"

A few excruciating beats of silence pass.

And then in a tentative voice, she says, "Hiding behind the bar."

More than two hundred pairs of eyes swing over to the long bar on the side of the room. Harper stands still, wide-eyed, looking guilty as hell. Her gaze darts down, instantly revealing Liv's location. She whispers to Liv for a moment before glancing back up at me. Liv's friend's brows raise in challenge, silently asking what I'm going to do about all this.

I jump off the stairs but then remember the box and spin back around to grab it.

When I reach her, she's sitting with her back against the wall, a large glass of wine in her hands.

"Baby. I'm so fucking sorry," I murmur, hoping the mic attached to my button-down shirt doesn't pick it up.

"Louder so we can all hear you, for Christ's sake. This shit is better than my soaps," someone shouts from the crowd.

Jesus.

Never again.

I stand in front of my gorgeous girl, sliding down to sit on the floor directly across from her, ready to lay it all out. Even if it's in front of hundreds of people.

A boom mic peeks overhead, and I give Liv a resigned shrug.

"Tell me I didn't fuck this up for good. Tell me you'll let me fix this."

"You walked away from me, Sawyer."

"Is that why you walked today, because you think I didn't want this—us?"

"You were either going to choose me because you had to choose *someone* or I was going to have to watch you date someone else–even if only for a week—and choose them at the end. Those were two profoundly lousy options." She toys with the hem of her skirt, shifting uncomfortably. "I needed you to be sure about us—apart from the show."

"Babe." Her eyes remain pointed down at her legs. I lift

her hands off her dress and interlock our fingers. "It's been you from the start. But I didn't want to take any chances. In the back of my mind, I figured the moment we became serious, it would all implode. I didn't want to risk it, so I put it off, wanting to keep things just as they were for a while longer."

Her little nose scrunches up. "That's so stupid, Sawyer Fletcher."

"Gorgeous, I was a walking, talking dating fail cautionary tale. And you cured me." A small smile pulls at her mouth. "But that's not why I fell in love with you."

"You love me?" she asks softly.

"I love you in a way that makes dreaming pointless. Being with you, I don't need to wish or want for a damn thing. You're it. You're everything."

Her breath whooshes out before she lunges at me, crawls into my lap, and crushes her mouth to mine.

"That's the cheesiest thing anyone has ever said to me," she murmurs against my lips.

Her hands find my hair, gripping me tight as if I'm going to pull away. Not a chance. I wrap my arms around her and bite down on her lush bottom lip with a tug that has her moaning. Taking advantage of those parted lips, I slide my tongue inside her sweet mouth.

Her barely audible whimper is the only warning I get before she pulls back.

I thread my hands through her waves, relishing the feel of her in my arms again.

A booming voice breaks through our heated kiss. "That was a level of pussy-whipped I didn't need to experience from my best friend, Fletch. But since it's my sister, I'm allowing it."

"Jaxon, those two are having a moment. Shut it or you'll be the second Vaughn brother to be escorted from the premises," Liv's mom shouts back at him.

Liv's forehead hits my chest, and I chuckle, rubbing her back and shifting her even closer.

She tips her head up, and sparkling green eyes lock on mine. "I love you, too, Sawy—"

I push in and kiss the words from her lips. That earns me a surprised giggle.

"I have something for you." Reaching over, I push the box I brought with me toward her.

"What's this?"

"It's something I put together for you. A girlfriend proposal."

She bites her bottom lip and tilts her head. "You're adorable."

"You mean hot."

"Sure."

"You want to open it or not, sassy?"

She wiggles on my lap, and I groan as a camera appears at the far end of the bar. Apparently the limited, semiprivate time we were given has come to an end.

She unties the ribbon and removes the lid. Liv laughs as she pulls out the first item.

"A first aid kit?" she asks, the cameraman approaching to get a better shot of the girlfriend survival kit I've put together.

"As my girlfriend, you may need it for one or both of us at any given time. Every date with you is perfection no matter what happens, but your safety is important to me."

She snorts and rolls her eyes. "I'm a medical professional, Sawyer. We'll be fine."

"You are, yes, and you amaze the fuck out of me. But I feel like my special kind of incidents and my human *male* physiology are a bit outside of both of our usual areas of medical expertise."

She scrunches her lips together as she considers this. "Fair. What's next?" She excitedly digs around before choosing the next item and holding it up. "Ew!" The crowd chuckles as she holds up the next item. "A rabbit's foot? You're a vet and you brought me a dead animal's body part?"

"For luck," I deadpan.

"*We* won't need it. Also, it's creepy."

She holds it between her thumb and forefinger as far away from her as she can get.

"It's not real, I just wanted to see your reaction," I say on a laugh. She tosses it at me, but her amused smile floods me with warmth.

Her eyes fill with curiosity as she feels around again. She pulls out a large, beige-coloured block.

"Cheese!"

Stinky, expensive cheese that has a name I can't pronounce.

My shoulders roll in an easy shrug. "Figured it might increase my chances of getting you to say yes."

Her teeth clamp down on her pretty bottom lip. She shakes her head and reaches back inside the box. "Not the worst idea. It better come with wine." Her hand dives back in, coming out with her favorite bottle of white wine.

Smirking, she sets it down and refocuses on the remaining contents of the box. She lifts out another bottle, one that has me leaning backward a few inches.

The label is facing me, so she spins it around to look at it.

"Coconut water?" she asks.

"In case you were feeling the need for a little retribution. Or any time I fuck up in the future. I grant you permission to coconut me in whatever way you see fit. Not so much that we'd have to call your idiot brother to give me a ride to the hospital. But maybe a bit in my body wash or lotion or something."

"Sawyer. Oh my god. No. You're crazy."

"Come on. You can't tell me it wouldn't be a *little* bit tempting on days I make you crazy. Or do something completely stupid. I give you the power to take me down a few itch-inducing pegs."

"I can do that without poisoning you or giving you a full-body rash, Stud. I'll just walk around naked, and then when you try to follow me into the bedroom, I'll lock the door."

Effective.

"Deal."

She mumbles a few choice words under her breath before dropping her voice. *"I give you the key to my fatality. Use it when I displease you,"* she mimics my deeper tone. "You are ridiculous. But I kind of love it."

I hit her with my full grin, both dimples on display. She brings her hands up to trace them.

"Speaking of keys . . ." I say, pointedly glancing at the box.

Her eyes search mine in confusion before her hand dives back in. Slowly she draws out the last gift. It's clutched in her fist, and she stares up at me in surprise.

"What's this?" she asks.

Someone in the audience yells, "Is it a ring? Show us!"

"It's not a ring. Not yet."

Liv's eyes bug out.

I open her hand and pluck the key from her palm.

"It's a key to my place—our place," I say, holding it up to her. "I want you there. All the time. I want my bed to be the one you get into after a long, hard night at work. I hope to wake up with you in the morning, share a pot of coffee, find you snuggled up with our dogs on the couch when I get home. You're not a guest or a visitor—I want you to use your key and walk right in because you belong there. With me."

"Oh shit," she whispers, wiping a tear from under her lashes.

"Are you going to take it?" I ask anxiously.

She nods and gingerly plucks it from my fingers.

"And what about my proposal?"

"Proposal?" she asks, slightly dazed.

"My girlfriend proposal. Think you're up for the challenge?"

Her expression softens. She grabs my face and lays another deep, intense kiss on me.

"On one condition."

I'm so fucking nervous, my jaw clenches as I reply, "Anything."

"I want the dimples. I want you to ask me, with dimples."

I laugh, clear my throat, school my face, and try again.

"Olivia Renee Vaughn, will you be my girlfriend and all that entails no matter the consequences, knowing I'll cherish you, please you"—I wink before letting loose the dimples—"and making any dream—secret or otherwise—come to life to the absolute best of my ability?"

Her face lights up. "Yes!" she shouts.

My lips find hers again

Her eyes plead with me, juicy lip sticking out as her fingertips trace the skin above the collar of my shirt. "Can we eat the cheese now?"

I bark out a laugh. "Fuck, I love you."

With an exaggeratedly sexy wink, she tucks the key I gave her down the front of her dress.

CHAPTER
FORTY-THREE
OLIVIA

W hen we finally manage to escape from all the family, friends, and guests who came out tonight, Sawyer convinces me to leave my vehicle at Rocky's and let him take me home.

Ducking his head down to my ear, he asks, "Ready to test out your new key and let me say sorry in all your favorite ways?" He grinds his hardness into my belly, and my core tightens. "I miss your pussy on my face, coming all over my dick, pulsing around my fingers."

Heat rises to my face, and my hips arch toward him. "Sawyer . . . we're still mic'd," I say as he freezes, brushing a hand down his chest where they normally clip it.

A dark, teasing laugh bubbles up out of me. "Kidding. That would have been really bad though. At least wait until we're out of the building and away from all this show insanity before using that dirty mouth on me."

He wraps me up closer, tucking his head into my neck, his scruff scraping against my collarbone, forcing a low moan from my lips.

The deep, satisfied breath he inhales has a tingling warmth

spreading through me. "Fuck, I missed you. You're lucky I don't use my dirty mouth on you right here."

His searing touch finds the hem of my dress, and fingertips skim up the backs of my thighs, causing my legs to tremble. When he reaches the edge of my ass cheeks, I need more.

I want those fingers to press in, move exactly where I need him. I clutch him to me, fingers digging into the muscled width of his shoulders.

He places an open-mouthed kiss to my neck. I pout as he pulls back. He has one hand locked on my hip as heated blue eyes bore into mine. Without a word, he spins us, my hand gripped in his and tugs me along to the staff-only hallway near the bar area.

A few people try to approach or call him over, but he ignores everyone, keeping a brisk pace as he leads us to the door marked *General Manager*. He launches us into Harper's office, and with a kick of his foot, the door slams closed.

This must be where he prepares before the show.

"Did you forget someth—"

He pushes me up against the door, my back hitting it with a deep *thud*. I peer up at him, my mouth hanging open. His hands are pressed on either side of my head as he stares down at me as if he's going to consume me whole.

"We're not making it home. I want you here. I want to claim every inch of you in this building. So every time we come here, all I'll be able to think about is the taste of you, the sound of your moans, and how you looked writhing against the door that confined me to this miserable dating game."

Biting my lip, I mess with him a little. "Hmm, I don't know. It wasn't so bad." His eyes narrow at me. "You think we would have gotten here, with you about to drop to your knees, if we hadn't done the show?"

"Yes." No hesitation.

I hum, doubtful. "You never looked at me before like you do now."

"I couldn't then. Now I can."

He surges forward, taking my mouth in a crushing kiss.

"Might have taken me a bit longer to let myself have you though. I'll give you that."

I smirk at him, then before I can even open my mouth to respond, his lips are right back on mine.

"Sawyer . . ." I try breaking away, but his lips follow mine. "We can't have sex in here. Someone could hear, or we could—"

"There's not a single bad thing that could happen while your pussy is on my face."

"No. You just wouldn't care at the time."

"Same thing." His lips are on me again, tongue stroking against mine, working me into a frenzy.

When my fingers sink into his hair, he groans, and his hands move from their place on the door to cover mine for a moment before slipping them out of the sleek, chocolaty strands.

"Hands on the door." He positions them as he says it. Palms down at my sides, pressed to the door. "Don't move. If you touch me, I'm going to fuck you. Hard. Rough. But first I want to apologize. I'm going to choose you, put you first every damn day, always." My chest heaves, an ache in my throat forms as the words I've longed for hit their mark.

He follows up with a possessive kiss that has my hips flexing in desperation toward him. His pillowy mouth leaves a cooling trail down my neck, between my breasts. His hands press, hot and firm along my ribs to my waist, squeezing when they get to the flare of my hips.

Sawyer drops to his knees, inching my dress up until he uncovers the scrap of lace between my thighs.

He places a kiss on my pubic bone, humming in approach. The tip of his nose runs along the seam, through my panties, kissing me there one last time before ripping the material down.

I step out of the thong, my eyes staying locked on him as he hooks one of my legs over his shoulder. His hand runs along the outer edge of my thigh to latch on to my bare ass.

He dives right in, tongue running through my slit, mouth sucking, nipping. A scorching heat burns through my veins, and all I can do is grind against his mouth, chasing that high, needing the release only he can deliver.

When his attention shifts from the apex of my mound to my entrance, fucking me with his tongue, I gasp and tilt my hips for more.

"You need more?" He stops to ask.

I whimper, my teeth biting harshly on my lower lip to keep from crying out.

Sawyer draws back, setting my leg back down.

My hands leave the door and grip his neck. "No! Don't stop. Sawyer . . ."

"I'm not stopping, gorgeous." He sits on the floor, spinning around so his back is to me, then lowers down. "Just changing positions. Get down here and ride my face."

I'm still breathing hard, so desperate for the release I'm promised, my attempts to veto this idea are feeble at best. "The floor? I-It's . . . Sawyer . . ."

"Don't care. Come take what you need from me."

I gently lower myself over him, my lack of experience at riding a sexy man's scruffy face making me falter. I settle both my legs on either side of his head.

"Fucking amazing view." He groans, taking my hips and yanking me down to meet his mouth.

His hands slide down to grip my thighs at the first stroke directly against my clit. I settle over him, grinding on him as his fierce tongue works me over.

I pump my hips, chasing my orgasm as my legs shake, scraping against his scruff every gyration. That quick spark of pleasure starts in my lower belly and moves lower. He growls into my pussy, his fingers tightening on my thighs. Without a doubt, I'll have faint marks tomorrow as a sexy reminder.

Reaching up, he takes my small breasts in his hands, squeezing before running his thumbs over my nipples. I groan, moving faster. He does something different with his tongue, and I'm lost—my head thrown back, a gasp of surprise and utter rapture explodes from my mouth.

I reach down with one hand, threading my fingers through his dark, disheveled strands. Clutching feverishly at him, my clit throbs, my heart thunders, and fire burns through my body.

I do exactly what he demanded—I take what I need. My climax hits me like a freight train, the air in my lungs rushing out in a fevered cry.

Collapsing against the door, I'm only somewhat conscious enough to avoid completely smothering the gloriously filthy man beneath me. Before I've fully regained use of my limbs, Sawyer slides out and snatches me up from the ground.

I move to face him, but he takes my hands instead and lifts them to press against the wooden door once again. "Keep them there," he demands.

Tingles race up my thighs as the rasp of his zipper echoes through the room, followed by his pants hitting the floor.

"Show me that incredible ass, gorgeous."

I tilt my pelvis and push my ass back, giving him a shimmy. He slaps one cheek, drawing a gasp from my lips.

His hands circle my waist. "Good girl," he rumbles, his cock plunging into my entrance. He stretches me to the edge of discomfort, filling every part of me in exactly the way I need.

I twist, leaning back to kiss him, my teeth scraping along his bottom lip. His hips slap against the softness of my ample ass in fast, powerful strokes.

"Fuck, you feel amazing. You're all mine, gorgeous. Just knowing I'm the man who gets to be inside you, that my come is

going to be dripping out of this pussy as we walk out of here—
I'm too fucking close to blowing."

"Come inside me. I need it. Please, Sawyer."

He groans, his hand shifting from my lower stomach, fingers
stretching down to circle my clit. I reach back and grab a handful
of his hair, bringing his head down for a kiss.

My legs start to shake, so he wraps his left arm around my
waist, pressing me closer to him.

"Yes, Sawyer. God. It's so good. How is it so freaking good?"

"It's perfect, baby. Tell me you know we're it." He kisses along
the top of my shoulder, keeping his thrusts deep and steady.

I lean back, resting my head on his pec, and whisper, "I
know." I grin up at him. "Pretty sure I knew before you, Stud."

Hips jerking against me in wild thrusts, he pinches my clit
gently between his fingers. His shaft drags against my walls,
swelling impossibly larger as I begin to spasm around him. I crest
the peak on a low moan, letting go, free-falling into waves of
pleasure.

His tone is deep and raspy as he tells me how perfect I am,
how he's going to fill me up. I'm still clenching around him as he
stills, his loud growling moan filling the space around us. The
twitches of his release triggers another wave of spasms, and I
bring his fingers back to my clit so he can get me off one last
time.

He works me hard and fast. "Good girl, milk every drop."

His voice in my ear sets me off, my orgasm hitting so
intensely, it's a heady mix of pain and pleasure. I collapse against
him and he holds me, keeping us locked together to ride out the
last blissful remnants of our sexy office fun.

"Best. Boyfriend. Ever," I say between breaths.

He chuckles, sliding out of me and turning me around. "I love
you so damn much, Liv."

I wrap my arms around his neck and, with a shaky voice,
admit, "You're the kind of dream guy I told myself I never

wanted"—confused amusement washes over his face—"but always hoped I'd be lucky enough to find. And if it weren't for all your staggeringly bad luck in relationships, I might never have gotten the chance to become this lucky."

He murmurs, "Fuck," before capturing my face in both his hands and pressing a lingering kiss to my swollen mouth.

Smiling against his lips, I break away long enough to say, "I love you, Sawyer."

He grins at me—with dimples.

"Let's get you home. As fun as this was, and as much as I appreciate the significantly better memories I'll now have of Rocky's, I need you in my bed."

"You want to go another round?"

"To sleep, babe. From now on, I need you in my arms, your wild hair in my face, and your scent all over my sheets every morning when I wake up."

I wasn't sure anything could top sex with Sawyer, but waking up to him every single day just might.

And I'm sure I could convince him to add some morning sex in there too.

EPILOGUE

SAWYER

SIX MONTHS LATER . . .

We pull up to Liv's mom's house for a Vaughn/Fletcher family brunch and park next to Brody's patrol car. He doesn't tend to roll up in it unless he didn't have time to switch to his personal vehicle. And since he exclusively rides his motorcycle as soon as the warmer weather hits, it's unlikely he'd choose to bring the cruiser.

Liv glances up at me, a quick check-in to see if I noticed. I did.

"It's probably nothing. Maybe his bike is in the shop."

I nod with a smirk. Being with Liv helps me ignore all the stupid shit that might or *does* happen and focus on her.

My hand is on Liv's hip as we enter her mom's house. The scent of fresh coffee lingers in the air, the faint sizzle of pancakes on a griddle a welcome sound as we make our way to the kitchen.

"There they are!" Lilah Vaughn shouts, tossing the towel that was draped over her shoulder to the island. "How was your weekend in Tahoe? You two look all glowy and happy. I imagine that's not just from the spa . . ."

"Mom! No," Jaxon grumbles. "They went hiking, got a massage or a facial or something. That's it."

I lean down and whisper in Liv's ear, "You definitely got a facial, didn't you, gorgeous?"

Her face blooms a pretty pink as she shushes me.

A hard smack hits the back of my head.

Confused, I glance up to find my best friend glowering at me, murder in his eyes. "Jesus, Jax. What was that for?" I ask, rubbing my head.

He points at me. "You fucking know."

At the end of the breakfast nook, casually reading something on his kindle, my dad chuffs out a laugh.

I wrap an arm around Liv and shrug innocently at Jax. He's had enough time to get used to the fact that Liv's mine and I'm hers. I imagine he'll milk this shit for as long as he can though.

With a sweet smile, she mouths, *Love you.* I bend to kiss the sweet words off her lips but keep it to two much too quick pulls of her mouth. God, she's fucking addictive.

"What did I miss?" Brody asks, stomping into the kitchen as he rakes a hand through his unkempt hair. He glances around, eyes landing on his brother first, then on us. "Looks like I'm going to need a lot more coffee to deal with whatever happened to put that manic grin on Livvie's face and the disgusted expression on Jax's."

Brody snags a mug from beside the coffee pot, pouring himself a cup.

"You definitely don't want to know," Jaxon grumbles.

Brody's phone blares from its position at his hip. "Ah, shit." His thumb jabs at the screen as he answers, "This better be good, Sergeant. I just left there and had no plans on returning until tomorrow." He strides out the back door, grumbling as he shuts it behind him.

My mom pours coffee for Liv and me. I pass the first mug to Liv, revelling in the sweet smile she gives me. My woman gets the coffee first. She gets a lot of things first . . . and I'm all too happy to give it to her.

Mom hands me the other mug, watching us closely.

Liv brings the coffee up to take a sip, both hands wrapped around the wide mug.

Mom freezes, mouth gaping, her hands held out. She flaps her arms and squeals.

Ah. There it is. She's finally noticed.

"Jane! What on Earth are you—?" Lilah begins to ask.

My mom points frantically at Liv, who beams at them both, holding up her left hand.

Both women rush us, screaming.

"Did this happen in Tahoe?"

"Let's see the ring again!"

"How did he propose?"

"Is there a date yet?"

"Did you get a 'wife' box this time?"

They hit us with question after question, most of which I let Liv handle since I can't keep up in a manner that appeases either of them.

Dad saunters over, clapping a hand over my shoulder. "Not sure if you can hear me over the ruckus, but congrats, bud. We love seeing you happy. And I also enjoy that your mother will have less to worry-spiral about each night before she goes to bed. Now it'll just be Cole."

I shake my head. "Glad I could help."

He nods at me, gives me a final pat on the back, then makes his way over to Liv for a hug.

Jaxon approaches, his mouth a firm, indecipherable line. The slight sheen to his eyes is the only hint I get before he jumps me, both arms coming around my midsection, smothering me in his version of an affectionate hug. He's the leanest of the Vaughn men, but he's not small by any means.

"You're about to officially join the Vaughn family. How

pumped are you?" he says, a strain in his voice as he lifts me off the ground a few inches, shaking me with fervor.

"Jax. Man." I grunt, trying to catch my breath. "Put me down."

He does, a grin on his face. "Dude. We're going to be brothers." He inhales deeply, his eyes flitting around the room. "Speaking of brothers, where the hell is Jensen?" His face turns serious. "Wait. I'm your best man, right? Does Anders know yet? I bet that cocky asshole thinks he's got it in the bag. You can tell him to lick my balls—that title's mine."

Lilah whips around, pulling away from Liv and my mom. "Jaxon. Don't use that language in my kitchen." She tsks at him and then throws both hands up. "Now, who's in for celebratory mimosas?"

My mom squeals in agreement, beelining for the fridge. "Yes, and Liv can tell us all about the proposal. That pavé solitaire-style engagement ring is breathtaking." Those words sound vaguely familiar, but I don't recall what they mean. I chose the ring I thought would make Liv smile every time she saw it sparkling on her finger. "So I can only imagine what your romantic weekend away proposal story entails. No need to include any post-engagement naked time details. We can leave that mother-son boundary intact."

"Uhhh . . ." I stall, looking at Liv for help. "It was nice. Super romantic. We went on a private sunset sail boat tour of the lake. I proposed on the dock beforehand, and we spent the rest of the evening enjoying a catered meal, bottle of wine, and some slow dancing on the deck."

Both moms smile sweetly at me. "And?" Lilah asks. "What did you say? Did you get down on one knee? What was her response? Were there people around?"

"Yeah, honey. That was the cliff notes version. We want every moment, every detail."

Liv takes a breath and holds it. I clutch her hand. I let the excruciating silence pass for several long seconds before sneaking a peek at her. She's struggling to hold it in, but keeping our proposal story a secret is a lost cause.

Her eyes cut to me. I sigh and lace my fingers through hers. "Go ahead, let it out," I tell her.

She turns back to my family and hers. "Sawyer fell off the dock." The words explode from her mouth.

"What? Sawyer . . . Good lord," my mom says.

"Dude. How the hell did you—?"

Brody barges in from the patio, frowning deeper than usual. "Jax, did you steal Jensen's fire gear from the station and fuck around town with it?"

Jax grimaces. "Who's asking? My brother or the chief of police?"

Brody's stony glare is all the answer Jax needs. Both sides of Brody are itching to kick his brother's ass.

"Because of you and Jensen's antagonistic, identical twin bullshit, my deputies have been fielding several complaints this morning."

"I'll go sort it out, bro. Honestly, it was just—"

"And Jensen is in the hospital," Brody adds.

"What?" Liv and Lilah shout.

"He's fine. Mrs. Langerham called while I was on the phone with my sergeant to inform me about an incident between him and Grace Parker this morning. There was an altercation that ended with Grace allegedly pushing Jensen down some stairs. Jensen is waiting on X-rays."

Lilah gasps and Liv frowns, uttering a resounding, "No way."

"Hold up." Jaxon steps forward, his tone practically gleeful. "Gracie finally kicked his ass? Oh this is too good. Did Mrs. L. put it up on The Vine yet? If someone called it in, I can almost guarantee there are photos."

Jaxon gets on his phone while everyone else asks questions on top of each other.

Brody simply holds up a hand. "I don't have any official information yet. I'll go in and figure out this mess. In the meantime, I don't want you all barging into the hospital. Wait to hear from me. Got it?"

He gets a few nods, but the rest stay quiet since they're probably not going to follow those instructions.

"Oh, and congrats you two," Liv's brother says, trying for his best version of a smile but failing. "I heard the news from the patio. Might have to back burner the celebration for a bit. It's going to be a long day."

With an affectionate squeeze of Liv's shoulder and a kiss on his mom's cheek, he leaves. Once his patrol car starts up, I scrub both hands down my face and try to make sense of what our happy, news-sharing brunch became.

A hand caresses down my back. "You feel like we caused this? That this is your unlucky love stuff striking?"

"Nope." A slow smile spreads across my face. "I think your brother is an idiot and shat all over our big announcement."

"Which brother?" she asks.

"All of them?"

She tilts her head to the side, lips pursed. "You know . . . if you think about it, this is actually kind of lucky."

"Really? Instead of celebrating our engagement, Jensen is in the hospital, possibly assaulted by a sweet, tiny woman, while Jaxon has been let loose on the town, attempting to fix whatever he did—that sounds lucky to you?"

"Brody busting in when he did with that awful story saved you from explaining how you almost drowned proposing to me."

"I *did not* almost drown. The water by the dock is shallow. I was at greater risk of a broken limb or concussion than drowning."

"That's not the way I was going to tell it. See? Lucky."

I fight a grin, shaking my head. "Olivia Vaughn," I grumble, my voice low and menacing. "I fucking love you."

She plants her hands on my chest. "Love you right back, Stud." She rises on her toes to kiss me, but before her lips touch mine, she pulls back and says, "Oh, and my brothers are going to try to convince you to change your last name to mine so you can be a Vaughn brother. Expect them to ambush you with that soon." She takes my mouth in a quick kiss, giving my bottom lip a sultry bite.

"Is this what you want?" I ask. Would I change my last name for Liv? Hell yeah, I would. And I wouldn't give a single fuck what anyone thought. "Because I've been yours the moment you demanded my dimples when I smiled at you. Every part of me is yours, gorgeous."

Her face softens, those hazel eyes brightening. "I've always been a Vaughn and wasn't sure that would ever change. But now that I'm yours, Sawyer, you better believe I'm claiming your last name."

Hugging her closer to me, I dip my head down until my lips brush hers and murmur, "No take backs."

———

THANK YOU SO MUCH FOR READING SAWYER & OLIVIA'S LOVE STORY.

WANT THE DISASTROUS PROPOSAL DETAILS?
Sign up to read this *exclusive* BONUS SCENE.
https://rebrand.ly/BonusFFTB

———

READY FOR A VAUGHN CHRISTMAS ROMANCE?
FALLING FOR THE GRINCH

ALSO BY AMY ALVES

The Landry Love Series
(Complete Series)

The Experiment (Emma & Jess)

The Denial Game (Lauren & Taylor)

The Forever Plan (Willa & Evan)

The Love Words (Chloe & Hayden)

The Surprise Seduction (Aria & Garrett)

The Road Home (Sadie & Sean)

Vaughn Brothers Series

Falling for the Bachelor (Sawyer & Olivia)

Falling for the Grinch (Declan & Dani)

JOIN MY FACEBOOK READERS GROUP!

ACKNOWLEDGMENTS

To those of you who have been waiting months for this book, **thank you** for being patient with me. Sometimes life (specifically "mom life") can throw a wrench into our plans.

Accidentally writing a full-length novel when this story was *supposed* to be a novella definitely didn't help either...Oops!

There are a lot of people I want to thank for getting me through this book with less hair pulling than there could have been:

First, Adrienne, a special reader who *encouraged* me to write Sawyer's book. Thank you for your passion...and your keen proofreading eye.

Katie, you accept my crazy and pull me through the hard days. Love you to bits!

My beta readers, Sara and Jeanine—your suggestions and comments are gold! I love chatting plot and characters with you, knowing you will take my ramblings and help make sense of them.

My reality TV show guru, Jenna—thank you for helping me make LoveVine fun and realistic.

My ARC & Street Teams—you are kind, hilarious, book-loving rockstars. Thanks for doing this with me.

Laetitia, my editor—filter and filler words were a burden we shared and one you helped me conquer. Thank you (but also, sorry).

The graphic designer goddess who put up with my indecisive ass—Kim Wilson. Thank you, thank you. I love the covers you brought to life for this series.

And last but not least...my hubby, who listens to all my story ideas, and pumps me up. Even though you'll likely never see this because you read the beta versions of my books, you are the best partner a gal could ask for.

ABOUT THE AUTHOR

Amy Alves lives in Alberta, Canada with her husband and two crazy cute kids. She is a romance-obsessed reader, a lover of wine and fuzzy socks, and a loather of laundry. For over a decade, she was a high school science teacher, but now substitute teaches in between writing novels and being a mom.

Find Amy In All The Places
She Gets Distracted:

NEWSLETTER SIGN UP
(WWW.AMYALVESBOOKS.COM/LINKS)
GOODREADS (GOODREADS.COM/AMYALVESAUTHOR)
INSTAGRAM (INSTAGRAM.COM/AMYALVES.AUTHOR)
TIKTOK (TIKTOK.COM/@AMYALVES.AUTHOR)
FACEBOOK PAGE (FACEBOOK.COM/AMYALVESAUTHOR)
FACEBOOK READER GROUP
(FACEBOOK.COM/GROUPS/AMYALVESREADERS)
BOOKBUB (BOOKBUB.COM/PROFILE/AMY-ALVES)
AMAZON PAGE (HTTP://AUTHOR.TO/AMYALVES)
WEBSITE (WWW.AMYALVESBOOKS.COM)

Made in the USA
Monee, IL
29 May 2023

34926986R00206